OLIVIA JOULES

and the

OVERACTIVE IMAGINATION

Also by Helen Fielding

Bridget Jones's Diary

Bridget Jones: The Edge of Reason

Cause Celeb

HELEN FIELDING

OLIVIA JOULES

and the

OVERACTIVE IMAGINATION

VIKING

VIKING
Published by the Penguin Group
Penguin Group (USA) Inc., 375 Hudson Street, New York, New York 10014, U.S.A.
Penguin Books Ltd, 80 Strand, London WC2R 0RL, England
Penguin Books Australia Ltd, 250 Camberwell Road, Camberwell, Victoria 3124, Australia
Penguin Books Canada Ltd, 10 Alcorn Avenue, Toronto, Ontario, Canada M4V 3B2
Penguin Books India (P) Ltd, 11 Community Centre,
Panchsheel Park, New Delhi – 110 017, India
Penguin Group (NZ), Cnr Airborne and Rosedale Roads, Albany, Auckland 1310,
New Zealand
Penguin Books (South Africa) (Pty) Ltd, 24 Sturdee Avenue,
Rosebank, Johannesburg 2196, South Africa

Penguin Books Ltd, Registered Offices: 80 Strand, London WC2R 0RL, England

First American edition
Published in 2004 by Viking Penguin,
a member of Penguin Group (USA) Inc.

1   3   5   7   9   10   8   6   4   2

Excerpt from "Whispers of Immortality" from *Collected Poems 1909–1962* by T. S. Eliot
reprinted by permission of Faber and Faber Ltd.

LIBRARY OF CONGRESS CATALOGING IN PUBLICATION DATA
Fielding, Helen, date.
Olivia Joules and the overactive imagination / Helen Fielding
p.   cm.
ISBN 0-670-03333-2
1. Women spies—Fiction.   2. Women journalists—Fiction.
3. Terrorism—Prevention—Fiction.   4. British—Foreign countries—Fiction.   I. Title.
PR6056.I4588O44 2004
823'.914—dc22   2003069469

This book is printed on acid-free paper. ∞

Printed in the United States of America
Set in Bembo with AG Schoolbook
Designed by Daniel Lagin

To Kevin

ACKNOWLEDGMENTS

With warm thanks to the following for their help with the writing of the book: for anecdotes, editing, expert knowledge, practical support and mysterious info re micro subaquatic GP locators: Gillon Aitken, Luis Anton, Craig Brown, Tim Burton, Andreas Carlton-Smith, Fiona Carpenter, Gil Cates, the CIA's Office of Public Affairs, Richard Coles, Marie Colvin, Nick Crean, Ursula Doyle, Harry Enfield, the Fielding family, Carrie Fisher, Piers Fletcher, Linda Gase, John Gerloff, Sara Jones, Jules' Undersea Lodge, Key Largo, Andrew Kidd, Paula Levy, Hugh Miles, John Miller, Michael Monteroso, Detective Joe Pau of the LAPD bomb squad, Maria Rejt, Mia Richkind, Sausage, Lesley Shaw, the Sunset Marquis Hotel, Beth Swofford, Russ Warner and those who are too secret to be mentioned even with an X.

I'm particularly grateful to J. C. for his time, sharing of specialized knowledge and for showing me how to fire a gun using a biro.

And thanks above all to Kevin Curran for his enormous contribution in terms of plotting, characters, jokes, ideas, multiple reads and edits, spelling and punctuation, and most of all for advising me that the way to write a thriller was not to put the whole plot down in the first chapter as soon as you thought of it.

OLIVIA JOULES

and the

OVERACTIVE IMAGINATION

1   LONDON

"The problem with you, Olivia, is that you have an overactive imagination."

"I don't," said Olivia Joules indignantly.

Barry Wilkinson, foreign editor of the *Sunday Times*, leaned back in his chair, trying to hold in his paunch, staring over his half-moon glasses at the disgruntled little figure before him, and thinking: *And you're too damned cute.*

"What about your story about the cloud of giant, fanged locusts pancaking down on Ethiopia, blotting out the sun?" he said.

"It was the Sudan."

Barry sighed heavily. "We sent you all the way out there and all you came up with was two grasshoppers in a polythene bag."

"But there *was* a locust cloud. It was just that it had flown off to Chad. They were supposed to be roosting. Anyway, I got you the story about the animals starving in the zoo."

"Olivia, it was one warthog—and he looked quite porky to me."

"Well, I would have got you an interview with the fundamentalist women and a cross amputee if you hadn't made me come back."

"The birth of Posh and Becks's new baby you were sent to cover live for BSkyB?"

"That wasn't hard news."

"Thank God."

"I certainly didn't imagine anything there."

"No. But nor did you say anything for the first ten seconds. You stared around like a simpleton, fiddling with your hair live on air, then suddenly yelled, 'The baby hasn't been born yet, but it's all very exciting. Now back to the studio.' "

"That wasn't my fault. The floor manager didn't cue me because there was a man trying to get into the shot with 'I'm a Royal Love Child' written on his naked paunch."

Wearily, Barry leafed through the pile of press releases on his desk. "Listen, lovey . . ."

Olivia quivered. One of these days she would call him lovey and see how he liked it.

". . . you're a good writer, you're very observant and intuitive and, as I say, extremely imaginative, and we feel on the *Sunday Times*, in a freelancer, those qualities are better suited to the Style section than the news pages."

"You mean the shallow end rather than the deep end?"

"There's nothing shallow about style, baby."

Olivia laughed. "I can't believe you just said that."

Barry started laughing as well.

"Look," he said, fishing out a press release from a cosmetics company, "if you really want to travel, there's a celebrity launch in Miami next week for some—perfume?—face cream."

"A face-cream launch," said Olivia dully.

"J.Lo or P. Binny or somebody . . . there we go . . . Devorée. Who the fuck is Devorée?"

"White rapper slash model slash actress."

"Fine. If you can get a magazine to split the costs with us, you can go and cover her face cream for Style. How's that?"

"Okay," said Olivia doubtfully, "but if I find a proper news story out there, can I cover that as well?"

"Of course you can, sweetheart," smirked Barry.

2   SOUTH BEACH, MIAMI

The lobby of the Delano Hotel was like a designer's hissy fit on the set of *Alice in Wonderland*. Everything was too big, too small, the wrong color, or in the wrong place. A light in a ten-foot-high shade hung in front of the reception desk. Muslin curtains sixty feet long fluttered in the breeze beside a wall dotted with miniature wall lamps and a snooker table with beige felt and ecru balls. A dark man was sitting on a white molded chair that looked like a urinal, reading a newspaper. The man looked up as a slender girl with blunt-cut blond hair stepped into the lobby. He lowered his newspaper to watch as she looked around, amusement flickering across her features, then headed for the reception desk. She was wearing jeans and a thin black top, carrying a soft tan-leather tote, and dragging a battered tan and olive carry-on behind her.

"Awesome name," said the receptionist. "Is that Jewels as in Tiffany?"

"No. J.O.U.L.E.S. As in the unit of kinetic energy," the girl said.

"No kidding? Ah yes, here we are," said the receptionist. "I'll have the bellboy bring in your luggage and send it to your room."

"Oh, don't worry. This is all I've got."

The dark man watched as the small, determined figure marched off towards the elevators.

Olivia stared in consternation at the elevator doors, which seemed to be made of quilted stainless steel. As they were closing, a beautiful bellboy in a white T-shirt and shorts forced his arm between them and leapt into the elevator beside her, insisting on helping her take her luggage—despite the lack of it—to her room.

The room was entirely white: white floor, white walls, white sheets, white desk, white armchair and footstool, white telescope pointing at a white venetian blind. The charmingly shaggable, white-clad whippersnapper pulled up the blind, and the startling aquamarines and electric blues of Miami Beach burst into the room like a tiny, vivid oil painting in the center of a thick white frame.

"Yeees. It's like being in a hospital," she murmured.

"Rather more comfortable, I hope, ma'am. What brings you to Miami?"

His skin was like an advert for youth, peachlike, glowing, as if it had been force-fed vitamins in a greenhouse.

"Oh, you know," she said, moving closer to the window. She looked down at the lines of umbrellas and loungers against the white sand, the pastel lifeguards' huts, the surreally blue sea crisscrossed by yachts and Waverunners, a line of big ships following each other along the horizon like ducks in a shooting gallery. "My God, what's that?" One of the ships was three times as big as the others: oddly big, like a pelican in the middle of the ducks.

"That's the *OceansApart,*" said the bellboy with proprietary pride, as if he owned not only the ship, but Miami and the ocean too. "It's like an apartment block—only floating? Are you here on business or pleasure?"

"They built it already?" she said, ignoring the nosy young whippersnapper's rudely interrogatory manner.

"They sure did."

"I thought it was still just an artist's impression."

"No, ma'am. This is the maiden voyage. It's going to be anchored in Miami for four days."

"This is the one on a permanent cruise from Grand Prix to Australian Open to Masters kind of thing, and the people fly in by helicopter to find their Picassos and dental floss laid out waiting?"

"You got it."

"Sounds like it might make a good story."

"Are you a journalist?"

"Yes," she said, pride in her quasi foreign-correspondent status overcoming her discretion.

"Wow! Who for?"

"The *Sunday Times* and *Elan International* magazine." She beamed.

"Wow. I'm a writer too. What are you writing about here?"

"Oh, you know. This and that."

"Well, if you need any help, just give me a call. My name's Kurt. Anything else I can do for you at all . . . ?"

Well, now you come to mention it . . . she felt like saying. Instead, she chastely tipped him five bucks and watched the delightful little white-clad bottom depart.

Olivia Joules liked hotels. She liked hotels because:

1. When you went into a new hotel room, there was no past. It was like drawing a line and starting again.
2. Hotel life was almost Zen-like in its simplicity: a capsule wardrobe, capsule living. No debris, no nasty clothes you never wore but couldn't throw away, no in-tray, no dishes full of leaky pens and Post-it notes with chewing gum stuck to them.
3. Hotels were anonymous.
4. Hotels were beautiful, if you picked right, which, after hours and sometimes days looking at hotel Web sites on the Internet, she inevitably did. They were temples of luxury or rusticity, coziness or design.
5. The mundanities of life were taken care of and you were freed from domestic slavery hell.
6. No one could bother you: you simply put DO NOT DISTURB on the door handle and the telephone and the world had to bugger off.

Olivia had not always loved hotels. Most of her family holidays had been taken in a tent. Until the age of twenty-two her only hotel experience had been of dingy yet embarrassingly formal Crowns and Majestics in northern British seaside resorts—strange-smelling, with bizarrely patterned carpets and wallpapers, where the guests spoke in intimidated whispers and forcedly posh accents, and her entire family would freeze with shame if one of them dropped a fork or a sausage on the floor.

The first time she was sent to a hotel on business, she didn't know what to do or how to behave. But when she found herself in an elegant, untouched room, with a mini-bar, crisp white cotton sheets, room service, high-end soap, no one to answer to and free slippers she felt like she'd come home.

Sometimes she felt bad about liking hotels so much, worried that it made her a spoilt lucky bitch. But it wasn't just posh hotels she liked. It wasn't really to do with poshness. Some posh hotels were disgusting: snobbish; overly fancy; not providing the things you needed at all, such as phones that worked, food that arrived hot on the same date as the one on which it was ordered; noisy air-conditioning units; views of car parks; and, worst of all, snooty, unfriendly staff. Some of her favorite hotels weren't expensive at all. The only real criterion of fineness she trusted was whether, on arrival, the toilet paper was folded into a neat point at the end. In the Delano, it was not only neatly pointed, it had a white sticker on saying THE DELANO in cool gray capitals. She wasn't sure about the sticker. She thought it might be taking things too far.

She put the case on the bed and started lovingly to unpack the contents that would become her home until she was forced back to London. Last thing out of the bag, as always, was her survival tin, which she tucked under the pillow. It wasn't clever to carry the survival tin through airports, but it had been with her for a long time. It looked like an old tobacco tin. She had bought it in an outdoor adventure shop on the forecourt of Euston station. The lid was mirrored underneath, for signaling. The tin had a handle to transform it into a miniature pan. Inside was an edible candle, a condom for water carrying, cotton wool, potassium permanganate for cleaning wounds and fire lighting, fish hooks, a rabbit snare, a wire saw, water-proof matches, a flint, fluorescent tape, razor blades, a button compass and a miniature flare. She hadn't used any of the items except the condom—which had been several times replaced—and the cotton wool in the occasional hotel that didn't offer cleansing pads. But she was certain that one day the tin would save her by helping her to collect water in the desert, strangle a hijacker, or signal from a palm-fringed atoll to a passing plane. Until then it was a talisman—like a teddy or a handbag. Olivia had never thought of the world as a particularly safe place.

She turned back to the window and the view of the beach. There was a laminated instruction card hanging from the telescope. She looked confusedly at it for a second, then gave up and peered into the eyepiece, seeing a green blur of magnified grass. She adjusted a dial to reveal the seafront upside down. She carried on, adjusting to the upside-down world moving down—or up?—to a jogger, ugh, without a shirt on (why boastfully revolt others?) and a yacht smacking awkwardly into each wave. She moved on upside-downedly sideways until she came to the *OceansApart*. It was like the white cliffs of Dover heading for Miami.

She dragged her laptop out of her bag and banged out an e-mail to Barry.

Re: Fantastic new story
1. Miami Cool, going really well.
2. Great Style story: *OceansApart*—obscenely large new floating apartment block—docked in Miami on maiden voyage.
3. Can cover but would need one or ideally two more nights here?
Over and out. Olivia.

She read it, nodding with satisfaction, pressed "Send," then looked up at the mirror and started. Her hair was quite mad, and her face horrifying in its puffiness: the product of sixteen hours spent in planes and airports—five of them stuck in Heathrow because someone had left a laptop in the ladies' loo. The face-cream party was at six. She had twenty minutes to transform herself into a dazzling creature of the night.

3

Fifty-eight minutes later she emerged, breathless, from the elevator, scrubbed and polished. A line of white limos stretched from the front of the lobby all the way up the avenue, horns blaring. The hotel bouncers were in their bossiest of elements, throwing their weight around in little white shorts and talking into headsets with the gravitas of FBI agents. Two girls with huge breasts and no hips were posing with rather desperate grins on a red carpet. They looked like weird man-woman hybrids—the upper part buxom female, the lower adolescent boy. They were striking identical poses, standing side-on to the flashbulbs, one leg in front of the other, bodies forced into an *S* shape, as if they were trying to duplicate a diagram from *InStyle* magazine or were desperate to go to the loo.

The greeting table displayed a precarious pyramid of tubs of Devorée—Crème de Phylgie, very surgical-looking, plain white with plain green writing. Olivia gave her name, took one of the glossy press packs and headed, reading it, towards the throng, shuddering at the list of repulsive-sounding algae and sea-critter-based ingredients.

A woman in a black trouser suit powered over, arranging her face into the sort of frightening white-toothed smile that looks like that of an angry monkey. "Hi! You're Olivia? Melissa from Century PR. Welcome. How was your trip over? How was the weather in London?" She marched Olivia towards the terrace, asking inane

and ceaseless questions without pause for answer. "How is your hotel room? How's Sally at *Elan*? Will you give her my regards?"

They stepped out on the deck where *le tout* fashionista and
musico Miami *monde* was artfully arranged around a selection of
wrong-sized furniture, and spilling down some steps into the garden below, where white-covered comfy chairs, giant indoor table
lamps and cabanas surrounded the turquoise-lit pool.

"Have you tried the Devorée martini? You got the press release
about the chef who's prepared the special dishes we'll be sampling
tonight?" Olivia let Melissa's autowitter wash over her. Usually, she
tried to let annoying people do their thing and hoped they'd buzz
off as soon as possible. Night had fallen with tropical suddenness.
The landscaping was lit with flaming torches, and beyond was the
ocean, crashing in the darkness. Or maybe, she thought, it was an
air-conditioning unit. There was something odd about this party. It
felt controlling and tense, like Melissa. The wind was lifting press
releases and serviettes, ruffling dresses and hair. There were people
around who didn't fit, moving and watching too anxiously for
Party Funland. She focused on a group in the far corner, trying to
figure them out. The women were actress slash model types: big
hair, long legs, small dresses. The men were harder to place: dark-
haired, olive-skinned, high mustache quotient. They were making
a show of being rich, but they weren't quite getting it right. They
looked like an advert from Debenham's in-house magazine.

"If you'll excuse me, there's someone I need to bring over. Oh
look, there's Jennifer . . ." Melissa powered off, still talking, leaving
Olivia standing on her own.

For a throwback second, she felt residual feelings of insecurity.
She stamped on them hard, as if they were a beetle or cockroach.
Olivia used to hate going to parties. She was too sensitive to the
signals given off by other people to glide through any social gathering unscathed. She liked to have proper conversations, not mindless
insincere moments, and she could never quite master the art of
moving smoothly from group to group. As a result, she used to

spend entire evenings feeling either hurt or rude. Dramatic events, however, made her decide she would no longer give a shit about anything. Over time, she had painstakingly erased all womanly urges to question her shape, looks, role in life, or effect upon other people. She would watch, analyze and conform to codes as she observed them, without allowing them to affect or compromise her own identity.

One of her favorites on her Rules for Living list was "No one is thinking about you. They're thinking about themselves, just like you." This was a particularly useful rule at parties. It meant, by implication, that no one was watching you either. Therefore, you could just stand on your own and observe, and no one would think you were a sad act. No one, for example, was thinking now that she was Olivia-no-mates-Joules just because she was on her own. Or worse, Rachel-no-mates-Pixley. No one would say, "Rachel Pixley, you're a dropout from Worksop Comprehensive. Leave the Delano Hotel this instant and go to the Post House Hotel on the Nottingham bypass."

When Rachel Pixley was a normal schoolgirl, living with two parents in Worksop, coming home to tea in a warm house, she used to think that an orphan was a glamorous thing to be, like Alona the Wild One in *Bunty* or *Mandy* comics—an orphan who was wild and free and galloped her horse bareback along the shoreline. For a long time after it all happened, she thought she had been punished for this fantasy.

When Rachel was fourteen, her mother, father and brother were run over by a lorry on a zebra crossing. Rachel, having lagged behind buying sweets and a magazine, saw the whole thing. She was put in the care of her unmarried Auntie Monica, who had cats and read newspapers all day in her nightdress. Her flat smelt of something indefinable and bad, but despite the fag ash that festooned her like snow, and her eccentric and inaccurate application of lipstick, Auntie Monica was beautiful and had been brilliant. She had studied at Cambridge and still played the piano wonderfully—

when she wasn't drunk. Playing the piano when drunk, as Rachel came to realize during the time she spent *chez* Auntie Monica, was like driving when drunk—inadvisable, if not criminal.

Rachel had had a boyfriend at school who was a couple of years above her but seemed much older than everyone else. His father was a nightwatchman and a maniac. Roxby was not exactly good-looking, but he was his own man. He used to work nights as a bouncer in Romeo and Juliet's. And when he came home—because by this time he and Rachel were living together in a room above the Hao Wah Chinese takeaway—he used to sit at the computer investing his bouncer earnings in stocks and shares.

Rachel, who had only ever understood money as something you earned in very small quantities by working, was initially resistant to the notion of making money out of money. "Money doesn't buy happiness," her hardworking father had told her. "If you work hard and you're honest and kind, then nothing can harm you." But it had. A lorry had run over him. So Rachel threw in her lot with Roxby and worked every weekend at Morrisons' supermarket, and did evening shifts after school in a corner shop run by a Pakistani family, and let him invest the money for her. When she turned sixteen, her father's life-insurance policy was turned over to her. She had twenty thousand pounds to invest. It was the beginning of the eighties. She was on the way to becoming, if not a rich woman, at least a woman of independent means.

When she was seventeen, Roxby announced that he was gay and moved to the canal district of Manchester. And Rachel, fed up with knock after knock, took a long hard look at life. She had seen her friends' older sisters, radiant and triumphant, flashing minuscule H. Samuel's solitaires on their engagement fingers, spending months obsessed with dresses, flowers and event-planning, only to be found a couple of years later in the shopping center, fat, broke and hassled, pushing prams through the rain, moaning about being hit, or belittled, or left. And she thought: *Sod that.* She started with her name. "Olivia" sounded glam. And the attractiveness of the word "Joules" was the only thing she remembered from physics lessons. *I'm all I've got,* she thought. *I'm going to be complete in myself. I'm going to work out my own good and bad.* *I'm going to be a top journalist or an explorer and do something that matters. I'm going to search this shitty world for some beauty and excitement and I'm going to have a bloody good time.* And this, Olivia Joules thought, leaning back against the Delano pillar, *is a lot more beautiful and exciting than Worksop. No one is watching you, just go with the flow and enjoy it.* Unfortunately for the Rule for Living, however, somebody *was* watching her. As she continued to scan the party, a pair of eyes met hers in a second of highly charged interest, then looked away. She also looked away, then glanced back. The man was standing alone. He was dark and rather aristocratic-looking. He was wearing a suit that was a bit too black and a shirt that was a bit too white—too flash for the Delano. And yet he didn't look like a flash person. There was a stillness about him. He turned, and suddenly his eyes met hers again with that thrilling unspoken message which sometimes transmits itself across a room and says, "I want to fuck you too." That was all that was needed: a look. No need to flirt, to maneuver, to chat. Just that moment of recognition. Then all you had to do was follow, like in a dance.

"Everything going okay?" It was the hyperactive PR woman. Olivia, realizing she was staring lustfully into space, remembered that she had a piece to file by tomorrow and had better get on with it. "There's lots of people I want you to meet," said Melissa, starting to bustle Olivia along. "Have you had something to eat? Let me see if we've got some people for you to talk to. Have you met Devorée?"

Putting thoughts of shagging strangers firmly to one side, she turned her attention to the business of quote-gathering. Everyone wanted to be in British *Elan* and the launch was easy pickings for sound bites. After an hour or so she had vaguely face-cream-based quotes from Devorée, Chris Blackwell, the manager of the Delano, a couple of handsome men whom she suspected were for hire, the

guy who did the list at Tantra, the PR for Michael Kors and
P. Diddy. It was more than enough for the solitary paragraph which
would inevitably prove the sum total of *Elan's* coverage. Moving
on to the *Sunday Times* "Cool Miami" piece, she quickly filled
her notebook with the grandmother of one of the models, who
had lived on the South Shore Strip twenty years before it became
fashionable again; a cop who claimed to have been on the scene
after the Versace shooting and was plainly lying and—*la pièce de
résistance*—Gianni Versace's former cleaning lady.

"Olivia?" Damn, it was Melissa again. "Can I introduce you to
the creator of Devorée's Crème de Phylgie? Though, of course,
Devorée has selected the ingredients personally herself."

Olivia let out an odd noise. It was the man who had been
watching her. He was a compelling mixture of soulful and powerful:
finely drawn features, a straight nose, fine, arched brows, hooded
brown eyes.

"This is Pierre Ferramo." She was disappointed. The name
sounded like something you'd find in gilt-plastic faux handwriting,
pinned on an overpriced tie in a duty-free shop.

"Ms. Joules." He was wearing a ridiculously over-the-top gold
watch, but his hand was rougher than she expected and the hand-
shake strong.

"Pleased to meet you," she said. "Congratulations on Crème de
Phylgie. Does it really contain sea slugs?"

He didn't laugh, he glinted. "Not the sea slugs themselves, only
an essence: an oil secreted by their skin."

"It sounds like something you'd want to wipe off rather than
put on."

"Does it, indeed?" He raised his eyebrows.

"I hope you won't be writing that in your piece," trilled Melissa
with a brittle laugh.

"I'm sure Ms. Joules will write with infinite subtlety and grace."

"Infinite," she said.

There was an extremely charged pause. Melissa looked from one to the other then started twittering. "Oh look, she's leaving. Will you excuse us? Pierre, I just want you to say hello to one of our very special guests before she leaves."

"Very well," he said wearily, murmuring to Olivia as he left, "sea slugs indeed."

Melissa introduced Olivia to more of her client base: two members of a boy band called Break whose gimmick was surfing and who had a "Beach Boys meets Radiohead fusion vibe." Olivia had never heard of the band, but the two boys were rather sweet. Beneath the surf-white hair, their complexions displayed a fascinating mixture of sunburnt crispiness and acne. She listened as they chattered on about their careers, Beavis-and-Butthead-type nervous sniggers punctuating a fragile veneer of bored arrogance. "We're auditioning for parts in this, like, movie? With surfers?" Their strange interrogatory intonation seemed to suggest that someone as old as Olivia might not understand words like "movie" or "surfers." "It's going to launch the single off the album?"

Two hits and they'd be off, but they didn't know it. She felt like giving them a motherly chat, but instead she just listened and nodded, watching Pierre Ferramo out of the corner of her eye.

"That's the guy who's, like, the producer? Of the movie?" whispered one of the boys.

"Really?"

They all watched as Ferramo made his stately way towards a mysterious-looking group of dark men and models. He moved gracefully, languid almost to the point of being fey, but exuding a sense of tremendous latent power. He reminded her of someone. The group parted like the Red Sea to receive him, as if he were a guru or god rather than a face-cream creator slash producer slash whatever. He settled himself down gracefully, crossing one leg over the other, revealing an expanse of bare leg, black shiny slip-ons and thin silky gray socks. A couple close to the group rose to leave their sofa.

"Shall we sit a bit nearer?" said Olivia, nodding towards the empty seats.

It was a silly, too-big sofa, so Olivia and the surf boys had almost to climb onto it, and then either virtually lie down or sit with their legs dangling like children. Ferramo looked up as she sat and graciously inclined his head. She felt her senses quicken and looked away. She breathed slowly, remembering her scuba-diving training: just keep breathing, deep breaths, be cool at all times.

She turned back to the boys, crossing her legs and smoothing her hand across her thigh. She moistened her lips, laughed and played for a second with the delicate diamond and sapphire cross at her throat. She could feel his eyes on her. She raised her lashes, preparing to look straight into those penetrating dark eyes. *Oh.* Pierre Ferramo was staring down the cleavage of the tall, unbelievably beautiful Indian model on his other side. He said something to her and the two of them rose, his arm around her, his hand on her hip, guiding her away from the table. Olivia looked at one of the spotty boys. He leaned forward and whispered, "It was doing it for me," and traced a tiny circle with his finger on her thigh. She laughed her deep throaty laugh and closed her eyes. It had been a while.

Halfway across the terrace, Pierre Ferramo heard Olivia's laugh and raised his head, like an animal catching a scent. He turned to Melissa, who was hovering at his elbow and murmured a few words to her, then he continued his dignified progress towards the lobby, the tall, silken-haired Indian model at his side.

As she sipped her apple martini, Olivia was struggling to think who it was that Ferramo reminded her of: the hooded eyes, the sense of intelligence and power, the languid movements.

She felt a hand on her arm and jumped.

"Olivia?" It was the wretched Melissa. "Mr. Ferramo would like you to join him for a small private party he is having in his apartment tomorrow night."

Olivia could hardly breathe. The small hairs were rising on the back of her neck and her forearms.

"All right," she said, brave and resolute, eyes darting this way and that in terror. "I shall be there."

Melissa looked at her oddly. "It's only a party."

But Olivia had suddenly realized exactly who Ferramo reminded her of. It was Osama bin Laden.

4

If Olivia had not yet brought her overactive imagination to bear, she was at least beginning to recognize the symptoms of a flare-up. As she let herself into her all-white hotel room, she was alive with excitement, mind racing through myriad wild scenarios. She kicked off her sandals, rubbed a blister on her left foot with one hand and reached for the phone to call Barry. *Stop, breathe, think,* she told herself, replacing the receiver in the nick of time. *Don't be crazy.* She sat on her hands and tried to distance herself from her whirling mind.

But it's brilliant, the whirling mind continued to tell her. Where better for al-Qaeda to hide than in the center of a hip urban scene? Everyone thought operatives were geeky types: engineers in grungy clothes who lived in grim apartments in Hamburg, or faded thirties terraced houses in faded London suburbs, eating takeaways together, praying in makeshift mosques and faxing their instructions from post offices in Neasden. Al-Qaeda operatives didn't drink apple martinis in cool hotels wearing Armani. Al-Qaeda operatives didn't produce movies and have hyperactive PRs to up their profiles. It was the perfect way to forge contacts. It was the perfect cover.

She jumped up to her laptop and Googled Pierre Ferramo. Hardly anything appeared on the screen. There was an Austrian jeweler in Salzburg who made cheap knockoffs of Fabergé eggs. There was a chain of ladies' boutiques in the north of England. And Google asked, "Did you mean Ferrari?" But nothing about a film producer or a perfumier, or anything that related to the man she'd met. It didn't add up. Even "Olivia Joules" would throw up a couple of hundred entries. As her hand crept towards the phone again, she told herself to get a grip, thinking back to the conversation with Barry.

You're having an overimaginative attack, she told herself. *And it's certifiably non-PC. Just because someone has dark hair, an accent and reminds you of Osama bin Laden, that's no reason to decide he's a terrorist.*

She took a hot bath and fell into a fitful sleep, then awoke suddenly half an hour later hearing Ferramo's voice again in her head, analyzing the accent. It was hopeless trying to sleep with jet lag. She changed position, moved her head this way and that, her thoughts becoming crazier and crazier. Then she sat up, glanced at her watch, picked up the phone and dialed.

"It's me," she whispered urgently into the receiver.

"Olivia, it's the middle of the bloody night." An English girl's voice—posh, confident.

"It's not the middle of the night."

"Olivia, eight o'clock on a Saturday morning is, to all intents and purposes, the middle of the night."

"Sorry, sorry. But it's important."

"Okay, what? Don't tell me. You've discovered Miami is a giant hologram designed by aliens? You're getting married to Elton John?"

"No," said Olivia, smiling in spite of herself. Kate O'Neill was her friend but also the Middle East correspondent for the *Sunday Times.* Olivia wanted her approval more than she could quite admit to herself.

"What? Come on."

"I can't sleep. I think I've . . . I've just got a hunch there might have been some al-Qaeda at that party last night. I met this guy. He kind of reminds me of Osama bin Laden."

Kate started laughing. She laughed for quite a long time. Olivia's shoulders slumped and she blinked rapidly, hurt.

"Okay," Kate said eventually. "How drunk are you, exactly?"

"I am not," Olivia said indignantly, "drunk."

"You're sure it's not a resurrected Abraham Lincoln?"

"Shut up," said Olivia. "But seriously. Just think about it. Where better could they hide than in plain sight where no one's expecting to see them?"

"I could think of, ooh, three, maybe four hundred places, just off the top of my head. Who is the guy? Is he six foot four, late forties?"

"No, but—" Her mind was racing again. "Look, I'm not saying it's actually him, but people can completely alter their appearance, can't they? He could easily have had some length taken out of each leg and his face changed."

"Right, right. So, if you look at it that way, Osama bin Laden could be Oprah Winfrey, Britney Spears, or Eminem. Why have you fastened upon this guy?"

"It's something about him. It's his features—well, more his expression, in fact. He's sort of languid."

"Oh, why didn't you say? *Languid?* Well, it's definite then. I mean, bin Laden is number one on the FBI's Most Languid List."

"Shut up. He says he's called Pierre Ferramo. He's pretending to be French, but I don't think he is. He kind of rolls his *r*s."

"Right, right. Was Osama bin Ferramo drinking alcohol?"

"Yes," she said doubtfully.

"Did he flirt with you?"

"Yes."

"Olivia, Osama bin Laden is a Muslim. Do you know what a Muslim is?"

"Of course I know what a Muslim is," Olivia hissed. "What I'm saying is that maybe this is a new form of hideout. They're very clever—they're constantly changing tactics. Maybe drinking and womanizing on the Miami South Shore makes a better hideout than a cave in Tora Bora."

"Hmm. I'm not sure they could pull it off."

"He hasn't. I've rumbled him. Anyway, the bin Ladens are a

really posh, rich international family. Don't you remember that guy from the *FT* who used to date one of bin Laden's sisters?"

"Oh yeah, right before he'd done any atrocities."

"And he asked her about her brother's reputation as a black sheep and she said, 'Oh, honestly, the worst one can say about Osama is that he's rather socially difficult.' "

Kate laughed. "Okay, point taken. But promise me something."

"What?"

"Promise me you won't ring up Barry and tell him you've found Osama bin Laden at a face-cream launch."

Silence.

"Olivia, are you listening to me? You remember the Sudan locust cloud? The Surbiton Moonies who turned out to be a corporate training scheme? The Gloucestershire ghoul that turned out to be steam from an air-conditioning vent? The *Sunday Times* has only just started to trust you again. So, please: do your Miami story on time, to length, nicely, and don't bugger things up for yourself. And go to sleep."

"Okay. Thanks, Kate. Call you in a couple of days," she said, reaching for her laptop.

She e-mailed Barry. She didn't tell him what the story was, she just asked to stay on and check out a lead. She had to do something, otherwise she'd be back in London writing articles that began, "Suddenly there is more wallpaper everywhere!!" Then she clicked off the light and lay staring at the ceiling, thinking.

Olivia believed in independent thought. Ever since the Twin Towers were hit, when the authorities told people to stay where they were and not evacuate, she kept asking herself: would she have been one of the ones who did as they were told and stayed, or would she have thought for herself and set off down the stairs?

5

She sat outside a café on the South Shore Strip waiting for Barry's morning call and wishing it would stop being so windy. It was sunny and humid, but the wind was a roaring, flapping constant in the background. Breakfast was Olivia's favorite meal: coffee and something piggy like a muffin. Or a smoked-salmon-and-cream-cheese bagel. Or banana pancakes. And as many newspapers as possible spread before her. But this morning the *New York Times*, the *Miami Herald*, *USA Today* and two British tabloids had to be restrained under the salt and pepper. She had ordered cinnamon-apple French toast in order to eradicate the remnants of last night's apple martinis. Treat apple with apple—like snake bite with snake venom.

She poured maple syrup onto the cinnamon-apple French toast triangle, stuck her knife in and watched the pureed apple ooze out, imagining confronting Osama bin Ferramo at his party that night: "Killing is so very wrong. We, as nations, must learn to honor our differences and live in peace." Osama bin Ferramo, breaking down, would sobbingly agree that his Holy War must end and that he would work tirelessly in future for world peace alongside President Carter, Ginger Spice, et al. Olivia would be internationally fêted, elevated to foreign correspondent, awarded an honorary Pulitzer . . . her mobile rang.

"Hi," she answered, in a tense, urgent voice, glancing behind her to check for al-Qaeda spies. It was Barry.

"Okay, *numero uno:* this floating apartment-ship story . . ."

"Yes!" said Olivia, excitedly. "It's a really good story. It's huge. And the people live on it all year round and just fly in by helicopter. I could do it in a couple of extra days." Olivia had the phone wedged between her ear and shoulder while she tucked into the apple French toast.

"Oh, I agree it's a good story. So good, in fact, that, as you apparently failed to notice, we covered it in a full-page spread in the Style section last week."

Olivia paused with her toast halfway to her mouth.

"That's a section of the *Sunday Times,* the newspaper you're supposed to be working for. Indeed, the very section of the *Sunday Times* you are supposed to be working for. You do, I assume, read the *Sunday Times* occasionally, are familiar with it, at least?"

"Yes," she said, brows lowered.

"And this other 'fantastic news story' you've found. What might that be? Miami invaded by walking dolphins, perhaps? The former Iraqi information minister spinning vinyl in the lobby?"

Thank God she hadn't e-mailed him after all.

"Well, actually it's something I've just started working on. I'll tell you more in a couple of—"

"Shut up. How are we getting along with the story we are supposed to be doing? The story we've been sent out to Miami, at considerable expense, to cover? Any chance of us turning our attention to that at some point? At all?"

"Oh yes, yes. I'm doing that. It's all fine. But I'm onto some really good leads for another story. I promise you, it's really good. If I could just stay one more night and go to this party, then . . ."

"No. En. Oh. No. You file 'Cool Miami' by six o'clock your time tonight. Fifteen hundred words. Spelled correctly. With normal punctuation, not an assortment of strange markings put in randomly, to help. And then you do not go to parties, go shopping, or get waylaid by any other form of irrelevant entertainment. You go to the airport, get the night flight and come home. Got it?"

By a supreme effort of will, she refrained from telling him that:

1. He was missing the biggest story of the twenty-first century.
2. One day he would be sorry.
3. Re his punctuation slur: language was a beautiful free-flowing, evolving thing which should not be fettered by artificial rules, regulations and strange markings imposed from without rather than within.

"Okay, Bazzer," she said instead. "I'll do it by six o'clock."

Elan had not yet called to nix the *OceansApart* story, so she thought it wouldn't do any harm to nip quickly down to the harbor to take a look, just in *case,* so that if *Elan* did happen to call and say yes, then she would have some more material. Plus, she could be picking up more local color for the *Sunday Times* piece while she was at it. It was nine already, but she figured that if she got back from the *OceansApart* by ten-thirty, she'd still have seven and a half hours to write the article for Barry. And spell-check it. And e-mail it. But it would definitely be fine. Definitely. That was only about two hundred words an hour. And she could run! It was, after all, vital to exercise.

Unfortunately, Olivia did not have a proper grasp of the passage of time. In fact, both Barry and Kate had noted on several occasions that Olivia thought time was personal, that it moved at the speed she wanted it to. Their view was that this was not a belief compatible with being a newspaper journalist with deadlines to meet and so on.

Jogging along the South Shore Strip, even at breakfast time, was like flipping through radio channels: a different beat blaring out from each café. Waiters were hosing down the pavements, gardeners blowing away leaves. The lines of hooting cars were gone, the party people only recently tucked into bed. Olivia passed a café playing salsa music; inside, everything—walls, tables, plates, menus—was covered in the same lurid jungle print; the waitress, even at that hour, was wearing a leopardskin, halter-neck catsuit. She crossed the road to get a better view of the campy grandeur of the Versace mansion and the art deco hotels—whites, pinks, lilacs, oranges—the Pelican, the Avalon, the Casa Grande, curves and funnels suggesting trains and ocean liners. It was hot already, the shadows of the fluttering palm trees crisp against the white pavement. She started working out her piece as she ran.

"Think Miami is full of old people's condos, the hum of electric wheelchairs and people shooting each other? Think again!" . . .

"Suddenly there are more revamped art deco hotels everywhere!" . . .

"If Paris is the new elevator music, Miami is the new Eminem." . . .

"If Manchester is the new Soho, then Miami is the new Manhattan." . . .

"If Eastbourne had a makeover from Ian Schrager and Stella McCartney, then forced all its inhabitants into a giant tanning booth . . ."

Oh God. She couldn't do this stuff anymore. It was nonsense. It didn't mean anything. She had to find a proper story.

At the south end of the strip were huge apartment blocks, and behind them, gliding smoothly, she could see a huge ocean liner. She must be close to the docks. She jogged along the street, the area becoming rougher and tattier, until she reached the water at South Pointe Park, where the deep shipping lane passed straight in front of the apartments and marina. The liner was moving fast, its bulbous rear disappearing towards the docks: big, but not the *OceansApart*. She peered at the skyline beyond it: the tower blocks of downtown Miami, the arched bridges of the highways crisscrossing the big expanses of water, the cranes marking the docks. She started to run towards them, but they were farther away than they seemed; she

kept thinking she was so nearly there, it would be stupid to turn
back.

She had stopped at the end of a traffic bridge, trying to get her
breath and pushing a damp strand of hair from her forehead, when
she suddenly realized that what she had thought was an office block
beyond the liner was in fact the *OceansApart*. Here, in the harbor, it
dwarfed all the other ships around it, making them look like toys or
miniatures. It was monolithic. It looked too big to be safe, as
though it might topple over.

Across the way, a small crowd of people was gathered on a patch
of grass, a group of taxis parked alongside. Olivia made her way
over. She counted the decks: there were fifteen of them, lines of
portholes, then layer upon layer of balconies. There were people
sitting out on white chairs at tables, eating breakfast. She glanced
around at the crowd. Some of them were clearly passengers, taking
photographs with the *OceansApart* in the background, dressed in
the garish and bizarre outfits which seem to go with the cruising
life. Olivia smiled at the sight of a lady with a bright orange face
and red lipstick, which had missed her mouth, wearing a little
white boxy jacket with epaulets and a captain's hat, and an embarrassed husband in pastel, infantilized cruise gear beside her, posing
while a taxi driver took their photos.

"Excuse me, love." It was a northern English accent. Olivia
turned to see an old couple, the auburn-haired lady in an elegant
green dress with a cream handbag and matching cream shoes. The
cream shoes made Olivia think of holidays in Bournemouth. The
man, who was only slightly taller than the lady, and stockily built,
was holding her jacket. It was sweet the way he was smoothing it
proprietorially, as if he was proud to be holding it for her.

"Would you mind taking our photo in front of the ship?" The
lady held out a disposable camera.

Olivia smiled. "Where are you from?"

"Leeds, love. Just near Leeds."

"I'm from Worksop," said Olivia, taking the camera.

"Ee, 'ecky thump," quipped the old man. "You look out of breath. Have you been running? Don't you want to get your breath back a minute?"

"No, I'm fine. Closer together," said Olivia, peering through the viewfinder. "Ooh, hang on. I'm going to have to move back a bit to get it all in."

"Don't bother, love. Just get a bit in. We know what it is, don't we, Edward?" The lady was a charming mix of elegant looks and broad Yorkshire accent.

Olivia clicked the camera, looking at the beaming couple through the viewfinder. It suddenly felt as though all the scariness and bad things in life had receded, and she was in a lovely granny-and-grandpa world of biscuit tins and doilies. To her horror, she felt tears pricking her eyelids.

"There you go. Souvenir of Miami," she said slightly too cheerily, handing back the camera.

The lady chuckled. "Running. It makes me feel jiggered just looking at you. Do you want a cough sweet?" She began to rummage in her bag.

"So, love," said the old man, "what are you doing so far away from Worksop?"

"I'm a journalist," said Olivia. "I'm trying to get my magazine to let me write something about the *OceansApart.*"

"Eee, right fair. A journalist. That's grand, that is."

"We can tell you all sorts about the ship, love."

"Do you live on it?"

"Yes!" said the man proudly.

"Well, only part of the time," said the lady.

"That's our cabin. Look, halfway up, in the middle, with the pink towel," said the man, pointing.

"Oh yes, looks nice. Lovely balcony. I'm Olivia, by the way."

"Elsie, and this is Edward. We're on our honeymoon."

"Your honeymoon? Have you known each other a long time?"

"Fifty years," said Edward, proudly. "She wouldn't have me when she were eighteen."

"Well, you started courting someone else. What did you expect?"

"Only because you wouldn't have me."

Olivia loved people's stories. Scratch the surface of anyone and you'd find something strange and complicated going on.

"Do you want a lift anywhere?" said the man. "We're taking a taxi to South Beach."

"Ooh, yes please," said Olivia. "As a matter of fact, I've made myself a bit late."

"So, carry on with the story," Olivia said as the taxi pulled out onto the highway.

"Well," said Elsie, "anyway, he thought I weren't interested, and I thought he weren't interested, and we lived in the same town for fifty years and never said 'owt. Then my husband died, and Vera, that was Edward's wife as was, she died, and then . . ."

"Well, here we are. We was married two weeks ago and we've got a lot of missed time to make up for."

"That's so sad," said Olivia. "All that time, wasted."

"Aye," said Edward.

"Nay, lass," said Elsie. "You can't go regretting stuff because there wasn't anything else that could have happened."

"What do you mean?"

"Well, you know, it's cause and effect. Every time anything happens it's because of all the other things happening all over the world. Any time you make a decision, there wasn't anything else you could have done because it were who you were, like, and it was all the things that had happened up to then that made you decide that. So there's no point regretting anything."

Olivia looked at her, nodding thoughtfully. "I'm going to add that to my Rules for Living," she said. Her mobile rang, dammit.

"You can answer it, love, we're not bothered."

It was a commissioning editor from *Elan,* gushing at her that they wanted the *OceansApart* piece, and she could stay another two nights to do it. "But we don't want any white shoes and blue rinses, right?" Olivia flinched, hoping her new friends couldn't hear. "We want hip people, not hip replacements."

Olivia said good-bye and clicked the phone off with a sigh. It rang again immediately.

"Where are you?" bellowed Barry. "I've just rung the hotel and you're not there. What the fuck are you doing?"

"I. Am. Do. Ing. It," she said. "I'm just doing a bit of extra research."

"Get the fuck on and write it," he said. "Six o'clock, finished, fifteen hundred words. Or that's the last time I'm sending you abroad."

"He sounded a bit aerated," said Edward.

"I don't like men what shout, do you?" said Elsie.

She arranged to come and talk to them the following morning at eleven. They said they'd introduce her to the residents' manager and show her round their apartment and "all the amenities." They dropped her off in front of the Delano. She looked at her watch and realized that, unfortunately, it was nearly quarter to twelve.

"If sex is the new elevator music, then Miami is the new Manhattan. If . . ."

It was quarter to four and she still hadn't got an opening paragraph. She sat back from the computer with her pen in her mouth. Then, glancing behind her guiltily, as if she was in the newsroom, she brought up AOL and hit Google, typing in "Pierre Ferramo." Still nothing there. It was definitely weird. If he was for real, there would be something at least. She typed in "Olivia Joules." You see, even she had two hundred and ninety-three entries. She started to read them: articles from the years she'd been trying to make it as a journalist, the first one about car alarms. Crufts Dog Show. She smiled fondly at the memories. Then she thought she'd have a little look through her clothes to think about what to wear for the party. As she stood up, she caught sight of the clock.

OhmybloodyGodandfuck! It was four-thirty-five, and she hadn't written a word.

Olivia dived back to the desk and hit her sleek titanium iBook with a sudden frenzy.

"In the capital of England the worlds of fashion, music, TV, theater, movies, literature, newspapers and politics combine in one small city like a writhing knot of snakes. In America these areas are separated out into capitals of their own. Traditionally, it was politics in Washington, literature, arts and fashion in New York, entertainment in LA. But within the last few years Miami—formerly the capital of guns, shady business dealings, smugglers and sun-seeking geriatrics—has exploded onto the capital-city scene in a burst of hot light, art deco and leopardskin as the center of extravagant cool, with the glitz of music, fashion and entertainment increasingly drawn there as if by the force of a giant pink and ice-blue magnet."

There. She would rephrase it and start with a bit of color. The phone rang. It was Melissa, the PR girl, "just asking" how she was getting on with the article and checking that she was coming to Pierre Ferramo's "little gathering." Olivia tried to type with one hand, the phone tucked under her chin, desperately waiting for a gap between sentences which never came. No sooner had she got rid of Melissa than the phone rang again. This time it was the commissioning editor from *Elan,* in a leisurely mood, wanting to talk more about the *OceansApart:* the angle, the length, the style, people who might be good for interviews. It was nearly five o'clock. It was hopeless, hopeless. Why the fuck had she got herself into this mess? She was doomed—doomed to write articles beginning: "Suddenly there are more hats everywhere!" She would never be allowed out of the office again.

6

Back in London, in the *Sunday Times* office, Barry Wilkinson was pacing in front of the big old-fashioned clock, cursing Olivia.

He watched, furious, as the second hand clicked towards eleven o'clock, poised to pick up the phone.

"Okay, the silly cow's flunked. We're going to have to run the standby."

Barry's deputy burst into the room brandishing a printout. "She's filed it!"

"And?" said Barry, witheringly.

"It's great," said the deputy.

"Humph," said Barry.

Meanwhile, Olivia too had been glancing furiously at the clock as she tried to get ready in a negative amount of time. Why did people in America do everything so bloody early? Lunch at noon. Dinner at seven. It was like being back in 1960s Worksop except that she was headed for a party hosted by either a perfumier slash producer or a terrorist, depending whether she was mad or not.

She was ready within minutes. Eight years earlier, as part of the Rachel-to-Olivia metamorphosis, she had made one supreme effort to change herself from plump to thin, to arm herself with a great body as a useful tool in life. What had startled her was how differently the world had treated her old plump self and her new thin self. It was then that she realized she could manipulate reactions. If you wanted to create a stir and have everyone notice you, that wasn't so hard. You just wore something very small and attention-seeking, like a wannabe movie star does at a premiere. If you wanted no one even to realize you were there: ill-fitting jeans with hankies in the pockets, flat shoes and a baggy sweatshirt, no makeup, glasses, and hair all over the place. She became, in her instinctive way, a master of disguise. Dressing was all about uniforms and codes. People didn't look much beyond that outside Worksop, until you got to know them, if you ever got that far.

Tonight, she decided, she needed a look which was attractive, but not so tarty as to offend any possible Muslim sensibility (tricky), and shoes which enabled one to walk or at least stand still without getting blisters. She had packed her rich, attention-seeking uniform (designer slippy things, enough posh jewelry to carry off some flashier fakes) and also her usual equipment: pepper-spray pen, spyglass, hatpin (an old fail-safe of her mother's to counter would-be assailants) and survival tin, of course.

After a very small number of attempts, she arrived at a simple pale slip dress and a Pucci wrap to cover her shoulders. She thought about covering her head as well, then realized she was getting carried away. She gave her reflection a rousing, almost cheerleader-like smile, and called downstairs for a cab. At the last moment, she stuffed the hatpin, pepper spray and survival tin into the Louis Vuitton clutch along with her miniature address book, just in case.

She flicked on CNN before she left to see if anything exciting had happened. They were doing a story about a time capsule from fifty years ago being discovered in a school.

"A message from the past"—dramatic pause—*"from those who lived in it,"* concluded the presenter sententiously. Olivia loved the CNN riddle-me-ree phraseology: *"He's tall, he's bad and he hid in a hole—Saddam Hussein!"* *"It's wet, it's see-through, but without it we'd die:*

waterrrrr!" Then her eye was caught by the text strip running underneath the pictures: alongside *"Yankees 11, Red Sox 6"* it read: *"Osama bin Laden sighted in southern Yemen. Sources call sighting 'conclusive.' "*

She stared at it, blinking. "Oh," she said eventually. "Oh dear. Though, obviously, that's good."

7

Olivia's feelings of sheepishness escalated as she arrived at Ferramo's apartment block and realized she had been expecting a cross between an overpriced Knightsbridge hotel and the interiors favored by Saddam Hussein in his early promotional videos: fitted carpets, square beige sofas, stilted flower arrangements in front of long net curtains, curly gilt chairs and bulbous lamps. In her fevered mind, Ferramo had sprouted a beard, a turban, flowing robes and a Kalashnikov. She was expecting sweet Middle Eastern musks and perfumes, Turkish (for some reason) delight and Ferramo sitting cross-legged on a prayer mat next to one of the bulbous lamps.

But the block was an ultramodern building, the public areas designed in a ruthlessly minimalist style with a nod in the direction of the nautical—everything was white or blue and dotted with porthole accents, i.e., round things. There were no bulbous lamps or curly chairs. Pierre Ferramo's penthouse occupied the entire nineteenth and twentieth floors. As she stepped out of the white metallic be-portholed elevator, she gazed awestruck at the spectacle in front of her.

The twentieth floor was one vast, glass-walled room, leading out onto a terrace which overlooked the sea. An illuminated lap pool—bright electric blue—stretched the entire length of the terrace. At the back of the room, through one of the walls of glass, the sun was setting behind the Miami skyline in a flamboyant burst of oranges and salmon pinks.

Ferramo was seated at the head of a vast white table, where a card game was in play, an almost palpable air of gravitas and power emanating from his dark, elegant figure. Behind him, the tall Indian model was resting a hand, consortlike, on his shoulder. Her long black hair shone against a pure white evening dress, the whole effect set off by a dazzling array of diamonds.

Olivia looked away, ashamed, afraid that Ferramo somehow knew what lunacies had been running round in her brain. He looked like a clever, dignified businessman: a rich man, a powerful man certainly, but not a terrorist. Thank God she hadn't said anything specific to Barry.

"Your name?" said the boy at the entrance, holding out a list.

"Olivia Joules," she said, fighting the urge to apologize, just in general.

"Ah yes, come this way."

The young man led her to a waiter holding a tray. She carefully selected a glass of sparkling water—no drunken fuck-ups for her tonight—and looked round the room, reminding herself: *No one is thinking about you; they're thinking about themselves, just like you.*

Two young girls in T-shirts and tight jeans, the waistbands almost indecently low, were exchanging air kisses. She recognized them as the girls who'd been posing, S-shaped, on the red carpet the night before.

"Oh. My. God." One girl's hand shot to her mouth. "I have that T-shirt."

"You're kidding me."

"The exact same T-shirt."

"Where did you get it?"

"The Gap."

"So did I! I got it in the Gap."

"Oh. My. God."

The two girls stared at each other, overcome by this almost magical coincidence.

"Hi. How do you two know each other?" Olivia ventured with a

friendly smile, fighting down the sense of being the most unpopu-
lar girl in the playground. Would that she had the Gap T-shirt too.

"Oh, we both work at—"

"We're actresses," snapped the other. They, like the T-shirts, were
almost spookily identical: big breasts, tiny hips, long blond hair,
brown pencil outlining their glossed collagen pouts. The only dif-
ference was that one was much prettier than the other.

"Actresses! Wow," said Olivia.

"I'm Demi," said the less pretty one. "This is Kimberley. Where
are you from?"

"England."

"England. Is that London?" said Kimberley. "I want to go to
London."

"You're lucky, living here."

"We don't live in Miami, we're just visiting. We're from LA.
Well, not *from* LA."

"My family's part Italian, part Romanian and part Cherokee,"
explained Kimberley.

"Olivia," she said, shaking hands and feeling awfully English.
"So you're just visiting? Are you working here?"

"No," said Kimberley airily, pulling at her jeans. "Pierre just
flew us over for the launch."

"Generous guy."

"Yes. Are you an actress?" said Kimberley suspiciously. "Do you
know him from Paris?"

"Can't act for toffee. I only met him last night. I'm a journalist."

"Oh. My. God. Which magazine are you from?"

"Elan."

"Elan? That's British *Elan,* right? You should come to LA. You
should give us a call. You could maybe do a profile on us."

"Okay," Olivia said, taking her little book out of her bag, hiding
the survival tin. "What's the number?"

The two girls looked at each other.

"Actually we're between addresses at the moment," said Demi.

"But you can reach us through Melissa. You know, who does Pierre's PR."

"Or you can ring us at work, at the Hilton."

Kimberley looked furiously at Demi. "We're just working there temporarily," she said sharply, "to keep us busy between auditions and rehearsals."

"Of course. Which Hilton?"

"The Beverly Hilton?" said Demi eagerly. "On Santa Monica and Wilshire? Where they hold the Golden Globes? I usually get to host the ladies' powder room during the Globes. It's awesome: four makeup stations, every kind of perfume. All the big stars come in for touch-ups: Nicole Kidman, Courteney Cox, Jennifer Connelly, you get to meet them close up."

Oh, for God's sake. Osama bin Ferramo indeed. He was just a playboy . . .

"Wow. What's Nicole Kidman like?" said Olivia.

"Oh my God," said Demi, hand to her heart.

"But actually"—Kimberley leaned forward conspiratorially—"we're going to be starring in the movie Pierre's producing. You've heard about that . . ."

. . . a cynical playboy, playboying on the dreams of innocent little wannabes.

"May I interrupt you, ladies?"

Olivia turned. A short man had joined them, dark chest hair protruding from a yellow polo shirt. The chest hair, like the hair on his head, was very tightly curled, like pubic hair. He smelled of nasty sweet perfume. He held out his hand, glancing at her breasts. "Hi, baby. Alfonso Perez. And you are . . ."

"Olivia Joules," she said coldly. "I met Pierre last night at the Devorée launch."

"Ah yes. And you are an actress too? Perhaps we can find a role for you?" He had a thickly accented voice with heavily rolled *r*s.

"No, thanks. I can't act my way out of a paper bag."

"That's funny," said Kimberley. Why did Americans say "That's funny?" They said it instead of laughing, as if funniness were something you observed from afar rather than something you participated in.

"Really, Ms. Joules? You do not wish to be an actress?" It was Ferramo.

There was a collective intake of breath from Demi and Kimberley. They gazed, lip-lined pouts momentarily ajar. Pierre Ferramo's legs were encased in neatly pressed blue jeans. His shoulders looked broad in a soft gray cashmere sweater. Olivia forced herself to breathe normally and looked into the dark, penetrating eyes. He raised his eyebrows quizzically.

"I tried acting once. I was given some roles in a comedy revue. One by one all my parts were taken away from me, apart from that of Miss Guided, the mute chambermaid."

The wannabes and the little oily man looked at her, baffled.

Ferramo showed a glimmer of amusement. "You will excuse us?" he said to the group, taking her arm and beginning to guide Olivia away.

As the wannabes glowered, Olivia had to fight down playground-level feelings of smugness and one-upmanship, feelings she deeply disapproved of in any circumstances. *Divide and rule.* Ferramo was dividing his roost of girlies in order to rule it.

A waiter hurried up with a tray of champagne.

"Oh, no thank you," said Olivia quickly as Ferramo handed her a long-stemmed glass.

"But you must," he murmured. "It is French. It is the finest."

Yes, but are you? His accent wasn't easy to place.

"*Non, merci,*" she said. "*Et vous? Vous êtes français?*"

"*Mais bien sûr,*" he said, with an approving glance. "*Et je crois que vous parlez bien le français. Vous êtes, ou—je peux?—tu es une femme bien educatée.*"

I wish. Worksop Comprehensive, she thought, but merely smiled mysteriously, asking herself if *educatée* was a proper French word and resolving to look it up later.

Olivia had an ear for languages, and had discovered that even when she couldn't speak a foreign tongue, she could often understand it. Even if the words were double Dutch, she could usually guess at what the person might be saying, or figure it out through her sensitivity to nuances of expression. There had been a time when her lack of university education had made her sad, so she had made up for it herself. With books and tapes and visits she had developed fluency in French and passable Spanish and German. A couple of visits to the Sudan and the Muslim islands of Zanzibar and Lamu had given her the rudiments of Arabic. Unfortunately, the world of style-and-beauty journalism was not giving her much chance to use all this.

Taking a large swig of champagne, Ferramo led her through the party, ignoring the bids for his attention. It was like being with the star at a film premiere. Eyes followed them, particularly those of the tall Indian beauty. "But of course, Ms. Joules, the French are not exactly *populaire* in your country," he said, leading her onto the terrace.

"Nor in this," she laughed. " 'Cheese-eating surrender-monkeys,' Homer Simpson called them." She looked up at him, smiling while gauging his reaction. He leaned against the cruise-ship-type railing and smiled back, gesturing for her to join him.

"Ah, Monsieur Simpson. The fount of all human wisdom. And you? You were at one with the French *sensibilité*?"

She leaned on the cool metal rail and looked out to sea. The wind was still raging. The mood appeared from time to time behind ragged, racing clouds.

"Were you?" she asked.

"I was ashamed of my countrymen." *Yes, but which countrymen?* "And you? What was your position?" *Why was he asking her this?*

"I always find it a bad idea to talk politics at parties."

"Not when asked for an opinion directly, surely."

"I was against the invasion."

"You *were*? And why was that?"

"Well, since you ask: there was no evidence of weapons of mass destruction, there was no connection between Saddam Hussein and al-Qaeda or September 11, and they were punishing a breach of international law by breaking international law themselves. I thought it was mad, unless there was something they weren't telling us, which it turns out there wasn't."

"You are right," he laughed, "you are not an actress."

"Because I've got an opinion? That's a bit sweeping, isn't it?"

"Actors. Do you know that, every day, over five hundred young people arrive in Los Angeles, expecting to be actresses, flocking after fame and wealth like so many locusts? There is nothing else of value in their lives."

"You seem to have taken rather a lot of them under your wing."

"I wish to help them."

"Sure you do."

He glanced at her sharply. "It is a brutal profession."

"Pierre?" The tall Indian beauty came out onto the balcony and touched him possessively on the arm. She was accompanied by a good-looking, well-toned man of maybe forty with a wide smile which turned up at the edges—a cross between that of Jack Nicholson and Felix the Cat. "Can I introduce you to Michael Monteroso? You remember, the genius facial technician who's been helping us? He's the toast of Hollywood," she added, wrinkling her nose at Olivia in an attempt to be girlishly conspiratorial. "Backstage at everything."

For a fleeting second a look of contempt crossed Ferramo's fine features, then he composed his face into a gracious smile.

"But of course, Michael. A pleasure. I am delighted to meet the maestro at last." Monteroso and he shook hands.

"And may I introduce my friend from London, Olivia Joules," said Ferramo. "A writer of great distinction." He pressed her arm as if to suggest a shared joke. "And, Olivia, this is Suraya Steele."

"Hi," Suraya said coolly, running her hand through her hair at one temple and flicking back the long shiny curtain so that it cascaded over her shoulders. Olivia stiffened. She hated women who did hair-flicking. It seemed so sneakily vain: disguising hair smugness and "everybody look at me and my lovely hair" attention-seeking as hair tidiness, as if they were flicking their hair back simply to keep it off their faces. In which case why not use a kirby grip or a sensible Alice band?

"Don't you write about beauty for *Elan*?" Suraya purred, slightly pitying.

"Really?" said Michael Monteroso. "Let me give you my card and my Web site. What I do is a special microdermabrasic instant-lift technique. I gave it to Devorée three minutes before the MTV awards."

"Didn't she look great?" said Suraya.

"Will you excuse me?" murmured Pierre. "I must return to the game. There is nothing worse than a host who wins, apart from a host who wins and then slides off."

"Yeah, we should definitely get back there." Suraya's accent was odd. It was a fluid mixture of drawling West Coast American and bookish Bombay. "Don't want rumblings of discontent."

As Michael Monteroso watched Ferramo's retreating back with evident disappointment, there was no need for Olivia to remind herself that no one was thinking about her. Monteroso looked like a man who had clawed his way to success late in life and was hanging on to it for all he was worth. He nodded at her vaguely, turned to see if there was anyone more interesting to talk to and broke into a white-toothed smile.

"Hey, Travis! How you doing, man?"

"Good, good. Good to see you."

The guy sharing a high five with Monteroso was one of the most overtly good-looking men Olivia had ever seen, with ice-blue, wolflike eyes, but she sensed desperation.

"How's it going?" said Monteroso. "How's the acting?"

"Good, good, you know. I'm doing like a little writing, and, you know, lifestyle management, and I'm making these kind of lifeline boxes, and, you know . . ."

So that would be bad, then, on the acting front, thought Olivia, trying not to smile.

"Olivia, I see you've met Travis Brancato! Do you know he's writing the script for Pierre's new movie?"

Olivia listened politely to Melissa's shtick, then escaped to find the giggly Beavis and Butthead guys from Break, who told her excitedly that they were going to be extras playing surfers on Ferramo's movie and introduced her to Winston, a beautiful black diving instructor who worked for various hotels on the Keys and was in town to take out clients on the *OceansApart.* He offered to show her round the ship the following afternoon, maybe even take her out for a dive. "I kinda get the feeling I won't be busy. I've only had one client so far, and I had to bring him back because he had a pacemaker."

Unfortunately, she was interrupted yet again by Melissa bearing a press release and a barrage of autowitter about Ferramo's new movie, including the news that Winston was going to be underwater consultant. Eventually, Olivia was forced to conclude that the reason she was there was not that Pierre Ferramo had noticed her, but because she was supposed to write an article promoting his new movie.

She left the throng and stepped out onto the terrace. There was nothing but blackness now towards the sea. She couldn't make out where the dunes ended and the beach began, but she could hear the waves pounding the shore. She noticed a metal staircase winding up from the balcony to a higher level and headed up, finding herself on a small private deck. She sat down, out of the wind, pulling her wrap around her, feeling disgusted with herself. It was insane to have let herself be manipulated by a publicist, to imagine that some ridiculous playboy was interested in her and then care enough to actually mind when it turned out he simply saw her as a marketing opportunity—and an overopinionated one at that. Worse, she realized, a part of her she wouldn't admit to anyone else was frankly disappointed that Ferramo wasn't a terrorist. She was just as bad as those fame-driven journalists she despised, always trying to make their names out of other people's misfortunes. *Pull yourself together,* she told herself. *You're Olivia Joules now. You need to get out of this daft party and get on.*

There was a sound on the metal staircase. Someone was coming up.

"Why, Ms. Joules. You are roosting up here like a little bird."

Ferramo was carrying champagne and two glasses. "Now you will join me, surely, in one glass of Cristal."

He was very attractive. It had been a very long day. She took a sip of the exquisite, ice-cold champagne and thought, *Rules for Living number seven: sometimes you just have to go with the flow.*

"Now tell me," he said, raising his glass to hers. "Can you relax? Is your work complete? Do you have your story?"

"Yes," she said. "But I've moved on to another. The *Oceans-Apart.* You know? The giant apartment ship?"

"Oh really? How interesting." His face said the opposite. "And with the *OceansApart* you will do what? Interviews perhaps? A visit to the ship?"

"Yes. Actually I met a couple of passengers who come from very near my home town. I'm going to go see them tomorrow and . . ."

"At what time?"

"Um, in the morning at—"

"I really do not think that is a good idea," he murmured, taking her glass away and drawing her closer.

"Why not?" He was so close she could feel his breath against her cheek.

"Because," he said, "I hope that tomorrow morning you will be having breakfast . . . with me."

He reached out and touched her face, masterfully raising it to his, his eyes melting into hers. He kissed her, hesitantly at first, his lips dry against her mouth, then passionately, so that her body pulsed into life and she was kissing him passionately in return.

"No, no," she said, suddenly pulling away. What was she *doing*? Snogging a playboy with a roomful of his other snoggees downstairs.

He looked down, composing himself, steadying his breathing. "There is something wrong?" he murmured.

"I've only just met you. I don't know you."

"I see," he said, nodding, thoughtful. "You are right. Then we will meet, tomorrow, at nine. I will come to the Delano. And we will begin to get to know each other. You will be there?"

She nodded.

"You are true to your word? You can delay your interview?"

"Yes." She didn't need to. It wasn't until eleven.

"Then good." He stood, held out his hand and helped her up, smiling with a flash of his perfect teeth. "And now we must rejoin the party."

As Olivia was leaving, she saw the guest list, abandoned under crumpled napkins and dirty glasses on a white table by the door. Always good to hang on to a guest list. Just as she was reaching for it, a door opened behind the table and Demi emerged adjusting her top, followed by the dark youth who'd been in charge of arrivals.

"Hi!" giggled Demi sheepishly and headed back into the party.

"I think I gave you my jacket when I arrived?" Olivia said to the youth, giving him a conspiratorial grin. "Pale blue? Suede?"

"Of course. I will look for it straightaway. I like your accent."

"Thank you." She flashed him a dazzling smile. *I like your accent too,* she thought. *And it's no more French than your boss's.*

"Oh, gosh!" She hurried along the corridor after the youth. "I'm really sorry. I didn't come in a jacket. I'm an idiot."

"That's all right, ma'am."

"Brain like a sieve. Sorry. Thank you," she said, slipping him five dollars.

And she stepped into the elevator, the guest list folded safely inside her clutch.

8

"You *kissed* him?"

"I know, I know. Oh God." Olivia was stretching the phone to the end of its cord, looking out of the window at the ships' lights on the ocean, wondering if Ferramo was looking out there too. Then she realized what she was doing and hit herself hard on the forehead. *Idiot.*

"I'm going to have to be quick. I'm in the newsroom," Kate was saying on the other end of the phone. "So, let's just get this straight. Last night you call me to say he's Osama bin Laden."

"I didn't say he was actually . . ."

"Not twenty-four hours later you call me to say you've been snogging him on a rooftop. You're the most ridiculous human being I've ever met."

"Well, you were right," said Olivia. "He's not a terrorist."

"You didn't tell Barry?"

"Nearly," giggled Olivia. "But no. I'm going to meet him tomorrow."

"Who? Barry?"

"No, Pierre."

"Pierre bin Laden?"

"Shut up. I know, I know. But I'm not going to sleep with him. I'm just going to have breakfast with him. It's just a little, you know, pick-me-up."

"Right, right, sure," said Kate. "Oh, fuck, got to go. Call me after, okay?"

Once again Olivia couldn't sleep. Trying to steer her mind towards reality, she clicked the light on and surveyed the overdesigned white room. Within seconds, her scruffy North London flat and its eclectic contents were transformed into an outpost of Delano-style minimalist chic, the walls and contents purged and white: the living room lit by a single lamp in a shade ten times too big, the washbasin disguised as a stainless-steel bucket, a simple but stylish chain instead of a toilet roll holder. *I could have a chandelier in the garden,* she told herself excitedly. *Why bore neighbors with traditional dull landscape lighting? And a giant chess set and a white indoor sofa outside—when I get a garden, that is.*

Unfortunately, before long she also had Pierre Ferramo in the garden, on the sofa. She jumped out of bed and logged on to her e-mail. There was a message from Barry. "Re: Miami Cool."

She clicked "Read."

"Good."

That was all: "Good." Glowing with pride, she clicked "Reply" and typed:

Re: Good.
1. Thanks, Bazzer.
2. *Elan* keeping me on another day.
3. Do you want a story about wannabe actresses? 500 a day arriving in Los Angeles hoping to make it?
Over and out. Olivia.

Within the next hour, she knocked out seven hundred and fifty words on the face-cream launch for *Elan,* then impulsively sent them the idea for the Los Angeles wannabe article, as well as an article on making rash judgments when you first meet someone and how first impressions can be completely wrong.

The following morning Olivia was up and dressed freakishly early. By seven-thirty, she was powering along the South Shore, determined to eradicate all foolish fantasies from her brain, to separate logic and desire, while giving her cheeks a pleasing healthy glow. It was windier than ever; leaves and branches had fallen from the palms, shreds of them were littering the road. A waiter was running after a tablecloth as it flapped away from him.

Out on the beach, the hoboes were starting to stir. One of them was staring in lewd delight at an oblivious beachside yoga class: seven girls on their backs, opening and closing their legs. She found herself following the same route as yesterday, telling herself she'd get a taxi back and have plenty of time to make herself pretty for breakfast.

She came to a stop when she reached the grassy island where she had met the old couple. She sat down on a concrete wall to look at the *OceansApart*, once more overwhelmed by its enormity. There was the bing-bong of a loudspeaker on the boat followed by an announcement. A seagull dived into the water for a fish. There was the usual dockside smell, petrol mixed with fishy odors and seaweed. The warm wind was rustling the surface of the water, little frothy waves lapping against the man-made rocky shore. People were on the balconies. She raised her spyglass to her eye, looking for Elsie and Edward's cabin. There it was in the middle of the boat, third deck from the top. Elsie was sitting in a white wicker chair in a white bathrobe, her hair caught up loosely, robe fluttering in the wind. And there was Edward, also in his bathrobe, standing in the doorway. *Lovebirds.*

As she watched, a muffled boom came from deep under the water. Suddenly the whole monstrous edifice gave a lurch like a drunken stagger, then righted itself, creating a wave which surged across the calm channel towards her, flinging itself against the rocky shore. She heard shouts and more figures appeared on the balconies, peering over the side.

Instinct told her to get away. There were some prefab shacks two hundred yards to her right, raised a couple of feet off the ground, and a steel storage container. She started to walk fast towards them. She was maybe twenty yards away from the steel container when there was a flash followed by a sound like a giant door slamming underground.

As she turned, a single large plume of water was rising beside the ship. She broke into a run, heading for the steel container, stumbling on the uneven ground. A siren started up. There were shouts, another siren, and then a blinding burst of blue light and a second boom, louder than anything she had ever heard. A great wall of hot air hit her, full of shards of metal and debris, flinging her forward onto the ground. Hearing herself gasping, her heartbeat banging in her ears, she dragged herself the final few feet towards the container. There was a gap underneath it, and she forced herself into it, wriggling to squeeze herself in as far as she could. She made a space around her mouth with her hands and breathed, trying to keep out the acrid smoke, trying to calm down, trying to shrink into herself to nothing, to hibernate like a tortoise in a cardboard box filled with straw.

As the sounds of destruction died down, leaving an unnerving silence, Olivia opened her eyes. Don't panic, she told herself. Olivia had understood long ago how life can turn on a sixpence, in a fraction of a moment. Rule number one, the chief survival rule: never panic. Never let your mind be clouded by hysterics so you forget to look, forget to grasp what's really going on, forget the obvious thing. She was looking through bitter black smoke towards the dock, where a huge fire was raging. It was hard to see, but it looked as though the water itself was on fire. She could dimly make out the *OceansApart*, which seemed to have been blown in two. One side was still horizontal; the other had reared up until it was almost vertical. Elsie and Edward's balcony was right on the dividing line: where it had been was now a gash, showing the ship in cross-section like a diagram.

She decided to stay where she was. As she watched, the half of the ship which was still horizontal seemed to bend outwards. A wall of hot air hit her once more, as if she'd opened an oven, and there was another boom as the hull burst into a giant fireball. Olivia buried her chin in her chest, feeling the flesh on one hand burning. There was a deafening roar above her. She pulled herself out, relieved to find her legs just about holding up beneath her. She ran for her life, as behind her she heard the boom of the container exploding.

9

"**Y**ou all right, ma'am?"

Olivia was crouched, her arms wrapped around her head, against a low building which was shielding her from the docks and the *OceansApart*. She looked up into the face of a firefighter.

"Are you hurt?"

"I don't think so."

The traffic had stopped on the highways and bridges. The air was filled with the sound of sirens and helicopters.

He pulled out a water bottle. She took a small mouthful and handed it back.

"Keep it."

"No, you keep it." She nodded back towards the ship. "You get out there. I'm fine."

"Sure?"

"Sure."

She leaned back against the wall and looked down at herself. She was black. The back of her left hand was burnt, although it didn't seem to hurt at all. She felt her hair gingerly. It was on the crispy side but still there—a miracle the peroxide hadn't combusted. Her eyes were smarting. There were hunks of torn metal and debris everywhere, and fires burning in dozens of places. *It's absolutely fine,* she thought. *It's perfectly simple. I'll just go into the water and find Edward and Elsie and bring them to shore.*

Olivia moved round the edge of the building, glancing for a moment out towards the open sea, the yachts in the marina, the blue sky. Then she looked back at the *OceansApart* and remembered how life can be such different things all at once: it was like switching from a TV holiday program to a disaster movie. The vertical half of the ship was sinking fast, the water boiling around it. The other half had a vast blackened hole in the hull and was listing. Smoke and flames were still billowing from it. Fires were burning all over the channel. The firemen were starting to pour foam on the flames. In between the flames floated debris, the corpses of sharks and barracuda and, Olivia realized, human beings, some of them still alive.

The paramedics had arrived and were setting up a help station. Olivia could see a man in the water close to the shore. Only his head was visible, his mouth wide open. As he looked in panic towards the shore, he went under. Olivia kicked off her trainers, took her sweatpants off and stepped into the water. Hot mud belched up between her toes. The water was hot too and dirty and thick. When she was close to where the man had disappeared, she took a big breath, steeled herself and plunged beneath the surface. She couldn't see a thing and she groped around in the foul murk for what seemed like an agonizingly long time until she finally felt him. He was barely conscious and he was a big man. She dived down again, put a hand on either side of his waist and pushed him upwards until he broke the surface. Then she let go for a second, burst into the open air beside him and took hold of his head. She held his nose and started rescue breathing, but it was too hard to keep them both buoyant. She turned to the shore and waved, then tried again. He took a huge, rasping breath. She put her arm around his neck as she'd been taught, and started to drag him towards the shore. The paramedics came out to meet her in the shallows and took him from her.

She looked back at the channel. It looked as though more people had been washed from the wreckage. A team of divers had arrived on the bank. She walked unsteadily over to where they were setting up. No one took any notice of her. She asked for a mask and some fins and a buoyancy-control jacket.

She walked back to the water's edge, putting on the jacket, blowing into the tube to inflate it until it felt tight against her rib cage, then letting the air out. For a moment Olivia felt nausea rising in her throat again. She thought she would find Elsie and Edward because they had been on their balcony on this side of the ship facing the shore. And although she had only just met them, they had brought with them all the comfort and familiarity of home.

Olivia brought back quite a few people, she didn't know how many. She felt as if she was on automatic pilot and none of it seemed quite real.

She sat down by a tree, suddenly exhausted. One of the paramedics came over with some water, got her to put her sweatpants back on, put a towel round her shoulders and rubbed her hands. He said she should go to the medical center and helped her to her feet. The mobile phone in the pocket of her sweatpants rang as they walked along.

"Hey, Olivia. Listen, the *OceansApart* . . ."

"Hi, Barry," she said bitterly. "The *OceansRippedApart*, you mean."

"Listen, are you down there? What have you got for us?"

She gave Barry what he needed between his interruptions: what she had heard from the paramedics and divers and police, the fragments of recollections people had come out with as she brought them to the shore.

"Good. Any witnesses? Come on, where are you? Can you get me someone there? On the scene?"

She caught the eye of the paramedic who had brought her in. He took the phone, listened for a few seconds then said, "You sure sound like one hell of an asshole, sir," clicked off the phone and handed it back to her.

Olivia let the paramedics take her vital signs and cover the burns on her hand. She ate a piece of bread and took some rehydration salts. Then, with a blanket round her shoulders, she got up and walked around. She saw a woman with auburn hair being brought in on a stretcher. Olivia stood there, bewildered, melting down, the pain from the last few hours reawakening the pain from the past—like hitting an old bruise. She found an empty corner, pulled the blanket over her, and curled into a ball. After a long time, she straightened up and wiped her fist across her face.

A voice said, "Are you all right, love? Do you want a cup of tea?"

"Ooh, that looks too strong for her, love. Put a drop more milk in."

She looked up and there, holding out a tray, were Edward and Elsie.

10

As darkness fell, Olivia staggered back into the foyer of the Delano. She made her way unsteadily, her vision blotchy, to the front desk.

"Can I have my key, please? Olivia Joules, Room Seven-oh-three," she said thickly.

"OhmyGod. OhmyGOD," said the receptionist. "I'll call the hospital. I'll call the emergency services."

"No, no. I'm fine, really. I just need . . . my key, and some . . . some . . . some . . ." She turned, clutching her key, looking for the elevator. She couldn't see where the elevator was. Then the beautiful bellboy was supporting her, then two bellboys, then total whiteout.

For a second, when she woke, her mind was wiped clear, but then the memory of the disaster flooded her consciousness in a tangle of images. She opened her eyes. She was in a hospital. Everything was white except for a red light flashing on and off beside her bed. She was Rachel Pixley aged fourteen, lying in a hospital bed, looking at a zebra crossing, running out of the newsagent's with a packet of Maltesers and a copy of *Cosmopolitan*. Running to catch up with her parents. There was a shout, a screech of tires. She closed her eyes, thinking about a woman she had seen on television after the Twin Towers came down: a thickset woman from Brooklyn. She had lost a son and was talking tough. Then she said, "I used to think I'd always want revenge: an eye for an eye, but now I just think, 'How can the world be so . . . cruel?' " And her voice broke on the "cruel."

The next time Olivia woke, she realized it was not a hospital but the Delano, and the red flashing light was not a heart monitor but the message light on the phone.

"Hi, Olivia! Hope I'm not calling too early. It's Imogen from Sally Hawkins's office at *Elan*. We got your e-mail and we had a call from Melissa at Century PR about the wannabe story. Yes, Sally would like to go for it. We'll get onto the travel arrangements. Give us a call when you wake up. Oh, and good luck with the *OceansApart*."

"Hi, Melissa here. I've spoken to your editor. We'll be holding auditions in the Standard Hotel in Hollywood over the next week or so, so I'm really hoping you'll be able to join us."

"Olivia? It is Pierre Ferramo. I am in the lobby. Perhaps you are already on your way down for our rendezvous?"

"Olivia? It is Pierre at nine-fifteen. I will be waiting for you on the terrace."

"Olivia, it appears you have forgotten me. There has been the most terrible disaster, perhaps you have heard. I will telephone you a little later."

"Olivia, oh God. It's Imogen from *Elan*. Oh God. Call us. Oh God."

"Olivia, it's Kate. I'm just hoping you weren't anywhere near that ship. Call me."

The hotel front desk, the doctor, Kate, nothing more from Pierre. Kate again. Then Barry.

"Where are you? Listen, can you get out there again? There's a press conference down at the dock at six-fifteen your time. We've got a snapper there. I just need you to get a few quotes, then get off to the hospital for survivors and families. Call me."

She fumbled for the remote, clicked on CNN, and lay back against the pillow.

"More, now, on the OceansApart *in Miami. As the death toll continues to rise, investigators on the scene say there are signs that the explosion may have been caused by a submarine, possibly of Japanese construction, packed with explosives. The submarine may have been manned by suicide bombers. Again, signs that the terrible explosion on the* OceansApart *may have been the work of terrorist suicide bombers."*

The text strip underneath ran: *"OceansApart explosion: 215 dead, 189 injured, 200 missing. Terror alert rises to red."*

She sat at the desk and rested her head on her arms. She felt damaged, exhausted, scared and lonely. She wanted comfort. She wanted someone to hold. She reached for a card on the desk and dialed a number.

"Hi." It was a woman's voice, slight West Coast drawl.

"Could I speak to Pierre?"

"Pierre's not around. Who needs him?" It was the hair-flicking Suraya model.

"It's Olivia Joules. I was supposed to meet him this morning but—"

"Sure. You want to leave a message?"

"Just, er, just say I was ringing to apologize about missing our meeting. I was down at the docks when the *OceansApart* blew up."

"Yeah. God. That really sucked."

Sucked?

"Will he be back later?"

"No, he had to leave town." There was something odd about her tone.

"He left Miami? Today?"

"Yes. He had urgent business in Los Angeles. He's holding auditions for the movie. You want to leave him a message?"

"Just tell him I called, and, er, sorry about the meeting. Thank you."

Olivia put down the phone and sat on the edge of the bed, the sheet screwed tightly in her fist, staring straight ahead, unseeing. She was thinking of the night before: Ferramo leaning close to her on the rooftop deck as she told him about the *OceansApart* story and her morning appointment with Edward and Elsie.

"I really do not think that is a good idea"—his breath against her cheek—"because I hope that tomorrow morning, you will be having breakfast . . . with me."

She picked up the phone and dialed *Elan.*

"Imogen? Olivia. I'm fine. Listen, I'd like to go to LA and do the wannabe story. Straightaway. As soon as you can. Get me on the first plane out."

As Olivia looked down over Arizona, the sun was setting, turning the desert red. The great gash of the Grand Canyon was already in darkness. She thought of all the deserts she'd flown over before, in Africa, in Arabia. And she wondered: *Did Pierre Ferramo know that the ship was going to blow when he kissed me last night?*

11   LOS ANGELES

As the taxi rattled and bounced over the potholes towards the hills, Olivia wound down the window, relieved by the sense of freedom and vague lawlessness she always felt in Los Angeles. It was so deliciously shallow. She looked up at the giant billboards lining the road: "Looking for a new career? Be a star! Contact the LA county sheriff's office." "We're back from Rehab and Ready to Party," said an advert for a TV guide. A bench at a bus stop featured a poster-sized shot of a grinning big-haired Realtor: "Valerie Babajian: your hostess for LA Real Estate." Another billboard for a radio station said simply, "Jennifer Lopez's brother, George," and another, which seemed not to be advertising anything at all, showed an artist's impression of a platinum blonde in a tight pink dress with a figure like Jessica Rabbit. "Angelyne" was written underneath in giant letters.

"Is Angelyne an actress?" she asked the cabdriver.

"Angelyne? No." He laughed. "She just pay for these posters of herself and then she do personal appearances, parties, things like that. She been doing that for years."

As the gray-green hills grew closer, lights pinpricking through the dusk, they passed the Cedars-Sinai Medical Center with the Star of David raised on the side.

"I know what Ferramo's doing here," she said to herself suddenly. "The wannabe movie is bullshit. They're going to hit Los Angeles."

Her mind began to whir into a familiar overdrive: missiles launched from the top of the Runyon Canyon dog park, plummeting down into the executive offices at Fox Studios; suicide bombers at the *American Idol* final; manned torpedoes racing through the sewers. She felt like calling CNN and filing a report. *"He's handsome, he's good at kissing, but he's planning to blow us all sky high: Pierre Ferramo . . ."*

Stop it, she told herself. *Calm down. Don't rush to conclusions.* But Olivia was angry and disturbed. If Ferramo had anything to do with what happened in the docks at Miami she was going to find out.

The sign for the Standard Hotel on Sunset, in a declaration of wacky subversiveness, was upside down. The hotel, once a geriatric home, had been recently converted to a temple of Hollywood retro-chic. The contrast with its former clientele was dramatic. Seldom had Olivia seen so many beautiful young people gathered in one place talking on mobile phones. There were girls in camouflage trousers and bikini tops, girls in slippy dresses, girls in jeans so low their thongs were two inches above the waistbands, boys with shaved heads and goatee beards, boys in tight jeans which showed everything they had, boys in baggy jeans with the crotch at knee level. There were plastic podlike chairs suspended from chains. Shag-pile carpet graced the floor, walls and ceiling. A DJ was spinning vinyl at the entrance to the pool deck. On the wall behind the reception desk a girl wearing only plain white underwear was reading a book in a glass box. It made Olivia feel like a seventy-year-old obese academic who would shortly be asked to move on down the road to the Substandard.

The receptionist handed her a message from Melissa welcoming her to LA and saying that the auditions were starting in the morning, and the team would be easy to find around the bar and lobby. Once again, the bellboy insisted on accompanying her to the room, despite her lack of luggage. His head reminded her of a child's magnetic sketch pad, the sort where you add beards and mustaches to a face using metal filings. The boy, or rather man, had dyed black hair, a goatee beard, long sideburns and black-rimmed narrow glasses. It was a ridiculous look. His shirt was open almost to his waist, showing an Action Man–like chest.

He opened the door to the room. There was a low bed, an orange-tiled bathroom, a bright blue floor and a silver beanbag.

"How do you like the room?" asked the bellboy.

"It's like being on the set of *Barbarella*," she murmured.

"I think that was before I was born," he said.

Cheeky sod. He was definitely in his thirties. He had intelligent bright blue eyes, which didn't fit with his fashion-victim facial hair. He lifted her case onto the bed as if it was a paper bag. His body didn't fit with his facial hair either. But, hey, this was LA: bellboy slash actor slash bodybuilder slash brainbox: whatever.

"So," he said, pulling open the plate-glass window as if it was a net curtain. A blast of sound hit them. Below, the pool area was in full party mode, heat lamps were blazing, music pounding. Beyond was the LA skyline: a palm tree illuminated, a neon sign saying EL MIRADOR APARTMENTS, a jewel box of lights.

"Looks like I'm going to get a lot of rest," she said.

"Where did you just come in from?"

"Miami."

He took hold of her hand, firmly, authoritatively, like a professional, looking at the burns.

"Been making fondue?"

"Yorkshire pudding."

"What happened?"

"I don't want to talk about it."

"What brings you to LA?"

"Do the words 'air of mystery' mean nothing to you?"

He let out a short laugh. "I like your accent."

"They all talk like this where I come from."

"You working here? You an actress?"

"No. What are you doing here?"

"Being a bellboy. How about a drink later?"

"No."

"Okay. Anything else I can do for you at all?"

Yes, rub sweet oils into my aching bones and change the dressings on my poor burnt hand, you wonderful, wildly strong, intellectual-looking beefcake.

"I'm fine."

"Okay now. Take it easy."

She watched him go, then shut the door behind him, locked it and put the chain on. She unpacked her things, colonizing the room.

Then she turned on CNN.

"And the main headlines again. As the death toll continues to rise, it's believed that yesterday's explosion in Miami on the OceansApart, which claimed the lives of over two hundred people, was in fact the work of al-Qaeda terrorists. The toll currently stands at 215 dead, 475 injured and over 250 missing."

She called down and asked if the London *Sunday Times* was in yet: not until the following afternoon. She opened the laptop to look for it online.

There was a huge headline: OCEANS RIPPED APART. The byline at the top was Dave Rufford and Kate O'Neill. Kate! There were lots of Olivia's quotes in there and whole paragraphs of her description. Maybe her byline would be at the bottom. It said, "Additional reporting by *Sunday Times* writers." She ran a search for Olivia Joules. She wasn't credited anywhere at all.

"Fuck it," she said after a moment. "It's just bullshit. The main thing is, I'm not dead." She opened the French doors, so that the sound of fun rose up from the pool deck, and sat down at the desk. It was the northern Protestant work ethic which had helped her escape from the land of the northern Protestant work ethic. Olivia clung to work to keep her safe, like her survival tin.

At midnight she leaned back, stretched and decided to call it a day. The desk was covered with the spoils from Miami: the party list, business cards, scribbled phone numbers on the backs of credit-card slips, a diagram trying to draw some meaning from connections which made no sense.

She looked up at shots of Bagdhad on CNN and turned up the sound.

"Do you suffer from reduced bladder control?" The shot had inexplicably changed to show a gray-haired woman giving a ballroom-dancing demonstration to a roomful of people. Olivia clicked off the TV in exasperation. Why couldn't they give you some clue as to where the news bulletin ended and the incontinence-remedy adverts began?

She clicked on Avizon.com in her favorites list. It was a low-rent actress slash model agency Web site which she'd found amongst a horrifying 764,000 entries for "Actresses Los Angeles." There was Kimberley Alford, one in a whole page of startlingly similar Kirstens, Kelleys and Kims pouting provocatively at the camera for producers to mull over and the rest of the world to wank over. She clicked on Kimberley's nose and her photo appeared full page, with her credentials:

Modeling level: professional.

Acting level: professional.

Ethnic look: Cherokee/Romanian.

Then her bust size, waist size, shoe size, teeth quality ("excellent").

Professional skills: rollerblading, tap, speaks five languages. Has own cheerleader uniform.

Underneath was Kimberley's four-line personal message:

"I am a true four-cornered all-rounder. I can sing, dance, act, model and play guitar! I'm on the right path, and waiting for the door to open that will lead to stardom. Acting is in my blood. My father has done the follow spot at the Academy Awards for twenty-five years. If you turn your spotlight on me, I will blow you away!"

Olivia turned to Travis Brancato, the wolf-eyed wannabe. His

business card led her to a Web site called Enclave, listing the hapless
Travis as a "lifestyle budget manager":

What is Enclave?

Enclave is a groundbreaking soft-science-based interface grounded
in a qualitative value-increase-based proposition. Through this unique
lifestyle enhancement program Enclave enables clients to increase
qualitative lifestyle returns on investments to achieve maximum
enjoyment.

Clients allow Enclave to manage a minimum annual lifestyle budget of $500,000, to advise and direct where the money is spent and
to negotiate the purchase of qualitative-led concepts, experiences,
goods and services.

From tickets to a major sporting event, premiere or award ceremony, a copy of a rarely heard early Floyd recording, to a table at
the hottest new restaurant in Paris, many of LA's most senior CEOs,
movie actors, producers and recording executives are already enjoying the science-based maximization of pleasure interfaces which Enclave affords.

Olivia leaned back from the screen and grinned. The idea, it
seemed, was that clients would "give" Travis half a million dollars
a year to spend, and in return occasionally receive a pair of tickets
to a ball game or a free CD. She couldn't get anything but an answering machine on Enclave's twenty-four-hour hotline number. Pre-
sumably all the lifestyle managers were too busy managing hundreds
of thousands of dollars into soft-science-based enjoyment maximization to pick up the phone.

She Googled Ferramo again. Nothing new.

The indoor bar area of the Standard had a loosely desert theme: the walls were papered with a floor-to-ceiling frieze of Joshua trees, the floor was cork, the lamps like giant desert flowers. There were two—for some reason—fish suspended from the ceiling. Olivia sat enjoying her morning coffee and the sunlight blasting in from the pool area. Auditions were plainly about to start. A youth, sweating in the heat in thick camouflage trousers and a woolly hat, was wandering among the girls, sporting a clipboard and a rather confused expression.

Olivia saw Kimberley before Kimberley saw Olivia. Her unfeasibly large and perky breasts were bouncing in a thin white halter-neck above her nonexistent hips, which were swathed in a miniature version of an ecru cheerleader's skirt. Horribly aware of how attractive she looked, she was sliding her finger in and out of her mouth like a cross between a five-year-old and a porn queen. Suddenly she started talking to herself.

"I gotta get, like, get something worked out. I don't want to wait tables anymore. . . . Oh, yeah, she kept my reel and told me to call her and then she didn't take my call. She kept me on hold for ten minutes. I mean, I listened to three songs?"

Two men walked past, completely ignoring Kimberley's scantily clad perfection. Women who would turn heads in London and New York scarcely seemed to warrant a second look in LA. It was as if they had a tattoo on their foreheads saying, "Wannabe actress slash model. Will bore you with career aspirations: unstable." The beautiful people in Miami were much more fun, Olivia thought. In LA, their beauty and seminakedness seemed to be saying, "Look at this! Now make me a film star!" In Miami they just wanted to get laid.

"So," Kimberley continued, "when I finally got to meet with her she was so, like, not listening to me? She said the way I looked on the tape, I'm not, like—" Kimberley's voice trailed off miserably— "commercial enough."

A wire was protruding from her ear. So at least she wasn't completely insane. But, still, Olivia was starting to feel sorry for her.

"It's fine," Kimberley said bravely. "I'm thinking maybe I could do, like, body-part work? It's like body-double work, but they just use parts of you."

But what about today? thought Olivia. *What about Pierre's auditions? I thought you were all lined up for a big part?* Had even Kimberley sensed that Ferramo wasn't for real? Or had she just heard "I'm going to make you a star, baby" eighteen times too often?

She went over to Kimberley and said hi. Kimberley responded with the sort of defensive look which assumed that anyone who said hi was trying to hit on her.

"Olivia Joules. We met in Miami. I'm a journalist on *Elan*."

Kimberley stared for a second, rasped, "Gotta go," into the handsfree, then turned on a dazzling smile and launched into an "Oh. My. God." routine.

"Where's Demi?" said Olivia, once the incredible nature of the coincidence had been dealt with. "Isn't she auditioning for the film too?"

A strange *froideur* seemed to enter the proceedings.

"Has she been saying stuff about me? I mean, you know, I'm not going to say anything, like, bad about Demi. She has issues? You know? I mean, honestly? I think she's got a problem. But I'm not the kind of person who says anything bad about anyone."

Olivia was confused, trying to work out how long it was since the party when they were the best of friends. Two days.

"I mean, she's still in Miami, right, with that Portuguese guy?"

"I've no idea."

But Kimberley's attention had wandered. She had seen someone coming and started arranging her breasts in the halter top, like a bowl of fruit for a photo shoot. Olivia followed her gaze and found herself looking straight into the eyes of Pierre Ferramo.

He was dressed as an LA film producer in shades, jeans, navy jacket and whiter-than-white T-shirt. His manner, though, was as regal as ever. He was flanked by two dark-haired, flustered boys, who were trying to deal with a growing cluster of would-be auditionees. Ignoring the entourage, he made his way directly to Olivia.

"Ms. Joules," he said, slipping off his shades, "you are two days late and in the wrong hotel in the wrong city, but as always it is a pleasure to see you."

His liquid gaze burned into hers.

"Pierre." Kimberley teetered over and flung her arms round his neck. A fleeting glance of disgust crossed his features. "Can we, like, go right away? I'm so, like, psyched?"

"The auditions will be starting shortly," he said, disentangling himself. "You may go upstairs and prepare if you wish."

As Kimberley wiggled off, swinging her bag on her hip, Ferramo waved his aides away and spoke to Olivia in a low, urgent voice. "You did not make our appointment."

"I went for a jog first, down to the harbor . . ."

He sat down opposite her. "You were there?"

"Directly across the water."

"You are hurt?" He took her hand and examined the dressing. "You have had medical attention? Is there anything you need?"

"I'm fine. Thank you."

"And how did you come to be in the vicinity of the explosion?"

"I was jogging. I often jog in the mornings. I was trying to get a good look at the ship. Did you know anyone aboard?"

She watched his face, like a detective watching a grieving husband make an appeal to his missing wife's abductor. Ferramo didn't miss a beat.

"No, thankfully I did not."

What about Winston, your underwater consultant?

"I did."

"You did?" He lowered his voice, leaning closer to her. "I am so very sorry. They were people you knew well?"

"No. But they were people I very much liked. Do you know who did it?"

Was there a glimmer of a reaction to the oddness of her question?

"As you will have heard, the investigation is only just beginning. It has the marks of al-Qaeda, of course, but we shall see." He glanced around. "This is not the time or place for this discussion. You are here for some days?"

One of the boys appeared behind him, hovering with papers. "Mr. Ferramo . . ."

"Yes, yes." Different voice, harsh, authoritarian, dismissive. "One moment. I am in conversation, as you can see."

He turned back to Olivia. "We can reschedule our meeting perhaps?" *A-rrreeeeshedull owah meeting.* It was a harsh, staccato intonation.

"I'm here for a few days."

"You will join me for dinner? Tomorrow evening, perhaps?"

"Er, yes, I . . ."

"Good. You are staying here? I will call you and make the necessary arrangements. Until then. It is a pleasure to have you here. Yes . . . yes." He turned to the boy, who was holding out a document apologetically.

Olivia watched as he looked at the document and rose to his feet, heading back to the wannabes. "Actually, we should be through by four." He handed back the paper. "*Shukran.* And then we can reconvene to discuss the call-backs."

Shukran. Olivia looked down, trying not to betray any reaction. *Shukran* was Arabic for "thank you."

13

"**C**ome home," Kate said from London. "Come home now. Call the FBI and get on the next plane."

Olivia sat trembling on the silver beanbag, pushed up hard against the door to the room. "But last time we spoke, you said I was jumping to conclusions."

"The only evidence you offered was that he was 'languid.' You somehow overlooked the fact that he tried to persuade you not to go to the *OceansApart* the night before it blew up."

"I thought it was part of a crappy pick-up line about asking me to breakfast. You know: 'Shall I phone you or nudge you?' kind of thing."

"You are literally unbelievable. Listen. He lied. He told you he was French and then he starts talking Arabic."

"He only said one word. He still could be French. Anyway, even if he is an Arab doesn't mean he's a terrorist. It might be just that sort of prejudice he was trying to avoid. I'm doing a story. *Elan* is paying my expenses."

"They'll understand. You can always pay them back. Come home."

"Kate," said Olivia quietly. "This is my story."

There was silence for a second. "Oh God. It's that byline thing, isn't it? That was Barry. He said it would be a joint byline. I called him when I saw it and bawled him out."

Then why didn't you call me too?

"He said they took your name out to save space. You're not on staff. I'm not trying to nick your story. Just come home and be safe."

"I've got to go," said Olivia. "I'm supposed to be at the auditions."

She clicked off the phone and started feverishly to type a list on her laptop which fell under two headings:

1. Reasons for thinking Pierre Ferramo is an al-Qaeda terrorist plotting to blow up LA.
2. Reasons why it is prejudiced, overimaginative or otherwise wrong to think Pierre Ferramo is an al-Qaeda terrorist plotting to blow up LA.

Then she paused, frowning, staring straight ahead. Olivia thought of herself as a liberal-egalitarian humanitarian. But was she actually just a common garden racist?

14

"**Y**ou may be from the bright lights of LA, but here, in the desert, you will find out who you really are, what you mean . . . *mean*."

"Okay. Hold it there, hold it there."

Olivia sympathized with directors. She wouldn't have the first idea what to say to an actress who was fucking up her lines except, "Could you do it . . . better?" But this director didn't seem to have anything to say at all. He glanced feebly at Alfonso, who was there in some undetermined capacity, opened his mouth as if to speak, closed it again, then said, "Um."

Olivia looked at the director, bemused. His name was Nicholas Kronkheit. He didn't seem to have done anything at all except direct a couple of student music videos at Malibu University. Why pick him?

"Okay," Alfonso broke in bossily. "Let's take it again, baby, from the top."

The script, written by Travis Brancato, was, well, *worrying* to say the least. Entitled *Boundaries of Arizona*, it was the story of a Hollywood film star who realized Hollywood was meaningless and ran away to the desert, where he fell in love with a Navajo girl and discovered happiness and fulfillment through making ornamental lifeline boxes.

As Kimberley—dark, plaited wig doing its best to bring out the Cherokee in her—prepared to run through the lines yet again,

Olivia slipped out of the room with a strange crablike sideways gait which she'd never used before. It seemed to be a spontaneous and unconscious expression of guilt and apology for finding the whole thing so desperate.

She sat in the bar, sucking iced latte through a straw and pondering the various ways in which the production of *Boundaries of Arizona* made no sense. Was Ferramo going to finance the whole thing himself? In which case, why had he picked such an ill-qualified nitwit as a director? If he was looking for finance elsewhere, why would he have hired a director and started casting before he involved a studio? And how come he hadn't noticed that the script was total crap?

"Hi!"

Olivia started and choked on her latte at the sheer force of Melissa's arrival.

"How were the auditions? How did the interview with Nicholas go?"

Fortunately, there was no need to reply when Melissa was talking.

"Look, these are our surfers. Aren't they the cutest? They've been trying out at the beach all morning and now they're going to do lines. Are you going to come and watch? I'm sure you'll need a bit of that for the piece."

A bunch of bleached-blond youths were ogling today's girl-in-her-underwear in the glass box behind reception.

"Oh, and this is our voice coach, Carol. Have you met her already?"

The woman looked interesting and rather nice. She actually had a wrinkled face, which looked completely out of place in the Standard. It was like seeing someone in a rumpled old shirt in a room full of immaculately pressed outfits. Olivia started imagining the concierge rushing up, shrieking, "Oh. My. Gaaaaaad. Give it to me! We'll have it pressed!"

"Pleased to meet you," said the wrinkled one.

"You're English!" said Olivia.

"So are you. Northeast? Nottingham? North of Nottingham?"

"Worksop. You're good."

"So!" broke in Melissa. "I've got you down for dinner with Pierre tomorrow night. This afternoon I want you to talk to the surfers, and then drinks early evening with some of the other boys."

"Excuse me, Ms. Joules." It was the concierge. "Just to say we have your appointment for a facial with Michael Monteroso at Alia Klum at three-fifteen tomorrow. They do have a twenty-four-hour cancellation policy, so I need to give them a credit-card number. The cost is two hundred and fifteen dollars."

"Two hundred and fifteen dollars?" said Olivia.

"Oh, I'm sure we can get Michael to give you a complimentary treatment," said Melissa. "And Kimberley and some of the other girls are going to meet you here at eight, take you out and show you some of the hangouts."

"No, that's fine. I don't take freebies," said Olivia. "And I think I might have to skip the drink this evening. I've got some calls to make."

Melissa pulled a nasty quizzical face, with her head on one side.

"Can't just write about this one production, you know!" said Olivia in a hearty voice. "So many interesting things going on around here, don't you think?"

15

"Which city, please?" said the voice on the end of the phone.

"Los Angeles," said Olivia, drumming her pencil on the desk.

"And the number you're searching for?"

"The FBI."

"Pardon me?"

"The FBI."

"I'm not seeing any listing for that. Is that a business or a private number?"

Olivia snapped the pencil in half. She had fifteen minutes before she was supposed to meet Kimberley for the night out and she hadn't done her makeup yet.

"No, the FBI. The Federal Bureau of Investigation. You know: cops, detectives, *X-Files,* hates the CIA?"

The other line started ringing. She ignored it.

"Oh, right." A laugh. "I got you. Here's the number now."

"The number you require can be automatically dialed by pressing one now," said a jerky, electronic voice. "An additional charge will be made."

"Hello, this is the Federal Bureau of Investigation," said another recorded voice. Mercifully the other line stopped ringing.

"Please listen carefully to the following list of instructions. If you are enquiring about employment possibilities, press one now; for existing cases, press two . . ."

Damn it. The other line started ringing again. She pressed HOLD and picked up line two.

"Olivia? It is Pierre Ferramo."

"Oh, er, hi, Pierre," she trilled gaily. *I'm just calling the FBI on the other line to tell them you're an al-Qaeda terrorist.*

"Is everything all right?"

"Yes! Fine! Why?"

"You sound a little . . . tense, perhaps?"

"It's been quite a long day."

"I won't keep you. I just wanted to make sure that we are still scheduled for our dinner tomorrow night? I would hate for us to miss each other again."

"Absolutely. I'm looking forward to it."

"Excellent. I will have someone pick you up at six-thirty."

Six-thirty? That's a bit early for dinner, isn't it?

"That will be lovely."

"And how were the auditions?"

By the time he'd gone, so had the FBI.

———

"Hi. Is that the FBI? I just wanted to report a suspicion I have in connection with the *OceansApart.*" Olivia was pacing the room, practicing out loud. "It's probably nothing, but you might just check out a man called Pierre Ferramo and . . ."

"Hi, Joules here. That the CIA? International terrorism, please. I've got a hot lead on the *OceansApart.* Ferramo, Pierre Ferramo. Arabic, certainly, possibly Sudanese . . ."

She couldn't do it. She felt as though she was about to go into an audition and had lost her motivation. She was Rachel Pixley from Worksop getting carried away and the operator would just laugh; at the same time, she was a treacherous Mata Hari arranging dinner dates with her murderous lover then turning him over to her masters.

She decided to go out with Kimberley and pals and make the FBI call early tomorrow. She could order room service and make a morning of it.

16

Pierre Ferramo was wearing a green beret, speaking on al-Jazeera: "She is a pigdog and an infidel. Her stomach is too fat to grill. It must be roasted."

A phone was ringing in the background. Kimberley Alford produced an onion from her halter-neck and began to slice it, smiling to camera, blood oozing between her teeth. The phone was still ringing. Olivia fumbled for it in the darkness.

"Hi, Olivia? It's Imogen from *Elan*. I have the editor for you."

She snapped the light on and sat up straight in bed, pulling her nightie over her boobs, running a hand through her hair and staring wildly round the room. Sally Hawkins. The editor of *Elan*. First thing in the morning. After a whole evening of, like, you know, like, Kimberley and her, like, friends. The horror, the horror.

"She'll be right with you." Imogen's voice had that assistant's "I-don't-need-to-be-nice-to-you-any-more-because-you've-fallen-from-grace" tone.

"Olivia?" Crisp, I'm-very-busy-and-important Sally Hawkins voice. "I'm sorry to have to ring you so early. I'm afraid we've had a complaint."

"A complaint?"

"Yes. I understand you called the FBI and suggested they should be checking out Pierre Ferramo."

"What? Who told you that?"

"We don't know the source, but Century PR are absolutely furious and rightly so, if, indeed, you did call the FBI. I told Melissa I'm sure if you had some concern about one of her people, you would have called us first."

Olivia panicked wildly. She hadn't called the FBI, had she? Or rather, she *had,* but she hadn't got through, or rather she *had* got through but she'd put them on hold and not said anything.

"Olivia?" Cold, nasty tone.

"I . . . I . . ."

"We work with Century very closely on a lot of celebrity interviews and shoots. We have the awards season coming up, for which we'll be relying on them very heavily and, and, really . . ."

"I didn't call the FBI."

"You didn't?"

"Well, I *did,* but I never got through to a person. I can't understand why—"

"I'm sorry," snapped Sally Hawkins. "This really isn't making any sense. Did you call them, or didn't you?"

"Well, I started to call them, but . . ."

Olivia was staring at Century PR's press release for Ferramo's movie. Pierre Feramo, it said: Feramo with one *r.* No wonder she couldn't find him on Google. She had bloody well spelled his name wrong. Oh God. *Don't panic.*

"Olivia, are you feeling all right?"

"Yes, yes, it's just . . . I . . . I . . ."

Wedging the phone between her ear and her shoulder, she moved over to the desk and Googled Pierre Feramo. There were 1,567 entries. Oh dear.

"All right. I see." The editor was now talking to her as if she were a retarded child. "All right. Now you've had a very frightening experience in Miami. I understand that. I think the best thing is if you just take a good rest for a few hours and come home. You've done some of the research for the story?"

Olivia was scrolling down the first page of the 1,567 Google entries: producer credit on a French short which won the Palme d'Or; photographed with a model at "the Oscars of the perfume industry"; quoted in the *Miami Herald* after the Crème de Phylgie launch.

"Yes. No, really I'm fine. I want to finish the story."

"Well. *We* think it would be much better if you came home. Century PR are not happy about you continuing to work with their people. So perhaps you can write up your notes and e-mail them to Imogen, and I'll have her arrange a flight for you this afternoon."

"But, listen, I didn't say anything to the FBI . . ."

"I'm afraid I have to go, Olivia. I've got a conference call. I'll have Imogen call you with the flight details. Make sure you send the research over."

Olivia stared around the room, disbelieving. She hadn't called the FBI, had she? She had only *practiced* calling the FBI. Had they perfected reading people's thoughts over phone lines? No. The CIA possibly, but not the FBI. She sat down on the bed. Surely not. The only person who had known that she was going to call them was Kate.

Olivia was typing furiously, writing up as much of the wannabe story as she'd got together in the short time before she was so cruelly fired. Every few minutes she flicked to a document called *"Kate: FURY: RE VENTING OF"* and vented.

"I can't believe you fucking well did this to me. I thought our friendship was based on trust and loyalty and . . ."

Three more paragraphs of wannabe story. Back to *"Kate: FURY: RE VENTING OF"*: "Kate, I hope I'm not jumping to conclusions unfairly, but I don't understand . . ."

Wannabe story again. *"Kate: FURY: RE VENTING OF,"* more considered this time: "Listen, you fucking bitch-queen from hell, how the fuck dare you do me over by fucking telling them I called the fucking FBI when I fucking didn't, you fucking . . ."

Back to the article. She typed a final paragraph and read it over.

She made a few changes, ran spell-check, pressed "Send," then kicked the leg of the desk.

It wasn't fair. It wasn't *fair.* In a sudden moment of blind fury, she picked up the phone and dialed Kate's home number. It was on answerphone, but she decided to go for it anyway.

"Hi, it's me. Listen, *Elan* just called and fired me for calling the FBI about Feramo. I didn't call the FBI. The only person who knew I was even thinking of calling the FBI was you. I can't believe you just wanted to get me off the story so you could, you could . . ."

Olivia's voice cracked. She was really, really hurt. She put down the phone and sat on the beanbag, blinking and rubbing a tear away with her fist. She stared ahead for a long time, lower lip trembling, then marched over to the tan and olive carry-on case, took out a very old, tatty piece of paper, unfolded it carefully, and sat back on the beanbag with it.

Rules for Living by Olivia Joules

1. Never panic. Stop, breathe, think.
2. No one is thinking about you. They're thinking about themselves, just like you.
3. Never change haircut or color before an important event.
4. Nothing is either as bad or as good as it seems.
5. Do as you would be done by, e.g., thou shalt not kill.
6. It is better to buy one expensive thing that you really like than several cheap ones that you only quite like.
7. Hardly anything matters: if you get upset, ask yourself, "Does it really matter?"
8. The key to success lies in how you pick yourself up from failure.
9. Be honest and kind.
10. Only buy clothes that make you feel like doing a small dance.
11. Trust your instincts, not your overactive imagination.
12. When overwhelmed by disaster, check if it's really a disaster by

doing the following: (a) think, "Oh, fuck it," (b) look on the bright side and, if that doesn't work, look on the funny side.

If neither of the above works then maybe it is a disaster so turn to items 1 and 4.

13. Don't expect the world to be safe or life to be fair.
14. Sometimes you just have to go with the flow.

And then the new one from Elsie, added at the bottom:

15. Don't regret anything. Remember there wasn't anything else that could have happened, given who you were and the state of the world at that moment. The only thing you can change is the present, so learn from the past.

And then Olivia's own practical application of this:

16. If you start regretting something and thinking, "I should have done . . ." always add, "but then I might have been run over by a lorry or blown up by a Japanese-manned torpedo."

Nothing is either as bad or as good as it seems. There were always one or two of them which jumped out. *Trust your instincts, not your overactive imagination.* Did she really think, in her gut, that it was Kate?

No. She didn't. And the information hadn't come from the FBI because she never actually spoke to the FBI. The only place the information could have come from was right here, inside the room. She started systematically checking the lights, the phone, under the desk, in the drawers. What would a bug look like? She had no idea. Would it be like a microphone? Would it have batteries? She giggled. Or little legs?

She thought some more, then reached for the phone again and dialed information: "The Spy Shop on Sunset Boulevard. Spy

Shop. S.P.Y. You know, spies? James Bond? Kiefer Sutherland? English public-school nineteen-thirties homosexuals?"

Half an hour later, she was staring at a large bottom-cleavage, which was protruding from under the bed.

"Ohhh Kayyy. Here we go. This is basically your problem."

Olivia took a few steps back as the bottom-cleavage started wriggling out towards her. Connor the countersurveillance expert pulled himself awkwardly to his knees, joyfully holding out the square cover from the phone jack with the same smiley expression used by techies the world over—computer buffs, diving instructors, ski instructors, pilots—when they've found something only another techie would understand but which they have to explain to a lay person.

"It's a two-point-five MP with a pilger. Probably took him about ten seconds if he had a DSR."

"That's great." She tried valiantly to provide him with some sort of emotional reinforcement. "Great. Er . . . so this was actually tapping the phone line?"

"Oh no. Oh no. No. This is just a microphone. Just a simple XTC four-by-two."

"Right. So it would just pick up what I said? They wouldn't have any way of knowing whether I was actually on the phone or not?"

"You got it. They might pick up the dial tone but . . ." He sucked in air through his teeth and stared at the phone jack cover, then shook his head. "No way. Not with a gimper. They would probably just pick up what you actually said. You want us to do anything else?"

"No, no. I'll pop in later and pick up the rest of the stuff."

She had ordered a bug detector disguised as a calculator, an invisible-ink pen, a chemical-attack protection hood, an excitingly flat and tiny digital camera and, childishly, but most thrillingly, a spy

ring with a mirror you could flick up to see behind you. It was an
excellent stash of stuff to go with the survival tin.

After the countersurveillance man had left, she immediately called
Kate and left a message. "It's me. I'm sorry. Really sorry. Brain-
storm. Turns out the room was bugged. I owe you a big margarita
when I get back. Call me."

Then she started pacing the room, trying not to panic. It wasn't
a game anymore, and it wasn't her overactive imagination. Something really bad was going on and someone was after her. She
glanced at the Rules for Living again, breathed in and out deeply,
thought: *Oh, fuck it,* and tried to imagine the whole thing worked
up into an amusing anecdote to tell Kate. The trouble was, it didn't
seem all that funny.

17

Thirty-eight minutes later, she was on Rodeo Drive, lying under a sheet in a white room with six separate jets of very hot steam hissing at her face.

"Er, are you sure these steam things are all right? They seem a bit . . ."

"They're perfect, trust me. We need to engineer a radiant temperature in order to micro-collapse the epidermal cellafeeds and stimulate—"

"Right. They're not going to leave big red blotches, are they?"

"Relax. You're going to be *sooo* adorable."

She was feeling many tiny sucking movements all over her face, as if a set of toothless mini-piranhas had been let loose on it, along with the six Bunsen burners.

"Michael," she said, determined to get at least something useful out of the hideous two-hundred-and-fifteen-dollar experience, "how do you know Travis?"

"Travis? Who's Travis?"

"You know—Travis? The guy you introduced me to in Miami?"

"You've just flown in from Miami? Do you have jet lag? I could ionize your face."

"No, thank you. He's an actor slash writer, isn't he?"

"Oh, that guy. Right."

"He's the guy who's written the screenplay for Feramo's movie."

"You're kidding me. Feramo's movie is written by *Travis*? Would you like to take a jar of Crème de Phylgie? The larger one is excellent value; you get two hundred milliliters for . . ."

"No thank you. What's wrong with Travis writing the movie? Ow! What are you *doing*?"

"I'm lifting the initial resistance of your epidermis. You should try the ionizing. Even if you're not jet-lagged, it's an excellent rejuvenating exfoliant, hypoallergenic, totally free of free radicals . . ."

"No thanks."

". . . biocolic-balancing plant extracts," he oozed on, ignoring her.

"How do you know Travis?"

"Travis?" Michael Monteroso laughed. "Travis?"

"What's so funny?"

"Travis picks up the cash from the salon and takes it to the bank. He works for a security firm. Do you have a facial technician who works with you regularly?"

"No, I don't actually," she said. "Bizarrely enough—"

"If you like, I'll give you my card when you go. I'm actually not supposed to work outside the salon, but for special clients I can come to your home."

"You're very kind, but actually I don't live here."

The Bunsen burners stopped, and she felt herself being lulled by the eucalyptus scents and the steady flow of gibberish into a half-asleep state. She tried to fight it and stay alert.

"I could come to your hotel?"

"No. So how do you all know each other—all the people at the party?"

"I don't really know them. I just help out with the facials for the events. I think some of them met at the dive lodge down in Honduras—you know, Feramo's place on the islands down there. Now this is eucalyptus and castor oil I'm putting on you here." *Feramo had a dive lodge in Honduras?* She concentrated on not changing her expression.

"I actually use a range of dermatologically tested organic products. This is totally organic, additive free. I'll make you up a pot to take with you."

"How much is it?"

"Four hundred and seventy-five dollars."

"Just the facial will be fine, thanks."

When she got into the changing room, she looked in the mirror and let out a horrified sigh. Her face was covered in small red rings, as if she'd been attacked by a creature with tentacles or tiny parasites trying to suck greedily on her, tails wiggling. Which, in a way, she had.

———

Olivia stopped at the mall on the way home and returned to her room armed with books: books on Honduras, books on al-Qaeda, and a book by Absalom Widgett, a British scholar of Islam, called *The Arab Sensibility: The Unlikelihood of the El Obeid Plasma TV.* She climbed under the covers for comfort to read. As she flicked through the al-Qaeda books, she suddenly froze and stared, rereading the same paragraph:

> *Intelligence officials warn that the Takfiri, an offshoot of al-Qaeda, belie their Islamic roots by drinking alcohol, smoking, even drug taking as well as womanizing and dressing in sophisticated Western style. Their aim is to blend in to what they see as corrupt societies with the goal of destroying them.*
>
> *Professor Absalom Widgett, the British scholar of Islam and author of* The Arab Sensibility: The Unlikelihood of the El Obeid Plasma TV, *has described them as devastatingly ruthless: the hardcore of the hardcore of Islamic militants.*

It was six-fifteen. She was to leave for dinner with Feramo in fifteen minutes. Her palms were sweating, and her stomach kept being gripped by spasms of fear. As she dressed and made herself up, dabbing the red sucker marks with concealer, she tried to stop, breathe, think, act calmly. She tried to think of positive scenarios: Feramo was just a playboy. Feramo had never heard of the word Takfiri. Feramo knew nothing about the phone call or the room bugging. Maybe it was the nosy, overly chatty bellboy with the bulging muscles and strange facial hair. Maybe the bellboy was working for the tabloids and had thought a celebrity was going to be checking into Olivia's room and had planted the bug.

By six-thirty she had psyched herself into thinking it was all completely okay. It was fine. She would just have this last fun dinner and then go back to London and start to rebuild the tattered remnants of her journalistic career.

Then she stepped out of her room and lost her cool again. What was she *doing*? Was she out of her *mind*? She was about to have dinner, alone, she didn't know where, with an al-Qaeda terrorist who knew she was on to him. There *was* no positive scenario. Feramo didn't want to have her to dinner, he wanted to have her *for* dinner. Still, at least the blotches on her face didn't show now.

The elevator doors opened.

"Oh, my dear, what *has* happened to your face?"

It was the wrinkly voice-coach lady, Carol.

"Oh, nothing. I, er, had a facial," said Olivia, stepping inside. "Have you been working with the actors at the auditions?"

"Yes, well. Not just the audition people."

Olivia looked at her quickly. She seemed to be troubled.

"Oh, really? So you're not just working with the actors then?" She decided to risk a bit of boldness. "You work with the rest of the team as well?"

Carol looked her straight in the eye. She seemed to be thinking a lot of things that she couldn't say.

"I always thought it was only actors who needed voice coaches," said Olivia lightly.

"People change their accents for all sorts of reasons, don't they?"

The elevator doors opened to the lobby. Suraya was crossing their line of vision, radiant against the white walls.

"What do you reckon?" said Olivia conspiratorially, nodding towards Suraya. "Malibu with a touch of Bombay?"

"Hounslow," Carol said. She wasn't laughing.

"And Pierre Feramo?" whispered Olivia, as they stepped out of the elevator. "Cairo? Khartoum?"

"That's not for me to say, is it?" Carol said overbrightly, never taking her eyes off Olivia's. "Anyway. Have a lovely evening." She gave a brittle smile and, pulling her cardigan around her, headed off towards the parking valet.

18

Olivia approached the reception desk and asked to have the charges since her arrival and all future charges taken off the *Elan* account and moved onto her credit card. It was turning into an expensive trip, but a girl has her pride. As she waited, the nosy bellboy with the goatee beard and muscles appeared.

"Leaving, Ms. Joules?" he said. There was something far too clever and self-possessed about him for a bellboy.

"Not yet."

"Enjoying your stay?"

"Yes, apart from the microphone in the room," she said softly, watching his face.

"I'm sorry?"

"You heard."

The receptionist returned just as a vaguely familiar, nastily sweet smell invaded her nostrils. Olivia turned. It was Alfonso, chest hair protruding from a polo shirt, which this time was pink.

"Olivia, I was beginning to think you would never appear. I was going to call up to your room."

The accumulated stress erupted in a burst of irritation.

"Why? Are you coming to dinner as well?" she snapped.

For a second Alfonso looked hurt. He was a funny chap. All oiliness and bluster, but she had the feeling that underneath he was suffering from low self-esteem.

"Of course not. Mr. Feramo simply wanted me to make sure you arrived safely. The car is waiting for you."

"Oh. Okay. Well, thanks," she said, feeling a bit mean.

"My God, what happened to your face?"

It was going to be a long evening.

Alfonso led her out and proudly pointed to the "car." It was a white stretch limo, the sort that people from out of town ride up and down Sunset Boulevard in on bachelor nights, wearing brightly colored wigs. As the driver held open the door, Olivia climbed in, or rather fell in, tripped over the bump in the middle, and found herself looking at a pair of Gucci stilettos. Her eyes moved upwards past delicate olive ankles and a dusty-pink silk dress to discover she was sharing the limo with Suraya. What was this?

"Hello again," said Olivia, trying to crawl onto the seat while retaining some vestiges of dignity.

"Hi. My God! What happened to your face?"

"I had a facial," she said, glancing round nervously as the limo purred off onto Sunset.

"Oh no." Suraya started to laugh. "You went to Michael, right? He's such a bullshitter. Come here."

She clicked open her bag, leaned over and started dabbing at Olivia's face with concealer. It was an oddly intimate moment. Olivia was too startled to protest.

"So, you and Pierre, hey?" Suraya's voice didn't fit with the elegant beauty. She sounded stoned and what Olivia's mother would have described as "common." "Are you guys an item?"

"Heavens no! Just a friendly dinner!" There was something about Suraya which was turning Olivia into a hearty Girl Guide.

"Oh, come on," drawled Suraya, leaning forward. "He thinks you're very intelligent."

"That's nice!" she said brightly.

"Sure." Suraya looked out of the window, smirking to herself. "So you're a journalist, right? We should go shopping."

"Right," said Olivia, trying to work out the logic of this.

"We'll go to Melrose. Tomorrow?"

"I have to work," she said, thinking how nonencouraging it would be trying on clothes with a six-foot, eight-stone model.

"What do you do?"

"I'm an actress," Suraya said dismissively.

"Really? Are you going to be in Pierre's movie?"

"Sure. Movie, bullshit, whatever. Do you really think he's for real?" Suraya said conspiratorially. "Feramo, I mean." She opened her purse and checked her reflection, then leaned forward again. "Well?" she asked, slipping her hand onto Olivia's knee and giving it a squeeze.

Olivia started to panic. Were they planning a hideous seventies-style sex romp as part of the smoke screen? They were passing the pink palace of the Beverly Hills Hotel now. She wanted to open the window and yell out, "Help, help! I'm being kidnapped."

"Pierre? I think he's very attractive. Are we going out to a restaurant?"

"I dunno. Restaurant, order in, whatever," said Suraya. "But do you think he's really a movie producer?"

"Of course," said Olivia levelly. "Why? Don't you?"

"I guess. How long are you going to be in LA? Do you like the Standard?"

If she was trying to get information, she wasn't very good at it.

"It's great, but not the sort of place you feel like putting on a bikini. It's like being on the set of *Baywatch*. Though that wouldn't be a problem for you."

"Nor you," said Suraya, pointedly eyeing her breasts. "You've got a great little figure."

Olivia adjusted her dress nervously. "Where are we going?"

"Pierre's apartment?"

"Where's that?"

"On Wilshire? So why don't I call you on your cell tomorrow to fix up shopping?"

"Call me at the hotel," said Olivia firmly. "Like I said, I'll be working."

Suraya looked nasty when she wasn't getting her own way. They lapsed into an uncomfortable silence as Olivia glumly imagined what was ahead: Olivia tied naked back to back with Suraya, while Alfonso strutted round them dressed as a baby in rubber pants and Pierre Feramo minced to and fro, cracking a whip. If only she'd stayed in the hotel and ordered room service.

Pierre's apartment in the Wilshire Regency Towers was the pinnacle of vertical luxury living. The elevator doors swung open on the nineteenth floor to reveal a gold and beige temple to understated bad taste. This was more like it—mirrors, gold tables, a black onyx statue of a jaguar. There was only one elevator. She slipped the hatpin out of her bag and hid it in her palm, looking round for another means of escape.

"You want a martini?" said Suraya. She threw her bag casually onto the square beige-brocade sofa as if she lived there.

"Ooh, no. Just a diet Coke for me, thanks," trilled Girl Guide Olivia.

Why am I being like this? she thought, walking over to the window. The sun was beginning to redden over the Santa Monica mountains and the ocean.

Suraya handed her the drink and stood ridiculously close. "Beautiful, isn't it?" she purred romantically. "Wouldn't you like to live somewhere like this?"

"Ooh! I think it might make me a bit dizzy," joshed hearty Olivia, edging away. "How do you find it?"

"You get used to it. I mean . . . I don't actually live here, but . . ." Hah! A flash of annoyance in the beautiful dark eyes. So Suraya *did* live here. She had given herself away.

"Where are you from?" said Olivia.

"Los Angeles. Why?" On the defensive now.

"I thought I heard an English accent in there."

"I guess I'm mid-Atlantic."

"How long have you known Pierre?"

"Long enough." Suraya downed her drink in one, walked away and picked up her bag. "Anyway, I gotta split."

"Where are you going?"

"Out. Pierre will be here soon. Make yourself at home."

"Right," said Olivia. "Well! Jolly good! Have a lovely evening."

Olivia watched the elevator doors close on Suraya, listening for the groan and hiss as it moved downwards, until she was sure she was gone. It was silent now, apart from the hum of the air-conditioning. The apartment was either a high-end rental or it had been furnished by an insane designer. There was no personal stuff—no books, no dishes with pens in—just gilded mirrors, ornaments, miscellaneous onyx beasts of the jungle and strange paintings of women in peril from snakes and long, thin dragons. She listened, adjusting her hold on the hatpin, gripping the Louis Vuitton clutch tightly in the other fist. There was a corridor opposite the elevator. She padded silently across the plush carpet towards it, seeing a line of closed doors. Heart pounding and telling herself, if challenged, she could claim she was looking for the loo, she reached out for the first gilt handle and turned it.

She found herself in a large bedroom, one wall entirely window. The centerpiece was a four-poster bed, the pillars fashioned like thick ropes, bulbous lamps on either side. Again, there were no personal items. She pulled open a drawer, flinching when it creaked: nothing in there. She couldn't close it. It was stuck. Cursing herself silently, she left it open and continued her tiptoed search. The bathroom was huge, mirrored, ghastly, in pink marble. It led to a major closet lined with cedar shelves, with a central island for laying out clothes. But no clothes. She leaned back against the wall and felt

it move. A panel—two inches thick, steel—was sliding noiselessly
to the left to reveal another room. A safe? A panic room? The lights
came up. It was larger than the bedroom and painted white: win-
dowless and empty apart from a line of small Oriental mats lined up
against the wall. The panel started to close and impulsively, just before it closed, she darted through.

She stood, heart beating, looking around. Was it really a panic
room? Were they prayer mats? She turned to look at the wall behind her. There were three white posters with Arabic writing on
them. She took out her camera, put the bag on the carpet, started
to photograph them, then froze. There was a slight noise from the
other side of the sliding wall: muffled footsteps! Someone was in
the bedroom. The footsteps stopped. Then she heard the sound of
someone struggling to close the drawer.

The footsteps started again, slow, still muffled, but moving closer.
She felt as though she were trapped underwater, out of air. She
forced herself to breathe, stay calm and think. Could there be a second exit? She tried to visualize the corridor outside: a long break,
then a door. Another bedroom suite?

She heard the footsteps on the marble floor of the bathroom and
looked back at the panel, noting the slight change in tone of the
wall, then scanned the wall opposite. There! She tiptoed over and
leaned her shoulder against it. It started to open. She slipped through
the gap, willing the panel to move back, almost sobbing with relief
as it did. She was in another closet, this time full of men's clothes.
There was a faint smell of Feramo's cologne. They were his clothes:
shiny, almost dainty shoes; dark suits; crisply ironed shirts in pastel
shades; neatly folded jeans; polo shirts. Her thoughts came randomly and fast as she hurried through: *God, he had a lot of clothes for
a guy. Very neat, almost anal. She could really mess up a closet like this.
How was she going to explain her emergence into the corridor?* She stepped
into the bathroom. *That was it: perfect. She could pretend she'd just
come out to use the loo.* Her reflection looked back at her from every
angle. She heard the slight, almost noiseless movement of the slid-

ing panel. She tucked the miniature camera under her armpit and flushed the loo. Maybe good manners would keep whoever it was out of the bathroom.

"Olivia?" It was Feramo.

"Hang on a sec! Not decent!" she said brightly. "Okay."

She smiled, trying to look as natural as one could, with one arm concealing a miniature camera under it. But Feramo's eyes were deadly cold.

"So, Olivia, I see that you have discovered my secret."

19

Feramo moved past her, shut the bathroom door, locked it and turned to face her.

"Do you normally wander through your host's home without permission?"

Go with the fear, she told herself. *Don't fight it. Use the adrenaline. Go on the attack.*

"Why shouldn't I look around for a bathroom if you ask me for dinner and have me met by unexplained six-foot sex goddesses then leave me hanging around on my own?"

He slipped his hand inside his jacket. "I take it this belongs to you?" he said, holding out the Louis Vuitton clutch. Bugger. She had left it on the floor when she was taking photographs inside the secret room.

"You told me you were French. You made a great thing about speaking from the heart. And then you bloody well lied to me. You're not French at all, are you?"

He looked at her, impassive. His face, in neutral, had an almost aristocratic sneer.

"You are right," he said eventually. "I did not tell you the truth."

He turned and unlocked the door. She thought she was going to faint with relief.

"But come. We will be late for our dinner," he said, more pleasantly now. "We will talk about these things then."

He threw the door open, gesturing her out into his bedroom. It was a big bed. Olivia strode determinedly past it—there was his shirt on a chair, books by the bed—and out into the corridor. He closed the door and stood between her and the elevator, directing her the other way.

At the end of the corridor was yet another closed door. He moved ahead of her to unlock it, and she grabbed the chance to slip the camera into her bag as he pushed the door open to reveal a stairwell.

"Up," he said.

Was he planning to push her off the roof? She turned to look at him, trying to gauge if this was the moment to run. As her eyes met his, she saw that he was laughing at her.

"I'm not going to eat you. Up you go."

It was very confusing. Reality kept shifting to and fro. Suddenly, now, with his laugh, it felt like a date again. At the top of the stairs he pushed opened a heavy fire door, and there was a rush of warm air. They stepped out into a strong wind and a tremendous roar. They were on the top of the building, the vast panorama of Los Angeles surrounding them. The noise was coming from a helicopter parked on the roof, rotor blades turning, the door open, ready.

"Your carriage awaits," Feramo shouted above the noise. Olivia was torn between fear and wild excitement. Feramo's hair was streaming straight back from his face as though he were in front of a wind machine on a photo shoot.

Olivia ran across the concrete keeping low to dodge the rotor blades. She scrambled into the helicopter, wishing she hadn't worn a slip dress and the uncomfortable shoes. The pilot turned round and gestured towards the harnesses and ear protectors. Pierre was in the seat beside her, pulling the heavy door closed as the helicopter lifted into the air, the building shrinking away below them. They were heading towards the ocean.

It was impossible to speak against the din. Pierre didn't look at her. She tried to concentrate on the view. The sun was setting over the Santa Monica Bay, a heavy orange ball against a pale blue sky, red light reflecting back off the ocean's glassy surface. They followed the coast a little way, banking downwards against the dark line of the mountains towards Malibu. She could see the long line of the pier, the little half-built restaurant at the end, and beside it the surfers, black, seal-like figures, catching the last of the waves.

Feramo leaned forward, instructing the pilot, and the helicopter swung out towards the open sea. She thought of her mother, years ago, chastising her for her sense of adventure, her interest in danger-ous boys and life close to the edge: "You'll get yourself into trou-ble; you don't understand the world, you only see the excitement. You won't see the danger until it's too late." Unfortunately the ad-vice was only given in the context of Catholic boys or boys with motorbikes.

The sun was slipping behind the horizon, separating in two, one orb on top of the other like a figure eight. Seconds after it disap-peared the sky around exploded into reds and oranges, the lines of airplane trails white against the blue high above.

Well, she wasn't having this. She wasn't just being whisked out into the middle of the Pacific without so much as a by-your-leave. She dug Feramo indignantly in the arm.

"Where are we going?"

"What?"

"Where are we going?"

"What?"

They were like a geriatric married couple already.

She wriggled further up in her seat and yelled in his ear.

"Where are we going?"

He smirked. "You'll see."

"I want to know where you're taking me."

He bent to say something in her ear.

"What?"

"Catalina!" he bellowed.

Catalina Island—a day-tripper's island twenty miles offshore. There was one little cheerful seaside town—Avalon; the rest was wilderness.

Night fell quickly. Soon a dark shoulder of land was rearing up out of the gloom. Far away to their left, she could see the lights of Avalon—cozy and welcoming, cascading down to the little curved bay. Ahead of them was only blackness.

20 CATALINA ISLAND, CALIFORNIA

The chopper was descending into a deep, narrow bay on the ocean side of the island, well hidden from the Californian mainland and the lights of Avalon. She saw vegetation, palm trees flattening away from the chopper. As they landed, Feramo opened the door and jumped out, pulling her after him and gesturing at her to lower her head. The blades didn't stop. She heard the engine sound rise again and turned to see the chopper taking off.

He guided her along a path towards a jetty. There was no wind. The ocean was calm, the steep line of the hills on either side and the jetty black in silhouette against it. As the noise of the helicopter faded, there was silence except for tropical sounds: cicadas, frogs, the clink of metal against metal at the jetty. Her breath was coming short and fast. Were they alone here?

They reached the jetty. She noticed surfboards leaning against a wooden hut. What did he want with surfboards? Catalina was hardly fabled for its surf. As they drew closer, she realized that the hut was a dive shack, stocked with tanks and gear.

"Wait here. I need to get something." She gripped the wooden railing, listening to Feramo's footsteps die away into silence. She was both terrified and confused. Was she in danger? Should she just grab a dive rig and make her escape? But then if this was, by any remaining chance, just an *über*-romantic date, it would seem like a pretty extreme piece of strange behavior.

She tiptoed over to the dive shack. It was well ordered: a line of tanks, twenties, in brackets; BCDs and regulator rigs on hooks; masks and fins in neat piles. There was a knife lying on a rough wooden table. She picked it up and slipped it into her clutch, starting at the sound of Feramo's footsteps returning. She was in danger, she knew, of being overwhelmed by fear. She had to regain control.

The footsteps were getting closer. Terrified, she cried out, "Pierre?" There was no answer, just the sound of the footsteps, heavy and uneven. Was it some thug or hired hit man? "Pierre. Is that you?"

She drew the knife out of her bag and held it behind her back, tensed and ready.

"Yes," came Pierre's liquid, accented tones. "Of course it is me."

She exhaled, her whole body relaxing. Feramo emerged from the gloom, carrying a clumsy bundle wrapped in black.

"What are we doing here?" she burst out. "What are you *doing* bringing me to some isolated place and just dumping me and not answering when I ask if it's you when you're making weird footsteps? What *is* this place? What are you *doing*?"

"Weird footsteps?" Feramo laughed, his eyes flashing, then suddenly whipped the black cover from the bundle. Olivia felt as though her legs were going to give way. It was an ice bucket containing a bottle of champagne and two flutes.

"Look," she said, putting her hand to her forehead. "This is very nice, but do you have to be so melodramatic?"

"You do not strike me as the kind of woman who seeks out the predictable."

"No, but you don't have to scare me to death to keep me happy. What is this place?"

"It is a boat dock. Here," he said, holding out the black cloth, "in case you are cold. I should perhaps have warned you we would be putting out to sea."

"To sea?" she said, trying simultaneously to take the wrap, which turned out to be very soft indeed as if made from the feathers of some rare bird, and hide the knife in it.

He nodded towards the bay, where the silhouette of a yacht could be seen gliding noiselessly round the headland.

She was relieved to find that there was a crew aboard. If Feramo was going to kill her, he would, one would have thought, have done it when they were alone. And the champagne would have been a very odd touch.

She was feeling slightly more relaxed, having managed to stash the dive knife in the Louis Vuitton clutch under cover of the black, ultrafine pashmina. Feramo stood beside her at the stern, as they glided out into the blackness of the open sea.

"Olivia," he said, handing her a glass, "shall we drink a toast to our evening? To the beginning." He clinked his glass against hers and looked at her intently.

"Of what?" she said.

"You do not remember our conversation in Miami? On the rooftop? The beginning of our getting to know each other." He raised his glass, then drained it. She sipped at hers, smiling weakly, wondering if this whole performance was designed to wrong-foot her, making her feel threatened and terrified one moment, and safe and pampered the next, like leg-waxing with a smooth-talking but incompetent beautician.

"So, tell me. You are a journalist. Why?"

She thought for a moment. "I like to write. I like to travel. I like to find out what's going on."

"And where have you visited on your travels?"

"Well, not as many places as I'd like: South America, India, Africa."

"Where in Africa?"

"The Sudan and Kenya."

"Really? You have been to the Sudan?"

"Yes."

"And how did you find it?"

"It was extraordinary. It was the most foreign place I've ever been. It was like *Lawrence of Arabia*."

"And the people?"

"I liked the people," she said quietly.

"And Los Angeles? How do you find it here?"

"Deliciously shallow."

He laughed. "That is all?"

"Unexpectedly rural. It's like the south of France only with shopping."

"And this journalism you do, this froth for magazines, it is your speciality?"

"Froth? I've never been so insulted in my life!"

He laughed again. He had a nice laugh, rather shy, as if it was something he didn't quite feel allowed to do.

"I really want to be a proper foreign correspondent," she said, suddenly serious. "I want to do something that means something."

"The *OceansApart*. Did you do a piece anyway for the *Sunday Times*?" There was a slight change of tenor in his voice.

"Yes, kind of. But they put it under someone else's byline."

"Did that distress you?"

"Pretty trivial thing in that context. What about you? Do you like LA?"

"I am interested in what it produces."

"What? Beautiful girls with giant fake breasts?"

He laughed. "Why don't you come inside?"

"Are you trying to get fresh?"

"No, no. For dinner, I mean."

A deckhand in a white uniform held out his hand to help her as she stepped down the stairs. The interior was breathtaking, if just a tiny bit naff. It was paneled in shiny wood with beige, deep-pile carpets and lots of brassware. It was like a proper room, not a cabin on a boat. The table was laid for two, with a white cloth, flowers and very shiny glassware and cutlery, which, disappointingly, was not gold-plated. The cabin was decorated with a Hollywood theme, and there were some interesting old photographs of stolen moments on set: Alfred Hitchcock playing chess with Grace Kelly, Ava Gardner soaking her feet in an ice bucket, Omar Sharif and Peter O'Toole playing cricket in the desert. There was a glass case with memorabilia inside: an Oscar statuette, an Egyptian headdress, a four-stranded pearl necklace with a picture of Audrey Hepburn in *Breakfast at Tiffany's* behind it.

"This is my passion," he said. "The movies. I watched so many with my mother, so many of the great old movies. Some day I will make a picture which will be remembered long after I am dead. If I can fight my way through the stupidity and prejudice of Hollywood."

"But you've made movies already."

"Small movies, in France. You would not know these films."

"I might. Try me."

Was that a fleeting look of panic?

"Look," he said, "this is a headdress worn by Elizabeth Taylor in *Cleopatra.*"

"Is that a real Oscar?"

"Yes, but I am afraid not the most distinguished one. My dream is to obtain one of the statuettes awarded for *Lawrence of Arabia* in 1962. But for the moment I am having to make do with this, which is an award for best sound editing in the late sixties that I managed to find on eBay."

Olivia laughed. "Tell me more about your work. I might have seen something. I see quite a lot of French films in—"

"And look. These are the pearls that Audrey Hepburn wore in *Breakfast at Tiffany's.*"

"The real ones?"

"Of course. You would like to wear them for dinner?"

"No, no. I'd look ridiculous."

He took them out of the case and placed them round her neck, fastening them with the dexterity of a surgeon. She bowed her head, feeling his fingers against her neck.

He stood back to appraise the effect of the necklace. "You are beautiful," he whispered. "And what makes it all the more attractive is that you do not know it."

She met his eyes for a second, caught herself feeling a stab of Cinderella syndrome and was furious. Dammit, she *was* impressed with the bloody yacht and the apartments, the pearls and the helicopter, the beauty and the charm. She knew she was one in a long line of girls who had been wooed with this lot, and she didn't want to be. The ridiculous, delusional feelings which can afflict a girl in such situations were bubbling up. She was thinking: *I'm different; I don't like him for his money, I like him for himself. I can change him,* while simultaneously imagining herself installed on the yacht, an adored creature, slipping into the water for unlimited scuba diving with no additional charge for equipment rental, then emerging from the shower and fastening Audrey Hepburn's pearls around her neck.

Stop it, she told herself. *Stop it, you total sad act. Do what you're here to do.* "Pierre bin Feramo," she felt like yelling, *"can we get this straight? Are you wooing me, or are you trying to bump me off? Are you a terrorist or a playboy? Do you think I tried to put the FBI onto you or not?"* Right, she was bloody well going to tackle him.

She stood looking at the Oscar and the Egyptian headdress in the case, trying to calm herself.

"Why did you lie to me?" she said without turning round.

He didn't reply. She turned to face him. "Why did you tell me you were French? I *knew* you were an Arab."

"You did?" He looked very cool about it all, even slightly amused. "Might I enquire as to why?"

"Well, number one, your accent. Number two, I heard you say *shukran.*"

A second's pause. "You speak Arabic?"

"Like I told you, I've been in the Sudan."

"Was that a mosque in your apartment?"

The hooded eyes gave nothing away. "It is actually a panic room.

And it seemed an ideal place for privacy and contemplation. And as for the slight, shall we say, *inaccuracy* about my nationality, I was trying to do away with the encumbrance of racial stereotyping. Not everyone has your positive attitude towards our culture and religion."

"Isn't that like politicians pretending not to be gay—the pretending in itself has the effect of suggesting there's something wrong with being gay?"

"You are suggesting I am ashamed of being an Arab?"

His voice was terrifying: calm, pleasant, violent anger surging below.

"I'm interested in why you lied about it."

He fixed his dark, soulful eyes on hers. "I am proud of being an Arab. Our culture is the oldest in the world and the wisest. Our laws are spiritual laws and our traditions rooted in the wisdom of our ancestors. When I am in Hollywood I am ashamed—not of my ancestry, but of the world I see around me: the arrogance, the ignorance, the vanity, the stupidity, the greed, the salivating worship of flesh and youth, the flaunting of sexuality for fame and financial gain, the lust for the new in the absence of respect for the old. This shallowness you joke of finding delicious is not sweetness but the very spores of rot within the ripe fruit."

Olivia held herself motionless, gripping her clutch, thinking of the knife inside it. She sensed that the slightest misjudged word or move would trip the wire of his carefully controlled rage.

"Why are the richest nations on earth the unhappiest? Do you know?" he continued.

"That's a rather odd generalization," she said lightly, trying to shift the mood. "I mean some of the richest nations in the world are Arab nations. Saudi Arabia's rather well off, isn't it?"

"Saudi Arabia, pah!"

He seemed to be having some kind of private battle. He turned away, then looked back, composed now.

"I am sorry, Olivia," he said in a gentler tone. "But spending time in America, as I do, I am often . . . hurt . . . by the ignorance and prejudice with which we are pigeonholed and insulted. Come. Enough. This is not the evening for this discussion. It is a beautiful night, and it is time to eat."

God, Pierre Feramo could drink. One martini, a bottle of Cristal, an '82 Pomerol and the best part of a '96 Chassagne-Montrachet later, he was calling for a Recioto della Valpolicella to go with dessert. In most men, it would have seemed as though there was a problem. In a Muslim, it seemed downright bizarre. But then, Olivia found herself thinking, just say for most of his life Feramo never drank a drop of alcohol. Just say he'd only started drinking recently, as a smoke screen. How would he know he had a problem? How would he know that everyone didn't drink like that?

"Aren't Muslims supposed not to drink alcohol?" she ventured. She was feeling rather full. The food was superb: scallops on pureed spring peas with white truffle oil, sea bass in a lightly curried sauce with pumpkin ravioli, peaches stewed in red wine with mascarpone ice cream.

"Ah, that depends, that depends," he said vaguely, filling up his glass. "There are different interpretations."

"Do you dive from this boat?" she asked.

"What, scuba dive? Yes. Well, actually, no, not from here, not personally. It is too cold. I prefer to dive in the Caribbean, on the reef off Belize and Honduras, and in the Red Sea. You dive yourself?" He moved to fill her glass, not noticing that it was already full.

"Yes, I love diving. Actually, I was thinking before I came of suggesting a diving story to *Elan:* diving off the beaten track. I was thinking of the Red Sea coast of the Sudan as well."

"But, Olivia," he said, raising his hands expansively, "you must come to my hotel in Honduras. I insist. The diving off the Bay Islands is unsurpassed. We have walls which fall for a thousand feet, intricate tunnels, the rarest of marine life. You must ask your magazine to let you cover it. And then go on to the Sudan. It is wonderful there, the visibility is the best in the world. It is totally untouched. You must do it. You must do it at once. I am leaving for Honduras tomorrow. You must telephone your magazine and join me there as my guest."

"Well, there's a problem," she said.

"A problem?"

"They've fired me."

"They've *fired* you?"

She watched him carefully for signs of bluffing. "Yes. Someone from your PR office called the editor and complained that I'd called the FBI to suggest they check you out."

"But how ridiculous."

"Exactly. I didn't. But someone bugged my room and was listening to me talking to myself."

"Talking to yourself? Suggesting to yourself that I should be checked out by the FBI?"

He looked genuinely hurt. She was growing increasingly confused. He was plausible. He seemed like a man with integrity. She could see why he might fudge his racial identity in such a climate.

"Look," she said, leaning forward, "Pierre, I'll be honest. I did wonder about you after what happened in Miami. When we were together on your roof deck, you seemed so determined I shouldn't go down to the *OceansApart* the next morning. And after it was blown up you immediately left town. You told me you were French, and then I heard you speaking Arabic. I do get a bit carried away and talk to myself—imaginary conversations, I guess, because

I spend so much time alone. But I can't understand who would have bugged my room."

"You are certain the room was bugged?"

"I found a device in the phone jack."

His nostrils flared.

"My dear Olivia," he said eventually, "I am so sorry that this has happened. I had no idea. I cannot imagine who would have done this, but as you know, we live in paranoid times."

"Yes. And you can see how—"

"Oh yes, yes. Of course. You are a journalist and a linguist. You have an enquiring mind. I would probably have been suspicious myself. But, then, I assume that had you retained these suspicions, you would not be here."

"It would have been a bit daft to come," said Olivia, carefully avoiding the lie.

"And now you have lost your job."

"Well, it wasn't exactly a job. But apparently your PR people called them in a fury."

"I will put this right immediately. You must write down the contact details of your editor and I will make a phone call in the morning."

He took her hand, his brown eyes melting into hers. "I am so sorry that this has happened." He really was the most beautiful man: gentle, charming, gracious, kind.

Don't fall in love with him, stop it, stop it, pull yourself together, she told herself. *I'm like one of those female aid workers who falls for the leader of the rebel army or gets kidnapped and falls for her kidnapper. I've got Stockholm Syndrome.*

"You will come? To Honduras?" he said. 'I shall organize a plane for you, and you must be my guest."

She steeled herself. "No, no. You're too kind, but I never accept hospitality when I'm writing a story. It interferes with the impartiality. I might find a cockroach in the soup and then where would we be?"

"Then this invitation to dinner must also interfere with your impartiality?"

"Only if I were writing a story about you."

"And you are not? Ms. Joules, you disappoint me. I thought you were about to make me into a star."

"I'm sure you're the one person in LA who's not looking for stardom."

"Not in this life, anyway," he said. "I will save stardom for the afterlife and my seventy virgins."

As she laughed, he reached out and ran his hand delicately across her cheekbone. The touch of his lips on hers sent shock waves through her system.

"Ms. Joules," he murmured, "you are so wonderfully, irrepressibly . . . English."

He stood up, took her hand, raised her to her feet and led her up to the deck.

"You will stay here with me tonight?" he said, looking down at her.

"It's too soon," she murmured, giving in as he brought her head against his chest, putting his arms protectively around her, his hand moving to stroke her hair.

"I understand," he said. The only sound was the soft lap of the waves against the side of the boat. "But you will join me in Honduras?"

"I'll think about it," she whispered weakly.

22   LOS ANGELES

"Weesh tuminall?' yelled the cab driver.

Olivia was heading for Los Angeles airport. They were passing the Los Angeles oil field where nodding donkeys bobbed up and down improbably as if they were in southern Iraq, not southern California.

"Weesh tuminall?" yelled the driver again. "Tuminall? Internassyunall? Or domestic fly? Weesh airline?"

"Oh, oh, er," she stalled, having no idea where she was going. "International."

The sun was setting among the clouds with the detail and splendor of an oil painting, the tangle of telegraph wires silhouetted against it. She felt a stirring of premature nostalgia for Los Angeles and America: the America of deserts, gas stations, road trips, and reinvention.

"Weesh airline?"

Oh shut up, she felt like saying. *I haven't bloody well decided yet.*

She tried to think clearly and sensibly, which was proving very difficult that morning. It was a perfectly simple problem: she told herself she had fallen in love with a man. It was the sort of thing that could happen to anyone—apart from his being an international terrorist.

Something about the combination of glamour, fear, and sexual promise last night had tipped her over the edge. The symptoms

were familiar: only thirty percent of her brain was operational. The
rest was taken up with a combination of fantasy and flashback.
Every time she tried calmly to evaluate her situation and make a
plan, her mind was overwhelmed by images of an entire future
with Feramo, beginning with scuba diving in crystalline Caribbean
waters, followed by shagging in Bedouin tents in the Sudanese
desert, concluding with Grace Kelly–Prince Rainier-style married
life in yachts and palaces with a Feramo who, in an astonishing feat
of mental gymanstics, had been transformed form a terrorist into
a major movie director/philanthropist, and also possibly a doctor/
scientist/other unspecified manly professional, who could also fix
cars. She should never have gone on the Catalina date.

She tried to pull herself together, struggling to separate logic
and desire. I am not, she told herself, ever going to go stupid over a
man again. We women have evolved and learnt to do everything
that used to be men's work, and they have responded by regressing.
They cannot even mend things anymore. She tried to focus on the
pressing question of where exactly she was going once she got to
the airport. But by now, Feramo, dressed in a rather fetching boiler
suit, was tinkering with the engine of his helicopter, watched by an
admiring crew. With a final twist of his spanner, the engine roared
into life, while the crew clapped and cheered. Feramo grabbed her
by the waist, flung her head back and kissed her passionately, before
sweeping her aboard his chopper.

Her mobile started ringing. The screen said OUT OF AREA. Feramo! Had to be.

"It's me," said Kate. "I was woken by transatlantic thought vibes.
You're about to do something bad, aren't you?"

"No, no. Just, er, Pierre has a dive hotel down in Honduras
and—"

"Don't you *dare* follow that man to Honduras. It's insane. What
have you been working for all these years if you're just going to
succumb to the charms of some ridiculous Dodi al-Fayed–style

playboy? He's probably got a hairy back. Four years down the line he'll be forcing you to stay at home in a burka while he travels all over the world shagging wannabe actresses."

"It's not like that. You don't know him."

"Oh please. Neither do you. Just come home, Olivia. Mend your fences at the *Sunday Times*. Get on with building a career and a life that no one can take away from you."

"But what if it's real? What if he is al-Qaeda?"

"Come home even quicker. You'll end up minus a head, let alone a career. And no, I'm not trying to nick your story."

"Sorry about that," said Olivia, sheepishly.

"It's all right."

"I'm not planning to spend the rest of my life with him. I just thought I'd have a little—"

"You don't need to go to fucking Honduras to have 'a little . . .' Get on a Heathrow flight tonight, and I'll see you tomorrow."

The cab was rounding the concrete curve towards the departure bays.

"Okay, we here. International tuminall," the driver cut in. "Weesh airline?"

"Just here."

"You're too susceptible to men."

"Well, at least I haven't been married twice," said Olivia, trying simultaneously to get out of the cab, tip the driver, get her carry-on and wedge the mobile under her ear.

"That's because you were startled into premature clarity by what happened to your family. Otherwise you'd have got married by the time you were twenty like everyone else in your school."

Olivia had a sudden intuition. "Have you had a row with Dominic?" she said, trying to indicate to the taxi driver that she hadn't actually intended to give him a twenty-dollar tip on a thirty-dollar fare.

"I hate him."

"Oh, you mean it's still on."

"Shut up. I hate him. So you'll be landing about three tomorrow, right? Come straight round."

"Yes, er, I'll call," said Olivia doubtfully, heading into the terminal.

Olivia loved traveling alone: on the move, one small carry-on, responsible only for herself. She smirked as the automatic doors slid apart to receive her. How did they *know* to open? It made her feel so important.

She sat down on one of a row of plastic seats and watched the airport world go by: a worried family dressed in the comfy shoes, pastel jackets and bum-bag uniform of tourists, clutching their bags, looking around fearfully, huddled together against an alien world. A fat Mexican girl with a baby, following an angry-looking boy. She thought about what Kate had said. Would she have stayed Rachel Pixley and had an ordinary life if it hadn't been for the accident? *Naaah,* she thought. There *was* no ordinary life. Life was fragile and bizarre and turned on a sixpence. It was up to you to snuffle out the fun.

She pulled out a crumpled printout of an e-mail and read it again.

Sender: editor@elan.co.uk
Subj: Pierre Feramo

My dear Olivia,

We were contacted this morning personally by Pierre Feramo. M. Feramo explained that his people had made an unforgivable mistake which was not in any sense of your doing. He spoke of you in the highest terms and asked that we reinstate you on the story immediately.

I cannot apologize enough for misjudging you. We have received the copy you sent, which is excellent. There is enough there already, I think, to make the piece. Would you like to continue the piece your-self, or would you prefer to move on to the Honduras diving story M. Feramo mentioned? We could, if you wish, have the "wannabe" copy cleaned up by the subs and you could retain your byline. Let us know.

Apologies again, and looking forward to many more superb pieces from you in the future.

Sally Hawkins

Editor, *Elan*

She put it back in her bag and pulled out the Expedia flight-detail printouts. There was a Virgin flight at 20:50 to London, and an AeroMexico flight to La Ceiba in Honduras at 20:40, connect-ing in Mexico City. All she had to do was decide.

23

Unfortunately, however, Olivia could not decide. She was plunged into the Land of Indecision, which she knew was a treacherous place where she could wander for days, increasingly lost in a maze of pros and cons and possibilities. The only way to escape was to make a decision—any decision—and then at least she could get out and see straight.

Brow furrowed with earnest resolve, she ran her eye down the departures board to check for the London flight: Acapulco, Belize, Bogotá, Cancún, Caracas, Guadalajara, Guatemala, La Paz. *What am I doing?* she thought. *If I go back to London, I'll be sitting in the pissing rain writing articles about dining rooms.*

She opened the guidebook to Honduras. "A paradise of white-sanded beaches and rain-forested peaks, surrounded by crystalline Caribbean waters. The Bay Islands offer the most spectacular diving in the Caribbean."

Mmm, she thought, flicking through to find Popayan, the island which housed Feramo's ecodiving resort.

"The smallest island in the archipelago, Popayan offers a flashback to the Caribbean of the 1950s. Many of the population are a mixture of black, Carib, Hispanic and white settlers—the direct descendants of shipwrecked Irish pirates. The village's only bar, the Bucket of Blood, is the center of all gossip and social life."

Her eyes lit up. It sounded like major fun. Then, remembering her mother's remarks about excitement and danger, she took out her book about al-Qaeda and opened it at the turned-down page headed "Takfiri."

Olivia had made her decision. She headed for the mailbox and dropped in an envelope addressed to her flat in London. It contained a CD copy of her hard drive, including the photos she had taken in Feramo's "panic room."

"One seat to La Ceiba, Honduras," she said to the lady on the desk.

"Would that be single or return?"

"One way."

24   CENTRAL AMERICA

The journey progressed from the anesthetic cleanliness of LAX to the craziness of Central America at a dizzying pace. Olivia thought it was like a speeded-up version of a Victorian exploration: Burton or Speke setting out from London to Cairo in starched wing collars, then plunging deeper and deeper into the African continent, losing their sanity, possessions and teeth.

Mexico City's airport was wild: the seats were of worn cowhide; men walked past in cowboy boots, sombreros and big mustaches; women sashayed in tight jeans and stilettos, bulging from sequined tops like game-show hostesses; while the game shows and music videos on the big screens teetered on the wrong side of soft porn.

Olivia was busy. She called Sally Hawkins, said she'd like to do the diving story, but stalled her for a few days. She decided to snuffle round the Bay Islands incognito and find out what she could before alerting anyone to her presence. She bought cheap jeans and a sweatshirt, found a drugstore and a shower and dyed her hair red and then switched to her old passport (which she'd rather fraudulently claimed to have lost when she changed her name) and became Rachel Pixley. The thought of airport food usually repulsed her, but here she was seduced by the smells and ate a giant plate of burritos with refried beans, salsa, guacamole and chocolate sauce.

The ATAPA connection to La Ceiba in Honduras was five hours late, the atmosphere at the gate increasingly festive. By the time the motley bunch of passengers boarded the tatty plane, the delay had turned into a full-scale party with free Styrofoam sandwiches and tequila-laced lurid green drinks all round. The man beside Olivia kept offering her swigs of tequila from a bottle, but, as she explained, she was too full of refried beans *au chocolat* to fit in anything else at all. Forty minutes into the flight, the mindless movie, which had been raucously ridiculed by the passengers, disappeared from the screen and the captain's voice came over the address system—first in Spanish, then in English.

"Ladies and gentlemen. Is your captain talking. I regret to announce you that this plane is problem and no landing in La Ceiba anymore. We go another place. We let you know. Bye."

Fear set all her senses on high alert. As she reached into her bag for the pepper-spray pen, keeping her eyes on the cockpit door, her mind was racing. As her thought activity increased, time seemed to slow as people said it did when they were drowning. It was a hijacking, clearly. Since 9/11, she knew, everything in this situation had changed. The important thing now was not to lie low but to act and act decisively.

25   TEGUCIGALPA, HONDURAS

The most effective way to overpower a hijacker was to work as a team. As Olivia looked aorund the cabin for suitable teammates, the man next to her held out the tequila bottle. This time she gratefully took an enormous swig. She handed it back to him and was puzzled to see him grab it with a cheerful grin. Glancing around the plane, she realized that no one was behaving appropriately for those on the verge of death. The air hostess was making her way down the aisle with another tray of lurid drinks and a fresh bottle of tequila.

"Is okay," said the man beside her. "Is no worry. ATAPA Airlines is never know where they go. Is stand for Always Take a Parachute." He roared with laughter.

The landing in Tegucigalpa was rather like a tractor hitting a corrugated-iron roof. But the assembled passengers clapped and cheered the pilot regardless. The first drops of rain were falling as they climbed onto a rickety bus, and soon, as they rattled through the scruffy streets of the town past crumbling colonial buildings and wooden shacks, a full tropical rainstorm was hammering on the roof. It was kind of cozy.

Olivia considered the El Parador hotel to be of the highest standard. The point on the toilet paper was faultless in terms of both sharpness and neatness. The only problem was that the bathroom floor was under two inches of water. The phone, when she tried to reach Reception, gurgled in reply. She headed down herself, requested the speedy dispatch of a mop and bucket and returned to the room, where she sat cross-legged on the brightly colored bedspread and started to organize her possessions.

She spread out her stuff in front of her and started two lists: *Essentials for Rest of Trip* and *Items Surplus to Requirements*. *Items Surplus to Requirements* now included the sweatshirt and ugly jeans (far too hot) and the beautiful this-year's Marc Jacobs tan-leather tote (too heavy, too identifiable and too posh).

There was a knock on the door.

"Un momento, por favor," she said, concealing her research materials and spy equipment under the blanket.

"Pase adelante."

The door opened, followed by a mop and a smiling Hispanic girl holding a bucket. Olivia made as if to take the mop, but the woman shook her head, and so the two of them did the floor together, Olivia emptying the bucket and the girl keeping up a steady stream of Spanish, mainly about what fun was to be had in the bar downstairs. When the floor was dry, the two of them stood back, admiring their handiwork. Olivia felt it was her honor—and hoped it wasn't neocolonialist—to replace the tip for this happy spirit with the leather tote, as well as some clothes and other *Items Surplus to Requirements*. The woman was very pleased, though not quite pleased enough to suggest she realized it was actually this season's Marc Jacobs, or maybe she was just a spiritual person who eschewed labels. She embraced Olivia and nodded down at the bar.

"Sí, sí, más tarde," said Olivia.

Better stay off the margaritas, Olivia told herself as she stashed her valuables in the safe and zipped her *Essentials for Rest of Trip* firmly in the tan and olive case. But hang it all, she thought when she reached the festive courtyard. *Everyone else is as pissed as a fart.* She took a sip of her first sensational margarita. *Salud!*

A handsome, white-haired man with a mustache, dazzlingly drunk, crooned along to his guitar as the shambolic crowd of hippie travelers, businessmen and locals joined in. When the inebriated *mariachi* started to lose the plot, he was abruptly replaced by blaring salsa. Within moments the dance floor was filled with locals dancing intricate, detailed steps exquisitely, and the indeterminate writhings of the tie-dye-clad gringos. Olivia, who had briefly gone out with a Venezuelan Reuters correspondent and developed a penchant for salsa, was mesmerized by the sight of dancers brought up on its rhythms doing the real thing. Through the mass of bodies, a guy with cropped, bleached-blond hair caught her attention. In the middle of all the festivity and mindless drinking, he sat at a table, leaning forward, chin on hands, watching the crowd intently. He was dressed in baggy hip-hop clothes, but he was too cool-looking and focused to be a backpacker. He reappeared a few minutes later, directly in front of her. He didn't smile; he just raised an eyebrow towards the dance floor and held out his hand. Sexy boy, cocky too; he reminded her of someone. He was a great dancer. He didn't move much, but he knew what he was doing, and all she had to do was follow. Neither of them spoke, they just danced, bodies close, his arm leading her where he wanted her to go. After a couple of numbers, an elderly local man cut in with immense courtesy. The blond guy ceded his position graciously. The next time she looked, he was gone. Eventually she took a break from the dancing; as she stood there, wiping her forehead, she felt a hand on her arm. It was the maid to whom she had given the tote bag.

"Go back to your room," said the girl quietly in Spanish.

"Why?" said Olivia.

"Someone was in there."

"What? Did you see someone?"

"No. I have to go," she said nervously. "You go and have a look. Go quickly."

Sobering up fast, Olivia made her way to the room, taking the stairs, not the elevator. She slipped the key in the lock, paused and flung the door open. The room was a mass of strange shadows thrown by the streetlights shining through the palm trees and the mosquito screens against her window. Still in the doorway, she reached for the light and clicked it on: nothing. She listened again, shut the door behind her and checked the bathroom: again, nothing. She went to the safe. It was untouched. Then her eye fell on her case. It was partly open; she knew she had left it zipped up. The clothes she had left folded inside were messed up. She slipped her hand underneath them and came across what felt like a polythene bag full of flour. She pulled it out, frantic, saw it was full of white powder and at the same moment heard footsteps in the corridor. She ripped open the bag, dipped in a finger and ran it along her gum, confirming her suspicion, with a not-unpleasant frisson, that it contained cocaine, and a sizable stash of cocaine. Just then, the footsteps stopped outside her room, and there was loud shouting and banging on the door.

"*La policia! Abra la puerta!*"

"*Un momento, por favor.*"

It was a simple choice: open the door to the police with a large bag of cocaine in her hand, or take a jump straight down from the fifth floor.

Stop, breathe, think. She stepped into the bathroom and flushed the loo. With the flush masking the sound, she gently lifted the mosquito screen away from the window and stood back. Taking as long a run at it as possible, she hurled the plastic bag out of the window with all her might, thinking: *Someone over there is going to find their evening just looked up.* Then—hearing a distant splash—she replaced the screen and calmly opened the door.

Once she actually saw the police, they weren't scary at all. They were spotty teenagers and actually rather apologetic. She sat on an upright chair, watching them search the room, trying to work out if they knew what they were looking for and where it was. Were they real police? Military? Actors? Resting actors slash lifestyle coaches?

"Todo está bien," said one of them finally. *"Gracias. Disculpenos."*

"No tiene importancia," she said, which wasn't strictly true, but then she was English and believed in the hot air of politeness, for, as the *Girl Guide Handbook* says, "There's nothing but air in a tire, but it certainly makes the wheels go round more smoothly!"

"Un cigarillo?" said the younger boy, holding out a packet.

"Muchas gracias," she said, taking the cigarette and leaning forward for a light. She hadn't had a cigarette in years. It hit her as though it were a joint. She wished she had some tequila to offer the policemen. They looked as though they'd be susceptible to getting drunk and telling her who sent them.

"Por qué están aquí?" she ventured anyway.

The two boys looked at each other and laughed. They had, they claimed, been tipped off. They all laughed some more and finished their cigarettes, and the two boys took their leave as if they were lifelong friends of hers who'd just been round for a party. When she was sure they had gone, she sank down with her back against the door. Eventually, she pulled herself out of her funk of fear and confusion and asked herself, in accordance with Rules for Living number seven, *Does it really matter?* The answer, unfortunately, was yes. She decided to call the British Embassy in the morning. If there was a British Embassy.

Olivia had a terrible, hot, anxious, sleepless night. She was relieved when a rooster started crowing to signal that it was over. When the sun appeared through the glistening tops of the palm trees, it gave a disappointingly pale light, not full-on Caribbean morning sun. She opened the window, looking down on a tranquil harbor and corrugated-iron rooftops, smelling the heavy, spicy air. There was a group of local women talking and laughing in the street below. There was clumsy *mariachi* music coming from a radio. She realized there had been no word to the passengers as to how or when they might reach their intended destination. She wondered if they would all just stay there forever, the party continuing day after day, until they did nothing but drink tequila and sleep under trees from dawn to dusk.

Down at Reception, a scruffy piece of paper taped to the wall said: *Pasajeros de ATAPA para La Ceiba. El autobús saldrá del hotel al aeropuerto a las 9 de la mañana.*

It was eight o'clock already. Olivia's mobile, it emerged, did not work in Honduras. She asked the receptionist if she could use the phone. He said the phones weren't working, but there was a call box outside. Down the road a dilapidated blue and yellow sign featuring what was either a telephone or a sheep's head was hanging at an angle off a wooden shed.

She started with Honduran directory enquiries, expecting a lengthy and frustrating round of engaged signals, nonanswers and repeated yelling and spelling of words, culminating in a dial tone. Instead, the phone was immediately answered by a charming girl who spoke perfect English, gave her the number for the British Embassy and informed her that it opened at eight-thirty.

It was eight-fifteen. Should she wait? Or rush back and pack her bag so that she'd be in time for the bus? She decided to stay where she was. At eight-twenty-five, a woman with two small children appeared, hovering insistently. Olivia briefly attempted to ignore her, but decency got the upper hand and she ceded her position. The woman began a lengthy emotional argument. By eight-forty-five, she was yelling, and the smallest child was in tears. By eight-forty-eight, both the children were in tears, and the woman was banging the receiver against the wall of the shed.

She was going to miss the bloody bus and the plane and be marooned in Tegucigalpa. In the end, it was quite simple, really. She opened the door, said, "You. Out," and dialed the Embassy.

"Hello, British Embassy."

"Hello, my name is"—dammit, what?—"Rachel Pixley," she said quickly, remembering that was the name on the passport she had used when she booked the flight.

"Yes. What can we help you with?"

After briefly explaining her problem, she was put through to a man whose crisp English voice made her almost tearful. It was like bumping into a British daddy, or a policeman after being chased by brigands.

"Hmmm," said the chap, when she had finished. "I'll be honest with you, this is not uncommon with the flight from Mexico City. You're sure there isn't anyone who could have tampered with your bag there?"

"No. I had repacked it just before I left the room. The drugs weren't in there. Someone came to my room when I was down in the bar. I'm worried about some people I met in LA, a guy called

Pierre Feramo and some rather odd things that happened . . ."
There was a slight buzz on the line.

"Can you hold on a minute?" said the Embassy chap. "Just got
to take another call. Back in a mo."

She glanced nervously at her watch. It was three minutes to
nine. Her hope was that all the passengers would be so hungover
that everyone would be late.

"Sorry about that," said the man, returning to the phone. "Miss
Pixie, isn't it?"

"Pixley."

"Yes. Well, look. No need to worry about the drug business.
We'll let the powers that be know. Any more problems, just give us
a ring. Can you give us an idea of your itinerary?"

"Well, I was planning to get the plane today to Popayan, stay in
the village for a few days, and then maybe move on to Feramo's hotel, the Isla Bonita."

"Jolly good. Well, we'll let everyone know to watch out for you.
Why don't you pop in on your way back and let us know how it all
went?"

When she put down the phone, she stared straight ahead for
a moment, biting her lip in concentration. Did the phone really
buzz when she mentioned Feramo, or was it just her overactive
imagination?

Back at the hotel the receptionist informed her that the bus had
left ten minutes ago. Fortunately, she ran into the recipient of the
Marc Jacobs tote, who said she'd get her husband to drive her to the
airport in his van. He took a while to turn up. By the time they rattled up to the Departures area, it was ten twenty-two. The plane
was due to leave at ten.

As Olivia careered across the tarmac, dragging the little case behind
her and waving frantically, two men in overalls were starting to pull
the stairs away from the plane. They laughed when they saw her
and shoved them back again. One of them bounded up ahead of

her and banged on the door until it opened. As she entered the crowded cabin, a ragged cheer went up. Her fellow passengers from the night before were pale and fragile, but still jolly. As she flopped gratefully into her seat, the pilot was making his way down the aisle greeting everyone individually. She felt quite reassured until she realized it was the drunken *mariachi* with the mustache from the salsa party the night before.

At La Ceiba airport she bought a ticket to Popayan and headed desperately for the newsstand, only to find no foreign newspapers except a three-week-old copy of *Time*. She picked up La Ceiba's *El Diario* and slumped into an orange plastic chair at the gate, waiting for the flight announcement, flicking through the paper and trying to find any update on the *OceansApart*. She was mildly cheered by the sight of her dancing partner from the previous night—the one with the serious expression and cropped peroxide hair. He reminded her of Eminem. He had the same combination of the grave and the subversive. He came over and sat beside her, holding out a bottle of mineral water.

"Thanks," she said, enjoying the slight contact as he handed it over.

"De nada." His face was almost expressionless, but he had compelling eyes, gray and intelligent. "Try not to puke now," he said, getting up again and heading for the newsstand.

Concentrate, Olivia, she said to herself. *Concentrate. We are not a skittish backpacker on our gap year. We are a top foreign journalist and possible international spy on a mission of global significance.*

27   POPAYAN, BAY ISLANDS

The island of Popayan came into view, and soon they were descending over a crystalline turquoise sea towards white coral beaches and greenery. The little plane landed with a horrifying bounce, then veered off the unpaved airstrip and turned right over a rickety wooden bridge, quite as if it thought it was a bicycle, before coming to an abrupt halt next to a rusty red pickup truck and a wooden sign which said WELCOME TO POPAYAN: DANIEL DEFOE'S ORIGINAL ROBINSON CRUSOE ISLAND.

There was a problem opening the door. The pilot was tugging at it from the outside, and inside a hippie backpacker was staring at the handle with unhurried fascination, poking at it from time to time as if it were a caterpillar. The blond guy got up, moved the hippie, gripped the handle, put his forearm against the door and opened it.

"Thanks, man," muttered the backpacker sheepishly.

Someone had left a British newspaper on a seat. Olivia grabbed it eagerly. Outside, as they loaded themselves into the back of the pickup, she sniffed the clear air appreciatively and looked around.

It was fun sitting in the back of the truck with all the backpackers. They bounced along a sandy track, then hit the main street of West End. It was like a cross between a Western movie and the Deep South. The houses were clapboard, with porches. Some of them had swing seats, some of them had battered, comfy-looking sofas.

An elderly lady with white permed hair and pale skin, wearing a yellow tea dress, was walking along with a parasol, a tall, extremely good-looking black guy a few paces behind.

Olivia turned back to the truck and found the blond man looking straight at her.

"Where are you staying?" he said.

"Miss Ruthie's Guest House."

"You're here," he said, leaning over and banging on the driver's door. She saw the muscles beneath his shirt. He jumped out to help her down, unloaded her bag and carried it up the steps to the green wooden porch. "There you go," he said and held out his hand. "Morton C."

"Thanks. Rachel."

"You'll be all right here," he said, shouting over his shoulder as he jumped into the back of the truck. "See you at the Bucket of Blood."

Spots of rain were starting to fall as Olivia knocked on the yellow door. A warm smell of baking wafted out. The door opened and a very tiny old lady stood before her. She had fair skin and red-gold hair in curls and was wearing an apron. Olivia suddenly felt as if she were in a fairy story and she would go inside to find a wolf in a red-hooded sweatshirt, several dwarfs and a beanstalk.

"What can I be doing for you then?" The old lady's accent had a strong Irish lilt. Maybe it was true about the Irish pirates.

"I was wondering if you had a room for a few nights."

"To be sure," said Miss Ruthie. "Come in and sit yourself down. I'll get you some breakfast."

Olivia half-expected a leprechaun to hop out and offer to help with her case.

The kitchen was constructed entirely of wood and painted in a fifties mixture of primrose yellow and pixie green. Olivia sat at the kitchen table as the rain hammered down on the roof and thought how making a home is nothing to do with a building and everything to do with how different people make it feel. She was sure Miss Ruthie could have moved into Feramo's minimalist Miami penthouse and still managed to turn it into Snow White's cottage or the Little House on the Prairie.

She ate a breakfast of refried beans and corn bread from a plate with two blue stripes, which reminded her of her childhood. Miss Ruthie said there were two rooms available, both looking out over the water. One was on the first floor and the other—which was a suite!—was on the top floor. The first room was the equivalent of five dollars a night, and the suite fifteen. She chose the suite. It had sloping ceilings, a covered deck and a view on three sides. It was like being in a little wooden house on the end of a pier. The walls were painted pink, green and blue. There was an iron bedstead and, in the bathroom, wallpaper which sported a repeat motif saying *I love you I love you I love you.* Most importantly, the toilet paper was folded to a faultless point.

Miss Ruthie brought her up a cup of instant coffee and a piece of ginger cake.

"You'll be diving later, will you?" said Miss Ruthie.

"I'm going straightaway," said Olivia. "As soon as I've unpacked."

"Get yourself down to Rod's shack. He'll take care of you."

"Where is it?"

Miss Ruthie just looked at her as if she was mad.

Olivia took the coffee and cake on to the deck with the newspaper and lay down on a faded flowery daybed. There was a story headed AL-QAEDA LINK IN ALGECIRAS BLAST. She started to read, but fell asleep to the sound of the rain bouncing down on the calm waters of the bay.

28

Sixty feet below the surface, it was like being in a dream or on another planet. Olivia, dressed in a red swimsuit and diving gear, was on the edge of a precipice, a sheer cliff falling away a thousand feet into the abyss. You could simply throw yourself over and somersault and fall at your own pace. She was following an orange puffer fish. It was a lovable little thing, bright orange and shaped like a football, with huge round eyes and ginger eyelashes, like something out of a Disney cartoon. A shoal of extraordinary blue and green fish burst up around her like a design on a fifties bath towel. Drew, her diving buddy, a slight, twenty-two-year-old, long-haired hippie, banged his fists together for her to check her air. She held up the gauge. Fifty minutes had passed and it felt like five. She looked up to where the sunlight dappled the surface. It gave her a shock to realize that she was so far down; she felt utterly at home. All you had to do was remember not to panic and to breathe.

She made her way reluctantly upwards, following the wisplike figure of Drew with his lankly flowing mane, keeping the pace slow, feeling the air expand in her BCD, letting it escape in short bursts. She broke the surface and stared, startled, at the other world: brilliant sunshine, blue sky, the cheerful line of clapboard houses on the shoreline deflatingly close. She had felt as though they were five fathoms deep, a million miles from civilization, and now the water was so shallow they could almost stand up.

She and Drew swam to Rod's Dive Shack jetty, where, holding

onto the edge of the ladder, they took off their masks, euphoric from the dive. They swung their weight belts up onto the wooden platform, unfastened their tanks and waited for help to hand them up. A small group was huddled on the benches outside the shack, deep in conversation. No one had noticed them.

"Dudes! What's up?" Drew called over. He pulled himself onto the jetty, then helped Olivia up.

"Hey, Drew," one of them replied. "You see anything uncool down there?"

"No, man. It's beautiful. Blue water."

Olivia's legs felt a little shaky as they walked along the warm wooden slats of the jetty. It had been a long dive. Drew was rinsing out the gear in a barrel of fresh water. He handed her a bottle of cold water. "You've gone blond," he said.

She put her hand to her hair. It felt thick with the salt.

"Suits you better than red."

"So much for six to eight washes," she said, starting to dunk her gear in the barrel.

"Hey, Rod. What's up? Something happened?" said Drew, as he and Olivia moved over to the group.

Rod, a stocky Canadian with a mustache, was older than the rest. He had the air of a college lecturer about him.

"They've started on the marker buoys above Morgan's Cave," said Rod, making a space for Olivia, then reaching into a cold box and handing her a soda. "Frederic went down there with a bunch of clients and met a party of Arturo's from a Roatán boat in the tunnel coming the other way. Arturo said he'd left a marker buoy, but it wasn't there when Frederic went down. It has to be Feramo's lot."

Olivia stiffened at the name but tried to act normally.

Another of the guys joined in. "Saturday someone put a buoy there when no one was down. Arturo saw it and went down to check it out, and no one was in there. The only way to stop it is to sit on top of the dive sites all day with a boat."

"Yeah, well, we might just have to do that and not just with a boat," said Drew in a dark, threatening voice.

The party started to break up. Drew wanted to walk her back to Miss Ruthie's.

"Who were they talking about back there?" she asked innocently.

"Guys from the hotel over Pumpkin Hill. They've got this luxury ecoresort thing going. Some people say it's owned by an oil sheikh. They're trying to clear out all the other dive operations and take over the caves and tunnels for their own clients. It's a pile of shit."

"Is it a dive hotel?"

"Well, yeah, but I think that's bullshit. He's got all these commercial divers and welders down there. He's got this fucking huge pier. I mean, what does he need a pier like that for on Popayan?"

Olivia's mind was racing.

"Welding? Can they do that underwater? What do they use for the blowtorches?"

"Acetylene."

"Is it explosive?"

"It is if you mix it with oxygen."

"Even underwater?"

"Oh sure. Anyway, here we are. You coming to the Bucket of Blood tonight?"

"Er, yes, okay," she said vaguely. "See you later."

She hurried back to her room and leafed through the newspaper, looking for the Algeciras bomb story she had seen earlier. There had been a blast in a tourist complex, and it was being attributed to al-Qaeda.

"Preliminary investigations suggest that the device was acetylene-based. Acetylene is readily available and routinely used by divers in the field of commercial welding."

The Bucket of Blood was quite a place. It was a wooden shack with a stone floor, a rough wooden bar and a barman with no teeth.

There were three locals sitting at the bar. The tables and benches were filled with backpackers.

The sexual politics of the backpacker scene was something Olivia found relaxing. Obvious displays of sexuality or financial solvency were frowned upon. You would no more turn up to a backpacker party wearing a halter-neck top and a miniskirt than you would in a Marks & Spencer's business suit or fisherman's waders. The standard dress was faded, threadbare clothes which might have fitted when they left Stockholm or Helsinki but which, after six months of diving, rice and peas and dysentery, were now two sizes too big.

Drew gave her a wave as she walked in, beckoning her to sit beside him. A loud guffaw emanated from the three locals at the bar. She looked over and saw that one of them was telling an anecdote and was bent over with his arse in the air.

The gang from Rod's made room for her on the wooden bench. One of them was telling a jargon-filled dive story, which seemed to involve Feramo's people.

"So he catches one of them in Devil's Jaw without leaving a buoy, and the guy just turns off his air."

Olivia lost her composure as Morton C. walked into the bar.

"Jesus. What did he do?"

"He cut through the other guy's AS . . ."

She watched as he joined a group at the back of the bar, greeting the other guys in a manly fashion, like they were gang members from south LA.

". . . and breathed from his BCD . . ."

Morton C. caught her watching him and raised his beer bottle. There was a slight change in his expression which might or might not have been a smile.

". . . then did an ESA until he managed to get his deck off and reopen the valve."

A man approached their table; he had a seventies hippie look—a big handlebar mustache, long hair, bald on top. "Hey, Rod. You wanna take a party out on the boat to Bell Key?"

"Any particular reason?"

The man gave a slow, delicious smile. "We got the share."

"Yay! Let's go. You coming, Rachel-from-England?"

It turned out that a large bag of cocaine had been washed up on the shores of Popayan the night before and was being shared democratically between the inhabitants of West End. Olivia wondered if it might be the bag that she had chucked out of the hotel window: highly unlikely, but there would be a pleasing circularity to that.

Most of the clientele of the Bucket of Blood headed out to the key in a small flotilla of dive boats, one of which conked out on the way. Olivia was aroused to observe that it was Morton C. who came to the rescue. He pulled at the starter cord, messed around with the throttle, then hauled the outboard motor out of the water. After tinkering for a few minutes, he put it back, pulled at the starter cord a few times and the engine started perfectly.

There had been a whip-round for a plastic gallon container of rum and a couple of gallons of orange juice. Once on the island, which was a hundred yards across and uninhabited, they lit a fire and mixed the drinks in coconut shells. Initially she was reminded of parties at school, everyone working out who they were going to snog later under a veneer of cool punctuated by bursts of nervous laughter. There was a bit of singing and guitar strumming while lines of coke were cut and joints passed around. People started to sit down around the fire and Olivia joined them.

She found herself acutely conscious of Morton C., watching him out of the corner of her eye and panicking slightly if she saw him talking to another girl. It was all deliciously teenage. He didn't acknowledge her at all, but their eyes met a couple of times, and she *knew*. He settled himself on the opposite side of the fire and she sipped her drink, declining the cocaine, but taking the occasional drag on a joint as it was passed round and watching his serious face in the firelight. Drew leaned over into her line of sight, his lank hair flopping over his face. "Rachel," he whispered solemnly, "you see over there, those trees? There's a helicopter in there. You see it? They've covered it in cotton wool." He glanced around furtively, then loped off towards the trees in an apelike manner.

It appeared that the cocaine was taking hold. An excited discussion started up to her right which consisted entirely of people agreeing with each other.

"That's it, that's it, man! That's it, that's it."

"Yeah, I mean, like, that's, like, so, like . . ."

"That's what I'm saying! That's exactly what I'm saying! That is *exactly* what I'm saying!"

Someone started walking towards the fire, murmuring, ". . . the senses might give us an experience of reality that seems to be that reality and is actually related to that reality but is not literally that reality," then stuck his toe in the fire, cursed and fell over.

Olivia lay back and closed her eyes. Someone had brought a boom box and put on French ambient music. The grass was great—very light, very giggly, very sexy.

"You changed your hair."

She opened her eyes. Morton C. was sitting beside her, staring into the fire.

"It was the sun."

"Yeah, right."

He slid back and leaned on one elbow, looking down at her, eyes moving over her face. He could have leaned forward just a couple of inches more and kissed her.

"You want to take a walk?" he whispered.

He helped her up and led her by the hand to the beach. She liked the feel of his hand: it was rough and capable. The path led round a rock, out of sight of the fire, and he stopped, brushing the hair away from her face, looking at her with those intense, gray eyes, the fine line of his cheekbone and jaw outlined in the moonlight. He looked adult and tough, as though he'd seen a lot. He took her face in his hand and kissed her, bold, insolent, leaning into her against the rock. He was a great kisser.

He moved his hands confidently down her body. She slipped her arms round his neck, drinking in the kiss, exploring the muscles of his back. There was a strap under his shirt. She followed it down towards his hip with her fingers and felt him push her hand away.

"Are you carrying a gun?"

"No, baby," he whispered. "Just pleased to see you."

"It's in rather an odd place."

"We aim to surprise," he said, slipping his hand expertly into her jeans. God, it really was like being sixteen again.

There were shouts. Drew appeared round the side of the rock. He stared at them, chewing violently on a stick of gum. He looked really sad for a second then turned away. "Hey, man, the boat's going back," he said huffily.

They pulled themselves together, adjusting their clothing. Morton C. put his arm round her and they walked back to join the others. He gave a short laugh. "Jesus, how are we going to get this lot into the boats?"

Rod was halfway up a coconut palm, perhaps searching for a helicopter, cotton-wool bound or otherwise. Drew was darting skittishly along the beach, still chewing. A splinter group had taken to the lagoon, where they were dancing in the water, arms waving above their heads. By the dying embers of the fire, more people had joined in the excited agreement-discussion and were yelling over each other.

"That's *exactly* how I see it, that's *exactly* how I see it!"

"Exactly! That's it exactly!"

Morton C. sighed and started to round everyone up.

The wind had dropped and the sea was inky black and calm. The talk turned to Feramo. Drew was agitated, staring off towards the lights at the end of the island, chewing frantically.

"You have to watch every fucking word you say on Popayan now because you never know who's working for them and who isn't. I'm going to go there tomorrow, man. I'm going to go down there and give them something to think about."

"Hey," said Morton C. "You're loaded, man. Take it easy."

"We should take them on," said Drew. "It's crazy, man. We know these caves better than they do. We should take them on." He stared straight ahead, still chewing, one leg jiggling maniacally up and down.

Olivia shivered. Morton C. pulled her close to him, wrapping his sweater round her shoulders. "You okay?" he whispered. She nodded happily. "You know anything about these people?"

She shook her head, not meeting his eyes. She was really embarrassed, suddenly, about the Feramo connection. "Only what everyone says. Do you?"

Someone passed him a joint and, taking a heavy drag, he shook his head. Olivia noticed that he blew the smoke out straight away, without inhaling.

"Like to see the place, though. Would you?"

"I was going to go. I thought it would be good for my article. Sounds scary now, though."

"You're a journalist?" Their fingers touched as he handed her the joint.

Drew was still going on about Feramo and Pumpkin Hill: "We should set something up and really scare them. Like surprise them. Like do something really creepy in the caves so they won't go back."

"Who do you work for?"

"Freelance. I'm doing a diving story for *Elan* magazine. What are *you* doing here . . . ?"

Olivia caught her lower lip in her teeth as Morton slipped his hand onto her knee, pressing with his thumb as he slid his hand slowly up her thigh.

Outside Miss Ruthie's they made out in the shadows under a tree. For a second, looking over his shoulder, she thought she saw a

curtain pulled aside inside the guest house, a head silhouetted
against the glow of a lamp. She ducked back into the shadows.

"Can I come in?" he whispered into her neck.

With a tremendous effort of will she pulled away slightly and
shook her head.

He looked down, composing himself, breathing unsteadily, then
looked back at her.

"No overnight visitors, huh?"

"Not without a chaperone."

"You diving tomorrow?"

She nodded.

"What time?"

"Around eleven."

"I'll come and find you after."

Back in the room she paced around, frantic. The nunlike self-denial
was torture. She didn't know how much longer she would be able
to keep it up.

29

A s Olivia walked along the main street early the next morning, a rooster was crowing and the smell of breakfast cooking drifted out from the small wooden houses. Children were playing on the balconies, old people nodding on the porch swings. A lugubrious man with pale skin and an undertaker's suit raised his hat to her. At his side was a young, red-haired black girl and a fair-skinned child with a flat nose, broad lips and tightly curled hair. The blond, pale lady she had seen when she arrived was walking elegantly along, still protected by her parasol and her handsome companion. Olivia started to imagine she was in a weird land of incest and interbreeding, where fathers would sleep with their nephews and great-aunts have secret affairs with donkeys.

She headed for a hardware shop and chandler's she had spotted the previous night, full of tin buckets, coils of rope and washing-up bowls. She loved the feeling that in hardware shops everything was useful and sensibly priced. Even if you spent really quite a large amount of money, it wouldn't be wasteful or extravagant. The sign above the window looked like something out of a funeral home in nineteenth-century Chicago: curly, intricate black writing which read HENRY MORGAN & SONS was peeling off now, showing the weathered wood beneath.

Inside, a tall man in a black suit was measuring rice out of a big wooden vat with a metal scoop—no Uncle Ben's boil-in-the-bag in Popayan. The man was muttering away to his customer in an

Irish accent as thick as Miss Ruthie's. Olivia bent over the counter, fascinated by the array of things on sale: fishhooks, torches, string, small triangular flags, cleats, shoe polish. There was the jangling of a bell as the door opened; the conversation stopped abruptly and a heavily accented voice asked for cigarettes.

"We're all out of smokes. I'm sorry."

"You do not have cigarettes?" It was a guttural, heavily accented voice, the *r* rolled, the *t* so emphasized it almost incorporated a spit.

Quick as a flash, Olivia flipped up the mirror on her spy ring, wild with excitement at a first chance to use it. The man, who had his back to her, was short and thick-waisted, clad in jeans and a polo shirt. She moved her hand slightly to get a better view and gasped as she saw the tightly curled black hair: it was Alfonso. She looked down quickly and peered into a cabinet, feigning an intent interest in a barometer. Alfonso was expressing some threatening-sounding skepticism about the alleged absence of cigarettes.

"Oh, but to be sure we'll have some Thursday when the boat comes in," said the tall man. "Try Paddy at the Bucket of Blood."

Alfonso cursed, then swung out of the shop, slamming the door behind him and making the bell jingle hysterically.

There was silence for a moment, then the storekeeper and customer started talking in lowered voices. At one point she picked out "in the caves" and "O'Reilly's goats are dead," but she thought that might be a line from an Irish ditty she had learnt at school and reminded herself sternly not to romanticize the situation.

Eventually she turned and asked for a ball of string, a map of the island, a bag of carrots and a large knife, adding casually, "Oh, and a packet of cigarettes."

"To be sure. What type will you be wanting?" said the shopkeeper.

"What have you got?"

"Marlboro, Marlboro Lights and Camels," he said, casting a merry look out into the street.

Olivia followed his gaze. Alfonso was deep in a conversation, but Olivia couldn't see who he was talking to. He moved slightly to the left and she caught a glimpse of cropped peroxide hair and baggy hip-hop clothes. She gripped the edge of the counter, her cheeks reddening, feeling a lurch of pain. It was Morton C. Morton C. was in cahoots with Alfonso. The sneaky bastard. How could she have been such an idiot? She couldn't visit Feramo now. Feramo wouldn't want a girl in his harem who had casually snogged one of his minions. She had managed to ruin the whole objective of her surveillance mission with one pathetic lapse of self-control.

She watched till the two men finished talking and went their separate ways. Then, carrying her map, carrots and cigarettes, slipped down the path at the side of the shop to sit by the sea, hidden from view in the tall grass. Her hand was shaking as she lit a cigarette, coughed and put it out immediately. She didn't know if she was more hurt or more angry or just both. *You can't trust anybody,* she told herself, brushing a tear from her cheek with her fist. *Not anybody.*

After a while she straightened up, jutting her chin defiantly, and walked back along the path.

The secret of success lies in how you emerge from failure, she told herself. She had two hours before her dive. That should be enough time to get to the top of Pumpkin Hill and see what was going on. At least she would get something out of this debacle: photos, at least, and maybe clues.

Following the map, she headed out of the village along a path with numerous forks and turnoffs. At every point of potential confusion she left a carrot pointing the way back. Ahead of her, Pumpkin Hill rose up from the undergrowth like a grassy hillock on the South Downs, a sandy path zigzagging up it, exposed and unprotected. On the right, the undergrowth continued up a narrow valley on the side of the hill. As she grew closer, she crouched down and trained her spyglass on the summit. She caught movement behind a tree and peered through the glass, trying to focus. A figure stepped out in camouflage gear, carrying what looked like an automatic weapon, and surveyed the area. She whipped out her miniature camera and snapped. *This is outrageous!* she thought. *Pumpkin Hill is common land. People should have the right to roam and certainly should be able to do so without men pointing machine guns at them.* Olivia did not agree with weapons of destruction, mass, individual or otherwise.

Dropping a carrot to mark the spot, she left the main path and went into the narrow wooded valley to the right of the hill. She marched ahead angrily, brushing branches aside, her agitation unleashing her imagination. Her mind started racing with notions as to what Feramo was cooking up in his fraudulent *soi-disant* eco-lodge. She became certain it was acetylene-based and headed for LA. Maybe he was training commercial diver/welders to take jobs in the sewers. Maybe they were going to release gigantic acetylene and oxygen bubbles, mix them and set them alight underwater. Maybe they were going to get into the cooling systems of nuclear power stations and set the bubbles off there. It was brilliant. A commercial diver could go into the plant with nothing more than the normal tools of his trade and blow the place sky high.

The trees and undergrowth reached almost to the summit. In places, the ground beneath was almost sheer. The climb left her covered in small cuts and scratches. As she neared the top, her spirits lifted, until she saw that her way was barred by a ten-foot fence with spikes on top. If she veered to the left, she would emerge onto the hill in plain view of the guard. She went to the right instead and came to a deep ravine. There was a ledge on the other side with a tree growing out of it, above which was a fairly easy climb. Olivia weighed things up. If it wasn't for the fifty-foot drop below, she told herself, she wouldn't think twice about jumping across. For God's sake, she had seen it done a thousand times by blond-haired princes in tights in Disney cartoons.

Before she had really thought it through, she jumped and found herself on the other side, slithering on some incredibly slimy substance which smelled revolting. She only just stopped herself from falling into the ravine by grabbing the bottom of the tree, which was also covered in the disgusting slime. As she turned her head to look, she knew there was something bad about the slime. Her nostrils weren't having any of it. Calling on the training afforded by innumerable smelly Third World toilets during her hippie traveling years, she expelled her breath sharply and didn't take in any more air until she was out of stink range. Then, lungs bursting, she turned her head heavenwards, took a tentative sniff, then took a deep breath of delicious pure Popayan air and started peeling off her clothes.

She lay on her stomach in her bra and knickers, her slime-coated jeans, T-shirt and shoes hidden at a distance so she couldn't smell them. She was out of sight of the guards, round the side of the hill, and peering through her spyglass at Pierre Feramo's resort. A turquoise coral lagoon was ringed with a perfect white beach dotted with palms and wooden sun loungers with cream linen cushions. In the center, a square pool was set into a wooden deck. A large thatched structure behind was obviously the reception area and restaurant. A wooden jetty stretched over the lagoon, leading to a thatched bar. On either side two further walkways stretched over the water, three thatched huts leading off each. Each hut had a shaded wooden veranda with a wooden staircase leading directly into the sea. Six more guest huts were scattered among the palms on the edge of the beach. *Mmmm,* she thought, slipping without noticing into holiday hotel mode. *Maybe I should visit, after all. I wonder if I could get one of the huts over the water. Or maybe it would be nicer to be back on the edge of the beach? But what about sandflies?*

The clientele dotted on the sun loungers and bar stools looked like *Vogue* models. A couple paddled kayaks across the lagoon. A man was snorkeling. Two girls were wading to the edge of the reef in scuba gear, aided by an instructor. To the right of the resort was a parking area, where there were trucks and diggers, a compressor and tanks. A rough roadway snaked round a headland. Beyond, a substantial concrete pier led out past the coral to the point where the water turned from turquoise to darkest blue. She put the spy-glass down and took some more snaps. Then she put the spyglass back to her eye, but for some reason couldn't see anything.

"It's the wrong way round."

She started to scream, but a hand was over her mouth, the other holding her arm behind her back.

30

She wriggled round to find herself looking at her ex-favorite gray eyes. "Oh God, it's you," she grunted through his fingers.

"What are you doing?" Morton C. sounded mildly amused, in sharp contrast to the hand over her mouth.

"Gerroff," she demanded with as much dignity as she could muster under the circumstances.

Morton released his grip and rested one finger against her throat. "Keep your voice down. What are you doing here?"

"Sightseeing."

"In your underwear?"

"I am also sunbathing."

"How did you get up here?"

"I jumped."

"You *jumped*?"

"Yes, and I nearly fell in. The ledge is covered in slime and so are my clothes."

"Where are they?"

She pointed. He scrambled down the slope. She could hear small sounds and rustling. She started to turn over.

"I said, don't move." He reappeared over the edge of the hill. "Is this yours?" he asked, holding up a carrot.

She glowered at him.

"Don't be sulky now. Come down here onto the ledge, slowly. Sit down on that rock." As she did, she realized she was shaking.

Morton C. crossed his arms, pulled his shirt over his head and handed it to her.

"Put this on," he said.

"Not with your stink on it."

"Put it on." He stood back, watching her put on the shirt. "You're not a journalist at all, are you? What are you doing here?"

"I told you. I came for a walk up Pumpkin Hill. I wanted to see the resort."

"Are you out of your mind?"

"Why shouldn't I check out the lovely hotel? What if I want to stay there?"

"Well, you ask at the lovely tourist office in the lovely village, and if they have a lovely room, they'll take you round in a lovely boat."

"Well, maybe I just will."

"Well, get you."

"Anyway, what are *you* doing here?"

"Are you always this difficult?"

"You're working for Feramo, aren't you?"

"What you need to do is get yourself back to the village without being spotted, and if you have any sense at all, you'll say nothing about coming up here."

"What a shitty thing to do, hanging around all the divers, pretending to be one of the lads, then grassing on them to that horrible, sinister acolyte like a telltale tit."

"I have no idea what you're talking about. Have you got any of that stuff on your skin?"

"My hands, but I wiped it off."

He took hold of her hands, held them two feet from his face and sniffed. "Okay," he said. "Off you go. I'll see you after the dive."

No, you won't, you two-faced bastard, she thought furiously, sitting in the mangroves and watching through her spyglass as Morton casually smoked a cigarette with the guard at the top of the hill. *I'm going to have one last dive, then I'm going back to the British Embassy, tell them what I've found out and go home.*

When Olivia turned up for her eleven o'clock dive, a group was huddled around the crackly television in Rod's shack, watching the news.

"They're small, they're green, they're widely available, but they're about to poison the world: castor beans!

"Experts believe these commonly grown beans may be the source of Tuesday's poison attack on the cruise ship Coyoba, an attack which has so far claimed the lives of two hundred and sixty-three passengers. The attack, believed to be the work of the al-Qaeda network, has been traced to the poison ricin, placed in the salt pots in the ship's dining room."

Up popped a scientist in a white coat. *"Ricin, of course, was the substance used in the so-called 'umbrella attack' on London's Waterloo Bridge in 1978. The Bulgarian dissident writer Georgi Markov was killed by a pellet filled with ricin and fired from an umbrella. The problem with ricin—which is highly toxic to humans—is that the source material, the castor bean, is widely grown in many regions of the world, and the poison can be produced in so many forms—powder, as in this latest attack, but also crystal, liquid and even gel."*

"That's what O'Reilly says they're growing over the hill," said Rod. "He thinks that's what poisoned his goats."

Fuuuuck, thought Olivia, sniffing her skin. "Just going for a swim!" she said brightly. "Very hot!"

She hurried to the edge of the jetty, stripped off her shorts and dived in. As she plunged deep into the lagoon, rubbing at her skin, her imagination was in overdrive: *Ricin, face cream, maybe Feramo was planning to poison Devorée's Crème de Phylgie with poison gel? Then Michael Monteroso would get it to catch on with his celebrity clients, and Feramo would slowly poison half of Hollywood before anyone suspected.*

As Olivia swam back, Rod was waiting at the end of the jetty with the gear. "Fancy taking on a tunnel?" he asked, with a flash of his white teeth.

"Er . . ." Olivia was dead against diving tunnels and wrecks. As far as she could see, as long as you kept breathing and didn't panic underwater, you were fine. If you went where you could get stuck, it wasn't so simple.

"I'd rather do the wall again."

"Well, I'm going to the tunnels. And Drew's not around. So if you want to dive today, you'll have to do tunnels."

Olivia did *not* like being bossed around in this manner.

"Fine," she said cheerily. "I'll just go for another swim instead."

"Okay, okay. We won't go in any caves or tunnels. I might show you the odd crevice, though."

Olivia tried to ignore the unattractive image this conjured up in her mind's eye.

31

Once underwater, Rod turned into a classic Smug Techie. He was the same breed as the man from the Spy Shop who had come to check out her room at the Standard, or the Smug Computer Expert who tinkers with your computer with a smirk and a vocabulary of unintelligible jargon, as if privy to a whole fabulous world which you cannot hope to understand, giving you a mere tasting menu of its delights suitable for a three-to-five-year-old, in order to bask in your childlike wonder and snigger about you with his techie friends later. Rod was somehow managing to convey a tech-esque smirk, in spite of the fact that he was eighty feet underwater and had a mask on his face and an oxygen pipe in his mouth.

Olivia followed him through a crevice and then, when she realized that the crevice was actually a tunnel and that it was getting too narrow to turn, panicked so much that she dropped the regulator out of her mouth. For a few seconds she broke the golden rule and started floundering. What if Rod was one of Feramo's men too and was going to kill her or lead her to Alfonso, who would perform female circumcision on her? What if she got trapped by an octopus? What if a giant squid wrapped its suckered tentacles around her and . . . *Calm, calm, breathe, breathe.* She collected herself, letting her air out slowly, and remembered what to do: lean to the right, run your hand down your thigh, and the regulator will be hanging just there—as indeed it was.

The tunnel was narrowing alarmingly. She started having fantasies about reporting Rod to the diving authorities and having him struck off. Could diving instructors be struck off? She wasn't breathing properly. A combination of fear and indignation was messing everything up. She had to force herself to do what she had been taught: breathe very very slowly and deeply, counterintuitively, as if, instead of being almost trapped in an underwater tunnel, she was lying down at the end of a yoga class imagining a ball of orange light sliding down her body. Soon she was hearing her own heavy breathing, like a sound effect in a horror movie.

After what seemed an unconscionable amount of time, she emerged into blue water. They were in an enormous cavern. There must have been a pretty large hole somewhere above because the water was clear and illuminated by shafts of sunlight. She looked up, trying to see the surface, but all she could see was diffuse light. Shoals of brightly colored fish darted this way and that. It was like being on some unbelievable acid trip. She swam to and fro, forgetting about time and reality, until she saw Rod in front of her tapping his hand on the air dial, communicating such patronizing sarcasm with each tap that she felt that the scuba world's gain had been the mime world's loss.

They had fifteen minutes left. She couldn't see the entrance back into the tunnel. Rod swam ahead of her, pointed to the gap and gestured to her to lead the way. It took longer than she remembered to get back. Something seemed wrong. She didn't recognize the route. The fear resurfaced: Rod was a terrorist, Rod had been talking to Morton, Rod was trying to get rid of her because she knew too much. As she turned a corner, she saw what was ahead and screamed into her regulator, screaming and screaming so that it fell from her mouth again.

32

Olivia was face-to-face with a diver whose entire head was covered in black rubber apart from holes for the eyes and an opening which flapped and sucked around his regulator like a fish's mouth. For a second, in the semidarkness of the tunnel, they stared at each other, mesmerized, like a cat and a goldfish. Then the diver took his regulator from his mouth and held it to hers, blowing out bubbles, holding her gaze until her breathing steadied, then took it back and took a breath himself. He kept his eyes trained steadily on hers as she breathed out into the water, then put his regulator back in her mouth to let her take in more air.

The instinct to flail and gasp was overwhelming. They were eighty feet underwater, under rock. She could feel Rod behind her, clawing and shaking frantically at her leg, pushing her. Did he think she'd simply stopped to look at the view? She kicked her fins to signal him to stop as the diver gently lifted the regulator to her mouth again.

Diving is a constant fight against panic. The phrase repeated itself in her head. She had stabilized, she was breathing from the regulator, but another wave of terror was starting to overwhelm her. She was sandwiched between Rod and the hooded man in the narrowest part of the tunnel. Even if she and Rod pushed their way back to the cavern, they might not make it in time. And if they did, they might not find air at the top; they might just die there.

The hooded man held up his finger for her attention. She kept her eyes on his, breathing his air, as he reached out along her body. Then he withdrew his hand and held up her regulator. Still holding her gaze like an instructor doing a demonstration, he breathed from it, then held it out to her. She thought there was something familiar about his eyes, but she couldn't make out the color. Who was he? At least he wasn't trying to kill her, or if he was, he was prone to self-defeating behaviors. He reached forward again, found her gauge, looked at it, and showed it to her. At this depth she had seven minutes of air left. Rod was shaking her leg frantically. She tried to turn her head. When she turned forward again, the diver was moving away from her, backwards, at a steady speed, as if he was being pulled. She started to kick and moved ahead. She felt a massive stinging burn on her shoulder. Fire coral. She had an overwhelming urge to kick Rod in the face with her fin. If she had planned to go into a tunnel she'd have put on a wetsuit.

The tunnel widened. The light ahead had a different quality. She could no longer see the diver in front of her. She moved faster and faster, bursting out into the open sea, looking up to see the light and bubbles of the surface misleadingly close. Resisting the urge to race her way up there, she turned to check for Rod, who was emerging from the tunnel, making his thumb and index finger into a circle.

She wished there was a signal for, "No fucking thanks to you, you irresponsible bastard."

Rod raised a thumb signaling the ascent, then jerked his head in a sudden, panicky movement. She looked up to see the shadowy form of a shark.

The shark was maybe twenty feet above them. Olivia knew that calm divers have nothing to fear from a shark. This one was moving fast and deliberately, as if towards prey. There was a flurry of movement and churning water, and then a red cloud started slowly to spread. She signaled to Rod to move away. His eyes were wide, terrified. She followed his gaze to see something falling down towards them, like a grotesque fish with a huge dark gaping mouth, trailing fronds which looked like seaweed. The object turned slowly to reveal a human face, the mouth open in a scream, bright red blood belching from the neck, long hair trailing behind. It was Drew's head.

33

Rod swam past her, thrashing dangerously, brandishing his knife and heading towards the shark. She reached out and grabbed his leg, pulling him back towards her. She held up the gauge, signaled with her fist across her throat to say out of air and pointed upwards. He looked down towards the head, still falling into the abyss, and then turned to follow her. She swam smoothly away from the scene, checking her compass for the direction of the shore, checking that Rod was still following, feeling the change in the regulator which told her that the air was almost gone, fighting the panic again. There were dark shadows above them. More predators were moving towards the bloodbath. She started a controlled, out-of-air ascent, blowing her air out very, very slowly, saying "Ahhh" out loud. She felt the air in her buoyancy jacket expand and tighten against her chest and found the air-release hose, taking a lungful of air from it, discharging it slowly into the water, looking up, seeing the magical light and bubbles and blue of the surface beckoning, closer than it seemed, and forced herself to take her time: *Breathe, don't panic, slow your ascent to the speed of the slowest bubble.*

As they broke the surface, gasping for air and retching, they were still far from the shore—the dive shack was a good three hundred yards away.

"What did you do to him?" yelled Rod.

"What?" she said, pushing her mask up and dropping her weight belt. "What are you talking about?"

She gave the signal for emergency towards the shore and blew her whistle. The usual bunch of guys were sitting around at the shack. "Help!" she shouted. "Sharks!"

"What did you do to him?" said Rod, through a sob. "What did you do?"

"What are you talking about?" she said furiously. "Are you mad? It wasn't Drew in that tunnel. It was someone in a rubber mask. He gave me his air and then just started zooming backwards."

"For fuck's sake. That's impossible. Hey!" Rod started shouting and gesticulating towards the shack. "Hey, get over here!"

She looked backwards and saw a fin.

"Rod, shut up and keep still."

Keeping her eyes on the fin, she blew the whistle and raised her hand again. Mercifully, a sense of urgency had finally communicated itself to the dive-shack guys. Someone had started up the boat's engine, figures were jumping aboard and seconds later the boat was powering towards them. The fin disappeared under the water. She drew her legs up close, mushroom floating, thinking, *Hurry, please hurry*, waiting for a sudden muscular movement, the feel of her flesh being ripped apart. The boat seemed to take an interminable amount of time to reach them. *What were they doing? Fucking stoneheads.*

"Leave the tanks—get in," yelled Rod, suddenly the capable dive instructor again, as the boat drew up. Olivia ditched her tank and her fins, reached out to the arms stretching over the side of the boat and, scrambling with her feet, got herself over and lay in the bottom, gasping for breath.

Back on the jetty, Olivia sat on the bench, a towel around her shoulders, her arms round her knees. The whole horrible ritual of death and its aftermath was unfolding around her. Out at sea, a shark cage containing Rod and a buddy was descending from a boat in a plainly hopeless quest to retrieve the remains of Drew, Popayan's only medical professional, an elderly Irish midwife, was standing helplessly on the jetty, holding her bag. At the sound of sirens, Olivia looked up to see a boat with flashing lights approaching: the medical boat from Roatán, the big island.

"You should be lying down, to be sure," said the nurse, lighting a cigarette. "We should be taking you off to Miss Ruthie's."

"She must be interviewed first by the police," said Popayan's one policeman grandly.

Olivia was dimly aware of the talk and theories gathering force around her: Drew had still been out of it on coke from the previous night; he'd gone down without a buddy; he'd been raving about teaching Feramo's lot a lesson. He could have made a mistake, cut himself and attracted the shark, or he could have taken on one of Feramo's people and got himself injured. Their voices lowered as they started talking about the figure in the tunnel. One of the boys touched her nervously on her shoulder, right on the fire-coral burn. She let out a slight moan.

"Rachel," the boy whispered, "sorry to ask, but are you sure it wasn't Drew in the tunnel? Maybe it was the shark pulling him back."

She shook her head. "I don't know. The guy was wearing a full body suit and head mask. I don't think it was Drew. I think if it had been, he would have let me know somehow. Sharks don't swim down tunnels, do they? And there was no hood on the h—" her voice broke—". . . the head."

Miss Ruthie was baking when she returned. Trays of buns and cakes were laid out on the stove and the yellow-painted dresser, and the smell was of cinnamon and spices. Tears started to prick Olivia's eyelids. Childhood images of comfort washed over her: Big-Ears's cottage, the Woodentops' house, her mother baking when she got back from school.

"Oh bejaysus, sit yourself down."

Miss Ruthie hurried over to a drawer and fetched a neatly ironed handkerchief with a flower and the initial *R* embroidered in the corner.

"Holy Mary, Mother of God," she said, taking a sticky-looking loaf out of a tin. "There we go. Now let's make us both a nice cup of tea." She cut Olivia a large slice of the loaf, as if the only response to a disembodied-head sighting was a sticky cake and a cup of tea. Which, Olivia thought, taking a bite of the most delicious, moist banana loaf, was quite possibly true.

"Is there a flight out today?" she said quietly to Miss Ruthie.

"To be sure. It goes in the afternoon most days."

"How do I book it?"

"Just leave your bag out on the step, like, and Pedro will knock on the door when he passes with the red truck."

"How will he know to stop? How will he know I want to get the plane? What if it's full?"

Once again, Miss Ruthie just looked at her as though she was stupid.

The knock came just after three. The red truck was empty. Olivia watched as her beloved tan and olive carry-on was loaded into the back, then climbed up in front, gripping her hatpin in the palm of her hand, running her thumb over the back of the spy ring, her pepper-spray pen tucked into the pocket of her shorts. The day was perfect: blue sky, butterflies and hummingbirds hovering above the wildflowers. The sweetness was unearthly, unsettling. She saw the Robinson Crusoe sign and the little bridge leading to the airstrip and started gathering her things together, but the truck turned off to the right.

"This isn't the airport," she said nervously, staying firmly in her seat as they ground to a halt on a patch of scrub by the sea.

"*Qué?*" he said, opening the door. "*No hablo inglés.*"

"*No es el aeropuerto. Quiero tomar el avión para La Ceiba.*"

"Yes, yes," he said in Spanish, lifting the bags to the ground. "The flight leaves from Roatán on Tuesdays. You have to wait for the boat." He nodded towards the empty horizon. The engine was still running. He waited impatiently for her to step out.

"But there's no boat."

"It will be here in five minutes."

Olivia got out suspiciously. "Wait just a few minutes," he said and started to climb back into the cab.

"But where are you going?"

"To the village. It's okay. The boat will be here in a few minutes."

He put the truck into gear. She watched as it rattled off, suddenly overcome with exhaustion, too weary to do anything. The sound of the engine gradually faded into silence. It was very hot. There was no sign of any boat. She dragged her case over to a casuarina and sat in the shade, swatting away flies. After twenty minutes she heard a faint whining sound. She jumped to her feet, scanning the horizon with the spyglass. It was a boat, heading towards her fast. She felt wild with relief, desperate to get away. As the boat drew closer, she saw that it was a flashy-looking white speedboat. She hadn't seen anything like it in Popayan, but then Roatán was much more of an international tourist hub. Maybe Roatán airport had its own private launch.

The boatman waved, cutting the engine and bringing the boat to the jetty in a perfect arc. It was beautiful, big, with white-leather seats and polished wooden doors leading to a cabin belowdeck. *"Para el aeropuerto Roatán?"* she said nervously.

"Sí, señorita, suba abordo," the boatman said, tying the boat up, swinging her bag aboard and holding out his hand to help her up. He pulled the rope loose, put the engine on full throttle and pulled out towards the open sea.

Olivia sat uneasily on the edge of a white-leather seat, glancing back as the coastline of Popayan faded into insignificance, then looking anxiously at the empty horizon ahead. The door to the cabin opened and she saw a dark head, slightly balding, covered in short, tightly curled black hair, emerging from the hold. He looked up and an oily, ingratiating smile spread across his features.

34

Olivia sat at the front of the boat in the white-leather passenger seat, fighting back surges of seasickness, her head bouncing up and down like a rag doll's as every few seconds she was slapped in the face by a wave. Meanwhile, Alfonso, also soaking wet, stood at the wheel, dressed in a ridiculous outfit of white shirt, white shorts, white three-quarter-length socks and a captain's hat. He was steering the boat inexpertly and much too fast into the prevailing wind so that it reared up and smacked into every wave head-on. He was gesticulating, oblivious, at the shoreline ahead and, completely inaudible above the roar of the engine, shouting things at her.

How, she thought grimly, *could I be such a bloody idiot? Miss Ruthie is working for Alfonso. Miss Ruthie probably poisoned the banana cake and cut Drew's head off. She's like the evil red-raincoated dwarf in* Don't Look Now. *She's going to reappear from the cabin in a Little Red Riding Hood outfit and cut my throat. What can I do?* The answer, she realized, was nothing. She still had the hatpin in her hand. The pepper-spray pen was in her pocket, but her chances of overpowering two burly men with a pen and a hatpin were, realistically, not very high.

"Where are we going?" she yelled. "I want to go to the airport."

"It is a surprise," Alfonso said gaily. "It is a surprise from Meester Feramo."

"Stop, stop!" she said. "Slow down!"

He ignored her, letting out a gurgling laugh and smacking the boat into another wave.

"I'm going to be sick!" she yelled, leaning towards the spotless white outfit and feigning a quasi-vomit. He jumped back in alarm and immediately cut the engine.

"Over the side," he said, waving his hand at her. "Over there. Pedro. *Agua.* Quick."

She did a convincing dry heave over the side—not much acting required—and leaned back, hand to her head. "Where are we going?"

"To Meester Feramo's hotel. It is a surprise."

"Why didn't someone ask me? This is a kidnapping."

Alfonso started the boat up again, looking at her with his oily smile. "It is a beautiful surprise!"

She willed the vomit to rise again. *Next time I'll do it for real,* she said to herself. *Right onto his little shorts.*

As they rounded the headland, an idyllic holiday scene spread before them: white sand and turquoise sea, bathers frolicking and laughing in the shallows. Olivia wanted to rush ashore and slap everyone, yelling, "It's evil, evil! This is all built on killing and death!"

The boatman approached the wheel, offering to take over, but Alfonso brushed him away impatiently, roaring towards the jetty as if in an advert for after-dinner mints, shower gel or tooth whitener. In the nick of time he realized he had misjudged it. He veered off to the left, scattering snorkelers and narrowly missing a jet ski, made a messy circle, churning up the sea, then cut the engine just a little bit too late so that he crashed into the jetty anyway, letting out a curse.

"Masterfully done," said Olivia.

"Thank you." He smirked, oblivious. "Welcome to La Isla Bonita."

Olivia sighed heavily.

Once she was on the stable surface of the jetty, feeling the sun drying her drenched clothes and the seasickness subsiding, things didn't seem quite so bad. A charming young man in white knee-length shorts took her bag and offered to show her to her room. Charming young bellboys seemed to be becoming a leitmotif of the trip. She thought back to the one at the Standard with the unnaturally bright blue eyes, large muscles, sideburns and goatee beard, whose face looked like one on a child's magnetic sketch pad, and made a mental note to check the room for bugs. And then suddenly it came to her: colored contact lenses. Morton with his bleached, cropped hair and gray, clever eyes; the hooded diver with the calm, steady eyes behind the mask; the Standard bellboy with the packed body, the bright blue eyes which didn't fit with his facial hair. They were the same person.

Trying to keep her composure whilst eyeing the current bellboy suspiciously, she followed him along a series of wooden walkways with ropes as handrails. The resort was fabulously eco, a barefoot paradise—pathways paved only with bark fragments, solar panels, signs carved in wood labeling the plants. She wondered whether there were neatly labeled castor-bean plants, and made a mental note to go for a nature walk in the morning and check for dead goats.

Her room—or, rather, ocean-view junior suite—was set back from the beach, standing on stilts on the edge of the jungle. She was disappointed not to be in one of the huts out over the sea, but even Olivia realized that in these circumstances it might not be appropriate to ask about a room change. The building was constructed entirely of wood and thatch, the linens and mosquito nets in soft whites and beiges. There were frangipani blossoms on her pillows. The walls were slatted to allow the sea breezes to join forces with the ceiling fan. The bathroom had modern chrome fittings, a deep porcelain bath with jacuzzi jets and a separate shower. It was all very stylish. The toilet paper, however, was not folded down to a neat little point. In fact, there was no fold in it whatsoever. It was simply left hanging against the roll.

"Mr. Feramo has asked you to join him for dinner at seven," said the boy with a sly smile.

He's going to poison me, she thought. *Feramo's going to poison me with ricin in the salt. Or he's going to serve me O'Reilly's poisoned goat. Or release an oxygen-acetylene bubble and set fire to me.*

"How lovely. Where?" she said smoothly.

"In his suite," said the boy with a wink. She tried not to shudder. She hated people who winked.

"Thank you," she said weakly. She wasn't sure if tipping was in order, but, deciding to err on the side of generosity, she handed him a five-dollar bill.

"Oh no, no," he said with a smile. "We don't believe in money here."

Yeah, right.

It was excellent to have a proper shower: an up-to-the-minute rainwater-style power shower with side jets and a chrome head the size of a dinner plate. She took her time, washing her hair in the high-end products, soaping herself, rinsing and moisturizing, then wrapped herself in the exquisite cream-colored Frette robe and padded across the wooden floor to the balcony, where she sprayed mosquito repellent onto her wrists and ankles, hoping it would work for diver-murdering Islamic kidnappers as well.

It was dark now and the jungle was loud with the sounds of frogs and cicadas. Flaming torches lit the pathways down to the sea, the swimming pool glowed turquoise through the palms and the air was sweet with jasmine and frangipani. Enticing cooking smells drifted up from the restaurant area, along with the murmur of contented voices. It was the seductive face of evil, she told herself, marching determinedly back into the room to find the bug detector slash calculator she'd bought from the Spy Shop on Sunset Boulevard.

She took it out of her case with some excitement, then stared at it, frowning. She couldn't remember what you were supposed to do. She had decided to throw away the packaging of all her spy equipment in order to protect the various disguises, overlooking the obvious flaw in the plan, which was that she would no longer have the instructions. She vaguely remembered that you were supposed to press in a preagreed code. She always used 3637, which was the ages of her parents when they were killed. She punched it in: nothing. Maybe you were supposed to turn it on first? She tried pressing ON and then entered 3637, then waved it around the room: nothing. Either there was no bug, or the bloody thing was broken.

She snapped. One little thing too many had been added to the cumulative stresses of the day, and she found herself hurling the little calculator passionately across the room as if it were responsible for everything: Drew's head, Morton C., Miss Ruthie, the subaquatic hooded rapist, the strange slime on the hill, the kidnapping, everything. She shut herself in the wardrobe with her back to the door and curled up into a ball.

Suddenly, she heard a tiny beeping noise. Raising her head, she opened the closet door and crawled across towards the calculator. It was working. The little screen had lit up. She was overcome with a rush of affection for the tiny gadget. It wasn't the bug detector slash calculator's fault. It was doing its best. She dialed in the code again. It started to vibrate very slightly. Excited, she got to her feet and started to walk around the room, holding the calculator out as if it were a metal detector. She couldn't remember how you knew when it found the bug. It beeped again, as if it was trying to help. That was it! It would beep if it detected something and start to vibrate increasingly when it got closer to the bug. She tried waving it at the power outlets: nothing. There were no telephone jacks. She tried the lamps: nothing. Then she felt the vibration change. It led her to a wooden coffee table with a stone flowerpot embedded in the center, from which emerged a stubby cactus plant. The calculator started practically jumping out of her hand, completely overexcited with itself. She tried to look under the table, but it was a heavy, boxlike thing. Should she disembowel the cactus with her knife? It would certainly be satisfying. She hated cacti. Spiky plants were bad feng shui. But then it was wrong to destroy life. What was it going to overhear anyway? Who was she going to talk to? She stared at the stubby little plant. Maybe it was a camera as well? She opened her case, took out a thin black sweater, pretended to put it on, then changed her mind and chucked it casually at the table, covering the cactus.

It was twenty minutes to seven. She decided she might as well try to look her best. A girl in a scrape had to use whatever resources were at her disposal. She dried her hair and then swung it around in the mirror in an imitation of the annoying Suraya, murmuring provocatively, "Leaves my hair shinier and more manageable!" The combination of seawater, sun and the remains of the red dye had turned it a lovely streaky blond. Her skin had caught some sun glow too, in spite of the lashings of sunblock. She didn't need much makeup, just a bit of concealer to tone down the red nose. She put on a flimsy black dress, sandals and jewelry and surveyed herself in the mirror. The whole effect was quite good, she decided, at least for the end of a shit day like this one.

"Okay, Olivia, you're on," she said sternly, then shot her hand over her mouth, worrying that the cactus had picked it up. Tonight she had to put on a performance. She had to present Feramo with the woman he wanted her to be. She had to pretend to herself that she had kissed no blond, gray-eyed, double-crossing youths, seen no disembodied heads, understood nothing about the links between al-Qaeda bombs and acetylene, and had never heard the word "ricin." Could she pull it off? It was going to be like "Don't mention the war" when dining with a German. "Would you pass the ricin please?" "It's very rice in the Bay Islands, isn't it?"

She started giggling. Oh dear, was it possible she was hysterical? What was she *doing*? She was about to have dinner with a *poisoner.* Her mind raced wildly, trying to summon antipoisoning strategies gleaned from movies: switching glasses, eating only from the same pot as the host. But what if the dishes arrived already on the plates? She stood still for a moment then lay down on the floor, repeating the mantra, "My intuitions are my guide; I still my hysteria and overactive imagination." She was just starting to calm down when there was a thunderous knock at the door. *They're taking me away to be stoned,* she thought, scrambling to her feet, hopping into her strappy sandals and reaching the door just as the maniacal knock came again.

A small plump lady in a white apron was standing outside. "You want turndown?" she said with a motherly smile.

As the lady bustled into the room, the bellboy appeared in the doorway behind her.

"Mr. Feramo is ready to receive you," he said.

35

Pierre Feramo was reclining on a low sofa, his hands resting on his lap with an air of controlled power. He was wearing loose clothes in navy linen. His beautiful, liquid eyes stared at her impassively beneath the finely arched brows.

"Thank you," he said, dismissing the boy with a wave of his hand.

Olivia heard the door close, stiffening as the key turned in the lock.

Feramo's suite was sumptuous, exotic, lit entirely by candlelight. There were Oriental rugs on the floors, ornate tapestries on the wall and a smell of burning incense which instantly took her back to her time in the Sudan. Feramo continued to stare at her scarily. Instinct told her to take control of the mood.

"Hello!" she said brightly. "It's nice to see you again."

In the flickering light, Feramo looked like Omar Sharif in *Lawrence of Arabia* when his blood was up.

"This is a beautiful suite," she said, attempting to look around appreciatively, "though in our country it is polite to get up when a guest enters, especially when you've had her kidnapped."

She saw the slightest flicker of confusion pass over his features, quickly replaced by a stony glare. *Oh, sod him, sulky bastard,* she thought. On the table in front of him was a bottle of Cristal chilling in a silver ice bucket, together with two flutes and a tray of canapés. It was, she noted with interest, the same table as the one in her room, right down to the cactus embedded in the middle.

"This looks nice," she said, sitting down and flashing him a smile as she glanced at the champagne glasses. "Shall I be mother?" Feramo's face softened for a second. She was, she realized, behaving like a northern housewife at the vicar's tea party, but it seemed to be doing the trick. Then his expression changed again and he fixed her with a fierce stare, like an annoyed bird of prey. *Okay,* she thought, *two can play at that game.* She settled herself down and stared back. Unfortunately, however, something about the impromptu staring competition made her want to laugh. She could feel the giggles bubbling up from her stomach, and suddenly they burst out through her nose, so she had to put her hand over her mouth, shaking helplessly.

"Enough!" he roared, leaping to his feet, which just made her laugh even more. Oh God, she had really done it now. She had to stop. She breathed in deeply, looked up, then collapsed in giggles again. Once something struck you as funny like that, when you really, really weren't supposed to laugh, you were doomed. It was like giggling in church or school assembly. Even the thought of him sweeping out a sword and lopping off her head struck her as hilarious as she pictured her head bouncing across the floor, still giggling, Feramo bellowing at it.

"Sorry, sorry," she said, pulling herself together, both sets of fingers over her mouth and nose. "Okay, okay."

"You appear to be enjoying life."

"Well, so would you be if you'd narrowly escaped death three times in one day."

"I apologize for Alfonso's behavior with the boat."

"He nearly killed a bunch of snorkelers and someone on a jet ski."

Feramo's mouth twisted oddly. "It was the fault of that accursed boat. Western technology, for all its promise, is designed to make a fool of the Arab."

"Oh, don't be so paranoid, Pierre," she said lightly. "I really don't think that's the first priority in modern speedboat design. How are you, anyway?"

He looked at her uncertainly. "Come, we must drink a toast!" he said, reaching to open the champagne. She watched him, fingering the hatpin hidden in the fabric of her dress, trying to assess what was going on. This was her big chance to get him drunk and find out what he was up to. She glanced around the room: there was a laptop closed on the desk.

Feramo seemed really quite desperate to get into the Cristal, but was having trouble with the cork. Clearly he hadn't had much practice either at opening champagne bottles or fucking things up. Olivia found herself frozen into an encouraging smile as if waiting for a man with a bad stammer to get the next word out. Suddenly the cork shot across the room and the Cristal spurted out, frothing all over his hand, the table, napkins, cactus and canapés. A strange curse burst from his lips as he started grabbing at things and knocking them over.

"Pierre, Pierre, Pierre," she said, starting to dab at the puddle of Cristal with a napkin. "Calm down. Everything's fine. I'll just take these . . ." she said, picking up the flutes and heading for the wet bar, "and . . . rinse them, so that they're pristine. Ooh, what beautiful glasses. Are they from Prague?" She carried on babbling as she washed them in hot water, then gave them a good rinse and swilled out the bottoms.

"You are right," he said. "They are fine Bohemian crystal. Evidently, you are a connoisseur of beauty. As am I." At this Olivia almost started laughing again. Clearly the Arab mind could be as corny as the shopping channel.

She replaced the glasses on the coffee table, ensuring that what had been Feramo's glass was now hers. She watched him carefully for the gestures of a thwarted poisoner, but instead she saw only the eagerness of an alcoholic on the verge of his first drink of the evening.

"Let us drink a toast," he said, handing her her glass. "To our rendezvous." He glanced at her seriously for a moment, then downed his champagne like a Cossack in a vodka-drinking competition.

Does he know you're not supposed to drink champagne like that? she wondered. It reminded her of Kate's mother, a lifelong teetotaler who, if she poured someone a G&T, would fill a tumbler almost to the top with neat gin with barely a nod in the direction of the tonic bottle.

"Come, let us eat. We have much to discuss."

As he rose to lead the way out to the terrace, she emptied her glass into the cactus. Feramo pulled back her chair for her, like waiters do. She sat down, expecting him to push it forward, like waiters do, only somehow he got it wrong, and she sat down on nothing, plunging to the floor. She thought she was going to start laughing again until she looked up and saw the intensity of his humiliation and rage.

"It's all right, Pierre. It's all right."

"But what do you mean?" As he towered over her, she imagined him commanding a mujahedin battalion in the Afghan mountains, pacing above prisoners, keeping his anger controlled, then suddenly blasting them with a machine gun.

"I mean it's funny," she said firmly, starting to get to her feet, noting to her relief that he hurried to help her. "The more a situation is geared up to be perfect, the funnier it is when something goes wrong. Things aren't *supposed* to be perfect."

"So that is good?" he said, the trace of a small-boy smile appearing.

"Yes," she said, "it's good. Right, I shall sit down on the chair, not under it, and we'll start again."

"I do apologize. I am mortified—first the champagne and then . . ."

"Shh," she soothed. "Sit down. You couldn't have found a better way to make me feel comfortable."

"Really?"

"Really," she said, thinking: *Now I don't have to worry about being poisoned every time I take a sip.* "I was intimidated when I walked in.

Now we know we're both just human beings and we don't have to pretend to be all fancy and perfect and we can just have a good time."

He grasped her hand, kissing it passionately. It was as if something about her acted as a trigger for him. His mood swings made no sense. He was dangerous, clearly. But she didn't have a lot of options here. Maybe if she just brazened it out and followed her nose she could keep control of the situation. Especially if she was sober and Feramo was drunk.

"You are the most wonderful woman," he said, looking at her almost wretchedly.

"Why?" she asked. "Because I'm good at washing glasses?"

"Because you are kind."

She felt terrible.

He downed another glass of champagne, leaned back and gave a vicious tug to a thick, dark-red bellpull. Immediately, the key turned in the lock and three waiters appeared carrying steaming casseroles.

"Leave it, leave it," Feramo barked as they twittered around, obviously terrified. "I shall serve it myself."

The waiters set down the dishes and hurried out, falling over each other in their haste.

"I hope," said Feramo, unfolding his napkin, "that you will enjoy our dinner. It is a great delicacy in our land."

She gulped. "What is it?" she said.

"It is curried goat."

36

"You will take some more wine?" said Feramo. "I have an 'eighty-two Saint-Estèphe which I think will go well with the goat."

"Perfect." There was a large potted fig tree conveniently placed beside her. As he turned to select a bottle, she quickly shoved a spoonful of goat from her plate back into the serving dish and emptied her glass into the plant pot.

". . . and a 'ninety-five Puligny-Montrachet for dessert."

"My favorite," she murmured smoothly.

"As I was saying," he said, pouring the wine before he had even sat down, "it is the separation of the physical and the spiritual which is the source of the problem in the West."

"Hmm," said Olivia. "But the thing is, if you have a religious government taking its cues from a deity rather than the democratic process, what's to stop any crackpot who takes power from saying it's the will of God that he spend the entire country's food money on eighteen palaces for himself?"

"Saddam Hussein's Ba'ath party was not an example of a religious government."

"I wasn't saying it was. I was just plucking an example out of the air. I'm just saying who decides what the will of God is?"

"It is written in the Koran."

"But the scriptures are open to interpretation. You know, one man's 'Thou shalt not kill' is another man's eye for an eye. You can't really think it's okay to kill in the name of religion."

"You are pedantic. The truth does not require sophistry. It is as clear as the rising sun above the desert plain. The failure of Western culture is evident at every moment—in its cities, in its media, in its messages to the world: the arrogance, the stupidity, the violence, the fear, the mindless pursuit of empty materialism, the worship of celebrity. Take the people you and I have witnessed in Los Angeles—lascivious, empty, vain, swarming to feed off promises of wealth and fame like the locust on the sorghum plant."

"You seem to be enjoying their company."

"I despise them."

"Then why do you employ them?"

"Why do I employ them? Ah, Olivia, you are not of their type and so you would not understand."

"Try me. Why would you want to surround yourself with waitresses and security guards and divers and surfers who all want to be actors if you despise them?"

He leaned forward and ran a finger very slowly down one side of her neck. Her hand tightened on the hatpin.

"You are not of their type. You are not the locust, but the falcon." He rose to his feet, moving to stand behind her. He started to stroke her hair, which made goose bumps rise on the back of her neck. "You are not of their type, and therefore you must be captured and tamed until you will want only to return to one master. You are not of their type," he whispered into her neck, "and therefore you are not lascivious."

Suddenly he wrapped her hair around his fist and jerked back her head. "Are you? Are you open to the advances of another man, the kisses, hidden, in the darkness?"

"Ow, get off," she said, pulling her head away from him. "What is the matter with the men on this island? You're all as mad as buckets. We're in the middle of dinner. Will you please stop being so weird, sit down and tell me what you're talking about?"

He paused, his hand still on her hair.

"Oh, come on, Pierre, we're not in a school playground. You

don't need to pull my hair to ask me a question. Now come along, sit back on your chair and let's have our dessert."

There was another moment's hesitation. He was prowling around the table like a panther.

"Why did you not come to me as you promised, my little falcon, my *saqr*?"

"Because I'm not a little falcon, I'm a professional journalist. I'm writing about diving off the beaten track. I can't cover the whole of the Bay Islands by heading straight for the most luxurious hotel."

"Is it also necessary to check out the local dive instructors?"

"Of course."

"Actually," he said icily, "I think you are perfectly aware of whom I speak, Olivia. I am speaking of Morton."

"Pierre, you do realize that what Western boys do at parties, especially when they've had a lot of rum and free cocaine, is try to kiss girls. It isn't a stoning offense in our countries. And at least I fought him off," she said, risking a white lie. "How many girls have you tried to kiss since I last saw you?"

Suddenly he smiled, like a small boy who has got his toys back after a tantrum. "You are right, Olivia. Of course. Other men will admire your beauty, but you will return to your master."

God, he was nuts. "Listen, Pierre. First, I'm a modern girl and I don't have masters." She was thinking very fast, working out how to get the conversation back on track. "Second, if two people are going to be together they have to have shared values, and I believe very firmly that killing is wrong. So, if you don't, we might as well sort it out now."

"You disappoint me. Like all Westerners you are arrogant enough to entertain only your own naïve and blinkered view. Consider the needs of the Bedouin in the harsh and unforgiving desert lands. The survival of the tribe must take precedence over the life of an individual."

"Would you support a terrorist attack? I need to know."

He poured himself another glass of wine. "Who in the world

would prefer war to peace? But there are times when war becomes a necessity. And in the modern world the rules of engagement have changed."

"Would you . . ." she began, but clearly he had had enough of this line of conversation.

"Olivia!" he said jovially. "You have hardly eaten at all! You did not like it?"

"I still feel a little ill from the boat ride."

"But you must eat. You must. It is a great offense."

"Actually, I would love a little more wine. Shall we open the Puligny-Montrachet?"

That did the trick. Feramo continued to drink and Olivia continued to tip her wine into the potted fig. He remained lucid, his movements impressively coordinated, but his passion and eloquence grew. And always she felt as though he was teetering on the precipice of some violent mood swing. It was all so bafflingly different from his controlled, dignified, public persona. She wondered if she was witnessing the effects of some psychological bruise, some wounded underbelly like her own: an early trauma, the death of a parent, perhaps?

A patchy map of his history emerged. He had studied in France. He made references which suggested the Sorbonne, but he was not specific. He was more expansive about his studies at Grasse on the Côte d'Azur where he had trained as a "nose" in the perfume industry. There had been a long period in Cairo. There was a father whom he seemed to both despise and fear. No further mention of a mother. She found it hard to draw him out on his work as a producer in French cinema. It was like trying to pin down one of the waiter slash producers in the Standard bar about his latest production. There was, clearly, a large amount of money sloshing around in his family and his life, and there had been major globe-trotting: Paris, Saint-Tropez, Monte Carlo, Anguilla, Gstaad.

"Have you ever been to India?" she said. "I'd love to go to the Himalayas, Tibet, Bhutan"—*don't hesitate*—"Afghanistan. Those

places seem so untouched and mysterious. Have you ever been up
there?"

"Actually, Afghanistan, yes, of course. And it is wild and beautiful and raw and fierce. I should take you there, and we will ride,
and you will see the life of a nomad, the life of my childhood and
my ancestors."

"What were you doing there?"

"As a young man I liked to travel, just as you did, Olivia."

"I'm sure you weren't traveling just as I did." She laughed,
thinking: *Come on, come on: dish. Were you training in the camps? Were
you training for the OceansApart, for something else? Now? Soon? Are you
trying to make me a part of it?*

"Oh, but I was. We lived as poor men in tents. My homeland is
the land of the nomad."

"The Sudan?"

"Arabia. The land of the Bedouin: the gracious, the hospitable,
the simple and the spiritual." He took another large gulp of Mon-
trachet. "The Western man with his lust for progress sees nothing
but the future, destroying the world in his blind pursuit of novelty
and wealth. My people see that the truth lies in the wisdom of the
past, and that wealth lies in the strength of the tribe." He poured
more wine, leaning forward and grasping her hand. "And that is
why I must take you there. And, of course, it will be perfect for
your diving article."

"Oh, I couldn't," she said. "No. I would have to get the magazine to send me."

"But it is the finest diving in the world. There are cliffs and
drop-offs plunging to seven hundred meters, coral pinnacle formations rising like ancient towers from the ocean floor, caves and tunnels. The visibility is unsurpassed. It is pristine! Pristine! You will
not see another diver for the duration of your stay."

Something in the latest bottle of wine appeared to release the
travel writer in Feramo.

"The pinnacle formations arise from great depths, attracting marine life in unbelievable numbers, including large pelagic species. It is an extraordinary Technicolor experience: sharks, mantas, barracuda, dog-toothed tuna, dog lips, jewfish."

"So, lots of fish then!" she said brightly.

"And tomorrow we will dive *à deux*."

Not with your hangover, we won't. "And are there nice places to stay?"

"Actually, the majority of the divers stay on the live-aboards. I have several residential boats myself. But you, of course, shall have the full Bedouin experience."

"That sounds wonderful. But I can only really write about what the readers can do themselves."

"Let me tell you about Suakin," he said. "Suakin, the Venice of the Red Sea. A crumbling coral city, the greatest Red Sea port of the sixteenth century."

After listening to a further twenty minutes of unbroken eulogy, she began to think Feramo's role in al-Qaeda might be boring his victims to death. She watched his drooping eyelids like a mother watches a child, trying to judge the moment when she could safely transport him to his cot.

"Let's go back inside," she whispered, helping him to a low sofa, where he slumped with his chin on his chest. Holding her breath, wondering if she really dared do this, she kicked off her shoes and tiptoed over to the desk and the laptop. She opened it up and pressed a key to see if it was merely sleeping like its owner. Dammit. It was shut down. If she started it up, would it make a sound: a chord or, God forbid, a quack?

Olivia froze as Feramo gave a shuddering sigh and shifted position, rubbing the tip of his tongue against his lips like a lizard. She waited until his breathing steadied again, then decided to go for it. She pressed the start-up button and prepared to cough. There was a slight whirring, then, before she got the cough out, a female voice from the computer said, "Uh-oh."

Feramo opened his eyes and sat bolt upright. Olivia grabbed a bottle of water and hurried over. "Uh-oh," she said, "uh-oh, you're going to have a terrible hangover if you don't drink some water."

She held the bottle to his lips. He shook his head and pushed it away. "Well, don't blame me if you have a horrible headache in the morning," she said, making her way back to the computer. "You should drink a whole liter of water at least and have an aspirin." She kept up a steady stream of mumsy chatter as she sat down at the computer and checked out the desktop, trying to keep her cool. There was nothing there except icons and applications. She glanced over her shoulder. Feramo was sleeping soundly. She clicked on AOL, then went immediately to "Favorites."

She clocked the first two:

Hydroweld: for welding in the wet.

Cut-price nose-hair and nail clippers.

"Olivia!" She literally jumped an inch out of the seat. "What are you doing?"

Calm, calm. Remember, he's had the best part of four bottles of wine.

"I'm trying to check my e-mail," she said without looking up, still clicking away at the computer. "Is this on a wireless network, or are you meant to plug it into the phone socket?"

"Come away from there."

"Well, not if you're just going to be asleep," she said, trying her best to sound sulky.

"Olivia!" He sounded scary again.

"Oh, okay, hang on. I'll just shut it down," she said hurriedly, quitting AOL as she heard him get to his feet. She put on an innocent expression and turned to face him, but he was heading for the bathroom. She darted across the room, opened a cabinet and saw a bunch of videotapes, some with handwritten labels: *Lawrence of Arabia, Academy Awards 2003, Miss Watson's Academy of Passion, Scenic Glories of the Bay Area.*

"What are you doing?"

"I'm looking for the mini-bar."

"There is no mini-bar. This is not a hotel."

"I thought it *was* a hotel."

"I think it is time for you to return to your room." He looked like a man who is just starting to realize how drunk he is. His clothes were crumpled, his eyes bloodshot.

"You're right. I'm very tired," she said, smiling. "Thank you for a lovely dinner."

But he was crashing around the room, looking for something, and merely waved her good-night.

He was a ruin of the dignified, mesmerizing man she had been so struck by at the hotel in Miami. *Drink is the urine of Satan,* she thought as she let herself back into her room. *I wonder how long before they start the al-Qaeda branch of AA?*

37

She had a hideous, sleepless night. She hadn't eaten anything since Miss Ruthie's slice of cake twelve hours before and, despite the luxury of the room, there was no mini-bar: no Toblerone, no jar of cashews, no giant pack of M&M's. She turned her head this way and that against the pillowcase, which felt like it was finest Egyptian three-thousand-thread count or something, but nothing helped.

Her thoughts began to run riot. At 5:00 A.M. she sat bolt upright and hit herself on the forehead. Caves! Al-Qaeda lived in caves in Tora Bora! Feramo was probably hiding the top tier of al-Qaeda senior management in a cave under Suakin. There was probably a Donald Rumsfeld wet dream of weapons of mass destruction in a cave underneath her right now, all neatly marked FORMER PROPERTY OF S. HUSSEIN.

Eventually, as dawn was beginning to dilute the darkness over the sea, she drifted into confused dreams: headless bodies in wetsuits, Osama bin Laden's head falling through the ocean in his turban while going on and on about fifteen-liter tanks, the virtues of neoprene drysuits, Danish BCDs and Australian drop-offs.

She woke to bright sunlight, the chirp of tropical birds and hunger pangs. There was the rich, humid smell that said "holiday." She pulled on the cotton bathrobe and slippers and padded onto her balcony. It was a perfect, almost cloudless Sunday morning. She could smell brunch.

The signs promising CLUBHOUSE led her to a tiki bar, where a bunch of young lovelies were laughing and joking together. She hesitated, feeling like the new girl at school, then recognized a familiar, like, Valley-girl voice?

"I mean, I, like, *get myself* so much more these days than I ever have?"

It was Kimberley with a huge stash of pancakes on her plate, playing idly with them with her fork and showing no interest in eating them at all. Olivia had to hold herself back from making a run at them.

"Kimberley!" she said brightly, barging into the group. "Great to see you. How's the movie going? Where did you get those pancakes?"

It was one of the major pig-outs of her life. She consumed scrambled eggs and bacon, three banana pancakes with maple syrup, one blueberry muffin, three small slices of banana bread, two orange juices, three cappuccinos and a Bloody Mary. As she ate, she felt the exhilaration of a hunch turned good: the first pieces of a puzzle starting to fall into place. One by one, familiar faces from Miami and LA began to show themselves at the bar or around the pool. As well as Kimberley, there was Winston, the beautiful black dive instructor—who, thankfully, had escaped the carnage of the *OceansApart*—Michael Monteroso, the facial technician, and Travis, the wolf-eyed actor slash writer slash lifestyle coach. All were displaying their fabulously oiled and worked-out bodies around the bar and pool. It was a recruiting camp, she was sure; it was the al-Qaeda version of Butlins. Winston was lying on a sun lounger holding a loud conversation with Travis and Michael Monteroso, who were sitting at the bar.

"Was that the vintage Valentino year, with the white stripe?" said Winston.

"That was the Oscars," said Michael bossily. "The Globes she was in backless navy Armani. And she made that speech about honeys— 'Everyone needs a honey to say "How was your day, honey?" Benjamin Bratt does that for me.' "

"And six weeks later they split up."

"I was on security for the *Oceans Eleven* premiere and I'm thinking, *I so can't ask Julia Roberts to open her purse,* and she just goes right ahead and opens her purse for me."

"You still doing that stuff?" said Travis the actor, schadenfreude glinting in the ice-blue wolf eyes.

"Not any more," snapped Winston. "Are you still driving a van for that place in south LA?"

"No."

"I thought you were," said Michael.

"Well, only, like, part-time."

"What place is that?" said Olivia.

"Oh, it's, like, so not anything." Travis sounded rather stoned. "It sucks, man, but you can make good bread. If you do, like, Chicago or Michigan and sleep in the van, you can clock up, like per diems and overhours, but, like, the best stuff always goes to the old guys."

"What's it called?" she said, then regretted it instantly. She sounded too much like a journalist or a policeman. Fortunately, Travis the actor seemed too out of it to notice anything.

"The security firm? Carrysure." He yawned, got up from his perch and ambled over to a table by a palm tree, where several candles were burning in what appeared to be a giant sculpture made out of wax. He put a half-smoked joint into his mouth, lit it again and started to manipulate the wax, molding it into strange, fanciful shapes.

"What's he doing?" said Olivia quietly.

Michael Monteroso rolled his eyes. "It's his wax cake," he said. "It releases his creativity."

Olivia glanced behind him and drew a sharp breath. Morton C.

was walking past the bar, wetsuit peeled down to the waist, muscles bulging. He was carrying a dive tank on each shoulder and was followed by two dark, Arabic-looking youths carrying jackets and regulators.

"I was at the Oscars that year," said Kimberley. "I was a seat-filler. I sat behind Jack Nicholson."

Olivia saw Morton C. spot her and looked away, furious. Two-faced git. He needn't think he was going to worm his way back into her affections now. She slipped the miniature camera from her wrap and surreptitiously snapped a few pictures.

"No kidding?" Winston was saying. "Those guys who, like, sit in the seat when Halle Berry goes to the bathroom?"

Olivia nudged Michael, nodding at Morton's retreating back. "Who's that?" she whispered.

"The blond guy? He's some kind of, like, diving-instructor-type thing?"

"My dad gets me the gig because he does the follow spot," Kimberley was saying proudly. "The second time it was for Shakira Caine, but she only, like, went to the bathroom during one break. But last year I sat in the front row for the whole of the first half."

"Anyone seen Pierre?"

"Alfonso said he was coming down for, like, for lunch, brunch, whatever. Hey! There's Alfonso. Hey, man. Come and have a drink."

The troll-like figure of Alfonso, shirtless, was heading towards them. Olivia found herself unable to stomach the sight of his very hairy back.

"I think I'm going to have a swim," she said, beginning to fear, as she slid off the stool, that she'd be drowned by the weight of the pancakes.

She plunged into the clear water, swimming strongly, holding her breath for as long as she could and surfacing a hundred yards farther on. She had won a race at school for swimming underwater in Worksop Baths before it was banned because someone got dizzy.

She surfaced, slicking back her hair so it didn't look mad, plunged down again and powered ahead for as long as she could, rounding the headland so that she could see the concrete pier. The sea was darker and choppier here; she was approaching the windward side of the island. She started to swim at a fast crawl until she was opposite the pier. It didn't seem to be in use. A tall fence with barbed wire along the top blocked entry from the hotel side. There were tanks and a storage shed close to the shore, and a surfboard which appeared to have been cut in half.

Beyond the pier was a long, windswept beach lashed by white-tipped waves. There was a small boat at anchor a couple of hundred yards out, tossing up and down. A diver stood up on the ledge at the back and stepped into the water, followed by three more. She dived down again and swam towards them. When she surfaced, the last of the four divers was beginning his descent. Thinking they'd be gone for a while, she started to swim towards the pier and was surprised, when she glanced back, to see all four of them had surfaced closer to the shore. Their pose was familiar as they waited in the water, like seals. Then one of them started paddling fast towards a wave and climbed onto a board. Surfers! She watched in fascination as they followed the wave in formation, zigzagging on the inner curve. She was getting close to the heart of the story. She could sense it. They landed, laughing together, and set off towards the pier. Suddenly one of them shouted and pointed towards her.

Olivia plunged down about five feet and headed for the concrete pier. Her lungs were bursting, but she kept going until she rounded the pier and then surfaced, gasping for breath. The surfers were nowhere in sight. She plunged down again and swam back towards the resort until the water grew calmer, warm and blue, and she was above a sandy bottom back in the shelter of the bay.

She surfaced with relief, floating on her back, trying to get her breath back. There was a raft a little way ahead. She swam slowly towards it, pulled herself up and flopped down on the Astroturf.

It was a cool raft. The Astroturf was blue—the same type as they had around the Standard Hotel pool in LA. She stretched out, getting her breath back, looking up at the sky where the moon was already visible. She relaxed, feeling the sun on her skin, the raft rising and falling softly with the waves, the water slapping gently against the side.

She was woken abruptly from her daydream. A hand was clapped firmly over her mouth. Instinctively, she pulled the hatpin from her bikini and sank it deep into the arm, which jerked in shock and loosened just long enough for her to wriggle free.

"Don't move." She recognized the voice.

"Morton, what is it with you? Have you been watching too many action movies?"

She turned and for the first time in her life found herself looking into the barrel of a gun. It was odd, really. She had wondered what it would be like, and, in the event, it was a strange, reverse-reality sensation. It made her think: *This is exactly like a film,* rather as when you see a beautiful view and you think it looks just like a postcard.

"What was on that needle?"

The gray eyes were icy, vicious. He was holding himself up on the raft with one elbow, still pointing the gun.

"That thing will never fire," she said. "It's been in the water."

"Lie down on your stomach. That's right. Now"—he leaned forward—"what was in that fucking syringe?"

He was scared. She could see it in his eyes.

"Morton," she said firmly, "it is a hatpin. I'm traveling alone. You frightened me. You're frightening me even more now. Put the gun away."

"Give me the pin."

"No. Give me the gun."

He shoved the barrel of the gun roughly into her neck and grabbed the pin with his other hand.

"This is very rude. I could easily just stand up and scream, you know."

"You'd be too late and they'd never find you. What the fuck is this?" He was staring at the pin.

"It's a hatpin. It's an old trick of my mother's to ward off sexual assailants."

He blinked at it, then let out his short laugh. "A hatpin. Well, that's just great."

"Bet you wish you hadn't pulled the gun, now, don't you?"

The gray eyes told her she was right. *Ha ha,* she thought.

"Shut up and talk," he said. "What are you doing here?"

"I wish I knew. I was kidnapped by Alfonso."

"I know that. But what are you doing on Popayan? Who are you working for?"

"I told you. I'm just a freelance journalist."

"Come on. A freelance fashion journalist who—"

"I am *not* a fashion journalist."

"Perfume journalist, whatever. A perfume journalist who's a linguist?"

"In *our* country," she said, drawing herself up indignantly, "we realize the necessity of speaking other languages. We are aware of the existence of other nationalities. We like to be able to converse with them, not just to talk in a loud voice."

"What are the languages? Gibberish? Bollocks? Gobbledegook? The language of love?"

She laughed in spite of herself. "Come on, Morton, stop brandishing that gun. I don't think your boss is going to be very pleased if he finds out you've been shoving a gun down my throat."

"That's the least of your worries."

"I'm not talking about me. What were you doing in that tunnel?"

"What tunnel?"

"Oh, don't give me that. Why did you kill Drew? An innocent hippie like that—how could you?"

He looked at her dangerously. "Why are you following Feramo?"

"Why are *you* following *me*? You're not very good at covering your tracks, are you? That fake beard and mustache you were sporting at the Standard were the worst I've ever seen in my life. And if you were going to stash a bag of coke in my hotel room in Tegucigalpa, it wasn't the brightest thing to sit making eyes at me five minutes before, then disappear and come back again."

"Do you ever stop talking? I said, why are you following Feramo?"

"Are you jealous?"

He let out a short, incredulous laugh. "Jealous? Over you?"

"Oh, I'm sorry. I was forgetting. I thought you might have kissed me because you fancied me. I'd forgotten you were a cynical, double-crossing, two-faced git."

"You need to leave. I'm here to warn you. You're getting yourself into deep water."

She looked down at him in the sea. "If you don't mind me saying so, that's like the kettle calling the frying pan 'dirty bottom.' "

He shook his head. "As I said, fluent in gibberish. Listen. You're a nice English girl. Go home. Don't meddle in stuff you don't understand. Get your ass out of here."

"How?"

"Oliviaaaaaaaaa!"

She turned to look behind her. Feramo was calling from the shallows, wading towards her, the water waist high. "Wait there," he shouted. "I will come."

She turned back to Morton C. but all that was left of him was bubbles.

Feramo approached the raft with sharklike precision in a powerful freestyle and pulled himself onto it athletically. He was toned and perfectly triangular: clear olive skin and fine features devastating against the blue water. *It's raining men,* she thought. She wished

Morton hadn't disappeared so she could have one on each side of the raft—one dark, one fair, both stunning against the blue water—and pick the prettier.

"Olivia, you look wonderful," Feramo said earnestly. "Wonderful." The blue water was evidently doing it for her as well.

"Let me call for a boat and some towels," he said, taking a waterproof bleeper from his pocket. Within minutes a speedboat drew up alongside them. A lithe youth in swimming trunks cut the engine, handed them fluffy towels and helped Olivia aboard.

"That will be all, Jesus," said Feramo, taking the wheel—at which Jesus walked to the back of the boat and simply stepped over the side, holding himself straight, as if he was going to walk back on the water.

Feramo turned to check that she was seated safely on the passenger seat and gently steered the boat in a wide curve through the millpond of the bay and off around the headland.

"I am so sorry I have left you alone all day," he said.

"Oh, don't worry. I slept really late too. Did you have a hangover?"

As she spoke, she was trying to gauge his mood, looking for anything she could use to manipulate him and get away.

"No, it was not a hangover," he snapped. "I felt as if I had been poisoned. My stomach was churning like the innards of an ape, and I suffered a headache of such terrifying ferocity it was as if there was a metal brace grinding into my skull."

"Er, Pierre. That's what we doctors call a hangover."

"Do not be ridiculous. That cannot be."

"Why not?"

"If that was a hangover," he said imperiously, "no one who has experienced it would ever drink alcohol again."

She turned her face away to hide her grin. She felt like a wife whose husband insists he knows exactly where he's going, when he's going completely the wrong way. It made her feel stronger. He was just a man. She had two choices now. She could concentrate on getting more information, or she could concentrate on getting away. But simple psychology suggested that the more information she extracted, the less chance she had of getting away.

"I need to leave," she blurted.

"That is not possible," he said, without taking his eyes off the horizon.

"Stop, stop," she said, allowing a note of hysteria to rise in her voice. "I need to leave."

Suddenly she knew exactly what she was going to do. She was going to cry. Under normal circumstances she would never dream of sinking so low, but (a) this was a very unorthodox situation, (b) she didn't want to die and (c) she had a feeling that the one thing Feramo wouldn't be able to handle was a crying woman.

She thought back to her ill-fated locust story in the Sudan, when she had attempted to cover the starving animals instead. A minder from the Sudanese Ministry of Information had flatly refused to let her into the zoo until she accidentally started crying with frustration, at which point he caved in, flung open the gate and insisted on giving her a full tour, as if she were a three-year-old on a birthday treat. Those tears had been an accident. The problem had been that in Khartoum Zoo there weren't any toilets. In general Olivia worked on the principle that she would never deliberately use tears to get her own way, and if they overwhelmed her by accident she would make sure she got to the loo before anyone saw.

Now, though, she was planning to use tears in cold blood. It was a matter of life, death and global security. But, then, did the end justify the means? Once you had violated a principle, where would it end? One minute you were crying in order to manipulate a man; the next you would be killing hippies.

Oh, fuck it, she thought and burst into tears.

Pierre Feramo stared at her in alarm. She sobbed and gurgled. He cut the engine. She cried more loudly. He recoiled, looking around for assistance as if under attack from laser-guided Scuds.

"Olivia, Olivia, stop, please. I beg of you, do not cry."

"Then let me go home," she said through paroxysms of tears. "LET ME GO HOME."

"Olivia . . ." he began and tailed off, staring at her helplessly. He didn't seem to have the capacity simply to comfort someone.

"I can't bear it. I can't bear to be trapped." And then, in a burst of inspiration, she declared passionately, "I need to be free, like the falcon." She sneaked a look under her eyelashes to see what effect she was having. "Please let me go, Pierre. Let me be free."

He was agitated. His nostrils flared slightly, his mouth turned downwards at the edges. He reminded her more than ever of bin Laden.

"Go where?" he said. "You do not enjoy my hospitality? We have not made you comfortable here?" She sensed the danger in his voice—jangling raw nerves and imagined slights on every side.

"I need to come to you freely," she said, softening, moving closer to him. "I need to come by choice."

She broke down again, this time for real. "I don't feel safe here, Pierre. I'm tired, so many weird things have happened: the ship blowing up, Drew's head being bitten off—I just don't feel safe. I need to go home."

"You cannot travel now. The world is not safe. You must stay here safe with me, *saqr,* until I have trained you always to return."

"If you want me to return, then you must set me free. Free, to soar like the eagle," she said, then wondered if she had overdone it with the whole bird thing.

He turned away, his mouth working.

"Very well, *saqr,* very well. I shall set you free and test you once again. But you must go quickly. You must leave today."

Feramo took her to Roatán airport himself in the white speedboat. He cut the engine as they were still a way offshore to say good-bye.

"I have enjoyed having you as my guest, Olivia," he said, touching her cheek tenderly. "I myself will be leaving for the Sudan within a few days. I will telephone you in London and arrange for you to join me and I will show you the life of the Bedouin."

Olivia nodded mutely. She had given him the wrong number.

"And then, *saqr*, you will begin to understand me better. And you will no longer want to leave." He looked at her in a burning, insane manner. She thought he might try to kiss her, but instead he did the strangest thing. He took her index finger, thrust it into his mouth, and *sucked* on it, wildly, obsessively, as if it were a teat and he was a starving piglet.

38

As the Roatán-Miami flight became airborne, Olivia could not quite believe either what had happened, or that she had got away. She felt as if she had been under attack from a wild animal, burglar or violent storm, which suddenly, for no apparent reason, had gone away. It was not reassuring. She tried to tell herself that it was all her doing, that it was her brilliant psychological manipulation of Feramo which had won her her freedom. But she knew it wasn't. It was just luck, and luck could change.

There was one thing of which she was certain: she had been given a warning and a reprieve. She had moved too close to the flame and, fortunately, had escaped only slightly singed. Now it was time to go home and play safe.

Her confidence improved in direct proportion to her distance from Honduras. *Falcon, my arse,* she told herself as she boarded the Miami-to-London flight with thirty seconds to spare. As the plane started its descent over Sussex, she was overcome with tearful relief. She looked down over rolling green hills, damp earth and chestnut trees, cows, lichen-covered churches, half-timbered houses, wiped a tear from her cheek and told herself she was safe.

But as she came through passport control and saw soldiers with guns, she remembered that you were never safe. People clustered around the television screens on the way through to the baggage hall. There had been another terror alert a few hours previously. The London Underground was closed. As she entered Customs, the doors to the Arrivals area opened and she saw the excited faces of waiting people and found herself irrationally hoping that someone would be waiting for her, someone's face breaking into a smile, hurrying up to get her case and take her home; or at the very least that there would be someone with a card saying OLIVIA JEWELS and the name of a minicab company. *Pull yourself together,* she said to herself. *You don't want to be taken home to cook supper in Worksop, do you?* But, actually, someone *was* waiting for her. She was pulled over at Customs, strip-searched, handcuffed and taken to the interrogation center in Terminal Four.

Two hours later she was still there, her spy equipment spread out on the table before her: spyglass, spy ring, miniature camera, bug detector, pepper-spray pen. Her laptop had been taken away for examination. She felt as though she had gone over the story three hundred times. "I'm a freelance journalist. I work for *Elan* magazine and the *Sunday Times*, sometimes. I went to Honduras to cover the cheap diving."

The officials' questions about Feramo made her nervous. How did they know? Had the Embassy tipped them off? HM Customs were barking up completely the wrong tree anyway. They thought he was trafficking drugs and that she was his accomplice.

"Did he give you his number?"

"Yes."

"Can we take it?"

"Won't that put me under threat?"

"We'll make sure it won't. Did you give him your number?"

"Nearly. I changed a couple of digits."

"We'll need that number as well. The one you gave him. You're ex-directory, aren't you?"

"Yes."

"Good. Why did you continue to follow him? Are you in love with him?"

She started to tell them about her terrorism theories, but she sensed she was dealing with the wrong people. They weren't taking her seriously. They were HM Customs and Excise. They were looking for drugs.

"I want to speak to someone from MI6," she said. "I need a terrorism person. I need a lawyer."

Finally, the door opened and a tall figure swept in in a flurry of perfume, hair and covetable clothes. The woman sat at the desk, bent her head, took hold of her hair and threw it back so it cascaded over her shoulders in a glossy black curtain.

"So, Olivia, we meet again. Or should I call you Rachel?"

It took Olivia a second to realize that she recognized the woman and another second to realize where from.

"Hmm," said Olivia. "I wonder what *I* should call *you*?"

"I'm going to ask you again," said Suraya in an annoying primary-schoolteacher tone. "And this time I want the right answer." She was as astonishingly beautiful as ever, but had lost her West Coast drawl and replaced it with a posh girls' boarding-school English.

Olivia's initial reaction to the revelation that Suraya was an undercover spy was to think, *That woman could never be a spy because no one would ever tell her anything because she's also an Undercover Bitch.* But then she remembered how stupid men could be when women were beautiful.

"I've told everyone about three hundred times. I'm freelance. I sometimes work for *Elan* magazine and the *Sunday Times*, when they're not pissed off with me about something."

"Born in Worksop." Suraya started reading bossily from her file. "Witnessed parents and younger brother killed on a pedestrian crossing aged fourteen."

Olivia winced: horrible, cruel cowbag.

"Left school before A levels. Changed her name to Olivia Joules. Started investing using parents' life insurance aged eighteen. Extensive travel. Small apartment in Primrose Hill. Freelance journalist, principally style and travel—ambitions to cover hard news. Plays piano, speaks fluent French, passable Spanish and German, some Arabic. Changes her appearance and hair color with regularity. Frequent visits to the States and various European cities. Other visits to India, Morocco, Kenya, Tanzania, Mozambique and the Sudan."

She paused, then added, "Currently unattached. So who are you working for?"

"Who are *you* working for?" snapped Olivia.

"MI6," Suraya Exoceted back.

"Did you put the bug in my bedroom in the Standard?"

Suraya tossed her hair disparagingly and started reading from the file again. "Rachel Pixley, writing under the name Olivia Joules, is considered by *Sunday Times* editorial staff to have an overactive imagination." She closed the file and looked up with a nasty smile. "So that explains the toys, yes?" she said, gesturing dismissively at the spy equipment. "Jane Bond delusions."

Olivia felt like hitting her on the head with a shoe. How dare she insult her spy gear?

Breathe, breathe, calm, Olivia told herself. *Do not stoop to the horrid witch's level.*

"So, tell me," said Suraya. "Did you enjoy sleeping with him?"

Olivia looked down for a moment, recovering her composure. It was fine, it was absolutely fine. Olivia's theory was that you could divide women into two types: those who were on the Girls' Team, and Undercover Bitches. If a woman was on the Girls' Team, she could be as beautiful, intelligent, rich, famous, sexy, successful and as popular as fuck, and you'd still like her. Women on the Girls' Team had solidarity. They were conspiratorial and brought all their fuck-ups to the table for everyone to enjoy. Undercover Bitches were competitive: they showed off, tried to put others down to make themselves look good, lacked humor and a sense of their own ridiculousness, said things which sounded okay on the surface but were actually designed to make you feel really bad, couldn't bear it when they weren't getting enough attention, and they flicked their hair. Men didn't get all this. They thought women took against each other because they were jealous. Quite tragic, really.

"Well?" said Suraya with a supercilious smile. "Did you, or didn't you?"

Olivia felt like yelling, "Oh, go fuck yourself, you ridiculous cowbag," but managed to stop herself by digging her thumb into her palm.

"I'm afraid the closest I got was to see him in his swimming trunks," said Olivia.

"Oh really? And?"

"They were quite baggy," said Olivia sweetly. "So sorry to disappoint, but I can't tell you much more. I'm sure you found all the information you needed from your own research. Why the interest, anyway?"

"That's for us to know and you to tell us more about," she said, as if Olivia were a seven-year-old child. "Now, I suggest you start by telling me why exactly you were following him."

Calm, calm, breathe, don't go mental, Olivia told herself. *Look on the bright side. The fact that MI6 has arrived initially in the shape of this horrible posh boarding school, hair-flicking, Undercover Bitch is neither here nor there. They are taking you seriously. Sooner or later, someone will lower his newspaper in a railway carriage, invite you for tea and biscuits in Pimlico, and pop the question.*

"I suppose you think staring into space like that is a clever technique," said Suraya, stifling a yawn. "Actually it's very childish."

"Did you spend a *very* long time learning how to interrogate people?" asked Olivia. "Did they tell you the best way to win people over was to really get on their nerves?"

Suraya froze for a moment, eyes closed, palms spread before her, breathing through her nose.

"Okay, okay, freeze frame," she said. "Rewind, yah? Let's start again." She held out her hand. "Pax?"

"What?" said Olivia.

"You know: pax, yah? Latin for peace?"

"Oh! Yah, yah. I mean sometimes I, like, *dream* in Latin."

"So look," said Suraya, still keeping up the crisp English tone, "let's come clean here. We've been looking at Feramo and his people for drugs. You know, Miami, Honduras, LA. It looked like a pretty obvious connection. As it turns out from our investigations,

Feramo is as clean as a whistle—an international playboy with an eye for girls with not much between the ears."

"You do yourself down."

"What?" said Suraya. "Anyway, you've mentioned a couple of times your suspicions about terrorism. We'd like you to tell us what that's based on."

But Olivia wasn't going to tell her what that was based on, or not all of it, anyway. She would wait until she was interrogated by someone she could at least stand.

"Well, first of all, I didn't believe he was French," she said. "I thought he was an Arab."

"Because?"

"His accent. And then, when the *OceansApart* blew up, I guess I, unfairly perhaps, put together some rather far-fetched clues to connect him to it. And then when I found out about the diving connection, I thought, ooh, maybe they'd used divers to blow up the ship. Silly, really, but there we are."

Now, Olivia thought, if *she* had been doing the investigation, her next question would have been, "And what do you think now?"

Instead, a tiny curl of satisfaction lifted the corner of Suraya's mouth. "I see," she said and got to her feet, picking up Olivia's file. She was wearing a very cool, short, seventies-style skirt with saddle stitching which looked like Prada, and a super-thin silk-knit sweater in an elegant shade of khaki.

"Excuse me one moment," Suraya said with a smile and slipped out of the room, taking the file with her. Olivia could just make out the word Gucci woven into the knit at the back of the sweater. They must pay them a lot in MI6, she thought.

She sat looking round the room, imagining that Suraya had gone to talk to her superior. Any second now, she would return with an elderly M-like figure, who would lean forward and murmur, "Welcome to MI6, Agent Joules. Now off you go to Gucci for the kit."

The door opened, and Suraya reappeared. "We're going to let you go," she said with a brisk finality, sitting down.

Olivia sank down in her seat, crestfallen. "I'll need these back, and my laptop," she said, starting to gather her spy things together.

"We'll be retaining these for a few days," said Suraya, putting out her hand to stop her.

"What about my laptop?"

"That too, I'm afraid. You'll have it back shortly."

"But I need it to work on."

"You can pick up a replacement and a copy of your hard drive on the way out. We'll contact you in a few days when we're ready to return the machine. In the meantime, Rachel"—Suraya had clearly picked up some pretty serious role-model stuff from the headmistress of her posh school—"I'm sure you are aware of the importance of not mentioning this to anyone. No harm done, but in future remember it's an extremely silly idea to get involved with any sort of drugs issues. You got off lightly this time, but in future there might be more serious consequences."

"What?" Olivia spluttered. "It was the British Embassy people in La Ceiba who told me it was safe to go to Popayan. They said it would be all right to hang out at Feramo's hotel."

"Well, how would they know?" said Suraya. "Anyway, excuse me, I must be getting on. They'll give you another laptop on your way out."

40

It was only back in the familiar surroundings of her flat—the plastic bottle of Fairy Liquid by the sink, the vacuum in the hall cupboard, the log McNuggets in the basket by the fireplace—that Olivia realized exactly how extraordinary the events of the last few days had been. Incredibly, it was less than two weeks since she had left London. The milk she had left in the fridge had gone off, but the butter was absolutely fine.

All the things that Olivia loved to escape to hotel rooms to avoid were here: an answering machine with thirty-one messages, the mail piling up in the hallway, the cupboard in the hall, which was full of things she hadn't got round to throwing away. It was freezing cold; the boiler had gone out, and she had to faff around pressing the ignition button over and over again, remembering as she did so how Morton C. had pulled the starter cord on the boat on the way to Bell Key, until the thing suddenly ignited and made her jump. She stood in the kitchen with a can of Heinz baked beans in her hand: all the clues and theories, wild imaginings and suspicions of the last two weeks whirling round her head like clothes in a washing machine. *MI6 have made a mistake letting me go,* she thought. *They should be using me.*

She looked out of the small arched kitchen window onto the familiar scene: the flat opposite with a piece of fabric instead of a curtain, and the floor beneath, where the man wandered around naked. In the street, she saw a man open the passenger door of a blue Ford Mondeo and get in beside the driver. The two of them looked up at her window, then, seeing her, looked quickly away. They didn't drive off. *Amateurs,* she thought, giving them a little wave, wondering who had made the bad employment decision: Feramo or MI6. She lit the fire, took a loaf of bread out of the freezer, made beans on toast and fell asleep in front of *EastEnders.*

Olivia didn't wake until noon the next day. The first thing she did was check the kitchen window. The men in the Ford Mondeo were still there. She was just wondering where they'd gone to pee in the night and hoping it wasn't on her doorstep when the phone rang.

"Olivia? It's Sally Hawkins. I'm so relieved that you're back safely." This was odd. Sally, Olivia realized, had no way of knowing she was back unless either the security services or Feramo had tipped her off. "How are you? How did the Honduras story go?"

"Well, er, I think maybe we need to talk about it," said Olivia, frowning, trying to work out what was going on. "I only got back last night."

"Pierre Feramo telephoned me. I think he spoke to you. He's offered us a trip to the Red Sea to do another leg of the diving-off-the-beaten-track story. We're very keen to set it up. I just wanted to make sure that you'd be happy to make the trip, you know, so we can . . ."

This was too weird. Sally Hawkins sounded scared.

"Sure," Olivia said casually. "It sounds pretty exciting, and the diving's supposed to be great. I might need a couple of days to turn myself around, but I'm definitely up for it."

"Good, good." There was a pause. "Er, just one more thing, Olivia." She sounded strangely wooden, like a terrible actress reading lines. "There's a chap I'd like you to meet, someone who's written for us a few times in the past. He's an expert on all things

Arabian. Very interesting man. Must be in his eighties by now. He happens to be in London today. It might be a good idea if you could meet for tea and get a few, er, travel tips."

"Sure," said Olivia, pulling a "She's mad!" face in the mirror.

"Excellent. Brooks's on St. James's. Do you know it? Just round the corner from the Ritz."

"I'll find it."

"Three-thirty. Professor Widgett."

"Oh yes. I read his book on the Arab sensibility when I was in LA. Some of it, anyway."

"Excellent, Olivia. Well, welcome back. And give me a ring tomorrow afternoon."

Olivia put down the phone and reached for her bedside drawer. She was going to need another hatpin.

There were two different men watching her door now, from a brown Honda Civic parked across the road.

She raised a hand to them, turned on her new MI6-issue computer and Googled Professor Widgett: Arabist.

41

Widgett was a distinguished professor at All Souls and the author of forty books and more than eight hundred articles on various Middle Eastern topics including *The Sinister West: The Arab Mind and the Double-Edged Sword of Technology*, *Lawrence of Arabia and the Junior Suite: The Bedouin Ideal and Urban Hospitality* and *The Arabian Diaspora: Yesterday and Tomorrow*.

She spent a couple of hours online, reading what she could find of his work, then got dressed for a February day. It felt weird putting on tights, boots and a coat, but she kind of liked it. She glanced out of the window. The shadows were still there. She moved to the back of the flat, climbed out of the bedroom window and down the fire escape, scrambled over the wall of Dale's garden downstairs, went through the post office and came out on the busy main road of Primrose Hill. There was no sign of anyone following her. Whoever they were, they weren't very good.

Brooks's was the sort of place which still didn't admit ladies, unless accompanied by a member, and offered three-course meals with savories as dessert. It had a porter's lodge at the entrance, a black and white tiled floor and a real coal fire in an ornate Victorian fireplace. A doorman with a nicotine-lined face and a worn waistcoat and tails showed her up to the library.

"Professor Widgett is right over here, miss," he said. The room was silent apart from the ticking of a grandfather clock. Four or five old men sat on the worn leather armchairs behind copies of the *FT* or the *Telegraph*. There was another coal fire, an ancient globe, walls covered in books and a lot of dust. *Ooh, I'd like to take a cloth and a bottle of Pledge to this lot,* Olivia thought.

Professor Widgett got to his feet. He was immensely tall and old. He made her think of lines in a poem she'd learned at school: "Webster was much possessed by death / And saw the skull beneath the skin." Widgett's skull was almost visible beneath his translucent, papery skin and the pattern of blue veins at his temples. His hair was all but gone.

The second he started to speak, though, Olivia was reminded of how ridiculous is the urge to patronize the old. Widgett was no kind, jolly old gentleman. As he spoke, she saw in his face the ruin of the beautiful roué he must once have been: the full, sensuous lips, the mesmerizing blue eyes—mocking, roguish, cool. She could see him galloping on a camel, scarf wrapped round his head, firing on some nineteenth-century desert fort. There was something theatrical about him: almost camp, but distinctly heterosexual.

"Tea?" he said, raising one eyebrow.

Professor Widgett's serving of the tea reminded her of someone doing a classroom chemistry experiment. It was such a performance: milk, tea strainer, hot water, butter, cream, jam. She suddenly realized why the English so loved their tea. It gave them things to fiddle with when they were bringing up other things which might stray into the difficult area of emotion and instinct. "Ahm . . . that too strong for you? Drop more hot water?" Professor Widgett huffed and harrumphed between enquiries about her take on the Arab world, which seemed strangely irrelevant to a travel piece on diving off the beaten track. What had been her experience of the Arab world? What, in her view, was the motivating factor behind the jihad? Had she ever found it odd that there was no piece of technical equipment in general Western use—no TV, no computer, no car—which was manufactured by an Arab country? Little more milk? Let me top up the pot. Did she think it a result of an Arabic disdain for manual labor or a product of Western prejudice? Was it, did she feel, an ineradicable source of Arab resentment of the West, given the Arabs' insatiable urge to use and own the new technology? Drop more milk in that? Sugar lump? Ever had a love affair with an Arab? Oh my God, this stuff is like cat's piss. Let's get the waiter over for another pot.

"Professor Widgett," she said, "did Sally Hawkins contact you, or did you contact her and ask her to contact me?"

"Terrible actress, isn't she?" he said, taking a sip of tea. "Absolutely appalling."

"Are you from MI6?"

He took a bite of scone, scanning her with cool, insolent blue eyes.

"A bit clumsy, my dear," he drawled in his slightly camp way. "Traditionally, one waits for the spook to pop the question."

He drank some more tea and ate some more scone, scrutinizing her. "So," he said. He leaned forward dramatically, putting his bony old hand on hers, and said in a stage whisper, "Are you going to help us?"

"Yes," she whispered back.

"You'll have to come now."

"Where to?"

"Safe house."

"How long for?"

"Don't know."

"I thought those were your people watching outside my flat."

"Yes. It's the others I'm worried about."

"Oh, I see," she said, composing herself for a minute. "What about my things?"

"Things, Olivia, things. One must never allow oneself to become attached to *things*."

"I quite agree. But, still, there are things I'll need if I'm going to come."

"Make a list. I'll have someone"—he waved his hand vaguely—"fetch the 'things.'"

"Why didn't you take me in at the airport and save all this trouble?"

"Operational blunder, darling," he said, getting to his feet.

42

Widgett carried himself like a sultan. He strode through the gridlocked streets of St. James's, elegant in a long cashmere overcoat, meeting anyone who crossed his path with a stare which was either hawklike or fond, depending on the subject. Olivia thought how dazzling he must have been at forty. She could imagine rushing through the same streets with him in evening dress to dinner and dancing at the Café de Paris.

"Where are we going?" she asked, beginning to fear that Widgett was not MI6 at all, but just mad.

"The river, darling." He led her on a complicated route through the back streets of Whitehall until they emerged onto the Embankment. A police launch was waiting. At the sight of Widgett, the officers, rather than loading him into an ambulance in a straitjacket, stood to attention. This was reassuring.

"Handsome fellows, aren't they?" he said, handing her into the launch.

"Where is the safe house?" she said.

"No need to know," he said. "Get some dinner and a good night's sleep. I'll be with you in the morning." He gave them an elegant wave and disappeared into the crowd.

Immediately, the launch swung out from the bank and into the central flow of the Thames, picking up speed and bouncing against the current. As they powered upstream, Big Ben and the Houses of Parliament were silhouetted against the moonlit sky. Olivia stood at

the prow, heart leaping with excitement, the James Bond theme
playing in her mind. She was a spy! She formed her fingers into a
gun shape and whispered, "Kpow! Kpow!" Then the boat banged
down hard against a wave, and a spray of thick brown river water
hit her in the face. She decided to spend the rest of the journey in
the cabin.

There was a plainclothes officer inside. "Paul McKeown," he
said. "I'm Scotland Yard's liaison with the security services. So,
what do you make of Widgett?"

"I don't know," she said. "Who is he?"

"Come on. You know who Absalom Widgett is."

"I know he works for MI6 and that he's a well-known Arabist,"
she said. "That's all."

"Absalom Widgett? He was a devil, he was. He seduced everybody's wives and daughters all over the Middle East and Arabia. He
had a chair at Oxford and a rug shop on the Portobello Road. He
used to pretend to be a gay oriental carpet specialist."

"Is he the head of something?"

"He was. He was pretty high up. But he grew disenchanted in
the seventies. It was never clear what happened in the end, whether
it was someone's wife, or drink, or opium, or an ideological row.
He was very much of the old school: chaps on the ground, native-
lingo-speakers, trusting to instinct—that sort of thing. He thought
all the new technology was the worst possible thing to happen to
Intelligence. Anyway, whatever happened, it was a mistake on
someone's part. The Arabic section was never the same, and they
pulled him out of retirement on the twelfth of September 2001."

Olivia nodded thoughtfully. "Would you tell me where I'm
going?"

"Not allowed to say. Don't worry. I think you'll find it's pretty
comfortable."

At Hampton Court she was ushered from the boat to a helicopter
and, after a short journey, into a car with darkened windows, which

purred through the country lanes of Berkshire and the Chilterns. They crossed the M40 and she recognized the Oxford ring road, then they plunged deep into the Cotswold countryside, glimpsing flickering fires and cozy-looking scenes through the windows of pubs and cottages. Then they were following the high walls of a country estate, and Olivia heard the crunch of gravel beneath the wheels as wrought-iron gates swung slowly open, the headlights beaming up a long drive. It was the sort of journey which she imagined would end with a uniformed butler opening the door holding a silver tray of Bloody Marys, or a bald midget in a wheelchair, a cat on his knee being stroked with a metal claw.

She was, indeed, met by a butler, an excessively courteous man in uniform, who informed her that her bags had already arrived and ushered her up stone steps into a magnificent hallway. Oil paintings covered the paneled walls, and a wide staircase of dark wood led on to the upper floor.

He asked if she wanted dinner or a "hot tray" in her room. She wasn't sure what a "hot tray" was, but the image it conjured was so beguiling—potted shrimps, Welsh rarebit, Gentleman's Relish, sherry trifle—that she decided she *would* like one, thank you very much.

At the sight of the bed, she lost all interest in her surroundings and sank, exhausted, between the crisp white sheets, noticing to her intense joy that there was a hot-water bottle with a quilted cover in exactly the right position for her feet.

Olivia never discovered the constituents of the hot tray. The next thing she knew it was morning and she had the traveler's syndrome of not remembering where she was. She fumbled for the bedside lamp. The room was in darkness, but bright sunlight was flaring around the edges of the thick curtains. She was in a four-poster bed with heavy chintz drapes. She could hear sheep. It didn't seem to be Honduras.

She swung her legs around and sat on the edge of the bed. She ached all over. She felt dehydrated and vile. She padded over to the window, pulled the curtains aside and found herself looking at a splendid English country-house garden: lawns, manicured hedges in ordered lines, a honey-colored stone terrace directly below her. Moss-covered steps, with a mock-Grecian urn on either side, led down to the lawn, on which there were croquet hoops. Beyond the lawn were chestnut trees, wintry and bare, and beyond that soft gray-green hills, dry-stone walls and smoke rising from the chimneys of gray rooftops clustered around a church spire.

She turned back to the room. Miraculously, her tan and olive case was there, containing the items from her flat she'd requested from Professor Widgett. There was an envelope under her door. It contained a map of the premises, a number to call when she was ready for breakfast and a note which said, *Report to Tech Op Room as soon as you have eaten.*

43   MI6 SAFE HOUSE,
THE COTSWOLDS

Olivia blinked at the computer screen. She was sitting in a booth in a room full of computers and operators. A technician was going through the shots she had taken with her digital camera.

"What is this one of exactly?" he asked.

"Er . . ." she said. The picture was of a muscled black male torso and thighs emerging from an extremely well-packed pair of red swimming trunks.

"Shall we move on?" she said brightly.

"Lovely framing," said a male voice. She turned. It was Professor Widgett, peering at the bulging red swimming trunks.

"I was shooting from the hip," she said lamely.

"Obviously. Has he got a name, or just a bar code?" said Widgett.

"Winston."

"Ah. Winston."

"Shall we look at the next one now?"

"No. So these are all the wannabes around Feramo's pool? What were they doing there? Servicing him?"

"I don't know."

"No." He looked at the screen then sighed, as if bored, and looked at her with his head on one side. "No, we rarely know. But what do you think? What do you scent?" He looked at her, opening his eyes wide and looking quite scary for a second. "What does your gut tell you?"

"I think he was recruiting. I think he was using them for something."

"Were they aware of that? Did they know what for?"

She thought for a moment. "No."

"Did you?"

"I think it's something to do with Hollywood." She looked back at the bulging swimming trunks. "Feramo hates Hollywood, and they all hang around there. Shall we move on to another shot?"

"Very well. If we must, we must. Next one, Dodd. Oh my word, what have we here?"

Olivia felt like crashing her head straight down onto the desk in front of her. What had she been thinking? The next shot was a close-up of a black rubber *V* with a zip at each edge. A bronzed, flat, rock-hard abdomen was emerging from the rubber.

"Oh dear. They're all a bit of a mess," said Olivia, realizing she was looking at a close-up of the crotch of Morton C.

"Wouldn't say that, darling," murmured Widgett.

"Try the next one. I'll be able to work out who it is."

The technician sighed heavily and moved on. It was Morton C. again, this time from the back, wetsuit peeled to the waist to show his impeccable torso. Morton C. was glancing over his shoulder in a pose which was oddly reminiscent of a fifties pinup.

"Very alluring," said Widgett.

"He's not alluring," she said, blinking angrily, humiliated. "He's the guy I told you about who pulled a gun on me. He's a creep."

Widgett's mouth twisted in amusement. "Ooh! A creep? He's the one who works for Monsieur Feramo, we think? And in what capacity do we think? A pimp? A toyboy?"

"Well, it looked as though Feramo had taken him on fairly recently to do diving trips with the wannabes. To be honest, I think he was playing everybody off against everybody else. He was pretending to be one of the divers. He was schmoozing up to everyone in the bar and on the boat. He was just using everyone."

Widgett leaned forward, raised his eyebrows wickedly, and whispered, "Did you have him?"

"No, I did not," hissed Olivia, staring furiously at the screen. The really annoying thing was that Morton C. looked bloody attractive. He had that dangerous, focused expression on his face which had first caught her eye in Honduras.

"Pity. Interesting-looking fellow."

"He's a shallow, double-crossing creep. He's little better than a common prostitute."

There was a slight cough at the back of the room. Professor Widgett studiously inspected his fingernails as a figure rose up from one of the computer booths, a familiar figure in unfamiliar clothes: a hip-looking dark suit, tie and shirt loosened at the collar. The cropped hair was no longer peroxide. Widgett glanced around.

" 'Little better than a common prostitute,' she says."

"Yes, sir," said Morton C.

"What was it she stabbed you with again?" said Widgett.

"Hatpin, sir," said Morton C. dryly, emerging from the booth.

Widgett unraveled himself and rose to his feet. "Ms. Joules, may I present Scott Rich of the CIA, formerly of the Special Boat Service and one of the brightest stars of the Massachusetts Institute of Technology." Widgett was overemphasizing his *t*s and *s*s as if he were Laurence Olivier on stage at the Old Vic. "He's going to be at the helm of our current operation."

"Finest computer genius you could hope to meet," added Dodd.

"Welcome to the operation," said Scott Rich, nodding slightly nervously at Olivia.

"Welcome to the operation?" she said. "How dare you!"

"I'm sorry?"

"Don't look at me in that tone of voice. You heard."

"Sorry about this," said Widgett to the computer tech. "Slightly wobbly moment approaching."

"What were you *doing*?"

"Surveillance," said Morton C. slash Scott Rich of the CIA.

"I know that. I mean, what were you *doing*? If you were work-ing for the CIA, why didn't you tell me?"

"Some might say you should have guessed."

"I thought you were working for Feramo."

"Likewise," said Scott Rich.

"What do you . . . are you suggesting . . . ?"

"Far be it from me . . ." Widgett murmured to the computer tech as if they were in a sewing circle. "But didn't she just call him a common prostitute?"

"If I'd told you, you might have told him."

"If you'd told me, we could have got to the bottom of what he was doing. I would have stayed."

"I agree with her," said Widgett, still in the gossipy voice to the computer tech. "Can't imagine what he was doing pulling her out so quickly. Some misguided notion of chivalry."

"Chivalry? Chivalry?" said Olivia. "You used me from the mo-ment you set eyes on me."

"If I'd really wanted to use you, I'd have made sure you stayed."

"You'd have used me before that if I'd let you, and you know perfectly well what I'm talking about."

"All right, all right," said Widgett, and Olivia heard the au-thority in his voice. The flash of cold detachment in his eyes told her he had given orders for harsh things in his time. "Sort your-selves out, and I'll see the pair of you by the steps on the front lawn. You'll find Wellingtons and Barbours in the boot room."

"I have no idea what you're talking about," said Scott Rich.

"Wet-weather gear, Rich. Can't have you tramping through the woods dressed like a waiter, can we?"

The housekeeper was waiting outside the operations room. Olivia and Scott Rich followed her down the dark, wood-paneled staircase and through to the kitchens, where there were scrubbed wooden tables, warm pipes and baking smells. The boot room was warm too and paneled in white-painted tongue-and-groove, with boots, scarves, socks and coats in neat lines on hooks and racks. It was soothing and comforting, but only up to a point.

"Why did you kill Drew?" hissed Olivia, putting on a pair of thick socks and green wellies.

"What are you talking about?" said Scott Rich, pulling a black sweater over his head. "I didn't kill that coke-crazed hippie. I tried to rescue him. Jesus!"

"Don't pretend it was the shark," she said, wriggling into a woolly jumper.

"If you really want the grisly details: Drew went after Feramo's divers on his own. He got into a fight underwater. Someone pulled a knife. The sharks were coming in. Feramo's people pulled him up onto their boat. I was following at a distance. The next thing I knew, bits of Drew were dropping over the side and every predator this side of Tobago was heading for the scene. And, by the way, your sweater's inside out and back to front."

She looked down uncertainly, then took it off and put it back on.

"It was you who put the cocaine in my bag in Tegucigalpa, wasn't it?" she said, as Scott Rich pushed open the door to let her go outside.

"No," he said.

"Don't lie."

He looked like a country squire. She realized she probably looked like a country squire's wife. The cold air hit her with a shock.

They rounded the corner and the full beauty of the house revealed itself: an Elizabethan manor with tall, square chimneys and mullioned windows, perfectly proportioned in honeyed Cotswold stone.

"I didn't put coke in your room."

"Then who did?" she said. "And what were you doing in that tunnel? You nearly killed me."

"Killed you?" said Scott Rich. Widgett was standing waiting for them on the steps. He saw them and set off to meet them halfway across the lawn, coat and scarf flapping. "I saved your life in that tunnel. I gave you my air. You guys were the idiots who went in without leaving a marker buoy. But look, for what it's worth, I'm sorry."

"So you did plant the coke?"

"No, I'm sorry I didn't take better care of you. I'm sorry I didn't tell you who I was."

"I can take care of myself."

"Oh gawd. You two are not still arguing, are you?" said Widgett as he joined them. "Come on, let's head for the woods. Olivia, when we get back to the house you'll be required to sign the Official Secrets Act. All right?"

"Yes, sir," gabbled Olivia, thrilled. "Absolutely, sir."

"Yeees, I rather thought you'd like secrets," said Widgett. "Everything you hear here stays here, understood? Or you'll be taken to the Tower."

It was a crisp winter day and the air was filled with English countryside smells, principally manure. Olivia followed the two spies along a path through the woodland, breathing in damp wood, rotting fungus, squelching through puddles in her Wellingtons, remembering the joys of being wrapped up warm outside on a cold day. She noticed a camera fastened to a tree, and then another, and then, through the misty woodland, a high-security fence with four layers of barbed wire on top of it and a soldier in camouflage gear behind it.

In the cold, Widgett's face looked even older. The red thread veins stood out through his skin, and there was a circle of bluish tinge, like a bruise, beneath each eye. He almost looked as if he was dead: a walking cadaver.

"There are two key questions," Scott Rich was saying. "One, what are they planning? We're picking up Intelligence chatter which points to—"

"Oh God, Intelligence chatter. I hate that term," said Widgett.

"Intelligence chatter. Intelligence chatter. Retarded intelligence, more like. Men on the ground is what we need. Human beings with human reactions to other human beings."

"We are picking up Intelligence chatter which strongly points to imminent attacks on London and Los Angeles."

"As well as Sydney, New York, Barcelona, Singapore, San Francisco, Bilbao, Bogotá, Bolton, Bognor and anywhere else where people send e-mails," muttered Widgett.

Scott Rich lowered his eyelids slightly. Olivia was starting to learn this would often be the only sign you got that he was rattled. "All right. We've got a real human being here. She's all yours," he said, leaning back against a tree.

Widgett appeared to be ruminating, chewing his lip or maybe his false teeth. He fixed her with his blue eyes. "Two questions. One: What does Feramo have up his sleeve? Divers in sewers, reservoirs—nuclear cooling systems? Two: They're trafficking explosives from the hotel setup in Honduras into southern California. How are they getting them in?"

"Is that what they were doing in Honduras?"

"Yes," said Scott Rich, expressionless.

"How do you know?"

"Because I found C4 at the top of that cave you were on your way out of."

Olivia looked down, frowning, thinking about herself swimming around in the cavern just looking at all the fish and thinking what bright colors they were.

"So . . . Agent Joules," said Widgett. "Any thoughts behind that stunning façade?"

She looked at him sharply. Her mind wasn't working properly. It had all got too important. She wanted to succeed as a spy too much.

"I need to think about it," she said in a small voice. Widgett and Scott Rich looked at each other. She sensed disappointment from the one, and dismissiveness from the other.

"Shall we walk on?" said Widgett.

The two mismatched figures walked ahead, talking seriously, the one precariously tall, trailing scarves, coat flapping, with theatrical gestures, the other powerful, contained, self-possessed. Olivia followed behind miserably. She felt like a fabled musical prodigy who had got onto the stage, made a few feeble squeaking noises on a violin and let everybody down. The stress of the whole bizarre experience started to crowd in on her. She felt exhausted and strung out, girly and useless. *Breathe, breathe, calm, calm, don't panic,* she told herself, trying to remember the Rules for Living.

Never panic. Stop, breathe, think.

Nothing is either as bad or as good as it seems.

When overwhelmed by disaster, think, "Oh, fuck it."

The key to success lies in how you pick yourself up from failure.

Olivia thought back to when she'd last used that Rule for Living: Lighting a cigarette behind the Popayan general store. She thought about Pumpkin Hill, looking down at the concrete dock, the dinner with Feramo, the wannabes around the bar, swimming round the headland to see the divers reappear with surfboards.

"Excuse me!" she said, hurrying to catch up. "Excuse me! I know how they're getting the explosive in!"

"Oh goody," said Widgett. "Do tell."

"They take it by road across Honduras, then up the Pacific Coast by boat."

"Yes, we had managed to get ourselves to that point," said Scott. "The question was how do they get the stuff into the States?"

"I think they transfer it to posh yachts and seal it inside surfboards, either on the yachts or at Feramo's place in Catalina."

Scott Rich and Widgett stopped walking and looked at her.

"Then they take the surfboards close into the California coast on the yacht. They weight and dead-drop them under the ocean either on the bottom or on a line. Then their surfers go down in scuba gear, pick up the boards, dead-drop their tanks, surf into shore at Malibu and drive off with the surfboards full of explosives in their camper vans."

There was total silence.

"Hmm, splendid piece of lateral thinking," said Widgett. "Based on . . . ?"

"I saw them practicing in Honduras. I swam round the headland in Popayan and saw them dead-dropping the boards, then surfing in."

"Wasn't that what you were supposed to be looking for, Rich?" said Widgett. "Or were you too busy getting her Burgundy out of your electronic bug? Puligny-Montrachet, wasn't it?"

"Shut up, please, sir."

"So you put a bug in Feramo's potted fig tree?" said Olivia.

"And his cactus. And your cactus, come to mention it."

"And you put a sweater over one, a glass of Cristal in the other, and a white burgundy in the third. Louis Jadot 'ninety-six, wasn't it?" said Widgett.

" 'Ninety-five," said Olivia.

"Must have hurt, pouring it away."

"It did," said Olivia.

"Karl, hey." Scott was talking into his phone. "Get the H section checking surfers on the SoCal coast, will you? Focus on the Malibu Lagoon break. Check the boards for C4 inside. And get some people onto Catalina—undercover—checking out the boat docks. Where was this place, Olivia? Olivia? Feramo's place on Catalina?"

"Oh, er. It was right of Avalon."

"*Right?*"

"East. North, maybe; you know, right when you're facing Catalina from LA. It's round the corner on the seaward side, towards Hawaii."

"Right, right," said Scott Rich. "Round the corner towards Hawaii." He sighed. "Just check all the landing stages," he said into the phone.

"Jolly good. Well, that's all sorted then," said Widgett. "Now what about the target? Any thoughts?"

She told them about her theories, about the face cream with ricin in, the acetylene bubbles in the cooling pipes of the nuclear power stations, the attacks on the studios.

"But it's too broad," she said. "I need to spend more time with Feramo to narrow it down."

"The perfect thing would be to take him up on this Sudan offer," said Widgett. "It would be fascinating under any circumstances."

"He'd be crazy to bring you out there," said Scott.

"He *is* crazy," said Olivia.

"He's crazy to have let you go," said Scott.

"Thank you," said Olivia, thinking maybe Scott Rich wasn't so bad after all.

"I meant because it was obvious you'd turn him in. As you have."

"He trusts me. He thinks I'm his falcon."

Scott let out an odd noise.

"Is something the matter, Scott, Rich, Morton, or whatever your name is?"

"Yes, Rachel, or Olivia, or Pixie, or whatever the fuck yours is today . . ."

"Oh God in heaven," drawled Widgett, taking out a hand-kerchief and wiping his forehead. "It is rather the form for spooks to assume multiple identities. I mean some of us spent two full seasons as a drag queen at the Aswan Cataract Hotel."

"*Spooks,* yes," said Scott Rich.

"Which is what makes Ms. Joules so interesting," said Widgett. "She's a natural spy. Now the question is, if *Pierre Feramo*"—he said the name with an exaggerated French accent—"telephones you as promised and beckons you to his Bedouin *lair* in the Red Sea hills, would you go?"

"Yup," said Olivia solemnly.

"Would you?" said Scott Rich, fixing her with his intense gray eyes. "Even if his only motive was to kill you?"

"If he wanted to kill me, he would have killed me in Honduras."

"Oh, absolutely," said Widgett. "A fellow could have a lot of perfectly good reasons for wanting to whisk Agent Joules off to the desert. Surely you've read *The Arabian Nights*, Rich? Profoundly erotic book. A girl swept away by a Bedouin could look forward to some most imaginative nights in his tent, I would wager."

"And then what?" said Scott Rich, striding angrily ahead.

44

It was five days since Olivia had left Feramo in the Bay Islands and he hadn't called. The team, which now, unfortunately, seemed to include Suraya the Undercover Bitch, had been holed up in a basement room since breakfast. Through some complex electronic maneuver, Scott Rich had routed the wrong number Olivia gave to Feramo through to the Tech Op Room so that, if Feramo rang, it would come to them direct.

The clock in the Operations Room was of the functional plastic type that Olivia remembered from school: a white face, black numbers and a red second hand. It was 4:00 P.M., 9:00 A.M. in Honduras on the fifth morning since—with a badly sucked finger—she had taken her leave of Feramo.

Scott Rich, Professor Widgett, Olivia, Dodd the tech op and Suraya were all, with varying degrees of subtlety or ostentation, glancing at the clock in turn and—in Olivia's mind—all thinking the same thing: *She's made it up. He wasn't interested in her at all. He's not going to call.*

"Rich, my dear fellow. Are you absolutely sure you got that number wired up properly?" said Widgett, picking at a morsel of foie gras and toast he had had sent up. "You seemed to be pressing an awful lot of buttons."

"Yes," said Scott Rich without looking up from the computer.

"He's not going to call, is he?" said Suraya.

"You should call him, Olivia," said Scott Rich.

"It will put him off," Olivia insisted. "He has to pursue."

"I thought you were his falcon," said Scott Rich, a twinkle in the clever eyes. "Or was it a budgie?"

He turned away and started talking to the technician, both of them focusing intently on the screen. One half showed Olivia's stolen shots of Feramo. The other was a slide show of known al-Qaeda terrorists. From time to time, they would stop and merge the shots to produce Feramo in a turban with a Kalashnikov, Feramo in a checked shirt in a bar in Hamburg, Feramo with a different nose, Feramo in a nightshirt with his hair standing on end.

"Actually, I agree with Scott," said Suraya, putting her long jean-clad legs up on the desk.

"If he doesn't call, then there's no point in my calling him because it means he has lost interest."

"Honestly," laughed Suraya, "this isn't *Blind Date*. You're just being insecure. He really likes you. Pierre prefers a strong woman. She should definitely call him."

Scott Rich leaned forward, elbows on his knees, chin resting on his thumbs, and looked at Widgett with the same intense focus which had first startled Olivia in the bar in Honduras.

"So what do you think?" he said to Widgett.

Widgett scratched the back of his neck and sucked air through his teeth. "There's an old Sudanese saying, 'Wherever man and woman are present, the devil is the third.' The Arab's stereotype image of a woman is almost as an animal: highly sexed and willing to have intercourse with any man, as if that is all they think about."

"Really?" said Scott Rich, leaning back, glancing at Olivia.

"The feeling persists even today in some quarters that a man and woman alone together will inevitably engage in sexual intercourse."

Olivia, distractingly, found herself flashing back to the night on Bell Key: Morton C. kissing her, pressing against her, slipping his hand into her jeans. She caught his eye for a second and had the disconcerting impression that he was thinking about the same thing.

"There was a survey not long ago," Widgett went on. "A group of Sudanese Arabs were asked, 'If you came home and found a strange man in your house, what would you do?' The answer came back almost unanimously: 'Kill him.' "

"Christ," said Scott Rich. "Remind me not to go out there disguised as a plumber."

"Thus the obsession, in some Arab cultures, with chastity—the veils, the burkas, the clitoridectomies. The woman is wholly eroticized: an object to be protected if she is one of your own, and pursued and conquered if she is not."

"Okay, so if in Feramo's eyes Olivia is an insatiable love beast anyway, why can't she just call?" said Scott Rich. "But, wait, how does sex outside marriage work with Islam?"

"Ah! Well! This is where it gets interesting," said Widgett. "Particularly with Feramo and all this Bedouin romanticism—wanting to sweep her onto a horse and gallop off into the desert sunset. The Bedouin ethos predates Islam. It's fundamental to the psyche. If you look at *The Arabian Nights*, you see that that way of thought, Bedouin desert-nomad mentality, overrides morality. When a hero's sexual conquests are the results of his courage, cunning or good luck, they are viewed not as immoral, but heroic."

"Exactly. So he needs to break down my will and overwhelm me," said Olivia. "He's not exactly going to feel heroic if I phone and give him my flight number."

Scott Rich handed her the phone. "Call him."

"Er, so the discussion we've just been having was meaningless?"

"Call him. Don't say anything about flying out there, or falcons. Just tell him you've got back safely and thank him for the fine wines and free hotel suite."

"Hmm," said Widgett, looking at Scott with cold blue eyes and chewing his toast.

"He's not going to call her," said Scott Rich tersely. "He's not going to ask her out to the Sudan, and we don't need her to go out to the Sudan. It's ridiculous. I just need to know where he is. Call him," he said, holding out the phone.

"Of course," said Olivia sweetly. "Do I just dial?"

"No, I'll do it for you," he said gruffly, turning back to the lines of screens and keyboards, giving a quick, disconcerted glance over his shoulder before going off with the tech op into some electronic zone-out, pressing and checking things and exchanging knowing looks. Scott Rich, for all his cool exterior, was a closet grungy techie. She tried to imagine him with a paunch and a big yellow T-shirt with something stupid written on it, drinking real ale with his mates.

He spun round on his chair. "You ready?"

"Sure," she said cheerily, putting the phone to her ear. "Say when!"

Buttons were pressed. The phone started ringing. Olivia felt a rising flutter of panic.

"Hello?" she said, her voice quavering.

"Hi"—a woman's voice—"my name is Berneen Neerkin. I'm calling from MCI Worldcom. We'd like the opportunity to introduce you to our new airtime package . . ."

Telemarketers! Olivia tried to compose her features. The infallible techno-god Scott Rich had got his wires crossed. She felt a giggle-bubble rising up as she caught a glimpse of his face. She tried to think of serious things, like death or getting a really bad haircut, but nothing worked. She started to shake and couldn't remember what position was normal for her own face.

Scott Rich got to his feet. He looked down at her very seriously, like a schoolmaster with a recalcitrant pupil. Noticing Widgett's shoulders shaking too, he shook his head and turned back to the computer.

"I'll just get a glass of water," choked Olivia, beetroot-red, and she staggered out into the corridor, where she leaned against the wall, shaking with laughter, wiping her eyes. As she made her way to the bathroom, the amusingness of the whole thing kept overcoming her. It wasn't until she'd splashed her face with water and stayed there a few minutes that she felt she had exorcised the last of the giggle-bubbles, and even then she didn't feel entirely safe.

As she made her way back along the corridor, she heard raised voices coming from the Tech Op Room.

"Look, we cannot shut down the whole of the state of California. We have C4, we have ricin, we have a possible commercial diving connection. Where does that take us? California is three times as big as your small, dark, benighted land."

"Yes, all right, all right," came Widgett's voice.

"Where do we start? In southern California alone we have major shipping ports in the Bay Area, Ventura, Los Angeles and San Diego. We have four nuclear-power sites and hundreds of miles of wide-bore tunnel water systems, sewage systems and drainage systems under every major city. We have aqueducts, bridges, reservoirs, dams and military bases. What do you propose we do? Evacuate the state? It's a needle in a haystack. Our only chance is to bust this Takfiri cell wide open and find out what they're up to. Now."

"Listen, young man, if you bust the cell, the danger is that the plan or device, whatever and wherever it is, is already in place; they'll know they're rumbled and they'll detonate early. My hunch is that you won't get anything out of them anyway because none of them is party to the whole scheme of things. The only person who might know more is Feramo, and that's why the powers that be got him the hell out of Honduras at the first whiff of trouble. If I were you, I'd get your people on shutting down any nonessential underwater maintenance and repair projects right away, and get your chaps down there to check out employees, commercial diving schools, anything suspicious."

"Have you any idea of the scale of that operation? All we need to do is find Feramo. If we find him, we can see into his freakin' laptop. We don't need Olivia."

"Listen, Rich, if we can work out what the bastards are up to without spending thirty million dollars reducing the whole of eastern Sudan to a pile of smoldering rubble and at the cost of one girl, we should get on with it."

No one heard Olivia slip back into the room

"Sir, she's a civilian. This is not an ethical path."

"She's an agent and she's willing to go. Sharp as a tack, that one. Going to snap her up for the Service when this is over, if . . ."

"If she's still alive?"

Olivia gave a slight cough. Four pairs of eyes turned to stare at her. A split second later the phone rang.

"Jesus! Jesus!" Dodd the tech op started panicking, flapping around, trying to find buttons. "It's him. It's Feramo."

45

Scott crouched beside her, listening through his earphones. He held her gaze, steady, reassuring, just as he had in the underwater tunnel, then cued her to go.

"Hello?"

"Olivia?"

"Yes, it's me," she said. There was frantic activity as Scott Rich and the technician attempted to trace the call. She closed her eyes and swung the chair so she had her back to them. She had to relate to Feramo as she had before, or it wouldn't work.

"Where are you?" she said, to save them the trouble. "Are you still on the island?"

"No, no. I am en route for the Sudan."

Olivia blinked, confused. Why was he telling her this on a mobile? Surely he couldn't be that much of an idiot. The old doubts returned. Maybe he wasn't a terrorist at all.

"Actually I cannot talk for long because my flight is departing soon."

"To Khartoum?"

"No, to Cairo."

"How fantastic. Are you going to look at the pyramids?"

"There will not be time. I will simply visit some business associates and then take a plane to Port Sudan. But, Olivia, you will visit me there, as we agreed?"

The quickening of attention behind her was almost tangible.

"Well, I don't know," she said. "I'd really like to come. I talked to Sally Hawkins, and she was keen, but I really need to get some more commissions to split the—"

"But that does not matter, Olivia. You will come as my guest. I will make the arrangements."

"No, no. You can't do that, I told you. Oh, and thank you so much for your hospitality in Honduras."

"Even though I had to kidnap you to force you to partake of it?"

"Well . . ."

"Olivia, my flight is about to depart. I must go, but I will call you from Cairo. You will be at this number tomorrow at around the same time?"

"Yes."

"But wait. I will give you a number. These are the agents in Germany of my diving operation. They will organize your flights to Port Sudan and visas. You have a pen?"

Four separate writing devices shot out in front of her. She selected Professor Widgett's ancient gold Parker.

"I must go. Good-bye, *saqr.*"

Scott Rich was gesturing at her to keep him talking.

"Hang on. When are you actually arriving in Sudan? I don't want to arrive and find you not there."

"I will be in Port Sudan the day after tomorrow. There is a flight from London on Tuesday via Cairo. You will take it?"

"I'll look into it." Olivia laughed. "You're so dramatic."

"Good-bye, *saqr.*"

The phone clicked off.

She turned to the rest of the group, trying not to smirk.

Scott and the technician were still pressing things. Widgett gave her a fleeting, approving and vaguely lecherous smile.

"Rich?" he roared. "Apologize."

"Sorry," said Scott Rich without looking up. Then he finished what he was doing, spun round on his chair and looked at her seriously.

"Sorry, Olivia."

"Thank you," she said. Then, feeling a rush of warmth and release from tension, she expanded. "I like people who apologize straight like that, instead of that sort of double-talking, passive-aggressive 'I'm sorry that you felt that . . .' fingers-crossed-behind-the-back non-apology which puts the blame on your own inaccurate understanding of the situation."

"Right," said Scott Rich, looking baffled. "What a *saqr*?"

"Falcon, you fool," said Widgett. "Now—and this is number one spook question at all times, Olivia—is he for real? Is *it* for real?"

"I know," said Olivia. "Why would he call from a mobile phone to say he's going to the Sudan if he's for real—I mean a real terrorist?"

"Well, I've always said he isn't," said Suraya. "He's a playboy who dabbles in smuggling, but he's not a terrorist."

"Did you get any further with those photo fits?" Widgett said to Scott.

"No. Nothing. No al-Qaeda fit."

"There is one thing that I didn't say," Olivia ventured hesitantly. The cool gray eyes met hers. "Yes?"

"Yes. It's just—You could check out his mother. I think he might have had a European mother, maybe someone vaguely connected with Hollywood. You know, a Sudanese or Egyptian father and a European mother, and I think she might have died when he was young."

"Why do you say that, Olivia?"

"Well, he mentioned his mother, and it's just—he reacts in an odd way to me sometimes, as though I remind him of someone. And then, when he said good-bye at Roatán, he . . ." She screwed up her face. "He shoved my finger in his mouth and sucked it, but manically, as if it was a teat and he was a piglet."

"Oh Christ," said Scott Rich.

"Anything else?" said Widgett.

"Well, yes. There is just one thing. He's an alcoholic."

"What?"

Four pairs of eyes were staring at her again.

"He's an alcoholic. He doesn't know he is, but he is."

"But he's a Muslim," said Scott Rich.

"He's a Takfiri," said Olivia.

They broke for dinner. As everyone was packing up and leaving, Olivia sat slumped at the table, thinking about the phone call. Widgett sat down opposite her, his mouth slightly twisted. He had an air of permanent disgust with the world which Olivia found refreshing.

"Your integrity—that's the fly in the ointment," he rasped. The blue eyes were cold, like a fish. Suddenly they flashed into life. "That's why you're a good spy," he said, leaning across the table, wrinkling his nose. "People trust you, which means you can betray them."

"I don't feel good," she said.

"Bloody good thing too," he said. "Never feel good. The corruption of the good by the belief in their own infallible goodness is the most bloody dangerous pitfall in the human spectrum. Once you have conquered all your sins, pride is the one which will conquer you. A man starts off deciding he is a good man because he makes good decisions. Next thing, he's convinced that whatever decision he makes must be good because he's a good man. Most of the wars in the world are caused by people who think they have God on their side. Always stick with people who know they are flawed and ridiculous."

46

The clock was ticking now. Suddenly there was high-level involvement on both sides of the Atlantic, and a new air of gravity permeated the operation. Olivia had three days to prepare for her departure. She was being rushed through an intense program of training in tradecraft, weaponry, desert survival and specialist equipment.

They were in what had been the servants' dining room, the full range of Olivia's equipment laid out on a long refectory table. She was inspecting a travel hair dryer, which had been doctored with ampoules containing a nerve agent attached to the front of the heating element.

"What about my real hair dryer?"

Professor Widgett sighed.

"I know you've gone to a lot of trouble, Professor," she said, "but the problem is, what am I going to actually dry my hair with?"

"Hmm. I see what you're saying. Is it conceivable that you might travel with two hair dryers?"

Olivia looked doubtful. "Not really. Couldn't you make the nerve-gas thing be curling tongs? Or maybe a perfume spray?"

There was a snort. She looked up defensively. Scott Rich was leaning against the doorframe, smirking.

"My dear Olivia," said Widgett, ignoring Scott, "we're trying to get the whole female thing right and so on, but this is a desert operation. Surely on such an expedition one would normally manage without a hair dryer?"

"Well, yes, but not if I'm supposed to be seducing the head of an al-Qaeda cell," she explained patiently.

"You're crazy," said Scott, straightening up from his leaning pose and joining the discussion.

"Well, it's all right for you two to say," she said, looking at Widgett's bald pate and the cropped head of the smirking Scott Rich. "Guys like women to look natural."

"Wrong," said Olivia. "They want women to look how they do when they've finished doing their hair and makeup to *look* natural. I really think in this situation the hair dryer is a more important tool than the nerve-agent dispenser."

"Take your point, Olivia. We'll look into some alternative," said Widgett hurriedly. She had the feeling he was being soft with her because he felt guilty about sacrificing her, which was not an encouraging thought.

"Now," said Widgett, "I've got the list of your usual equipment, and we've tried to stick to it as closely as we can." He cleared his throat. "Cosmetics: lip gloss, lip pencil, lip balm, eye shadow, eyeliner pencil, brushes, blusher, concealer, powder: matte, powder"— he paused slightly—" 'illuminating shine,' mascara: 'radiant touch,' eyelash curler."

"Jesus Christ," said Scott.

"It's all in very small containers," said Olivia defensively.

"Yes, though actually that's rather a pity," said Widgett. "We're trying to keep your normal kit externally identical because his people undoubtedly checked it out in the Americas, but we would actually do much better with normal sizes of all these things. Anyway: perfume, body lotion, mousse, shampoo, conditioner."

"They'll have those in the hotel," said Scott Rich.

"Hotel shampoos make your hair go funny. And, anyway, I'm not going to a hotel. I'm going to a bedouin tent."

"Then use asses' milk."

"Mechanical items," Widgett continued. "Survival items, short-wave radio, digital micro-camera, spyglass and the usual clothing: footwear, swimwear and—Rich, no contribution required, thank you so much—underwear."

"And jewelry and accessories," added Olivia anxiously.

"Quite so, quite so. Now," he said, striding to the other side of the room and clicking on a light, "we have prepared a pretty extensive armory based on these items. Actually quite interesting preparing a kit for a female."

"You must have done that before."

"Not in quite these circumstances."

The total inventory was scary. She was really going to have to concentrate not to get things mixed up. Most of her existing stuff had been converted into weapons of . . . if not mass destruction, then short-range, specific destruction. Her ring had been fitted with an evil-looking curved blade which would flick out the second she pressed her thumbnail against one of the diamonds. Her Chloé shades had a spiral saw in one arm and a slim-line dagger tipped with a nerve agent in the other. The buttons on her Dolce shirt had been replaced by miniature circular saws. She had a lip salve which was actually a temporarily blinding flash, and a tiny blusher ball, which, when the fuse was lit, emitted gas which could knock a roomful of men out for five minutes.

"Good. Will I get my old things back afterwards?"

"If this goes as they hope it will," said Scott, "you'll get a super-market sweep in Gucci, Tiffany and Dolce and Gabbana at the expense of Her Majesty's Government."

She beamed.

One of her Tiffany starfish earrings now contained a tiny GPS locating beacon, which would track her movements throughout the expedition.

"Brand new, top of the range, this," said Widgett. "Smallest ever produced. Even works underwater to around ten or fifteen feet."

"What about underground?"

"Unlikely," said Widgett, not meeting her eye.

The other starfish earring contained a cyanide pill.

"And now the gun," said Scott Rich. She stared at them aghast. They had gone over the daggers in the stilettos, the Dolce seventies retro belt made of real gold coins for buying her way out of a mess, the slim dagger and tranquilizer syringe made into bra underwirings. She'd rejected the brooch with the hand-ejected tranquilizer dart on the grounds that anyone under sixty wearing a brooch would immediately look suspicious.

"I'm not going to carry a gun."

They stared at her blankly.

"It will get me into far more trouble than it will save me from. Why would I be carrying a gun if I'm a travel journalist? And, anyway, Feramo knows I don't believe in killing."

Scott Rich and Widgett exchanged glances.

"Let me explain something," said Scott. "This isn't a romantic tryst. It's a highly dangerous, intentionally deadly and extremely expensive military operation."

"No, let *me* explain something," she said, quivering. "I know how dangerous this is and I'm still doing it. If one of your specially trained expert operatives could do what you're sending me to do, you'd be sending them. You need me, like I am. That's how I've got this far with it, by being like I am. So either shut up and let me do it my way, or go and seduce Pierre Feramo yourself in the Sudanese desert."

There was silence. Widgett began to hum a little song. "Pom, pom, pom," he went. "Pom, pom, pom. Any more questions, Rich? Any more penetrating insights? Any more helpful comments? Or shall we get on? Good. Now let's look at how you fire a gun, Olivia, and we'll make a decision about whether to give you one later."

47

Scott Rich stood behind Olivia, his hands over hers around the gun, easing her body into the right position.

"You're going to absorb the recoil through your arms without flinching. And then, *veery* smoothly"—he put her finger on the trigger—"without jerking"—he placed his finger gently on top of hers—"you're going to pull the trigger. Ready?"

The door burst open. It was Dodd.

"Sorry to interrupt, sir." He always looked as if he wanted to kiss Scott Rich's feet.

"That's fine. What's the problem?"

"We've had a repeated caller on Ms. Joules's mobile number, and Professor Widgett thinks she should call back straight away. He doesn't want her reported missing."

Scott gestured at Olivia to take the phone.

"I'll play you the last message. Have to put it on speaker, I'm afraid, Ms. Joules. That okay?"

Olivia nodded. Scott leaned back against the wall, arms folded.

"Olivia, it's Kate again. Where the *fuck* are you? If you've gone haring off to Honduras after your 'little fling' with that ridiculous Dodi al-Fayed–style playboy, I'm going to have your guts for garters. I've called you four *hundred* times. If you don't ring me back by the end of today, I'm going to report you missing."

"I'll call the number for you," said the tech.

"Er . . . okay," said Olivia. "Could you not put it on speaker-phone, please?"

"Sure."

"Kate, hi," she said sheepishly. "It's Olivia."

A barrage of indignation erupted from the earpiece.

"So anyway," said Kate excitedly, when she'd finished venting, "did you shag him?"

"No," said Olivia, glancing at the two men.

"Did you snog?"

Olivia cast her mind back. Did she snog in Honduras? "Yes!" she said. "It was great, only it, er, wasn't him . . ." She tailed off, glancing embarrassedly at Scott.

"What? You followed him all the way to Honduras and then you snogged someone else? You are literally unbelievable."

"Shhh," hissed Olivia. "Look, I really can't talk right now."

"Where are you?"

"I can't . . ."

"Olivia, are you all right? If not, just say 'no,' and I'll contact the police."

"No! I mean, yes, I'm fine."

Scott leaned over and handed her a note.

"Hang on a minute."

The note said:

Tell her you're having an erotic tryst—you're perfectly all right but you're in the middle of things and you'll call her tomorrow. We will pay her a visit to explain.

She looked up at Scott, who raised his eyebrows sexily and nodded encouragement.

"The thing is, I'm having an erotic tryst. I'm perfectly all right but I'm in the middle of things. I'll call you tomorrow and tell all."

"You are the worst. What about Osama bin Feramo?"

"I'll tell you tomorrow."

"Okay. Just as long as you're all right." It seemed to have done the trick. "Sure now?"

"Yes. Love you." Olivia's voice wobbled slightly. At that moment she'd have given a lot to sit down with Kate over a couple of margaritas.

"Love you too, you incorrigible slapper."

Olivia looked down at the note and laughed. Scott had signed it:

Uniquely yours—S. R.

48

Olivia sat by the fire in the snug, looking at a plate of plump truffles dusted with grated chocolate. She knew it was polite to wait, but the pressure was starting to get to her. She reached out and shoved one in her mouth. The daily recorded conversations with Feramo were making her feel like a creep. She had to concentrate on *OceansApart* flashbacks to keep her resolve. She had just stuffed another truffle into her mouth when the door opened and Widgett strode in, followed by Scott Rich.

"Something in your mouth, Agent Joules?" said Scott dryly, sitting down on the sofa and spreading maps out by the tea tray.

"Right," said Widgett. "So we're looking at the Red Sea hills here. Now the area is predominantly Arab, but with six percent of the population Beja. Kipling's 'Fuzzy-Wuzzies.' Wily bunch of nomads, amazing vertical hair. Tremendously fierce and resilient. If you can get them on your side, you'll be all right in a crisis. The ones to watch out for are the Rashaida Bedouin nomads with satellite dishes on their tents and giant SUVs herding the camels. They're smugglers. No one can catch up with them. Hilarious bunch. I always had rather a soft spot for them."

"This is where I think the caves might be," said Olivia, nodding and pointing to the map.

"Ah, Suakin, the ruined coral port. Wonderful place."

"Feramo told me all about it," said Olivia. "I think the al-Qaeda people are hiding there. I think they get into the caves underwater, like in Honduras."

"We're looking into it," said Scott Rich. "Bin Laden was pretty cozy with the Sudanese regime in the mid-nineties."

"I know," said Olivia quietly.

"When the Sudanese finally kicked bin Laden out in 'ninety-six, in theory the camps and cells were kicked out, but the more likely scenario is that they moved underground."

"Or underwater," said Olivia.

"Exactly," said Widgett excitedly. "So your primary goal is to find out specifically what the threat is facing southern California. The secondary goal is to find who Feramo is hiding or visiting."

"But it's still not too late to pull out," said Scott Rich. "It's important you know what you're getting into. We still don't know who Feramo is. But we know what sort of gracious hosts you'll be looking at in general. Port Sudan"—he pointed at the map—"is directly opposite Mecca. Iran has leases on bases in Port Sudan and Suakin. So you've got thousands of Iranian soldiers in training, rebel NDA camps and a tinderbox of hydroelectrics to the north, a separate lot of interests coming in from Eritrea to the south, a bunch of crazy nomads in the mountains, and al-Qaeda, if you will, under the water. Still fancying a romantic mini-break?"

"Well, I thought it was very nice there last time!" said Olivia brightly, to annoy him. "I'm looking forward to it. Especially with all my new accessories."

"Excellent. Have another chocolate," said Widgett.

"Olivia, it's not safe out there," said Scott Rich.

"Safe?" she said, eyes flashing. "When is anything ever safe? Come on, you know how it is. It's like diving off that wall under the ocean."

"Yeah," he said softly, sexily, "I know. Sometimes you just have to throw yourself over the edge, baby, and roll."

49 CAIRO, EGYPT

As the plane approached Cairo, Olivia experienced a bout of eu-phoria: *I wish I could freeze this moment in time and remember it forever. I'm a spy. I'm Agent Joules. I'm on a mission for the British gov-ernment. I'm in Club Class, drinking champagne with microwaved nuts.*

She had to stop herself grinning uncoolly as she strode through passport control. It was great to be on the road again. Away from the school-like atmosphere of the manor, she felt capable and as free as a bird of the nonfalcon variety. The connecting flight to Port Sudan was delayed by six hours. *Hell,* she thought. *I've never seen the pyramids. "Just jump over the edge, baby, and roll."* The GPS wouldn't pick up her earring signal until she reached the Sudan. She cleared Customs and hopped in a cab.

Back at the safe house in the Cotswolds, Scott Rich was about to leave for RAF Brize Norton. He would be taking an RAF flight to the aircraft carrier USS *Condor* anchored in the Red Sea between Port Sudan and Mecca. He was packed and ready and he had an hour. He was alone in the Tech Op Room, working on the com-puter by a single light.

He leaned back from the search, screwing up his eyes and stretching, then leaned forward again and blinked rapidly at the re-sult. As photographs and information began to appear on-screen, he fumbled for the phone in his jacket and dialed Widgett.

"Yes, what is it, man? I'm in the middle of dinner."

Scott Rich's voice was shaky. "Widgett. Feramo is Zaccharias Attaf."

There was a second's pause.

"Oh, God in heaven. Are you *sure*?"

"Yes. We need to get Olivia back from Africa. Now."

"I'll be with you in forty seconds."

Olivia's taxi was on a dual carriageway, weaving alarmingly between the lanes. There was a Christmas decoration hanging from the rearview mirror and a pale blue nylon garland of some kind arranged across the dashboard. The driver turned to look at her, flashing a smile and one gold tooth.

"You hwan carrpeet?"

"I'm sorry?"

"Carrpeet. I geeve you verry good price. My brother have carrrpeet shop. Very close by. No go marrkeeet. In marrrkeet very bad man. My brother carrpeeet verry, verry beautifful."

"No. No carpet. I want to go to the pyramids, like I said. Watch out!" she shouted, as cars started to swerve, horns blaring.

The driver turned back to the road with a curse, making a rude gesture out of the window.

"Pyramids. Giza," said Olivia. "We go to the pyramids, then come back to the airport."

"Pyramid verrry farr. Is no good. Is dark. No see. Better buy carpet."

"What about the Sphinx?"

"Sphinx is okay."

"So we'll go to the Sphinx, yes? And back to the airport?"

"Sphinx is okay. Very old."

"Yes," she said in Arabic. "Old. Good."

He roared off the dual carriageway at a crazy speed, plunging into a darkened residential area of dusty streets and mud houses. She wound down her windows, excitedly breathing in the smells of Africa: rotting rubbish, burnt meat, spices, dung. Eventually, the taxi ground to a halt beyond a labyrinth of unlit streets. The driver cut the engine.

"Where's the Sphinx?" said Olivia, feeling a twinge of alarm, flicking out her hook ring.

The driver grinned. "No farrr," he said, gassing her with his stinking breath. Suddenly, the total idiocy of her behavior hit her. What was she *doing* deciding to sightsee on a mission like this? She took out her mobile phone. It said NO NETWORK.

"Sphinx very beautiful," said the driver. "You come with me. I show."

She looked at him carefully, decided he was telling the truth and climbed out of the taxi. He took out a long object, which seemed to be a cosh. She followed him along the darkened road, feeling extremely dubious. There was sand underneath their feet. She loved the dry scent of the desert air. As they rounded a corner, the driver put a match to the cosh, turning it into a blazing torch. He held it aloft and pointed through the darkness.

Olivia gasped. She was looking at a pair of giant, dust-covered stone paws. It was the Sphinx—no barriers, no ticket counters, just *there,* in the middle of a dusty square, surrounded by low ruined buildings. As her eyes grew accustomed to the dark, the whole familiar shape began to reveal itself, smaller than she had imagined. The driver, raising the blazing torch, encouraged her to climb up onto the paws. She shook her head, thinking that if not actually illegal, it was certainly not right, and settled instead for following him around the perimeter, trying to get a sense of century upon century of oldness.

"Okay," she said, beaming. "Thank you so much. Better get back to the airport now."

It might not have been the most responsible decision, but she was awfully glad she'd come.

"You hwant carrpeet now?"

"No. No carpet. Airport."

They turned the corner to head back to the car, and the driver cursed loudly. Another car was parked beside their taxi, headlights full on. Figures emerged from the darkness, coming towards them. Olivia shrank into the shadows, remembering her kidnapping training: the first moments of the kidnap attempt are key, on your territory, not theirs, when you have the best chance of escape. The men were focusing on the driver. There were raised voices. He appeared to be trying to placate them with an oily smile, talking very fast, heading towards his taxi. Olivia tried to melt away into the shadows. She was a hundred yards from the Sphinx, for God's sake. There had to be some other people somewhere. One of the shadowy figures saw her and grabbed her arm. At the same moment her driver got into his taxi and started the engine.

"Hey, wait!" yelled Olivia, starting to run towards him. *Now, make a noise, make a fuss, raise the alert while you're still in a public space.* "Help," she started to yell. "Heeelp!"

"No, no," said her driver. "You go with him. Verry good man."

"Nooooo!" she yelled, as he slammed the car in gear and moved off. A rough arm restrained her as she tried to run after the car, its taillights disappearing into the labyrinth of streets.

Olivia looked round at her captors. There were three of them, young men in Western clothes. "Please," said one of them, opening the car door. "Farouk must leave for other customer. You come with us. We take you to airport."

As the man took hold of her, she jabbed him with the hook ring, breaking free as he yelled in pain, starting to run, yelling, as she'd been taught, in a way that left no doubt to anyone listening that she was under attack. "Help me, oh God, please help me. Heeeeeeelp!"

It was a wet, windy night in the Cotswolds. On the tarmac at RAF Brize Norton, Scott Rich was yelling into the phone, trying to make himself heard above the roar of the jet engine. "Where the hell is she? I said, where is she?"

"No bloody idea. Flight was delayed by six hours. Suraya's set up

Fletcher in Cairo to watch for her: messages at the desk, et cetera, et cetera."

"Suraya?"

"Yes. Anything wrong with that?"

Scott Rich hesitated. An aide approached, trying to rush him onto the plane. Scott waved him aside and headed into the shelter of the hangar. "I want you to give me your word that you'll order Olivia back."

Widgett gave a strange laugh. "You're asking a spook to give you his word?"

"Zaccharias Attaf is a psychopath. He has killed eight women in exactly these circumstances. He becomes obsessed—as he is with Olivia—and when they fail to live up to whatever his insane fantasy happens to be, he kills them. You've seen the pictures."

"Yes. He has a tendency to suck bits of them off, it would seem. Are you sure it's him? How did you get there?"

"It was what she said about Feramo's mother and the finger-sucking. There are no pictures of Attaf to go on, as you know, but everything else adds up. Pull her off the case. Bring her home. She's not a professional. Where is she now? You can't knowingly send her out to meet a psychopath."

"A psychopath who is also a senior al-Qaeda strategist."

Scott Rich lowered his eyelids. "You seem to view her as completely expendable."

"My dear fellow, Ms. Joules is entirely capable of taking care of herself. We have all risked our necks in our time for the greater good. That," said Widgett, "is the business we are in."

Calm, don't panic, breathe, calm don't panic breathe. Does it really matter? Yes. Oh fuck yes. Olivia tried to keep her head together and think as the kidnappers' car rattled through the blackness of the mazelike streets. They were Feramo's people, that much was clear. She'd failed on the first bit of kidnap training by allowing them to get her into the car. The next thing she'd been taught was to "humanize the relationship with one's captors." *Well, honestly,* she'd thought at the time, *how obvious could you get?* She fumbled in her bag for the pack of Marlboros she'd been given and held them out to the young man who had bundled her into the car. "Cigarette?"

"No. No smoke. Very bad," he said curtly.

"Quite right," she said, nodding fervently. Idiotic. She was idiotic. They were probably devout Muslims. What next? Slug of whisky, Muhammad? Dirty video?

There was a change in the streets outside: more light, figures, a donkey, a bicycle. Suddenly they burst out of the dark streets into a brightly lit souk. There were crowds of people, sheep, strings of fairy lights, music and cafés. The car ground to a halt at the entrance to a dark alleyway. The driver turned round. She clenched her fist, the hook ring outwards, clutching the hatpin in her other hand.

"Carpet," said the new driver. "You buy carpet? I give you good price, special for you."

"Yes," she whispered, slumping back against the seat, eyes closed, shaking with relief. "Very good. I buy carpet."

It was deemed necessary, unfortunately, to buy quite a large carpet. As they roared up the approach to the airport thirty-five minutes before takeoff, the carpet protruded precariously from either side of the car boot. Olivia was so tense she was having to dig her fingernails into her palms in an attempt to stop herself yelling pointless things like, "For God's sake, hurreeeeeeeee."

Then there were flashing lights, sirens, police cars and barricades and a line of red taillights. It was a massive holdup. Her mouth was dry. She had escaped death but, as is the way of things, her relief had immediately been replaced by another worry: missing the plane and therefore screwing up the mission. She felt herself trying to speed up the car by physically leaning forward as they slowed to a snail's pace. There'd been an accident, plainly. A man's body was lying on the tarmac, a pool of dark blood flowing from his mouth, a policeman chalking an outline around it. The driver leaned out of the window and asked what had happened. "Shooting," the driver yelled over his shoulder to Olivia. "Englishman."

She tried not to think about it. As the car pulled up at Departures, she almost threw the agreed fare of fifty dollars at the driver, grabbed her bag, leapt out and charged into the terminal, heading for the desk. Unfortunately, the two youths started to follow her, carrying the carpet.

"I don't want the carpet, thank you," she called over her shoulder. "Take it back with you. You can keep the money." She reached the Sudan Airways desk and flung her passport and ticket down. "My bag is already checked through. I just need a boarding pass."

The youths triumphantly dropped the carpet onto the baggage scales.

"You want to check in this carpet?" said the Sudan Airways attendant. "It is too late. You will have to take this carpet as hand luggage."

"No, I don't want the carpet. Look," said Olivia, turning to the youths, "you can take the carpet. No room on plane. You can keep the money."

"You no like carpet?" The boy looked devastated.

"I love the carpet, but . . . look. All right. Thank you, very nice. Please, just go away."

They didn't go. She handed them each a five-dollar bill. They left.

The airline lady started typing into the computer in the way the ground staff do at airports when you're late for a flight—rather as if writing a contemplative poem, pausing to stare at the screen searching for exactly the right word or phrase.

"Er, excuse me," said Olivia. "It's very important that I don't miss the flight. I don't actually want the carpet. I don't need to check it in."

"You wait here," said the woman, who walked off and disappeared.

Olivia felt like swallowing her own fist. It was ten past nine. The departures screen for the delayed SA245 to Port Sudan said *Dep 21:30. Boarding Gate 4A. Last Call.*

She was on the point of making a run for it and blagging her way through without a boarding pass when the woman returned wearing a sepulchral expression and accompanied by a man in a suit.

"All right, Ms. Joules?" said the man in a slight East London twang. "I'll see you through to the flight. Is this yours?" he asked, picking up the carpet.

Olivia started to protest, then gave up and just nodded her head wearily. The man rushed Olivia and the carpet past the queues and through security, taking her into an office a little way from the gate. He closed the door behind him.

"My name's Brown. I'm from the Embassy here. Professor Widgett wants to speak to you."

Her heart sank. He had found out. She had fallen at the first hurdle. Brown dialed a number and handed her the phone.

"Where the hell have you been?" bellowed Widgett. "Buying carpets?"

"I'm sorry, sir. It was a dreadful mistake."

"Never mind now. Never mind. Forget it. A man who never makes a mistake never makes anything."

"I promise it won't happen again."

"All right. If it makes you feel better, a certain unpredictability of movement is no bad thing. The agent we had lined up to meet you just got himself shot."

Oh my God. Oh my God. "Was that his body I just saw on the way into the airport? Was it my fault? Were they trying to get me?"

A dispatcher in a luminous yellow jacket put his head round the door.

"No, no, nothing to do with you," said Widgett.

"Better ring off," mouthed Brown. "They're about to shut the doors."

"Professor Widgett, the plane's about to leave."

"All right, jolly good. Off you go now," said Widgett. "Don't miss the flight after all this. Good luck and oh, er, with, er, Feramo . . . Probably best to play along with this little fantasy he has about you as long as you can."

"What do you mean?"

"Oh, you know . . . these types that build a girl up, put her on a pedestal, are inclined to turn a bit nasty when the imaginary edifice crumbles. Just, er, keep him where you want him. Keep your wits about you. And, remember, Rich is just a shout away in the Red Sea."

Olivia rushed onto the plane, finding the carpet thrust into her arms as the doors closed. She tried vainly to shove it into the overhead locker under the baleful stare of the stewardess. It was only as the captain turned off the FASTEN SEAT BELT signs and they were leaving the lights of Cairo behind, as she looked down at the vast, empty darkness of the Sahara, that she had time to digest what Widgett had said. She realized that the wiser course might have been not to get onboard the plane at all.

50   PORT SUDAN,
RED SEA COAST,
EASTERN SUDAN

Scott Rich stood on the deck of the CIA dive ship USS *Ardèche* waiting for the lights of Olivia's approaching flight to appear in the night sky. The shoreline of the Sudan, dotted with the flickering red lights of fires in the desert, was a black shape against the darkness of the sky. The sea was utterly calm. There was no moon, but the sky was bursting with stars.

He heard the roar of the jet engine before the lights appeared, as the plane began its descent over Port Sudan. He slipped back belowdeck and flicked switches, the control deck before him humming into life. In a few minutes' time, the GPS would pick up the signal from Olivia's earring. Abdul Obeid, CIA agent, holding a Hilton sign, would pick her up in Arrivals and bring her to the harbor and a waiting launch. Before the first light of dawn, she would be aboard the USS *Ardèche* and out of reach of Feramo.

Scott Rich's face broke into a rare smile as a red light flashed up on the screen. He pressed a switch. "We've got her," he said. "She's at the airport."

As Olivia followed the line of somnambulant passengers into the scruffy Customs hall, she found herself drifting into her usual African-airport, hibernating-tortoise mode. She saw the passport control guys in their brown Formica booths, drowning in bits of paper. It always baffled her how they kept track of anything without computers, but somehow they did. The one time she'd tried to enter Khartoum without the correct visa she had found herself spending twelve hours in custody in the airport. And the next time she had arrived, they somehow remembered and shoved her in the cage again. As she reached the front of the queue and handed over her papers, the man behind the desk stared at them, apparently blankly, and said, "One moment please."

Bugger, she thought, trying to maintain a pleasantly bland expression. There was no more stupid thing you could do than lose your temper with an official in Africa. A few minutes later the man reappeared, accompanied by a stout official in khaki military uniform, the belt squeezed far too tightly around his gut.

"Come with me please, Ms. Joules," said the stout man, flashing white teeth. "Welcome to Sudan. Our honored friends are expecting you."

Good old MI6, she thought, as the portly officer ushered her into a private office.

A man dressed in a white djellaba and turban appeared at the door and introduced himself as Abdul Obeid. She gave him a quiet nod of complicity. It was all going to plan. This was the CIA local agent. He would take her to the Hilton, providing her on the way with a gun (which she had resolved to lose as soon as possible), and give her an up-to-date briefing incorporating any changes of plan. She would call Feramo, take a night to rest at the Hilton and prepare her kit and meet him in the morning. Abdul Obeid escorted her to a car park at the side of the office, where a smart four-wheel drive was waiting, a driver at the open door.

"You heard that Manchester won the Cup?" she said, settling into the backseat as the vehicle roared out of the car park. Abdul was supposed to reply, "Do not speak to me of that because I am a supporter of Arsenal," but he said nothing.

She felt a slight twinge of unease. "Is it far to the hotel?" she said. It was still dark. They were passing corrugated-iron shanties.

There were figures sleeping by the roadside, goats and stray dogs picking at garbage. The Hilton was close to the sea and the port, but they were heading towards the hills.

"Is this the best way to the Hilton?" she ventured.

"No," said Abdul Obeid abruptly, turning to fix her with a terrifying stare. "And now you must be silent."

Eighty miles east, in the Red Sea midway between Port Sudan and Mecca, the full might of the American, British and French Intelligence services and special forces was gathered on the aircraft carrier USS *Condor*, focused on the whereabouts of Zaccharias Attaf and Agent Olivia Joules.

In the control room of the dive ship USS *Ardèche,* Scott Rich was staring, expressionless, at the small red light on his screen. He pressed a button and leaned forward to the microphone.

"*Ardèche* to *Condor*, we have a problem. Agent Obeid has failed to make contact at the airport. Agent Joules is traveling at sixty miles per hour in a southwesterly direction towards the Red Sea hills. We need ground forces to intercept. Repeat: ground forces to intercept."

Olivia calculated that they were about forty miles south of Port Sudan and somewhat inland, following the line of the hills which ran parallel to the sea. They had long ago left the road behind, and she was conscious of rough terrain, land rising sharply to their left and desert scents. She had made several attempts to extract weaponry from her bag until Abdul Obeid had caught her at it and flung the bag into the back. She had weighed up the possible benefits of trying to kill or stun the driver and decided there was little to be gained. Better let them lead her to Feramo, if that was where they were going. Scott Rich would be on her trail.

The vehicle screeched to a halt. Abdul opened the door and pulled her out roughly. The driver took her bag out of the back and threw it to the ground, followed by the carpet, which seemed to have become even more unwieldy and landed with a heavy thud.

"Abdul, why are you doing this?" she said.

"I am not Abdul."

"Then where is Abdul?"

"In the carpet," he said, climbing back into the car with the driver and slamming the door. "Mr. Feramo will meet you here at his convenience."

"Wait," said Olivia, staring horrified at the carpet. "Wait. You're not going to leave me here with a body?"

In response, the vehicle started to reverse, executed a dramatic hand-brake turn and roared off back the way it had come. If she had had a gun, she could have shot out the tires. As it was, she gave in, sank down on her bag and watched the taillights of the four-wheel drive until they disappeared, and the roar of the engine faded into nothing. There was the cry of a hyena, then only the vast ringing silence of the desert. She found herself thinking of Widgett talking about the terrorists' war on the West, and how it was rooted in deserts and history and real and imagined slights which couldn't be eradicated by armies or bluster; and she felt helpless. She glanced at her watch. The local time was 3:30 A.M. Dawn would come within the hour, followed by twelve hours of unforgiving blistering African sun. She had better get busy.

As the first rays of the sun crept over the red rocks behind her, Olivia regarded her handiwork wearily. Abdul was buried under a thin covering of sand. Initially she had placed a cross of sticks at the head because that was what seemed normal on a grave; then she realized that this was a pretty major faux pas in these parts and changed it to a crescent made out of stones. She wasn't sure if that was right either, but at least it was something.

She had carried her belongings a good distance away, trying to escape from the smell and the aura of death. Her sarong was stretched between two boulders to make some shade. The plastic sheet was spread out on the rocky earth below, and on it was a chair made out of her bag and bundled sweatshirt. The embers of a

small fire were burning beside it. Olivia was tending to her water-
collection point: a plastic carrier bag stretched above a hole she'd
dug in the sand, pebbles weighting it in the center. She lifted it,
carefully shaking down the last drops of water, and took out the
survival tin from underneath. There was half an inch of cold water
in the bottom. She drank it slowly, with pride. With the supplies
she had in her bag she could survive here for days. Suddenly she
heard hoofbeats in the distance. She scrambled to her feet and hurried to the shelter, rummaged in the bag and found her spyglass at
the bottom. Looking through it, she saw two horsemen, maybe
three, in colored clothing. Rashaida, not Beja.

   I hope it's Feramo, she thought to herself in denial, turning him
back into a romantic hero, because that was the best shot at mental
comfort she'd got. *I hope he's coming to get me. I hope it's him.*

   She ran a brush through her hair and checked her equipment.
Fearing separation from her kit, she had stashed as much weaponry
as possibly on her person—behind the booster pads in her bra, in
the lining of her hat and the pockets in her shirt and chinos. The
absolute essentials were in the bra—the dagger and tranquilizer syringe acting as underwiring. The flower in the center hid another
tiny circular saw and in the booster pad she had concealed the digital micro-camera, the blusher-ball gas diffuser, a waterproof lighter
and the lip salve, which was actually a flash.

   She ate one muesli bar, slipped another two into her chinos and
checked the contents of her bum bag: Maglite torch, Swiss Army
knife, compass. Hurriedly, she dismantled the water-collecting device, repacked her survival tin and shoved that in the bum bag too,
with the carrier bag.

   As the sound of hooves grew louder, she focused hard on her
training—keep your spirits up by looking on the bright side; keep
your mind alert and the adrenaline pumping by preparing for the
worst—when she heard a single gunshot. She didn't have time to
look, or think, as she flung herself flat on the ground.

51

At a little after 9:00 A.M. the heat was still bearable. The Red Sea was glassily flat, the red rocks of the shore reflecting in the blue water. In the operations room of the USS *Ardèche*, the smell of frying bacon drifted over from the galley. Scott Rich sat slumped over the desk as the sibilant voice of Hackford Litvak, the head of the US military operation, oozed over the system.

"We have had no movement whatsoever within the last four hours. The possibility of finding her alive is rapidly decreasing. What is your view, Rich?"

"Affirmative. In all likelihood she is dead," he said, without moving from his slump.

"Oh, don't be so bloody dramatic." Widgett's camp bellow burst out from the desk. "Dead? It's only nine o'clock in the morning. She's never been an early riser. Probably fast asleep with a Beja."

Scott Rich straightened up, a flicker of life returning to his expression. "This particular GPS is sensitive to an unprecedented degree. It picks up movements during sleep and at certain ranges can detect breathing."

"Oh la-di-da-di-da. You sure the bloody thing isn't broken?"

"Professor Widgett," purred Hackford Litvak, "in November 2001, your British security services berated us for delay in reacting to intelligence that bin Laden was hiding in the southern Afghan mountains."

"Quite right too," said Widgett. "Bloody bunch of idiots. Our lot were ready to go in, but oh no, you had to do it. By the time you'd finished arguing about who was going to do the honors, bin Laden had buggered off."

"Which is why, this time, we want to move in immediately."

"What's that English expression?" said Scott quietly on Widgett's private channel. "Hoist with one's own petard?"

"Oh, do shut up," said Widgett.

"Professor Widgett?" said Hackford Litvak.

"Yes, I heard. This is a completely different scenario. We have an operative on the ground, trusted by the target with whom she has a rendezvous. She is our best chance not only of finding him, but of finding out what he's up to. If you lot go barging in with all guns blazing, in this case I fear, quite literally, we'll get nothing. Hold back. Give her a chance."

"You are suggesting we give a chance to a dead operative?"

"Jesus Christ, Litvak, you sound like a machine."

"What is your view, Rich?" said Litvak.

Scott Rich blinked. It was a long time since he had found himself incapacitated by his emotions. He leaned forward, his hand on the microphone switch and paused for a second, collecting his thoughts. "Sir, I think you should send the Navy Seals into the Suakin caves," he said. "And get undercover operatives into the hills immediately to retrieve the GPS and"—a split-second pause—"the body."

"Oh dear," said Olivia, "I've lost my earring."

Clutching her bare earlobe, she pulled hard on the reins to bring her stallion to a halt and looked down, appalled, at the sand.

The Rashaida behind her slowed his mount, shouting to his companion to stop. "There is problem?" he said, bringing his horse alongside hers.

"I lost my earring," she said, pointing first to one ear, then the other, in helpful illustration.

"Oh," said the tribesman, looking genuinely concerned. "You want I search?"

As the other Rashaida, who was riding ahead of them, pulled up his horse and started to trot back, Olivia and the first Rashaida looked back across the landscape of sand and scrub they had spent the last five hours traversing.

"I don't think we're going to find it," she said.

"No," he said. They continued to stare. "Much money, he cost?"

"Yes." She nodded very hard then frowned. Oh dear. This was very bad. The GPS cost very, very much money. They were not going to be pleased about this. Nor were they going to be able to find her.

She thought for a moment. There was a chance she could turn on the transmitter in the short-wave radio. Her orders were not to waste the battery and to use it only when she was transmitting an important message, but surely this qualified as an important message? Her bag was on the horse of the other Rashaida. The scarier of the two, he was dressed in a red robe and black turban. He was Bad Rashaida Cop. The Good Rashaida Cop, despite his fierce appearance, was turning out to be a sweetie.

"Muhammad!" she shouted. Both men looked up. Unfortunately they were both called Muhammad. "Er, could I get into my bag?" she said, gesturing at the back of Bad Rashaida Cop's horse. "I need to get something."

He stared at her for a moment, flaring his nostrils. "No!" he said, turning his horse back to the path ahead. "We go." He dug in his heels, cracked his whip and shot off, at which the other two horses whinnied excitably and shot off after him.

Olivia's exposure to higher levels of horsemanship had, hitherto, been limited to the occasional two-minute canter during a pony trek. The insides of her thighs were so agonizingly bruised that she didn't see how she could go on. She had tried every conceivable position: standing up, sitting down, sliding back and forth with the horse, sliding up and down with the horse, and had succeeded only in bruising herself from every possible angle so that there was no millimeter left of her legs which didn't hurt. The Muhammads, camel-like, seemed to require neither food nor drink. She had eaten three muesli bars since dawn. Nevertheless, the whole thing still struck her as something of an adventure. When else would she get to gallop through the Sahara alone with two Rashaida, unencumbered by tour guides, jeeps from Abercrombie & Kent, overweight Germans and people trying to sell you gourds and getting you to pay them to do dances?

But then, Bad Cop Rashaida ordered them to stop. He trotted a little distance ahead and vanished behind an outcrop of rocks. When he returned, he ordered Olivia to dismount and blindfolded her with a rough, evil-smelling black cloth.

Back on the USS *Ardèche*, Scott Rich was directing the onshore team towards the GPS. Three separate operatives, dressed as Beja, were approaching on horseback in a pincer movement. The line from Widgett in the UK crackled into life.

"Rich?"

"What?" said Scott Rich, eyelids lowering dangerously.

"Agent Steele, Suraya?"

"Yes?"

"She's working for Feramo."

"The source?"

"A Deniable in Tegucigalpa. He was taken in on another count. The poor half-witted fellow tried to claim diplomatic immunity by saying he was working for us. He told them he'd planted a bag of the white stuff in Joules's room at our behest, then alerted the local police. The consular people got their local guys on the trail and it led straight to Suraya Steele."

"Where is she now?"

"In custody. Debriefing. She spoke to Feramo late last night, it would seem. Maybe it was all for the best, eh?" said Widgett. "They bumped Agent Joules off pretty quickly, it would seem. No time for Feramo to, you know, get—"

Scott brought his fist down on the switch, cutting Widgett off in midflow.

Olivia spent the last stretch of the journey clinging to Good Cop Muhammad on the back of his horse. Once they had left the flat sandy base of the desert floor and turned into the hills, the route had become steep and was pitted with rocks. Olivia, on her own horse but blindfolded, had become a danger to herself and everyone around her. Good Cop Muhammad was being very sweet and gentle, though, encouraging her, telling her that Meester Feramo was waiting to greet her, that all would be good and that there would be treats when she arrived.

Hours later, Olivia was to remember that even at this point, blindfolded and captive, she was idiotically oblivious to the gravity of her situation. Had she been less carried away by adventure, she might have tried to press her advantage with Good Muhammad, squeezing her arms a little more tightly around his waist, leaning in a little closer, playing on the Rashaida's gleeful lust for high-priced goodies by offering him the gold coins from her D&G belt. But she was light-headed from the heat and the jet lag, dehydrated, becoming delirious. Her imagination was full of the welcome ahead: Feramo with a bottle of chilled Cristal and a Bedouin treat prepared for the end of her journey—perhaps a torchlit feast with dancers, fragrant rice and three separate French vintages—in tented surroundings reminiscent of the trendier Marrakech holiday haunts featured in *Condé Nast Traveller*.

When she felt herself pass from sun to shadow, it was with relief. When Good Cop Muhammad dismounted and helped her down, even though her legs would barely straighten or bear her weight and her inner thighs were so bruised they were going to be black, she beamed with pleasure. She heard voices, both male and female.

She smelled musk and felt a woman's hand slip into hers. The hand
was guiding her forward. Olivia felt the brush of soft garments
against her arm. The woman put her hand on the back of her neck,
forcing her to bend it as Olivia caught her head against rock. There
were hands behind her, pressing her forward. She was moving
through a narrow, jagged entrance. She staggered unsteadily ahead,
feeling the ground moving steeply downwards and realizing, even
through the blindfold, that she was in blackness. The air was cool
and damp. It smelled stale and musty. The woman removed her
hand from Olivia's neck. As Olivia stood to her full height, the
woman's light tread retreated. It was only as Olivia heard the groan
and crunch of a heavy object being moved behind her that she realized what was happening.

For once in her life, *stop, breathe, think* was of no use at all. Her
bag was with the Muhammads. As she started to yell and grab at
her blindfold, a hand caught her viciously across the face, flinging
her against the rock. She was trapped underground without food or
water, in the company of a madman.

52

Well, *at least I'm not alone,* she thought, forcing herself to look on the bright side as she lay in the dirt, struggling to get up, checking with her tongue to see if her teeth were still there. She fumbled at the blindfold.

"Leave it!"

Her heart started to beat frantically in her chest, her breath coming in short, ragged bursts. It was Feramo's voice, and yet it didn't sound like Feramo.

"Pierre?" she said, trying to sit up.

"Putain!" came the chilling voice again. *"Salope."* He brought his hand down on her cheek again.

That did it. "Ow!" she said, pulling off her blindfold and blinking furiously in the darkness. "What on earth do you think you're doing? What's the matter with you? How dare you? How would you like it if I hit you?"

She pulled the hatpin out of her chinos and was almost on her feet when there was the crack of a whip and she felt the sting of leather across her arm.

"Stoppit!" she yelled and rushed at the dim figure in the darkness, sinking the hatpin into flesh, grabbing for the whip before retreating a few feet.

Her eyes were becoming accustomed to the dark now. Feramo was crouched before her, clad in the colored robes of the Rashaida. His face was horrible, mouth working and twisted, eyes crazy.

"Are you all right?" Her words came out, quite unexpectedly, with tenderness. Olivia always had a problem, close up, with divorcing herself from the humanity of another person. "What's wrong? You look terrible." She reached out gently and touched his face. She felt him grow calmer as she stroked his cheek. He reached his hand up to hers, took hold of it, moved it towards his mouth and started to suck.

"Er, Pierre," she said, after a few moments, "I think that's enough now. Pierre? Pierre? What do you think you're doing?" She wrenched her finger out of his mouth and began nursing her hand.

His expression changed dangerously. He stood up, towering over her.

"Lie down, lie down flat, on your face. Your hands behind your back."

He tied her hands with rope. There was a beeping sound. "Sit up."

He was sweeping her with a plastic detector stick. He took the hatpin, the belt and the bum bag containing the torch and the survival tin. He grabbed the remaining earring, the one containing the cyanide pill, from her ear, then twisted the hook ring from her hand and tossed it to the ground. He took hold of her blouse and ripped it, so that the circular-saw buttons fell to the ground, rolling in all directions.

"Where is the GPS?" he said.

"What?"

"The GPS. The tracking device. What are your people using to follow you? Do not feign innocence. You have betrayed me."

She shrank back, cowering. How did he know?

"Your mistake, Olivia," he said, "was to believe that all beautiful women are as treacherous and disingenuous as you."

Suraya. It had to be her. Undercover Bitch: undercover double agent.

"And now it is time for you to give us some information."

Feramo dragged Olivia behind him for a long time through a low, narrow tunnel, shining his torch ahead. Whenever she stumbled, he jerked on the rope as if she were a donkey. She tried to detach herself from the situation and observe it. She tried to remember her training at the manor, but instead she saw Suraya instructing her sneeringly in tradecraft—the art of dead-drops, hiding film in lavatory cisterns, swapping briefcases with strangers, giving secret signals by leaving windows half open and displaying vases of flowers. She must have been really enjoying herself. Olivia turned her mind, instead, to the Rules for Living.

Nothing is ever as good or as bad as it seems. Look on the bright side and, if that doesn't work, look on the funny side. She thought back to telling Scott Rich she was Feramo's falcon and imagined his amused reaction if he could see her now—Feramo's mule or tethered goat. She still had a chance. She wasn't dead yet. Feramo was nuts and unstable and therefore things could change. If he wanted to kill her he would have killed her in the cave. Maybe she would kill him first, she thought, as he jerked on her rope again. She had plenty of weaponry in the Wonderbra.

The next moment she hit rock head-on. Feramo cursed and jerked at the rope. The tunnel had turned a sharp corner. There was light and a change in the air. She could smell the sea! As her eyes adjusted to the new light, she saw that the tunnel was widening into a cavern. There was scuba gear neatly stacked on racks and hooks: tanks, wetsuits, BCDs.

On the USS *Ardèche*, Scott Rich was watching the radar, monitoring the approach of a motor launch.

"Rich?" Litvak's pureed tones oozed over the speaker. "I had a message. What's the problem?"

"They've found the GPS twenty miles west of Suakin. Plus a Rashaida acting friendly who says he'll take them to Olivia on horseback for fifty K."

"Fifty K?"

"She's with Feramo. I've authorized it. I'm going in."

"You need to stay on the *Ardèche*. You're commanding the intelligence operation."

"Exactly. I'm commanding the intelligence operation. We need human beings on the ground. I'm going in."

"Knew you'd come round to my point of view eventually," came Widgett's voice.

"Shut up," said Scott Rich. "You're supposed to be asleep."

Feramo had Olivia tethered to him twenty feet underwater with no air. She was reminded of a crocodile which weighs down its prey below the surface and comes back when it's ready to eat it. Feramo was making her breathe from his spare regulator—when he chose to let her. It was crazy, but good. It took all her mental energy to control her breath, to let it out slowly and not hold it. It slowed her into a rhythm and cleared her mind of panic. She allowed herself a moment to take in the extraordinary beauty surrounding her. Feramo was right. It was the best underwater landscape she had ever seen. The water was blue and crystalline, the visibility astonishing. Even this far down the rocks were red, and towards the open sea she saw coral pinnacles rising from the abyss. She caught Feramo watching her and smiled, making her thumb and first finger into an O to show her approval. There was a look of warmth in his eyes. He held out the spare regulator and gave her more air. He gestured to her to keep it, and they swam forward together, sharing air, following the line of the cliffs, for all the world like a couple on a honeymoon trip in the Maldives. *Maybe it'll be all right*, she told herself. *Maybe I can turn him round.*

A massive coral pedestal rock protruded from the shore supported by a low, narrow stalk, eaten away by the current. Feramo gestured to her to descend and swim underneath the rock. It was unnerving: there were only three or four feet between the rock and the seabed. Feramo swam ahead of her, jerking the spare regulator from her grasp, and suddenly stood up on the seabed, the top of his torso apparently melting into the rock. Olivia looked up and stared, wide-eyed. Above her was a square opening and a white room, lit by electric light.

Feramo was lifting himself up into the room. Olivia felt for the bottom with her fins, straightened up and broke the surface, pulling off her mask, shaking back her hair, gasping in the air.

There was an Arab boy dressed in swimming trunks whom she recognized from the Isla Bonita. He took the diving equipment from Feramo, and handed them towels.

"It's unbelievable," she said. "What is this place?"

Feramo flashed his white teeth proudly. "The air pressure is kept at exactly the same level as the water pressure, and therefore the water will never rise above this point. It is perfectly safe."

And easy to escape, she thought, until he led her through a solid-steel sliding door, opened by a punched-in code, and then through another and into a shower room. He left her alone to shower, telling her to change into the white djellaba she would find inside.

He was waiting for her when she emerged. His face was angry again. "And now, Olivia, it is time for me to leave you for a while. My people have some questions for you. I advise you to supply them with whatever information they need without resistance. And then you will be brought to me to say good-bye."

"Good-bye?" she said. "Where am I going?"

"You betrayed my trust, *saqr,*" he said, refusing to meet her eye. "And therefore we must say good-bye."

53

Olivia felt as though she'd been asleep for a long time. Initially, it was a woozy, not-unpleasant feeling, but as she regained consciousness sensation returned. The burnt spots on her hand were agonizing and there was new bruising on her back. She felt as though she had spent a night in a tumble dryer. There was a sack over her head. It smelled of farmyards and barns, incongruously comforting. Her hands were tied, but, hey, she thought, quickly remembering there was a mini circular saw behind the flower on her bra fastener. *I'm going to get out of this,* she told herself. *I'm going to survive.*

She made a few attempts to get at the bra with her teeth, realizing how ludicrous she must look, a white-robed creature with a bag on its head trying to eat its own bosom. She gave up and flopped back against the wall. There were voices not far off and the loud hum of the pressurized air supply. She strained to hear the voices. They were talking in Arabic.

She sucked, pulling the sack hood into her mouth, and started to bite. Before long, she had a small hole. Using her tongue and teeth and then her nose, she slowly made it wider, until she could almost see. There were footsteps. Quietly she flung herself down so she was lying on her face, hiding the hole. The footsteps came into the room, inches from her, and then retreated.

I've got to get into my bra, she thought. *I've got to get into the bra.*

She carried on chewing at the sack, spitting out string and straw. She lowered her head and pushed the hole upwards until it was opposite her eyes. Bingo! She could see! She had to stop herself shouting, "Yessss! Yessssss!"

She was in a passageway, hewn out of rock and lit by fluorescent strips. There were posters on the wall covered in Arabic writing and a Western calendar with, for some reason, a picture of a tractor on it. There was a date circled in red. She heard voices; they were coming from behind a curtain which hung over an archway to her left. Something was digging into her back. She twisted round. A valve protruded from a thin metal pipe running down the cave wall. She looked down inside the robe at her Wonderbra—it was a front fastener, which could be useful.

Very slowly, silently, she shifted herself round to face the valve and ripped at the sack, exposing more of her face. Then she shifted position, pushed the valve against the Wonderbra catch and pressed. Nothing. She tried again, and again, then tried to squeeze her shoulders and boobs together to loosen the pressure and leaned forward again. The Wonderbra sprang undone. It was such a relief not to have all the paraphernalia digging into her from the booster-pad pockets. She eased one cup against the valve to push it upwards and, after only three attempts, she caught the edge of the black lace in her teeth.

Olivia was unbelievably pleased with herself, so pleased she almost allowed herself to grin and drop the bra. She turned around too quickly so that her sandal scraped on the floor. The voices stopped in the next room. She was frozen with one half of a black Wonderbra in her mouth, like a dog holding a newspaper. Heavy footsteps started to move towards her. She shook the sack back over her face and lay down. The footsteps came very close. A foot poked her in the ribs. She shuddered and turned her head slightly, which she thought was a realistic touch. The footsteps retreated. She didn't move until the voices started again.

The Wonderbra cup was inside out, still held in her teeth. Slowly, she pulled it out from her djellaba and, still using her teeth, twisted round to hook it over the valve. It was awfully uncomfortable, but she managed to twist back and push the rope binding her hands against the saw. It was wretched, slow work. There was a horrible moment when the bra came away from the valve, and she had to go through the whole process of hooking it up there again. But, eventually, the little saw cut through enough fibers for her to break her hands free and untie her ankles.

Glancing anxiously towards the curtain, she opened the lip salve she had stashed in her bra. She set the timer to three seconds, replaced the cap and, aiming carefully, rolled it under the gap between the curtain and the floor. Then she curled up, eyes tightly closed, squeezing her face between her knees and her arms. Even so, the flash was almost blinding. There were shouts, screams and crashing noises from behind the curtain.

She leapt to her feet, ran to the curtain and yanked it open. In that split second, she took in an astonishing scene. Twelve men were clutching their eyes, blinded, blundering in panic. There were photographs and diagrams on the walls. Bridges—the Sydney Harbour Bridge, the Golden Gate Bridge, Tower Bridge, another bridge spanning a wide harbor with skyscrapers in the background. There were seven pictures in all. On a table in the center of the room, there was what looked like the bottom of a round plinth facing towards her, and beside it a jagged piece of metal, gold on the outside, hollow inside, like a piece broken off a chocolate Santa. She thought about grabbing it to use as a weapon. Then, behind the table, sitting crosslegged on a carpet, she saw an unmistakable, tall, bearded figure. He was sitting perfectly still, eyes closed, blinded by the flash like everyone else, but totally calm and totally terrifying. It was only a split second's sighting. But she could have sworn it was Osama bin Laden.

She had seconds. She photographed the bridges first—realizing halfway through that the flash wasn't working. Then she tried for a group shot. And then bin Laden. The camera was so tiny you couldn't see what you were doing—you had to guess. And it was hard to see anything after the flash. Could it possibly be him?

The man closest to her reacted to the sound of the shutter and turned towards her. She lit the fuse on the tiny gas ball and rolled it into the center of the room, retreated through the curtain and ran. They would be able to see again in a couple of minutes, but the gas would knock them out for five.

Once she was out of the anteroom and round the corner, she stopped, leaned panting against the wall and listened. The corridor was white-painted rock, stretching as far as she could see in both directions. It was hard to hear above the air-pressure system, but the sound to her left seemed to have a different quality. Was that the sound of the sea or of machinery?

She decided to go for it. As she ran up the slight incline, it began to seem familiar and, yes, there was the shower room and, in the distance, the metal door. As she grew closer, she realized it was wedged open by a body, like a suitcase stuck between elevator doors. It was an injured, semiconscious Feramo. He looked as though he had been trying to escape. She stepped over him, then hesitated. She put her face close to his. His eyes were slightly open. He was breathing with difficulty.

"Help me," he whispered. "*Habitibi,* help."

She pulled the dagger underwiring from her Wonderbra and pointed it at his throat, as she had been taught, straight at the carotid artery.

"The code," she hissed, jabbing him. "Tell me the code for the door."

"Will you take me with you?"

She blinked at him for a moment. "If you're good."

He could barely speak. She couldn't work out what they had done to him. What had he been thinking, bringing her here?

"The code," she said. "Come on, or you die." It sounded silly when she said it.

"Two four six eight." He could barely whisper.

"Two four six eight?" she said indignantly. "Isn't that a bit obvious? Are both doors the same code?"

He shook his head and croaked, "Zero nine eleven."

She rolled her eyes: *Unbelievable.*

"Take me with you, *saqr,* please. Or kill me now. I cannot take the pain and indignity of what they will do."

She thought for a second, reached into her bra and pulled out the tranquilizer syringe which formed the other cup's underwiring.

"It's all right, it's only temporary," she said, seeing Feramo's frightened eyes. She whipped up the djellaba he was wearing and expelled the air from the syringe. "There we go!" she said, matron-like, sinking the needle into his buttock.

Wow, it worked fast. She punched in 2468 and pulled him out from between the doors. Just before they closed, she had a brain wave, whipped off his sandals and shoved them between the doors, leaving a six-inch gap, too narrow to get through but wide enough to let water in. Dragging a prone Feramo behind her with her good arm, she tapped in 0911 at the next set of doors, feeling a great lightness of spirit as they opened to reveal the brightly lit entry room, the scuba gear and the square of seawater. This time she wedged a pair of fins between the doors.

She pulled off her djellaba and hovered for a second on the brink of the Land of Indecision. Should she just plunge into the water as she was, swim to the surface and wing it, or scuba? She reached for the BCD, weight belt and tanks, and put the whole kit together.

She was just stepping into the water when she glanced back at Feramo. He looked pitiful, crumpled and sleeping like a sad little child. She found herself imagining all the bossy men who try to organize the world—the Americans, the British, the Arabs—as fucked-up little kids: the Americans brassy and bullying, wanting to be stars of the baseball pitch; the British from their public schools priggishly determined to be righteous; and the Arabs, frustrated, repressed by their parents, blustering incoherently because there is nothing worse than losing face.

"He'll be more use alive than dead," she told herself, banishing her feelings of tenderness. Listening out for the sound of anyone approaching, she ripped off his robe, pausing for an essential second to admire the sublime, olive-skinned body, checked him for shark-luring cuts and found him clear, weighted and buoyed him, shoved him in a full head mask and rolled him into the water, leaving him bobbing in the square of the entrance. There was a pressure gauge on the wall. She grabbed a tank and rammed it at the gauge, breaking the glass, then took a piece of glass to pierce the pipe. Immediately there was a change in the hum. She looked down at the square of water where Feramo was floating. It was starting unmistakably to rise. Eventually it would hit the lights and short the electrics, and with all that pressurized oxygen it might even blow the place to pieces. And if that didn't happen, the water would rush in and they would all drown.

She lowered herself into the water, letting air out of Feramo's BCD to make him sink, then, taking hold of the tranquilized floating terrorist, she started to swim, heading out from under the pedestal rock, dragging him behind her with her good hand in a gratifying reversal of roles.

I'm quite clever, really, she said to herself.

Unfortunately, it hadn't occurred to her that it would be dark. Diving at night, especially without a light and with a rather flimsy dagger instead of a harpoon, was not a great idea. She didn't want to break the surface too near the shore in case al-Qaeda had scouts. She didn't want to break the surface too far out because of sharks. She didn't want to use up her air in case she needed to go down again.

She swam directly away from the shore at a depth of ten feet for about thirty minutes, then surfaced and settled for letting air out of Feramo's jacket so that he was neutrally buoyant two feet down. Then she pulled her legs in tight and sat on him. If the sharks came to feed, they could eat him first. All she could see was blackness: no lights, no boats. If the sharks stayed away, she could float here safely until dawn, but then what? She deliberated over whether to cut Feramo loose and swim back to shore, or further out to sea. She was so terribly tired. She felt herself beginning to drift off to sleep, when suddenly the force of a massive, living object burst to the surface from beneath her.

54

"There's something down there."

Scott Rich was in the navigator's seat of the Black Hawk watching the heat-seeking monitor. The electronic chatter filling the cockpit was crazy-making, but Rich was entirely composed, leaning forward, focused, intent, listening to simultaneous feeds from the ground forces, four separate air patrols and Hackford Litvak's Navy Seals.

"Sir, the ground patrol have found Agent Joules's clothing at the end of the tunnel. No sign of the agent herself."

"Anything else?" said Scott. "Signs of a struggle?"

"The clothing was torn and bloodstained, sir."

Scott Rich flinched. "And your position now?"

"At the coastline, sir, a ten-foot drop to the Red Sea."

"Anything else you can see there?"

"No. Only scuba equipment, sir."

"Did you say scuba equipment?"

"Yes, sir."

"Then goddammit, get it on and get in the water." He clicked off his microphone and turned to the pilot, pointing at the screen in front of them. "There. You see it? Let's get down there. Now."

Olivia screamed as Feramo burst up out of the water, forcing the dagger out of her grip with one hand, grabbing her round the throat with the other. She brought up her leg and kneed him hard in the balls, wriggling free the second he released her throat, swimming away and thinking fast. He had been under longer than she. He should be out of air—she had a good ten minutes' worth left. She could drop thirty feet and lose him.

She started to descend, pulling on the mask, clearing the regulator as she went down, but Feramo lashed out and caught hold of her wrist. She screamed in agony as he twisted the joint. She felt herself blacking out, drifting into welcome unconsciousness. The air was escaping from her buoyancy jacket, the weights were pulling her down, the regulator was yanked out of her mouth. Then, suddenly, there was an almighty clattering and roaring overhead, and bright lights shone into the water. A figure plunged towards her, silhouetted through the ghostly green water. It took hold of her, releasing the weight belt, and pulled her up towards the light.

"Falcon, indeed," Scott Rich whispered in her ear as they broke the surface, strong hands around her waist. "You look more like a baby frog."

Then suddenly Feramo reared up again like a whale in a BBC special, lunging at them with the flimsy dagger.

"Float for a second, baby," said Scott, as he grabbed Feramo's wrist and knocked him out with a single blow.

Olivia leaned nervously out of the Black Hawk. Scott Rich was still in the water, trying to tie up Feramo, who was slumped in the winch basket, but the rotor wash kept flinging him away.

"Leave him," Olivia yelled over the radio. "Come back up. He's unconscious."

"That's what you thought last time," came Scott's reply.

Olivia gripped the edge of the open hatch, scanning the circle of light on the water for predators.

"Here, ma'am," yelled Dan, the pilot, handing her a pistol. "If you see a shark, shoot it, but try to avoid Special Officer Rich."

"Thanks for the tip," she muttered into the radio.

Suddenly, there was a dull boom back towards the shore and almost immediately a siren started blaring on the instrument panel.

"Jesus! Let's get him up, get him up, up!" yelled Dan as a missile lit up the sky around them.

"Scott!" Olivia yelled, as the sea ahead seemed to explode into a huge fireball, throwing out a blast of air which sent the chopper reeling.

Olivia could hardly breathe, but seconds later Scott's scowling face appeared over the edge of the hatch and the Black Hawk swung upwards, out of reach of the burning sea.

They were heading back to the aircraft carrier. It was steamily hot. Both Scott and Olivia were dripping wet. Neither of them looked at the other. Olivia was wearing only her underwear and a US Navy–issue T-shirt which the pilot had flung at her. She knew that if she leaned her cheek into the warm skin of Scott's neck, or felt his rough, capable hand brush the soft skin of her thigh, she wouldn't be able to control herself.

There was a burst of fire and a series of violent bangs against the airframe. "Hold on, baby," said Scott. "We've taken a hit. Hold on tight." The stricken helicopter shuddered and seemed to stop in its tracks. Then it lurched horrifyingly and plummeted straight down, throwing them onto the floor. There was a loud metallic bang and a jolt. Scott scrambled towards her, grabbing hold of her as the engine screamed and the pilot struggled to bring the aircraft under control. Ahead, Olivia saw dark water rushing towards them, then the lighter color of the sky, and then water again. The pilot was cursing and yelling, "We gotta eject, we gotta eject!" Scott held her tight, pressing her head into his chest, trying to get them back towards a seat, yelling into his radio above the din, "Okay there Dan, hold steady. We're all right, bring her up, we're going to be fine." Then, to Olivia, above the roaring and clattering, "Hold onto me, baby. Whatever happens, just keep holding on as tight as you can."

Yards from the water, suddenly, miraculously, Dan regained

control. They hovered precariously for a few moments, stabilized, then swung upwards again.

"Phew, sorry about that, folks," said Dan.

In the rush of adrenaline and relief, Olivia raised her head to see Scott Rich's gray eyes looking down at her with immense tenderness. For an astonishing second she thought she saw a tear, then he pulled her to him passionately, his mouth searching for hers, gentle hands sliding up beneath the US Navy T-shirt.

"USS *Condor* at five hundred meters ahead, sir," said Dan. "Shall we make the descent?"

"Give her another once around the block, will you?" murmured Scott into the radio.

As Olivia stood on the vast deck of the aircraft carrier, debriefed, showered and fed, taking a last look at the calm water and the star-filled night, Scott Rich appeared through the shadows.

"They found part of Feramo's leg," he said. "The sharks got him."

Olivia said nothing, looking back towards the Suakin shore.

"I'm sorry, baby," he said gruffly, allowing her the confusion of her feelings. After a few moments, he added, "Not as sorry as the administration are, though. And nowhere near as sorry as I am that I didn't get to do the job myself, with my bare hands, or perhaps my teeth, after I'd extracted every last morsel of information from that smooth bastard in the most painful manner possible."

"Scott!" said Olivia. "He was a human being too."

"One day, I'll tell you exactly what sort of human being he was. And what he might have done to you if—"

"Done to me? What do you mean? I wouldn't have let him."

Scott shook his head. "They want you to go back to LA, you know that? They need you to help look into his entourage."

She nodded.

"You going to go or have you had enough?"

"Of course I'm going to go," she said, adding, as if it were an afterthought, "are you?"

A solitary hawk gliding silently over Hollywood—above the Kodak Theater, ringed by cables and TV vans; the blaring horns of Sunset; the pre-Oscar parties thronging the turquoise-lit pools of the Standard, the Mondrian and the Château Marmont—towards the darkness and coyote cries of the hills, might have spotted a single lighted window high on a promontory. Behind the glass wall, a slight, fair-haired girl and a man with close-cropped hair were lying in each other's arms among rumpled sheets, lit by the flicker of firelight and CNN.

"It was deadly, secret and would have brought the whole world to a standstill. Thwarted plans for a devastating al-Qaeda attack were revealed today by the White House," said a newscaster, who looked like a swimsuit model. *"The planned operation, on an unprecedented scale, was uncovered and foiled by the CIA."*

Olivia sat straight up in bed. "It wasn't the CIA. It was me!" she said indignantly.

The shot cut to a White House spokesman pointing at a map with a little stick:

"Plans were well advanced for simultaneous attacks on key bridges in Manhattan, Washington, D.C., San Francisco, London, Sydney, Madrid and Barcelona. As bridges blew and panic spread throughout the major cities of the civilized world, a secondary operation to detonate explosives at key traffic intersections would have come into play."

An excitable academic—captioned HEAD OF TERRORISM STUD-IES, UNIVERSITY OF MARYLAND—replaced the man with the map.

"It had all the hallmarks of the al-Qaeda high command: simplicity of concept and audacious left-of-field thought. Within minutes of the news hitting the international media, panic would have spread, causing motorists in already traffic-choked cities to abandon their cars and flee the roadways, generating gridlock on an unprecedented global scale: a gridlock made up of abandoned vehicles which would have proved a logistical near-impossibility to clear."

Up popped the president.

"Hour by hour, minute by minute, the men and women of our Intelligence services, step by step, are winning the war on terror. Make no mistake . . ."

He paused with that odd look in his eye, which struck Olivia as that of a nervous stand-up pausing for a laugh.

". . . the forces of evil who are conspiring in their holes against the mighty civilized world will not prevail."

"Oh, shut *up!*" Olivia yelled at the screen.

"Hey, baby, relax," said Scott. "They all know it was you. But if they put your picture up on the news, there'd be an Olivia Joules jihad. And where would that leave us?"

"It's not that. It's that every time he says 'civilized world,' he converts another five thousand to the anti-arrogance jihad. It's just downright dangerous. If—"

"I know, baby, I *know.* If only they'd listen to you. If only there were more women in charge in the Western and Arab nations then none of this would have happened, and the world would live in peace, joy and freedom. You should have taken bin Laden out in that cave. Then you could have launched your own presidential campaign with the twenty-five million."

"I know you don't believe me," said Olivia darkly, "but Osama bin Laden was in that cave. Once they get the water out of the camera, you'll see."

"You will get something, you know, for Feramo and the other guys. You won't get the full whack because you were an agent. But

I think you'll be able to buy as many insanely uncomfortable pairs of shoes as you like."

She pulled the sheet around her and stared intently at the glittering Lurex blanket of the city below. "Scott?"

"What is it, my falcon, my desert frog?"

"Shut up. I still think they're going to do something else. I think they're going to do something in LA. Soon."

"I know you do, but you're not going to figure it out by staring strangely into the abyss. You need to sleep. Why don't you rest your head right here and we'll get back on the case tomorrow?"

"But . . . ," she began, as he pulled her into the strong, manly muscles of his chest. *I don't need men . . .* she told herself, feeling his strong arm drawing her closer, feeling warm and safe. *Oh fuck it,* she decided, as he rolled on top of her and started to kiss her again.

The safe-house Operations Room was a chaos of computers, wires, communications systems and men in shirtsleeves trying to look world-wearily cool. In the middle of it all Olivia Joules sat motionless, staring intently at her widescreen computer. Kimberley, Michael Monteroso, Melissa the PR, Carol the voice coach, Travis Brancato the out-of-work actor slash writer, Nicholas Kronkheit the unqualified director, Winston the divine black diving instructor, and as many of Feramo's wannabe entourage as could be located had been rounded up and taken to a local CIA interrogation center, where they were all still in custody. Olivia had spent the last few hours going through the videotaped interrogations, cutting and pasting and scribbling notes. Sensing herself on the brink of a breakthrough, she paused, mind whirring.

"So I got the final take on Suraya."

Dammit. She looked up with an irritation which was overtaken by lust. Scott Rich was leaning against the doorframe, tie loosened, shirt collar undone. She felt like sliding up to him and removing the whole ensemble.

"What?" she said, catching his eye and looking away quickly.

They were at that thrilling stage of early shagging when nobody else knows about it. Of course, it was hard to be sure in a CIA safe house, but then they *were* both established masters of subterfuge.

"Suraya Steele has been working for al-Qaeda for ten years."

"No!" said Olivia. "Ten *years?*"

"Al-Qaeda enlisted her when she was nineteen. She was hanging out in Paris trying to find modeling work and/or rich men. We don't know exactly who the contact was, but it was someone pretty high up. They gave her a lot of money, I mean a *lot* of money, up front."

"That explains the Gucci and the Prada."

"What? She was studying drama and media studies at Lampeter University. The deal was that she would switch her course to Arabic, then try to get into the Foreign Office with a view to MI6. It sounds like naïve bullshit, but evidently it worked. It's sure put the wind up your security services, I can tell you. Every female operative under the age of seventy-five is going to be spending the next three months in intensive interrogation."

"My God. Heads must be rolling. How could they not have spotted it?"

"Al-Qaeda are smart—no electronic communication, just whispers, winks, dead-drops, pen and paper—old-fashioned direct contact as advocated by Widgett."

"How's he taking it?"

"He's fine. He was in retirement for most of her operational time. They rumbled her within months of him coming back on side."

"So she was on a winner either way?"

"If she pulled off something big for al-Qaeda she'd get a new identity and a multimillion-dollar fortune. If she pulled one of them in for MI6, she'd be fêted and promoted. All the agencies were crying out for Arabic speakers. Once she was inside MI6 the cell kept feeding her enough to make her look like an ace spy. They set her up with enough inside info to swing her the Feramo case."

"Did Feramo know she was working for al-Qaeda?"

"Sure. That's why he hated her."

"He *did*?"

"They put her onto him because they were afraid he was a loose cannon. She was watching him for her superiors and watching him for his superiors."

"So it was Suraya who bugged my room."

"I told you it wasn't me."

"No wonder she hated my guts."

"Well, aside from the way you look."

"That's not why girls hate each other."

"And the fact that Feramo was hotter for you than her. If you had rumbled Feramo to MI6, it would have made her look incompetent. If you had got too close, Feramo might have rumbled her to you. Once you'd actually blown the whole thing for her by hooking up with Widgett, she couldn't wait to get you out to the Sudan, grass on you and have them bump you off."

"What will happen to her now?" said Olivia. "*Please* don't tell me she'll be sentenced to fifty years in prison in a badly cut orange jumpsuit with all her hair cut off?"

"Probably a number of hundred-and-fifty-year sentences to run concurrently, if she's lucky and doesn't get shipped off to sample some Cuban cigars. Oh, and by the way, your friend Kate said hello."

"Kate? Who's spoken to her?"

"Widgett did. He filled her in. She said to tell you she was very impressed and she wanted to know who the other one was."

Olivia grinned. Kate meant the other snoggee.

"Excuse me, sir." A slight, neatly dressed man was hovering in the doorway. Scott Rich was treated with near reverence in US Intelligence circles.

"Mr. Miller has requested that you see him in the lab immediately, sir, with Agent Joules."

Olivia jumped to her feet. "They must have got the photos out," she said. "Come on!"

She steamed along the corridor towards the lab, with Scott following, saying, "Okay, baby. You gotta calm down here. Must be cool at all times."

Olivia burst into the lab, to find it filled with solemn faces. Every senior agency member in the area was gathered to see the proof that bin Laden had been in the Suakin caves. The bodies of several senior al-Qaeda operatives had been recovered from the collapsed and waterlogged cave network. But not bin Laden.

"Well done for getting them out of the wet camera," said Olivia. "Whoever did it."

A small girl at the back with curly red hair broke into a grin. "It was me," she said.

"Thanks and everything," said Olivia. "Really clever."

"Okay, so shall we take a look?" said Scott Rich. "May I?" He slid into the chair in front of the computer. The technician respectfully pointed out a couple of links, and Scott brought up the first photo.

"Okay, what have we here?" It was entirely gray. "Close-up of part of a whale?" murmured Scott.

"I hadn't got the flash working yet."

He flicked to the next shot. Half of it was burnt-out white, but you could make out the photograph and diagram of Sydney Harbour Bridge. Olivia tried to remember the sequence of events in the cave. She'd photographed the pictures and then attempted a nice group shot. Then she'd gone for bin Laden, then lit the fuse on the gas and bolted.

The CIA honchos crowded around the group shot. It was very hard to make anything out. All you could really see through the gloom were beards and turbans.

Scott glanced towards her. "They'll be able to work on it," he said encouragingly. "They'll enhance it. Did you take a close-up of bin Laden?"

"Yes," she said. "I'm pretty sure it's the next one."

The chatter ceased. All eyes were on the screen. Olivia dug her fingernails into her palms. She had been sure, amidst the confusion and terror in the cave, that she was looking at bin Laden. It was the demeanor: the sense of latent malevolent power, the intensity behind the languid calm. But then, she remembered Kate laughing at her about Osama bin Feramo on the FBI's Most Languid List, and thought she'd better keep her mouth shut.

Scott Rich leaned forward. She forced herself to breathe, watching Scott's weatherworn hand reach for the mouse and click. At first the image was hard to make out. Then it became clear. It was grubby white fabric, stretched across a pair of knees.

"Right," said Scott Rich. "It appears we have a shot of bin Laden's crotch."

56

Olivia was back on the computer within minutes, working off her fury and embarrassment, plowing through the snatches of interviews she had bookmarked and the sections of transcript she had cut and pasted together. Then suddenly it was as if the sheer energy of her rage burst through the clouds of overinformation and false leads like a shaft of light.

She leaned round the corner of the desk. "Scott," she hissed, "come over here."

"It's the Oscars," she said, as he leaned on the desk beside her, so close that she almost put her hand on his thigh out of lust and newly acquired habit.

"I know it's the Oscars. Do you want to watch the show?"

"No, I mean they're going to *hit* the Oscars. That was what Feramo was planning; that's why he lured the wannabes. He hated Hollywood. It's the essence of everything his people despise about the West. The entertainment industry is predominantly Jewish-run. The Oscars is the—"

Scott rubbed his hand wearily across his forehead. "I know, baby, but we've been through this," he said softly. "The Oscars would be the most incredible, obvious, fabulous symbolic target for al-Qaeda. Which means—with the possible exception of the White House or George W. Bush himself—the ceremony is also the best defended and most impossible to hit of all the potential targets in the Western world at this moment in time. The whole area from the sewers below to the airspace above is cleared and monitored. The full might of the FBI, the CIA, the LAPD and every high- and low-tech surveillance device on the planet and above is focused on the Kodak Theater. Any of those people will tell you: al-Qaeda are not going to hit the Academy Awards today."

"Listen to this," said Olivia, clicking on the screen. "Michael Monteroso—you remember? The facial technician? He was backstage at the Oscars last year, performing his insane one-minute microdermabrasic nonsurgical facial lifts to buff up the presenters before they went on. He would have been doing it again this year if he wasn't in custody. Melissa from Century PR worked on the PR team for the Academy Awards production office for three years before moving to Century. Nicholas Kronkheit, you remember? The director with no experience on *Boundaries of Arizona?*"

"Sure, but—"

"His father has been on the board of the Academy for twenty years."

"These kids are trying to make it in Hollywood. Of course they're going to have—or try to have—some connection with the Academy."

"Feramo had tapes of the Academy Awards at the lodge in Honduras."

Scott Rich stopped talking. The sudden seriousness of his reaction made fear flutter up in her stomach.

"Can we warn them?" she said. "Can we stop the show?"

"No. We don't get to stop the Academy Awards on a hunch from an operative. Go on. How do all these fit together?"

"They don't. That's the point. That's the mistake we've been making. I think Feramo was targeting the Oscars, but didn't have a plan. All these wannabes had a connection, and he was using them to find out how it works."

He watched her with that familiar expression she loved, leaning forward, hands clasped against his mouth, focused, intent.

"Kimberley, you remember Kimberley?" she said.

"Oh. My. God. Oh *yeah*."

"Shut up. Her father has done the follow spot at the Oscars for twenty-five years. If she wasn't in custody, this would have been her seventh year as a seat-filler."

"Seat-fillers? Those are the guys who sit in when the stars go to the bathroom?"

She nodded. He looked at her carefully for a moment, then picked up the phone. "Scott Rich here, this is urgent. Get me a complete list of the seat-fillers at the Academy Awards this year . . . I mean *urgent* urgent. Plus a list of all backstage passes issued this year."

"Can we get in there?" she said, glancing at her watch and looking anxiously out of the big plate-glass window at the city below.

"Honey," said Scott, "the way the chiefs of staff feel about you at this moment, you could take the Best Actress award if you asked for it. What time does it start?"

"Half an hour ago."

57

Los Angeles had been gearing up for the Academy Awards like London gears up for Christmas, although with rather less drunkenness. The windows of Neiman's, Saks and Barney's were dressed with evening gowns and Oscar statuettes. The front lawns of *le tout* Beverly Hills were covered with marquees. Publicists, agents, party planners, stylists, florists, caterers, facialists, trainers, hair and makeup artists, valet-parking organizers—all were in various stages of meltdown. Bitter phone calls had been exchanged over whether Gwyneth or Nicole had first call on the Valentino with the boxy pleats. In the Hermitage Hotel on Burton Way, the suites on two entire floors were converted into designer showrooms where any actress with the flimsiest claim to a red-carpet snap could wander in and help herself. The office in charge of the *Vanity Fair* post-Oscar party was in crisis, deluged by angry calls from agents and publicists. Charts on the walls showed a fluctuating schedule of what time each guest was allowed to arrive—the B list arriving just before midnight, the C list arriving before dawn next morning.

The Oscar race had been the traditional interstudio contest of marketing budgets, newspaper ads, screenings, lunches and media bombardment. The lead contenders had emerged as follows:

1. *Insider Trade!*, a musical set on Wall Street during the boom of the 1980s, in which the heroine, a commodity trader who longs to be a dancer, spends most of the action asleep at her desk,

dreaming about dancing with other commodity traders, the said
dreams being shared on cue with the breathless movie-goers.

2. The story of Moses, starring Russell Crowe in a big white beard
   and a nightie.
3. A Tim Burton movie called *Jack Tar Bush Land* about mini-
   humans whose bodies are on top of their heads and who live
   underground in woodland areas.
4. *Existential Despair*, in which five different characters confront
   their own mortality during the period of one lunch hour in an
   upscale retailer.
5. *East Meets West*, a comedy-drama with a message, featuring Anthony Hopkins as Chairman Mao, who, through an ancient
   curse, switches bodies with a young Los Angeles student during
   the Cultural Revolution.

Some of the other notable contenders included:

— A film about the early Amish, which nobody had seen but was a
  cert for cinematography because the director of photography
  had just died.
— An adaptation of a book about Oscar Wilde, which was in the
  running for special effects for the scene in which Oscar Wilde
  bursts in his Paris hotel room, although that bit wasn't actually in
  the book, and the author was furious about it.
— Kevin Costner's comeback playing a man having a midlife crisis
  who, over a period of three and a half hours, lumbers towards
  the realization that he actually really loves his wife.

The atmosphere in the Kodak Theater moved from brittle nervous-
ness at the start to restlessness as the minor awards went on and on,
and too many wives, lawyers and agents were thanked. By the time
Scott and Olivia arrived at the theater, the show had been under
way for nearly two hours. The stars were returning from the bar,

the seat-fillers were being replaced by the real celebrities and tension was mounting for the big ones.

Scott and Olivia slipped quietly into the auditorium, standing in the shadows of a door stage-right, a few feet from the podium. Olivia tried to keep her composure in the face of such a spectacle. The whole of the entertainment industry's elite was before them: actors, directors, producers, writers, agents, executives were all gathered under one roof in a glittering display of self-congratulation. The front rows were filled with some of the most beautiful, recognizable faces on the planet.

As Olivia scanned the audience, Scott Rich watched her without seeming to watch, as only a secret agent can. Her face was silhouetted in the red light and had that familiar look of earnest determination. The long, shimmering dress that had been hurriedly provided clung to her form in a way which made him ache. She was wearing an insane auburn wig which made even Scott Rich want to smile. Her hands were clenched tightly around a smart leather clutch bag which, he happened to know, contained the following:

— CIA ID
— chloroform pad
— syringe containing nerve relaxant
— syringe containing instant sedative
— stun gas pellet
— mini-spyglass
— tiny cellphone
— and, of course, a hatpin

What Scott didn't know, because he was a man, and a man whose skills lay more in his powers of logical deduction and technical brilliance than in his intuition, was that Olivia was almost overwhelmed by fear. She was more scared than she had ever been in Honduras, Cairo or the Sudan. She had the awful feeling that there was about to be a catastrophe over which she had no control. She was here, at the epicenter of where it was going to happen, and she didn't know what it was, where it would come from or how to stop it.

She checked the faces in the auditorium, row by row. If she saw one face—one actress, one girlfriend, one security guard, one seat-filler, one usher—she recognized from Feramo's crew, she would know. She would have them arrested and interrogated while there was still time.

Helena Bonham Carter was taking the microphone. "There are those who have argued that the nomination for Best Supporting Actor in *Moses* should have gone to the burning bush," she began. There was a roar of laughter. The audience was excited, ready to laugh. Shots of the five supporting-actor nominees appeared on-screen in various poses of ferocious staring, weak smiles or studied nonchalance. The shot cut to one of them dangling from a heli-copter above a choppy ocean, swinging to and fro, waving his legs wildly.

"If he carries on wriggling like that, the chopper'll be in the water," muttered Scott. Olivia had a flashback to her rescue from the Red Sea: the noise of the Black Hawk above the surface, the lights turning the water green, Scott's silhouette plunging towards her, kicking Feramo away, grabbing her, hauling her up to the sur-face and the unexpected warmth of the tropical night, then him knocking Feramo out and winching her to safety.

As the tearful actor ran up the stairs, putting his hands to his heart then out to the audience, Olivia wanted to point at Scott Rich and shout, "It should have been him, not you! He does it for real!" Then she imagined Scott attempting a sobbingly grateful "without whom none of this would have been possible" speech, and Widgett arriving for his lifetime-achievement-in-heroic-deeds-of-espionage award, posing for the camera, arms and scarves flap-ping everywhere, and she wanted to burst out laughing.

The tearful actor held the Oscar above his head in a triumphant salute, and she saw the bottom of the plinth with the gold shape behind it, and suddenly nothing was funny about the situation any more because she knew exactly where she had seen the same image from the same angle before. It was in the al-Qaeda cave beneath Suakin: the plinth lying on its side, the jagged layers of gold-plated metal behind it, hollowed out like a chocolate Santa or Easter bunny.

"Scott," she said, grabbing his arm, "it's the Oscars."

"Er, I know," he said, looking bemused.

"No," she hissed. "The statuettes. They've doctored the Oscars. The Oscars are the bombs."

Scott Rich neither changed his expression nor took his eyes off the audience. He simply drew Olivia into the shadows of the doorway and whispered, "How do you know? Tell me quietly."

"It was in the cave. They had an Oscar cut in half, hollow in the middle."

"You're sure?"

"Well, it was kind of hard to see, but . . . I'm pretty sure. And in Catalina he showed me an Oscar he'd bought off eBay."

"Oh Jesus," said Scott, scanning the audience, where the gold statuettes were scattered, cradled lovingly in the arms of the winners. "How many are out there already? Fifteen? Twenty?"

He pushed Olivia through the door ahead of him and started walking fast along the corridor, taking his cellphone out, thinking aloud as Olivia tried to keep up.

"It has to be C4. It's the only explosive that's stable enough. A pound of C4 in each one and a timer sealed inside some sort of metal alloy. They must have switched the load at some point. They probably wouldn't even run the dogs over the statuettes. Even if they did, depending on when they put the stuff in there, they might not have picked it up. Hello? Is that central control? Scott Rich, CIA. Give me the head of law enforcement. This is very urgent."

With Olivia following, he headed out of the building, walking fast, the wrong way down the red carpet, flashing his ID. "Hello?"

he said. "Tom. Scott Rich here. We have a tip-off. This is a secure line, right? Okay, get this: the Oscars have been doctored. They're devices. IEDs. They're bombs." There was a second's pause on the other end. Then Olivia heard the voice begin again. "I know. We have the agent here," Scott said. "She remembers seeing a doctored statuette in the al-Qaeda hideout in Sudan. What? Yes, I know, I know. But what do we do?"

As they hurried along, Olivia's mind was working very fast. She suddenly interrupted him. "Who're you talking to?" she whispered. "Ask him the name of the company that transports the Oscars."

A few seconds later the reply came back.

"Carrysure."

"Carrysure! That was the company Travis Brancato worked for! You remember? The flaky actor slash writer slash lifestyle manager with the wolf eyes? The one who wrote the script? He was a driver for them when he wasn't writing."

Scott blinked at her for a moment, holding the phone away from his ear. "Okay, Olivia, call the office," he said. "Tell them what you know and get them onto him in the interrogations unit." Then back into the phone, "Tom, okay, this lead is firming up. We need to move. Yeah, we're heading out towards you now. I can see the van, we'll be with you in two minutes."

"Shouldn't they just stop the show and get everyone out?" Olivia said, glancing at her watch as she waited to be connected: twenty-eight minutes to go until the end of the scheduled broadcast.

Scott shook his head and scowled, still talking. Olivia's connection came through, and she filled them in and told them to get onto the interrogation center and grill Travis Brancato, adding a few helpful hints on how to get him to talk.

They were approaching the big white van of the Command Post. Scott clicked off his cell and looked at Olivia. "Okay, baby," he said tenderly. "You've done your bit ten times over. You want to get out of here and go home?"

"No."

"Good," he grinned. "So let's get back in there," he said, nodding at the auditorium. "If the statuettes are on timers, you can bet there'll be a very nervous al-Qaeda operative in the auditorium with a device which can override the timers and detonate the bombs. It's probably a cellphone or a very, very big watch. If he sees any attempt to stop the show, get the Oscars out or evacuate the theater, his orders will probably be to blow the lot there and then, including himself. Just carry on looking for anyone you recognize from Feramo's entourage or anyone behaving suspiciously. They're going to be sweating, probably high on something, certainly very scared, like 'Shit-I'm-about-to-die' very scared. Should stand out among a bunch of actors playing gracious in defeat."

He looked at his watch. "If they're thinking big, they'll blow it in Best Picture, just before the end. We have maybe twenty-five minutes."

Inside the theater, Olivia was silently repeating her mantra: *Don't panic, stop, breathe, think; don't panic, stop, breathe, think,* in a breathless, panicky fashion. She walked down the side of the auditorium, scanning the rows one by one, praying to whatever divine force was up there: *Please, please, whatever you are . . . just help me out one more time, then I won't ask you again, I promise.* She was conscious of a subtle increase in the security presence, people slipping through side doors, taking positions against the walls. Here and there among the audience, she could see the glint of the golden awards, each a ticking time bomb, cradled against a sequined bosom or passed admiringly from one celebrity to another.

Anthony Minghella was opening the envelope for Best Director.

"And the winner is, Tim Burton for *Jack Tar Bush Land.*"

Olivia spotted Burton as he rose to his feet, fringe flopping over his thick blue-tinted glasses as he made his way along the row. She headed swiftly down the aisle towards him, ignoring the odd glances, threw her arms round him as if she'd been his agent for fifteen years, flashed her ID and whispered: "CIA. Major problem. Please keep talking as long as you can."

He caught her eye, saw how scared she was and nodded. "Thanks," she whispered. "Make it a long list."

A shudder went through the crowds on Hollywood Boulevard as the white SUVs of the LAPD bomb squad raced the two blocks between the Command Post and the theater. The Oscars still remaining backstage were being replaced. Guest lists, staff lists and plus-one lists were being scrutinized for clues. Officers were poised to remove the Oscars from the winners in the audience as discreetly as possible, as soon as the word came. But inside the Command Post there was silent pandemonium as the heads of the LAPD, the Fire Service, the FBI, the security firms and Scott Rich debated an impossible series of incalculable risks and decisions.

An attempt, however low-key, to extricate the Oscars from the clutches of their recipients might trigger an operative to detonate them. Stopping the ceremony might do the same. And, in any case, evacuating an audience of three and a half thousand could take the best part of an hour. To send the full might of the emergency services hurtling to the scene would generate equal panic, a panic which would surely, inevitably, seep into the auditorium, into the consciousness of whoever it was who had his finger on that override button. Someone suggested gas.

"Yeah, that went great in Moscow," murmured Scott.

"We'd have three dozen of the world's most famous celebrities choking on their tongues," said the man from the FBI.

And so the ceremony was proceeding. With twenty minutes to go, there were eighteen metal bombs spread around the auditorium, which could blow the Academy Awards sky-high with the whole world watching. But as far as anyone knew, it could all just be a figment of Olivia Joules's overactive imagination.

Onstage, Tim Burton was giving the performance of a lifetime. "What can you say about an assistant cinematographer who also makes a great pot of chamomile tea, and I don't mean with tea bags . . ."

At the CIA special interrogations unit, Travis Brancato's formerly stunning ice-blue, wolflike eyes were more like those of a drunk who has been on a four-day bender. His hair was wild, his chin against his chest. The interrogator's hand was poised to strike again, but he was getting nowhere. A woman appeared in the room and handed him a note—it was Olivia's suggestion for getting Travis to talk. The interrogator paused to read it, then leaned over to Brancato's ear.

"The head of every Hollywood studio is at that ceremony. You come up with the goods, you've saved the day. You don't, you'll never work in this town again."

Brancato's head jerked up, alert. "I didn't do anything," he gabbled. "All I did was leave the van unlocked for twenty minutes at a rest stop. That's all I did, man. I thought Feramo just wanted an Oscar for himself."

Back onstage, an increasingly desperate-looking Burton was doing his best. "Well, look at the time!" The audience was becoming restless, but he plowed gamely on.

"But seriously," he said, "how many of us *do* stop to *really* look at the time? I hope my accountant Marty Reiss does, because I gather he works by the hour . . ."

As Scott Rich strode through the backstage area, a man hurtled past him with four Oscars in his arms. He was wearing a T-shirt which said IF YOU SEE ME RUNNING, TRY TO KEEP UP. Scott did as it said and was joined by a man carrying more Oscars, this one in full protection gear: a dark green, eighty-pound suit lined with bulky, ceramic, blastproof plates and an air-cooled mask. They hurried out of the back of the building, where the area around the white bomb squad SUVs was cordoned off.

"Joe," Scott shouted, seeing a seasoned, wise-looking man with graying hair and glasses. "You run one through yet?" It was Joe Perros, a bomb-squad veteran of twenty-two years, now its head.

"Yup," said Joe grimly. "There's a pound of C4 in there with a Casio timer. We're just gearing up to open it by remote."

"You going to take the rest away or blow 'em here?" said Scott. "If they hear that lot go up inside the auditorium . . ."

"Yeah, that's the pucker factor," said Joe. "But as luck would have it, we brought a TCV."

He pointed to a five-foot steel ball, which the techs were draping in bomb blankets in the back of one of the vans. "We blow half a dozen in there, the audience won't know a thing."

"You got a team inside to work on the overrider?" Scott said, nodding back towards the auditorium.

"What do you think?"

"Great. I'm going inside," said Scott. "Call me with the bad news when you get to the timer."

Tim Burton had moved on to influences from his past. "None of this would have been possible without my cousin Neil, who let me play with his painting-by-numbers in the school holidays. Thanks, Neil, this is for you. And, finally, my first art teacher, a white-haired lady with the soul of Picasso. What the hell was her name? Mrs. Something . . . Lankoda? Swaboda? Hang on, I'll get it in a minute . . . Olim! Ms. Olim!"

Olivia, lurking in the shadows of a doorway and sporting her newly borrowed seat-filler pass, was using the miniature spyglass to scan the upper levels of the balcony. There was no one she recognized. No one was behaving more oddly than was normal for an Oscar ceremony. The music started up. She saw the relief on Burton's face as he stumbled desperately towards the wings and, at his glance, flashed him a huge thumbs-up.

Stars were pouring back into their seats during the applause. Olivia watched the woman in charge of the seat-fillers shepherding her charges into the key gaps. They had less than fifteen minutes left now. As Adrian Brody made his entrance to present the Best Actress award, all eyes turned to the stage, and she saw a security guard bend towards an Oscar winner in the stage-left aisle. The order must have been given to get them out. Olivia did one last despairing sweep of the center stalls—and there! There was a face she recognized, a blond girl with big hair, heavy lip liner and pneumatic breasts bursting out of a skimpy silver dress. It was Demi, Kimberley's ex–best friend from the party in Miami. She was taking her seat in the middle of the stalls, a seat-filler's ID pass hanging round her neck, sitting down next to a dark-haired boy. Olivia recognized the boy—he had stumbled out of the cloakroom with Demi, all disheveled, as she was leaving Feramo's penthouse in Miami. He was sweating. His eyes were darting wildly round the room. He had seen the security guard disappear with an Oscar, and his right hand was hovering nervously over his left wrist. Olivia dialed quickly and whispered into her cellphone, "Scott, I think I've got him. Stage-right stalls, ten rows back, on the right of Raquel Welch." She started moving up the aisle towards the boy and Demi, blood pounding in her ears.

Just then Brad Pitt appeared through the side door ahead and leaned against the wall, cool as fuck. Brad Pitt! Great. Olivia clocked his look of mild surprise as she approached. She flashed her new CIA ID and drew him back into the shadows of the doorway.

"We need you to do what I say," she whispered. "Just do whatever I say."

He met her eye reassuringly. "The girl in the silver dress," she whispered, standing on tiptoes to reach his ear. "Blond hair in a bun thing, two to the right of Raquel Welch. You got her? Get her to leave her seat and go outside with you."

"You got it." He gave a delicious, sexy smirk and set off towards

Demi. Olivia watched him play the moment like the pro he was. She watched Demi's head turn, as if drawn by Brad Pitt–vibes, saw him giving her a look and a nod. Demi's hand fluttered to her throat, disbelieving, then she got up, making her way along the row towards him. Olivia saw the dark-haired boy look round in a panic, and then back to the stage, where Adrian Brody was giving the longest preamble to the Best Actress nominations in the history of the Academy Awards.

"Olivia?" Two men in dark uniforms appeared behind her. "LAPD bomb squad. Where is he?"

She nodded towards the boy.

"Okay. Separate him and the detonator before he knows about it. We're right behind you."

There were murderous looks and shushes as Olivia pushed her way along the row, holding up her seat-filler pass, head down, making for the empty seat next to the boy, praying he wouldn't recognize her. She saw the bulge under his left sleeve, and the way his other hand kept moving towards it, covering it, as if protecting it. She had the chloroform pad concealed in her hand. She sat down, saw his face turn towards hers with a look of vague recognition, sweat dribbling down his temples. She gazed into his eyes and gave him her most dazzling smile, slipping her right hand onto his thigh as she did so. With one movement she covered his wrist and shoved the chloroform pad over his mouth, pulling the hand with the watch under her body, out of reach of his other arm, seeing his panicked eyes, hoping to God she was right. There was a commotion: heads turning, unbriefed security rushing towards them.

"Hold his other arm! Hold it! CIA," she hissed to Raquel Welch as she held the pad closer over his nose and mouth, feeling the boy's struggles begin to subside.

Raquel Welch grabbed the boy's free arm, shoved it under her famous bottom and sat on it. It was so great working with an actress who could take direction.

"Hold this," Olivia said, giving the arm with the watch on it to the startled man on her other side, whom, she later discovered, was a senior executive at DreamWorks. "He's a terrorist. Don't let go."

As the startled man gripped the boy's arm and up on stage the Best Actress finally got to find out who she was, Olivia pushed back his sleeve and wrested the watch off the now-limp wrist. A bomb-squad officer was halfway along the row, treading on people, pushing towards her. She reached out, handed him the watch, took her phone out and said, "Scott. He's out cold. The watch is with the bomb squad. We can clear the auditorium."

The danger of an override detonation was gone, but seventeen statuettes were still ticking away in the audience, primed to blow before the end of the show. They somehow had to get them out without starting a panic. Olivia saw officers appearing from the aisles and doorways and seats within the audience, attempting to collect the Oscars. Already it wasn't going well. The winner of the Best Foreign Language Film award, a lanky figure with a drooping mustache and striped bow tie, was refusing to hand his over, generating an unseemly tussle with a senior member of the fire department.

Out in the foyer, the area around the gentlemen's rest rooms was cordoned off. Officers were ushering any remaining stray guests out into the street. An Englishman in a dinner jacket was arguing with a security guard who was refusing to let him back into the hall. "But I'm nominated for Best Picture. My category's up next. I only came out to practice my speech in the bathroom."

"Sir, if I told you what was happening in there, you'd be straight back into that bathroom."

"I can't believe you're being so obtuse. What is your name and staff number?"

Two men in blast protection suits with BOMB SQUAD written on the back thudded at speed through the foyer, each clasping half a dozen Oscars in their arms. They dived into the men's rest room.

"You still wanna go back in there?" said the officer.

"Er, no, actually, no," said the Englishman, "no," and he ran for his life out of the exit and down the red carpet. There were sounds of panic from the auditorium. Another bomb-squad tech appeared with two Oscars and ran for the rest room. "Only one unaccounted for," he yelled.

Onstage, Meryl Streep was following orders, trying to surmount the rising pandemonium and keep the show running. "And the Academy Award for Best Picture goes to . . ." she said, drawing the card out of the envelope, *"Existential Despair."*

Just then, a burly uniformed figure strode on stage and held up his hand for calm. "Ladies and gentlemen," he said, but no one could hear above the uproar. As Meryl Streep helpfully gestured the police chief closer to the microphone, an enormously wide man, the executive producer of both *Existential Despair* and the Wall Street musical, lumbered onto the podium, followed by the two men who had actually produced the movie. As he put himself between the police chief and Meryl Streep, lunging at the replacement statuette, Scott Rich appeared on stage scowling, marched up to the large producer and punched him full on the jaw. At which the other two men joined in and punched him too. "I've been wanting to do that for years," one of them said rather loudly into the microphone.

"People," Scott Rich said, taking the microphone. "PEOPLE," he bellowed. For a moment there was total silence.

"Scott Rich, CIA. We had a serious situation. It is under control. Whether it stays under control depends on you and whether you behave like heroes. The world is watching. You need to leave the theater by the front exits only: that's here, and the first balcony here, and the next two balconies here. You need to move calmly, you need to follow instructions and you need to move fast. Okay, over to you."

As the audience filed out of the theater, the combined security forces were frantically scouring the building. Seventeen Oscars were buried under blast plates and blankets in the gentlemen's rest rooms, the surrounding area cleared. There were two minutes to go until the timers were set to blow, and one remaining Oscar was unaccounted for. The recipient, a thin, worried-looking girl who'd won the award for her role as Best Supporting Actress in the Chairman Mao film, was nowhere to be found. The crowds were still streaming out in a reasonably ordered fashion; only the security forces were aware of the bomb that might still be lurking in their midst.

Olivia stood flat against the wall, concentrating hard, then suddenly it came to her. She dialed her cellphone. "Scott," she said, "I bet I know where she is. No one's seen her since she went backstage. I bet she's throwing up."

"Okay, I'm on it," came Scott's voice. There was the sound of hurrying footsteps for a few moments. She glanced, terrified, at her watch again. "Okay. Now listen to me, Olivia. I'm right there. I see her; I'll get her out. I'll deal with it. There's nothing you can do. We have one minute left. Get out of the theater. Now. I love you. Bye."

"Scott!" she yelled. "Scott!" But the line was dead.

She looked desperately around and started heading for the stage, trying to keep to the outside of the crowd as if it were a current—sticking to the edges where it was less strong, so she could move more easily. But as she moved forward, a huge rumbling roar began from the foyer, the ground beneath them shook, and the walls seemed to bend outwards. There were screams and panic and a smell of acrid smoke—like fireworks only more acidic—and then more explosions followed immediately by another blast ahead, from backstage.

Olivia jabbed frantically at her phone. "Scott!" she yelled desperately. "Scott!" But it just rang and rang as the crowd started to scramble and surge in all directions. Olivia pressed herself against the wall and stood perfectly still in the middle of it, wide-eyed, watching. Slowly, she began to realize that it was all right. The bomb squad had done the job with the bombs in the rest room.

The walls were still standing, the blast had not penetrated the auditorium, there was no shrapnel, no blood, no bodies. No one seemed to be hurt. Except for the one man she loved.

She dialed the number again. It rang and rang and rang. She sank down on the floor miserably, one big tear starting to roll down her cheek, then suddenly someone picked up.

"Scott?" she said, nearly swallowing the phone in her eagerness.

"No, ma'am, this ain't Scott, but he's right here."

"He *is*? Is he all right?"

There was a silence. "Yes, ma'am. I guess you could say he's looking a little dirty, but he seems to be all in one piece. He managed to get the Oscar right down into the lavatory bowl with a bunch of drapes on top, and he and the young lady almost got themselves under the bomb-squad van. Oh, ma'am, he wants to speak to you." She waited, gulping, sniffing, rubbing her face.

"Is that you?" he said gruffly. "I told you not to call me at work."

"Can't trust you anywhere," she said, smiling and wiping away tears at the same time. "You just can't keep your hands off models and actresses, can you?"

59   MAUI, HAWAIIAN ISLANDS

As the air ambulance came in to land over the tropical waters of Maui, Olivia's mobile rang. She released her hand from Scott's for a second and pressed the button.

"Olivia?"

"Yes?"

"It's Barry Wilkinson here. Listen. Can you do us a piece? You were there, weren't you? The Oscars and the Sudan. We want a full I-was-there exclusive—front of the main section, whole of the News Review—and a piece for the daily, if you can run something off by eight o'clock. Just a few hundred words and some quotes. Olivia?"

"I don't know what you're talking about," she said. Because if there was one thing she knew, it was that she didn't want her face on the front of any newspaper. She was probably going to have to live in disguise for the rest of her life as it was.

"Listen, lovey, I know. I know about MI6. I know you went to the Sudan, because *Elan* told me. I know you were at the Oscars because I saw you on camera in a red wig. And—"

She held the phone away from her ear, glanced out of the window at where the plane was coming in to land over a curve of sparkling sea, palm trees and white sand, grinned gleefully at Scott Rich, put the phone squawking with Barry's irate voice back to her ear and said, "Oh don't be silly, lovey. It's just a figment of your overactive imagination."